PRAISE FOR JEANNE M. DAMS AND
THE BODY IN THE TRANSEPT

"Rings as clear and true as hand-bells on a Sunday morning . . . A lovely first mystery."
—Carolyn G. Hart

"I enjoyed *The Body in the Transept*, the company of people I would like, especially Dorothy Martin."
—Anne Perry

"A wonderful treat for lovers of the classic English mystery."
—*The Denver Post*

"Fans of cozy mysteries will delight in this debut novel. . . . Scores a '10' in every way, from plot to character to setting."
—*The Armchair Detective*

"Gleams with all the polish of a quaint English-village mystery. Nicely described small-town antics, a cleverly concocted plot, and a charmingly competent heroine."
—*Library Journal*

"Will delight lovers of cozies set on both sides of the Atlantic."
—*Publishers Weekly*

Books by Jeanne M. Dams

The Body in the Transept
Trouble in the Town Hall

Published by HarperPaperbacks

TROUBLE IN THE TOWN HALL

A Dorothy Martin Mystery

JEANNE M. DAMS

HarperPaperbacks
A Division of HarperCollinsPublishers

HarperPaperbacks

A Division of HarperCollins*Publishers*
10 East 53rd Street, New York, N.Y. 10022-5299

This is a work of fiction. The characters, incidents, and
dialogues are products of the author's imagination and are not to
be construed as real. Any resemblance to actual events or
persons, living or dead, is entirely coincidental.

ISBN 0-06-101132-0

HarperCollins®, ■®, and HarperPaperbacks™
are trademarks of HarperCollins*Publishers* Inc.

Cover illustration © 1997 by Pamela Patrick

A hardcover edition of this book was
published in 1996 by Walker Publishing Company, Inc.

First HarperPaperbacks printing: February 1998

Printed in the United States of America

Visit HarperPaperbacks on the World Wide Web at
http://www.harpercollins.com

❖ 10 9 8 7 6 5 4 3 2 1

To my mentor and biggest fan,
my wardrobe advisor and best friend,
my surrogate mother—
to the woman who is all those things,
my sister, Betty

Many people helped with the research for this book, but I owe special thanks to Sir Robert Bunyard, Retired Chief Constable of the county of Essex, for his invaluable expertise about the intricacies of English police procedure. If I've made mistakes, it is despite his excellent advice.

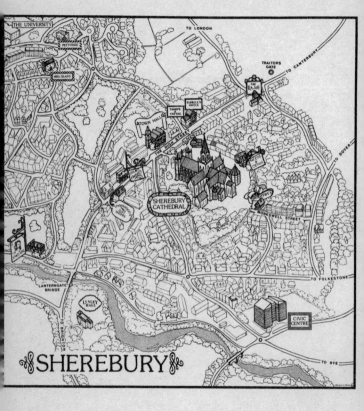

THE UNIVERSITY

TO LONDON

TRAITORS
GATE

TO CANTERBURY

PETTIFERS

MRS. TEAPOT

FARRELL'S
OFFICE

THE RAJAH

THORPE
& SWYTHE

TOWN HALL

TO DOVER

THE HIGH STREET

SHEREBURY
CATHEDRAL

MONKSWELL STREET

TO FOLKESTONE

LANTERNGATE
BRIDGE

LYNLEY
HALL

CIVIC
CENTRE

TO BRIGHTON

TO RYE

❦SHEREBURY❧

TROUBLE
IN THE
TOWN HALL

Prologue

THE CLOUDLESS HEAVENS had just begun to pale over the ancient cathedral town of Sherebury. As the last few stars flickered out in the brightening sky of that midsummer dawn, England turned its worshiping face to its oldest god, the sun—which divinity, with a beaming benevolence rare in those latitudes, poured out his blessings upon the city. The warm tide of light, paying tribute first to the newer creed, flowed over the topmost cross of the cathedral, washing its cool stone with golden glory, splashing down the spire. Treetops and chimney stacks were warmed and brightened, as were the roofs of the university on the hill and the clock tower of the Town Hall. The clock face showed 4:57.

Minute by minute, as the sun rose higher, its golden rays reached deeper, bathing the humbler roofs, the walls, the windows. In east-facing bedrooms, springs creaked and snores were interrupted as sleepers shifted to keep the brilliance out of their eyes.

The light at last reached the humble, dusty window of a broom closet, shining straight into the open eyes of the man on the floor who lay unblinking, unmoving.

The sunlight, indifferent, continued its stately progress.

1

THE JUNE DAY had started off normally enough with the cats' demands to be fed and let out. They'd been up very early—the birds' response to a brilliant midsummer sunrise had wakened all their hunting instincts—but there was, unfortunately, nothing unusual about that. By six I was functional myself and trying to do something about my flower beds, to the astonishment of my next-door neighbor. She restrained herself, however.

"Quite a job of work you've got there, Dorothy," she said mildly, leaning on the back gate and surveying the dejected-looking flower bed over the top of her glasses with a Churchillian frown.

"Jane Langland, don't you start making caustic remarks." I sat up, with sharp cracks from both knees, and looked over my scraggly flowers and flourishing weeds. "I know I've never been much of a gardener, and maybe I'm a little old to start now. But I've wanted an English garden all my life. Your climate in this country gives people pneumonia, but it does wonders for roses."

"Not doing much for yours," retorted Jane with brutal candor. "Why not find a gardener?"

"Even if I could afford it, the midwestern work ethic would protest. Frank and I always did things ourselves." And together. I brushed a sudden treacherous tear from my cheek, careless of the mud on my gloves, and Esmeralda woke from her nap in a patch of catnip and came over to rub her comforting, furry gray bulk against my legs.

"Frank loved gardens, too," Jane pointed out briskly. "He told me so, when you two were first thinking of moving here from the States. Said the flowers were the best thing about England. Expect he's up there shaking his head over the hash you're making of this."

"Probably." I managed a grin in appreciation of her unsentimental sympathy. "Anyway, I don't want to commit myself to a gardener while every-thing is so unsettled. I thought this morning, when those miserable beasts wanted out at the crack of dawn, that I should put in a cat door. But I can't do even a simple thing like that until I own the house, and I'm *not* going to buy it unless I can fix it up, and it looks to me as if this planning thing is going to go on forever." I waved away a heavy, furry bumble-bee and bent to my work again, viciously attacking a clump of large leaves while Samantha, my Siamese, chased the bee.

"Planning permission takes weeks," Jane pointed out, "especially for a listed building. I'd engage that gardener, meanwhile. Planning committee's more apt to believe you intend to preserve the character of the house if the garden is lovely and traditional. Which it won't be under your tender care." She chuckled richly in a deep baritone. "That 'weed' you just murdered was a delphinium, you know."

• • •

But I toiled stubbornly for the rest of that gorgeous, increasingly hot morning, until the phone call from Alan rescued me. I was delighted to accept a last-minute lunch date with Sherebury's chief constable, who had been so busy with constabulary duties that I'd hardly seen him for the past couple of weeks. So I dolled myself up in a smart new black-and-white dress and my best black straw hat, and sallied forth to do a little shopping before lunch at the new Indian restaurant we'd been wanting to try.

Or at least I tried to sally. A morning spent on my knees hadn't improved either them or my back, and black patent heels are impractical walking shoes for a woman of any age, let alone one who's—well, old enough to know better. So if sallying implies a certain briskness of pace, mine was more of a meander.

It suited the day, anyway. Sherebury High Street was, I thought critically, looking somewhat better than in recent months. The weather had brought out shoppers in droves, and the baskets full of petunias and geraniums hanging from the lampposts looked festive. The cathedral spire, just visible over the shops across the street, positively sparkled against the perfect blue sky.

There was still a certain gap-toothed look to the street, though. Every month or so another shop closed "for renovations" and never reopened. The depressed economy of my adopted town was showing, and I worried about it.

The worst blight of all was the poor old Town Hall, decaying from dry rot and the deathwatch beetle, and most of all from lack of money for repairs. Nothing could spoil its generous Elizabethan proportions, or its exquisite materials and workmanship, but with official city business having moved to a hideous new Civic Centre, the Town Hall exuded the bereft air of the abandoned. The great tubs of flowers that used to flank its studded oak doors had been taken away, the papers fluttering from the notice boards were torn and faded. Streaked, uncurtained windows looked in on a once busy, now deserted interior.

But it wasn't deserted. I stopped just as I was about to pass the building, and stared. I could have sworn I'd seen movement behind one of the windows—there it was again! I moved closer and peered into dimness; I thought I caught a glimpse of something, but then it was gone.

I tried the door—locked, just as it should be. Certainly it was no business of mine, but a confirmed snoop is never put off by a little thing like that. I knocked.

The shadow came closer. "Round to the side door! I 'aven't got me key to the front!"

The voice, female and strongly Cockney, reassured me utterly. Obviously she belonged there (and I did not), but I was committed now. Feeling silly, I went obediently to the side door, a dreary little portal I had never noticed before, opening onto the narrow passageway between the Town Hall and the modern building next door.

A large gray-haired woman stood in the doorway, dustcloth in hand. Appraising my going-out-to-lunch dress and hat, she spoke doubtfully. "Was you wantin' somethin', madam? On account of, there's nobody 'ere no more, you know."

"I know," I agreed apologetically. "I'm sorry to bother you, but when I saw someone in here I wondered—I mean, I didn't know the building was still being kept clean, Mrs.—?"

"Ada Finch. And as for keepin' it clean, that's in a manner of speakin', that is. Come in, then, luv." Seizing the opportunity for conversation, she led me round to the staircase in the front hall, settled herself with a comfortable grunt on the third step, and took up where she'd left off. "In the old days I'd 'ave bin 'ere at 'alf past five, to get everything spic *and* span for them as worked 'ere. Now, o' course, it's just keepin' the woodwork nice for them as is goin' to move in, so I only 'as a day now and again, and 'oo knows 'ow long that'll keep on." She fetched a gusty sigh from beneath the layers of sweaters that covered her ample bosom. "Breaks me 'eart, it does, to see the place like this after all the years I looked after it lovely."

"The woodwork is still beautiful, though. The carving on that staircase is in perfect condition."

"Never a crack in it," said Mrs. Finch triumphantly, giving the elaborate spiked newel post an affectionate rub with her rag, "for all it is 'undreds of years old. Lovely piece of work, that staircase is. Carved all the way to the top, and every landin' different. Makes a lot of work, but I keeps it nice. You should 'ave seen the job I 'ad, too, cleanin' it proper when I first come to work 'ere. More years ago than I care to remember, that was, and me just a young girl workin' under that sour old Mr. Jobbins." She sniffed. "More concerned about gettin' 'is tea regular than keeping the place up to snuff, 'ee was. Young I might've bin, but I knew better than to let the dust pile up in all them crevices. I bin trained right. Went at it with a nail file, I did, and sometimes a toothpick, month after month, until I 'ad it lookin' like new. Polishes up a treat, don't it?"

"It's magnificent," I said sincerely. "It's such a pity—"

"That's wot I says," Mrs. Finch broke in eagerly. "Terrible shame it'll be if that Mr. Pettifer and them pull it all about and turn it into one of them malls. I don't 'old with shoppin' malls. Give me proper shops, where you could 'ave a talk with the butcher, or greengrocer as it might be, friendly-like, and maybe get a nice little piece of liver for the cat, or a wilted lettuce, and do 'im a favor next time out.

"Ah, well, them days is gone forever; you've got to move with the times or get left behind. Speakin' o' time—" Mrs. Finch looked at the man's wrist-watch shoved far up on her left arm. "I always 'as me a cuppa just about now. Would you like one, Mrs.—?"

"Martin, Dorothy Martin," I said hastily. "I'm sorry, I should have introduced myself. And thank you, but I'm supposed to be meeting someone; I really have to—"

"You're American, ain't you?" she said as she clumped to a closet behind the stairs. "I've 'eard as 'ow they don't drink tea. Dunno 'ow they get through the day. Time was when I could 'ave a nice cuppa with me mates, the rest o' the cleaners, sit in comfort in a room they give us, put me feet up and 'ave a bit of a gossip. Now I keeps me tea things in the broom cupboard and 'as to make do with sittin' on the stairs by me lonesome, but still, tea's tea."

She opened the door as she spoke and took one step into the tiny room before she caught her breath in a sharp gasp and screamed.

So it was that, for the second time in six months, I found myself staring into the eyes of a dead man. The first experience, in Sherebury Cathedral on Christmas Eve, was something I didn't care to remember; I'd made a nuisance of myself to all concerned, including my new acquaintance Chief Constable Alan Nesbitt. But perhaps familiarity softens these blows. More likely, I was too taken up with Mrs. Finch's hysterics to have time for any of my own.

After the first frozen moment of shock, poor Mrs. Finch collapsed against the paneled wall of the hallway, gasping and whimpering, and I could get a good look.

On the whole, I wished I hadn't. The man was young, no more than a boy, really. His eyes, horribly, were wide open. I'd seen only that much when we were interrupted.

"Mrs. Finch! What is it?" The voice from somewhere behind us was loud, peremptory, and male, and I yelped. When I turned, heart pounding, and he came closer to our gloomy corner, I recognized him. Oh, marvelous. Archibald Pettifer, city councilman, real estate developer, and self-appointed minder of everyone's business. Just what we needed.

"Mrs. Finch! Mrs.—er—madam! What is the trouble?"

His stentorian bellow finally got through to the cleaning lady, who hiccuped and wobbled away to the stairs, sniffling into her apron. Mr. Pettifer stood for a moment looking down at the body on the closet floor. Then he shook his head like a bull ready to charge and took over.

"Now, then, what is all this?"

His shaking voice and dirty-ivory face belied his pompous attitude, and I nearly giggled. I've met Pettifer on only a couple of occasions, which was enough; he irritates me simply by existing. He must have noticed that I wasn't impressed, because he glared at me and cleared his throat.

"Madam, I am Archibald Pettifer, and I asked a question. What—"

I drew myself up. "I heard you, Mr. Pettifer, and we've met. Dorothy Martin, since you don't seem to remember. I didn't answer because I have no more idea than you. Mrs. Finch opened the door and found that man lying on the floor. He is apparently dead. I don't know who he is or what he's doing here." Two could play the pompous game.

He seized on my last words. "Ah! And what are *you* doing here, may one ask?"

I caught my temper by the tail just as it was about to lash out, claws fully extended. "I saw Mrs. Finch in here, through the window, and came in to make sure there was no problem. And may I point out, sir, that we should be taking care of Mrs. Finch and calling the police instead of questioning each other? I haven't asked why *you* are here, or how you got in."

His look this time ought to have turned me to stone, but he did offer an explanation of sorts. "I—er—heard a scream and came in the side door, which Mrs. Finch had no business to leave unlocked. Furthermore, *I* have legitimate business here. And I was about to suggest that, if Mrs. Finch insists on having hysterics, you take her to some place where she can sit down properly—" he looked about as if expecting a chair to materialize in the hallway "—and then summon the police. Unfortunately, no telephones remain in the building, and someone must stay here with the—to—er—must stand guard."

I seized at the idea of escape. There was a public phone at Debenham's, the big chain department store across the street, which also had a tearoom. I thought I'd have trouble moving Mrs. Finch, but once she took in the word "tea" she forged ahead like a horse nearing its stable.

When I had her settled at the one free table with a pot of tea and some biscuits, I slipped away to the phone. After the emergency 999 call I asked for Alan—an entirely separate office, since his job is purely administrative—and was told he was out to lunch.

Oh, good grief, of course he was—he was waiting for me. That call took a little longer.

"Alan, thank God I found you!" I babbled in relief. "I couldn't remember the name of the restaurant, so I had to talk to your secretary, and she had to call for the number, and—"

"Dorothy." His voice was sharp, official. "Tell me."

"There's been a murder, Alan! At least I think so. It's at the Town Hall, and I was there when—"

"I'll be there."

He hung up and I went back to Mrs. Finch, who had finished one cup of tea and recovered her volubility.

"And wot I'd like to know," she said with a sniff,

pouring another cup of repellent black brew and copiously adding milk, "is, 'oo is 'ee, and 'ow did 'ee come to be in *my* cupboard?" Her chins quivered with outraged dignity and her voice rose. "'Ooever 'ee is, 'ee'd no call to come and die 'ere! Look at the trouble 'ee'll cause! And no more than a layabout, to look at 'im."

"You got a close look?" I asked, lowering my voice in the hope that she would do the same, though the lunchtime crowd probably drowned us out.

"Well—not to say *look*. But 'is clothes and all . . ."

I understood. Mrs. Finch had barely glanced at the body before dissolving into hysterics, but she found comfort in the thought that the human being who had once inhabited that body was a stranger and a useless sort of person.

I was not so easily comforted. No matter who the dead man was or what his life had been, his end was pitiable. Mrs. Finch was certainly right about one thing, though: There was a great deal of trouble ahead for everyone concerned.

"Have you finished your tea? Do you think you're well enough to go talk to the police?"

"Go 'ome and 'ave meself a drop o' gin, is wot I'd like to do," she said wistfully. "Wot a 'ope! They'll be asking their questions till the cows come 'ome. Well, no 'elp for it." She heaved herself to her feet. "Thanks for me tea. Went down a treat; I'm meself again. Sure you won't 'ave any? There's a cup left in the pot."

I shuddered. I probably needed sustenance, and my nice lunch with Alan wasn't going to happen, but I was a little more upset than I liked to admit, and my stomach was in no state to deal with stewed tea. "I'm fine. Shall we go get it over with?"

The police had arrived in the few minutes since I had phoned. A crowd had gathered, but Mrs. Finch sturdily shouldered aside all would-be obstacles. When the constable at the Town Hall door barred our way, she stared him down, hands on formidable hips.

"'Ere, ducks, I'm the one wot found the body, and they want to talk to me. And this 'ere is Mrs. Martin, and she was with me. So just you get out of the doorway an' let us pass." Fortified by tea, she was beginning to enjoy her importance.

The scene-of-crime team was already busy inside the building, and just inside the front door Pettifer was arguing with a uniformed policeman. He apparently wanted to talk to the officer in charge, whose whole attention was taken up with directing his men.

Our constable escorted us to the officer in question and murmured something to him.

"Yes?" He looked us over. "I'm Inspector Morrison. I understand one of you ladies discovered the body?"

He was a man of about fifty, inconspicuous-looking save for a very sharp eye and a quick manner that stopped just short of impatience. He gestured us toward the stairs, the only place to sit, and was following when Pettifer accosted him.

"Look here, sir! Am I to be kept waiting about all day? I've told my story twice, what there was to tell, and I've pressing business to attend to. That ass over there said you wanted to talk to me. Well, here I am!" His face was red and his hands were clenched and shaking; I had a fleeting moment of

worry about his blood pressure. I may dislike
Archibald Pettifer and all his works, but I didn't
want him to have a heart attack on the spot.

"Presently, sir. Rest assured we'll not keep you
any longer than necessary. If you'd care to wait
over there?" The inspector pointed to a spot well
out of earshot. Pettifer scowled at all of us and
stomped off.

"Now then, ladies?"

We sat down on the hard oak steps, and the
inspector turned his attention to me. "You are . . . ?"

"Dorothy Martin. My address is Monkswell
Lodge."

His attitude sharpened slightly. "Ah, yes, the
American lady. Involved in the cathedral murders,
weren't you?"

"Involved is not exactly the word I would
choose."

He smothered a smile. "No, perhaps not. Now,
what can you tell me about this incident?" The uniformed man by his side began to take notes.

"Very little, I'm afraid. It's Mrs. Finch's story,
really." I related how I happened to be in the building and what I'd seen, trying to remember exact
times and failing, and feeling very silly about the
whole thing, and then it was Mrs. Finch's turn.

She was asked in excruciating detail about
every movement she had made since arriving at
the Town Hall, and she was pleased to oblige,
proudly describing her dusting and polishing
of almost every surface that might have been
expected to yield evidence. If the inspector
winced he tried not to show it; the woman was
simply doing her job and couldn't be expected to
know what was lurking in the broom closet. It

wasn't until she began to add anecdotes about how she had felt in her bones all morning that something was wrong that his fingers began to drum very quietly on the beautifully polished banister.

"Yes, well, thank you, Mrs. Finch. I think that'll be all—or, no, just one more thing. How did you get into the building this morning?"

She bristled at that. "With me key, 'ow do you think?"

"Of course," Morrison said soothingly. "I actually meant, by which door?"

"Oh." Mrs. Finch colored, ducked her head, and gave him a sideways grin. "Sorry, luv. I'm *that* upset—you mustn't take no notice. Come in the side door, same as always. Off Cat Lane?"

The inspector nodded. "And was the door locked?" he went on.

Mrs. Finch looked at him with pity in her blue eyes, her head to one side like an elderly robin's. "Naow. I always wastes me time unlockin' doors as is unlocked already. O' course it was locked!"

"And when you leave—you lock it up again with the key?"

That did it. Mrs. Finch stood up and transfixed the inspector with a look that might have cut through the solid oak paneling. "I'll 'ave you know, Mr. Fancy P'liceman, as Ada Finch 'as never gone off and left a door open in this 'ere ancient monument! Time was I 'ad the keys to every door in this place, leavin' out the big front door, as is barred. And all the keys was different, and big as 'orses. Now the pore old place is left to itself I only 'as the one, and I guards it with me life! 'Ere, see for yourself!"

She fished in her pocket, brought forth a large old-fashioned key all by itself on a ring with a big brass hotel-style tag, and waved it an inch in front of his face. "I put that tag on so's I'd 'ear it fall if I dropped it, and I could find it easy. An' I locks the door every time I leaves, or I'll eat me key, tag an' all, with 'orseradish sauce!"

She folded her arms, her lower lip protruding ominously, and while the inspector soothed and placated and assured her he didn't doubt her word, I pondered the point about the key. If the place was securely locked up, how had the dead man gotten in? And more to the point, how had the murderer gotten out, leaving a dead bolt locked behind him? Someone inside, presumably the murderer, could have unbarred the ancient front door to let the victim in, but you can't leave by a barred door.

The inspector was winding up with the disgruntled Mrs. Finch. "You've been very helpful, and I'm truly sorry to have kept you here so long. We'll have your statement typed and ask you to come down to the station to sign it, but there is just one more point. Did you, in the course of your work, see or move anything out of the ordinary?"

"Dirt an' rubbish was wot I moved," she snapped. "Look in the dustbin if you like."

I had no doubt he or his men would do just that. I had every doubt they'd find anything of interest.

"I know you must be longing for a bit of rest, Mrs. Finch. We'll let you know when you can resume your work here—soon, of course," he added hastily, seeing her face grow even grimmer. "We must seal the building as a crime scene for now, and I shall have to keep your key for a day or two." He tried a conciliatory smile.

Mrs. Finch was having none of his peacemaking; her honor had been impugned. "And 'oo's goin' to clean up the place, then?" she demanded, hands on hips. "Dustin' for fingerprints, they calls it; I calls it makin' a ruddy great mess! As if I didn't 'ave enough to do, trying to keep this place from goin' to rack and ruin while the muckety-mucks decide what's to be done with it, pore old place, left all any'ow so as they could go and 'ave their fine new offices in that fine new pile o' concrete as'll fall down about their ears in a year or so, I shouldn't wonder, and serve 'em right, too, makin' us common folks traipse out miles from anywhere to fill out their ruddy forms an' all, and bus fares bein' wot they are, too . . ." She grumbled her way out the door, heading for her drop of gin and a glorious gossip with the neighbors.

Inspector Morrison raised an eyebrow and smiled a little at her retreating back, shaking his head. "A vanishing breed, God bless her. Salt of the earth, but infuriating at times." He shook his head again, dismissed Mrs. Finch from his mind, and turned the full force of those disconcerting gray eyes on me. "Can you tell me, Mrs. Martin, your impression of Mrs. Finch when she found the body? Was she truly surprised, or . . . ?"

"If she wasn't flabbergasted and terrified, you can tell the Queen to hand her a knighthood, or a dameship, or whatever it is, for being the finest actress in the United Kingdom. I never saw a more genuine fit of hysteria. Anyway, you only have to look at her to know she's honest."

"Right." The monosyllable accepted what I'd said, without necessarily agreeing. "Of course, the one who finds the body is so often—however. Now, if we can go once more over—"

"Dorothy! There you are! Morning, Morrison, this one fell to you, eh? Bad luck on such a glorious day!"

Alan, a big man who looks like Alistair Cooke, made an impressive entrance. I was so glad to see him I looked up with what must have been a *Perils of Pauline* sort of expression; he smiled back affably and spoke again to the inspector.

"You haven't met Mrs. Martin, have you, Derek—except officially, I mean? Pity you had to meet over a corpse, but we may yet be thankful she was here. You'll find her a good witness, I believe."

"I had already drawn that conclusion, sir." His eyes softened. "I was just about to take her through it all again, but it's probably pointless; she was thorough and concise the first time. If you'd like . . ." He sketched an "after you" in Alan's direction.

There was something about his gesture that suggested he was deferring not only to his superior officer, but to an important friend of the witness. Ah, well, Sherebury is a small town, after all. So he'd known all along I was Alan's—what? Perhaps this was not the moment to try to define the relationship.

"No, indeed, I shan't interfere. But if you've actually finished, I'd like to give the lady some lunch. Dorothy? Do you need to brush yourself down?"

"No, Mrs. Finch keeps the place spotless. I'm just stiff. Is my hat all right?"

"Very nice indeed," he said with the almost hidden smile he addresses to all my hats, and offered me his arm.

I was glad enough to take it; reaction had set in. "Alan, I don't know if I can manage Indian food, after all. My insides are acting a little peculiar."

"I shouldn't wonder, but you do need to eat. How long ago was breakfast?"

"It feels like years."

"Right, then what about something simple and sustaining at Alderney's?"

Alderney's is the tea shop in the Cathedral Close and one of my favorite places in Sherebury. "Perfect. They have wonderful comfort food." He started to move toward the door, but I pulled at his arm.

"Alan, I have to know what they've found out. Did you have a chance to talk to anyone? Who is—he?" I jerked my head toward the broom closet. "Does this have anything to do with the preservationist battle over the Town Hall?"

"No idea. I did have a word with the men before I talked to you, but they don't know much yet. How in the name of all that's holy did you get mixed up in this, by the way?" His voice was quiet, but the concern he wouldn't display in front of Inspector Morrison was apparent.

"Pure accident, and I'm not 'mixed up' in it. I just had the bad luck to be here." I summarized what had happened. "Who is he?" I repeated.

"There was no identification on the body. Young, early twenties probably; you will have gathered that. I don't suppose he was at all familiar to you?"

"I didn't look properly. I could check now, I suppose."

Alan put his hand over mine, still clinging to his arm. "Only if you want to. There's little likelihood you would know him, after all."

"No, it's all right. You're a very reassuring person, you know."

"If you're certain." He took me to the door of the closet and said something to the policemen still working there, who moved aside.

The man lay on his back, arms and legs spread-eagled, filling the floor of the small room. He was dressed in a dirty black T-shirt and a pair of blue jeans, frayed at the knees and not, I thought, on purpose. He looked very young indeed. A scrabble of beard failed to hide a pasty, acne-scarred face. His hair, worn longer than my taste preferred, was of a color hard to determine, so greasy were the locks scattered against the floorboards. His eyes were shut.

"No," I said in a not very steady voice after a long look. I was shaken with pity for a young life ended, and perhaps, from his appearance, unhappy, meaningless even before the final blow of fate. "No, I've never seen him before."

We were on our way out of the building before I spoke again. "Alan, would they—the police, I mean—would they have moved the body?"

"Not at this stage; they haven't finished with photographs. Why?" He was all Chief Constable Nesbitt again.

"Because it's been moved. His arms were down at his sides when I saw him. I didn't see much, but I saw that. And—" I tried to control a shudder "—his eyes were open."

2

AFTER THAT, OF course, Alan stayed to talk to Inspector Morrison and his men for a few minutes, with the result that we hit Alderney's at the height of the lunchtime rush. Alan managed to get us a table. He usually does; I've never been sure whether it's those devastating blue eyes or the fact that a chief constable is an important person, rather like a medieval lord sheriff. It was definitely the eyes, though, that got a pot of tea on the table almost instantly. He poured me a cup and made me add a lot of sugar. He also poured a little brandy in it.

"Alan, you never cease to amaze me! Do you always carry a flask? I've never noticed it."

"Emergency stores only. I bring it when I feel I may be called upon to rescue a swooning lady. Drink that down."

I'd have disputed "swooning lady" if it hadn't been so close to accurate. As it was, I obediently drank my tea, relaxed, and suddenly recovered my senses.

"Alan, the bookshop! My job! What time is it? I have to go—"

"Sit still. I'll ring them up." He untangled his long legs from the maze of table and chairs, spoke to the hostess, and picked up her telephone at the desk.

"What did you say?" I demanded when he got back. "I wouldn't want Mrs. Williamson upset—"

"That you were being detained by the police to assist us with our inquiries."

"Alan, you didn't! She'll have a heart attack!"

"No, I didn't, actually. I said you'd been un-avoidably delayed and would be there as soon as possible. I did identify myself."

I sighed. "She'll worry herself into a stew, poor dear. I'd better hurry, so I can explain for myself."

"You'd do better to go home after you've had a spot of lunch. You're still quite white, you know."

"Oh. Well, no, I didn't, but really I'm fine, Alan, or I will be when I've eaten something. I have to get to the bookshop, Mrs. Williamson's counting on me. Anyway, work keeps me from thinking, and the cathedral is such an oasis of calm, I'll feel much better. I'm sure."

I was protesting too much, but Alan let it go and simply said, "Why on earth don't you call the woman by her first name? The English aren't all *that* formal, you know."

"Her first name is Ariadne."

"Oh, dear. Yes, I do see. What do the others call her?"

"Willie. Somehow I can't . . ."

"Quite." He looked at the menu. "How about chicken rolls and rice pudding for both of us? Nursery food."

"Sounds good." And when the sandwiches

arrived, crusty rolls with lots of white meat and let-tuce, I attacked mine like a starving woman.

"So how," I said when I could speak, "are plans for the royal visit coming along?" I wanted a respite from murder, and I figured Alan was good for sev-eral minutes on his chief headache of the moment, the impending visit of Prince Charles to open the new wing of the hospital.

Alan ran a hand down the back of his neck. "As smoothly as these things ever go, I suppose, actually. It's just that the Palace has got the wind up, rather. And so have I, much as I hate to admit it."

"About what—hecklers about the Diana situation?"

"Not so much that as these damned anarchists." He glanced casually around the room, which was beginning to thin out as those on limited lunch hours hurried off. The table next to ours was empty, but Alan lowered his voice all the same. "I can't be specific, but a recent episode is seen as a direct threat to Prince Charles. They managed to keep it out of the press, but—" He raised his hands in a gesture of exasperation.

"The Prince's people think there'll be a next time?"

"There will be, undoubtedly. The question I must deal with is, Will it be in Shrewsbury? That's what I want to know from MI5 and the rest of the security lot, what sort of threat I might have to contend with, and so far they've not been able to tell me."

"I can't get over being amazed at the idea of anarchists." I glanced at my plate, surprised to find it empty. Alan's prescription had been admirable. "It all sounds so quaint and dated, straight out of the twenties."

"Doesn't it? Unfortunately the current lot are

not at all dated. They organize their little games over the Internet."

"Good grief. Do you really think someone like that might be working in Sherebury?"

Our rice pudding arrived and we both tasted its creamy goodness before Alan replied.

"I don't know—and I should know—but I'm uneasy. I have a feeling something nasty is going on; I just can't put my finger on it." He ran his hand over his neck again and began to tick off points on his fingers. "There's the Town Hall business. Pettifer wants to turn it into his mall; the preservationists are fighting tooth and nail to save it. All right, but it's getting just that much more heated than one would expect. So is the controversy over that university housing scheme of his— did you know Pettifer's received two anonymous letters? No more than vague threats, but it's unusual in a preservation matter; the chattering classes are the ones who care the most, and they don't stoop to such tactics."

"And now—today—"

"Indeed. Can you talk about it now?"

One reason Alan has risen to such a senior police rank is his sensitive understanding of people. It's also one of the reasons I'm so fond of him. I smiled and put down my spoon.

"So long as we avoid the more graphic bits, I want to know what you know."

He sat back and tented his fingers in what I had come to know as his lecturing pose. "Well, I asked, of course, about the body, and got confirmation they hadn't moved it except to look for identification. There was none, as I told you. At that stage they hadn't even taken his fingerprints."

"That means Pettifer, doesn't it? He was alone with—him—" I couldn't make myself call that pitiful creature *it* "—while Mrs. Finch and I went to Debenham's."

"It looks like it. Though why . . . ?" Alan shrugged his massive shoulders. "They'll put him through it, of course, about that and about the question of keys."

"I've thought about that. I don't suppose there's a snap lock to any of the outside doors, so someone—the murderer—could have left it locked behind him?"

"No, I asked. There are only the two outside doors, front and side, and of course the front has that great medieval bar. Primitive, but very effective for all that. The back door—side door, whatever you want to call it—has an old-fashioned lock. You Americans call it a dead bolt, I believe—locks only with a key from either side. So, it looks as though our murderer—if it was murder—had a key."

"Assuming Mrs. Finch was right about the door being locked when she arrived this morning. I'm sure she wasn't lying on purpose, but she might have just assumed it was locked, because it always was."

Alan looked dubious. "An old lock like that is apt to be pretty stiff. I should think there'd be a fairly obvious click or screech when the bolt gave way. Hard to think she'd not notice a difference."

"True." I sat silent for a moment, absently sipping my tea. "Why did you say, 'if it was murder'?"

He shrugged. "Cautious habit, I suppose. They don't know the cause of death yet, of course. It could, stretching the limits of possibility, have been suicide or accident, but Morrison seemed to think the body had been moved to the broom cupboard, which would mean . . ."

I put down my cup, and Alan scraped back his chair.

"It's time we got you to that precious job of yours, if you're still determined to work this afternoon."

We strolled across the Cathedral Close together. Sherebury's Close, a broad area of grass and trees and flower beds surrounding the cathedral, is bordered not only by the administrative buildings of the cathedral and the homes of her clergy, but by a few commercial buildings. Alderney's, at the far end by the west gate, is followed by a bank, a jeweler, a gift shop, and my favorite pub, the Rose and Crown. The Olde English effect makes tourists go into ecstasies, especially on days like today.

The sun glinted off diamond-paned windows and shone warm on our backs. Someone across the Close was cutting the grass, the scent perfuming the air, as did the pink roses blooming profusely by the path. Birds sang in the tops of the oak trees while squirrels chased each other noisily round and round the trunks. Looming benevolently over all, the cathedral dozed in early-afternoon languor, and beyond it, on the other side of the precinct wall, we could just see the uneven gables and chimneys of my Jacobean house. I pointed.

"It does look picturesque, doesn't it?"

"Pure seventeenth century. Are you any closer to being able to bring it into the twentieth?"

I sighed. "Not really; I'm caught in a maze of bureaucracy. To begin with, I can't get anyone started on plans. It's just plumbing and wiring and windows and that kind of thing, but it seems I need a specialist in old buildings. There are only two firms like that left in Sherebury, and they're both so busy I can't get a commitment. Then after I have the plans I have to apply for grants to help with the cost, from the council and English Heritage, and even if I get the money I can't let anyone get started until I get planning permission, and listed building permission as well." I stopped, out of breath.

"That can take forever. When does your lease expire?"

"That's the trouble—end of August. The owner says he's willing to extend it a bit, since I've contracted to buy, pending all the approvals. But he's not being very pleasant about the delay, and I'm afraid he'll sell it out from under me if things go on for too long. I can't even stand to think about having to move. Where would I ever find another wonderful house like that?"

"It's frightfully inconvenient, of course, a really old house. And you do realize it costs the earth to maintain?"

"Yes, I know, but I love it, Alan. I know it isn't an important house—it's small, and nobody famous ever lived there or slept there or hid there while escaping from whatever—but it's important to me. In a way, it's the symbol of everything I love about England, the respect for the past, the fine workmanship . . . and as that loses ground to the shoddy and modern, as England becomes more and more Americanized, I want to cling to my little corner of grace and tradition."

I looked away, embarrassed, but there was more I had to say. "And, you see—it's home. It would have been Frank's and mine, he loved it, too, and

now—it's my security blanket, I suppose." I
blinked away a tear and Alan took my hand firmly
in wordless sympathy. We walked to the cathedral
door in silence.

Late as I was, I sat in the nave for a few minutes.
The great space was filled with light from massive
stained-glass windows, shafts of it coloring the dust
in the air, rainbow pools of it lying on the cool
stone floor. The voices of tourists and guides
seemed only to emphasize the essential quiet.
Women attending to the flowers shook the fra-
grance of roses into the air, to mingle with the scent
of old stone and the faint, lingering perfume of
incense. Somewhere a flute and a choir boy were
practicing Handel.

I stood, restored and ready for my job.

When Frank and I first visited England, I was
a bit taken aback by the bookshops in all the
cathedrals; visions of Jesus chasing the money
changers out of the temple sprang to mind. Once
I began to appreciate the finances involved, however, I changed my mind. It costs millions of
pounds a year to keep these magnificent buildings from falling down. If bookshops can help
preserve the cathedrals for their original purpose
of inspiring awe and worship, then I'm all for
them, especially as the prices are reasonable and
most of the labor is donated by overworked volunteers.

So when I began to cast about for something to
do in my adopted home, I tried the bookshop,
where Mrs. Williamson made me feel not only welcome but much needed.

I waved to her as I entered the shop, and as soon as she could free herself from a cluster of tourists with questions, she hurried to me with furrowed brow.

"Oh, Dorothy, I've been so *worried*! Has something dreadful happened? When the chief constable rang up—"

"No, no, I'm fine," I interrupted. With one eye on the far corner of the shop, where the other volunteer for the afternoon was working at the cash register, I tried to edge toward the staff room. "Just let me put my things away, won't you, and I'll be right out to help. I really am so sorry, Mrs. Williamson, I can see you're busy and I didn't mean to worry you. I—there was a—an accident that I happened to—er—witness. So I had to stick around for a while."

"You weren't hurt!" Her voice rose as the cathedral organist began to practice, and curious eyes turned toward us, including those of the anemic blond cashier.

"No, it was nothing like that." The shop was beginning to empty as the tourists followed the compelling voice of the organ. "I—um—can we talk about it later? I'll just leave my purse—"

But it was too late. The volunteer had dealt with the last purchase and was edging toward us like a nervous cat, pale blue eyes full of apprehension. Clarice Pettifer. Mrs. Archibald Pettifer.

"Oh, whatever happened, Dorothy?" she gasped. "Willie said you were with the police!"

There was no evading it. I had wanted a little time to organize my response before facing Clarice, but the shop had cleared. It was just the three of us. I had no excuse.

I took a deep breath. "Clarice, you'd better come back and sit down."

"Why?" Her voice rose and there were pink spots on her cheeks where her pale color had faded even more, leaving painfully obvious makeup. "What's the matter? It isn't—" her hand flew to her mouth "—it isn't Archie?"

"No, he's—I'm sure he's fine. Do sit down."

Mrs. Williamson, bewildered but cooperative, helped me get her into the staff room and onto a chair.

"Tell me, you must tell me!"

I was going about this very badly. Clarice was a fragile, nervy type. Mention of a dead body even in the abstract would upset her, and with her husband involved, I had hoped to break the news gently. Some hope.

"It's nothing to get upset about, really, but—well, it does concern your husband, in a way." I hurried on, trying not to meet Clarice's red-rimmed eyes.

"It's just that—well, I happened to be in the Town Hall—"

"The Town Hall?" Her voice dropped to a whisper, and her hand moved to her mouth again.

"Yes, I was talking to Mrs. Finch, the cleaning lady, and she happened to—um—" I cast about for a euphemism. There weren't any.

"I'm sorry, but she—we—found a dead man."

We were able to catch Clarice before she hit the floor.

Between us, we managed to move her to the shabby couch that, with a dilapidated overstuffed chair, a

tiny sink, and an electric kettle, constituted the luxury of the staff room. I bathed her forehead with
cool water while Mrs. Williamson ran distractedly
into the shop to shoo out two or three browsers and
put the "Closed" sign on the door. When she got
back, Clarice was beginning to stir.

"I think we'd better have the doctor, don't you?"
said Mrs. Williamson. She hugged her midriff; her
ulcer must have been giving her fits.

"Oh, no," said Clarice, weakly but quite dis-
tinctly. "I'm quite all right, really." She struggled
to sit up and went white again. "No, if I could
just—rest for a bit—really, I don't want a doctor—Archie wouldn't like—might I have a glass
of water, do you think?"

I got the water. "Are you sure you don't need a
doctor? You're still terribly pale."

"No."

I recognized in the set of the little rosebud
mouth the stubbornness sometimes found in normally compliant people. "Then I'm taking you
home. Do you have your car?"

"Oh, no, I'm sure I can manage. We can't leave
Willie—the shop—"

"Don't be silly." Mrs. Williamson's voice was
suddenly crisp. "You've both—had a shock. If I
can't cope alone, I'll recruit some emergency help
or leave the shop closed."

It was a noble sacrifice at the height of the
tourist season, and I said so. "That's very kind of
you, Mrs. Williamson. If I see someone on my way
out, I'll—"

"You will not; you've enough to do. I'll see to it.
And I do wish you'd call me Willie. You make me
feel like your grandmother. Clarice, can you walk?"

It was a long way from the bookshop to the cathedral parking lot, but one of the vergers helped with Clarice. And then Clarice's car turned out to be a BMW, and the thought of driving it on the left side of the narrow Sherebury streets nearly undid me. But Clarice was in no shape to drive and my own sturdy little VW was in my garage, so there was no help for it. I got in the driver's seat and prayed, and somehow we made it without a scratch.

I don't know what kind of house I'd expected the Pettifers to live in. I suppose, knowing they were rich, I'd imagined a stately old manor house of some sort. I couldn't have been more wrong. The house, built at the crest of one of Sherebury's many hills, was certainly close to the million-pound class, but it was brand, spanking new and seemed at a glance to consist mostly of white stone and glass. The entry hall was tiled in black and white; the stairway was marble and chrome—the spotless, sterile home of a wealthy, childless couple.

Over her feeble protests I helped Clarice up to bed in her frilly, feminine bedroom, an interesting contrast to the rest of the house, and then went down to the kitchen to make the universal English cure, a nice cup of tea.

The kitchen, full of all the latest gadgets, was so clean and neat I wondered if Clarice or anyone else ever cooked in it. I took extreme care not to spill anything as I made the tea. Back upstairs, I somewhat guiltily slipped into Clarice's bathroom and explored the medicine chest before I went into the bedroom with the tea.

"I couldn't find any biscuits," I said cheerfully as I set the tray on the bedside table and poured out a cup. "You'd better have a lot of sugar in the tea, though." Not only is sugar good for shock, it would help disguise the taste of the sleeping pill I'd dropped into the cup.

"Oh, I always take four lumps," Clarice said. "Archie says it's a low taste. You're being very kind, Dorothy."

"Don't be silly. How are you feeling?"

"I'm quite all right, really." A tiny bit of color came into her cheeks. "I expect you think I'm a frightful bore, fainting like that."

"Not at all. I should have been more tactful—"

"It was just that—Archie has been spending so much time at the Town Hall, and I was afraid—of course, I realize you'd have told me if . . ." She trailed off and looked at me anxiously.

"Oh, he's fine. He was there, as a matter of fact; he came in just after we—made our discovery."

"When . . . ?"

"Very close to noon."

"Then why didn't he ring me? I was at home until after one. Why hasn't he come home?"

There was panic in her voice again. I did my best.

"The police kept us quite a long time, asking questions, and Mr.—your husband was still there when I left. I expect they wanted to discuss the—er—layout of the building. And so on." And may St. Peter, or whoever keeps an eye on liars, forgive me. "Would you like me to try to find him for you? I don't think you should be alone."

That threw her back into a dither. "Oh—well—he'll be annoyed, if he's busy—but perhaps—I *should* like to talk to him—but if he's doing something important—I don't know, I'm sure—"

"I'll tell you what." She was working herself up again, and I wanted the sedative to take effect. "I'll see if I can track him down, and then he can decide what to do. You finish that tea, and I'll be right back. No, I'll use the phone in the kitchen; it may take several calls and I don't want to disturb you."

Before I left the room, I managed to unplug the phone beside the bed. I had all too good an idea where Archie might be, and I didn't want Clarice to hear.

3

AFTER A FEW anxious minutes, I managed to reach Alan, but it was a few more before he could check with his men and call back with news that wasn't as bad as I'd feared.

"Then they're going to let him go?"

"Oh, yes, certainly, nothing to hold him for. Remember, we're not even certain it's murder, yet. Pettifer's being questioned closely as a matter of routine."

I snorted.

"Oh, heard that one before, have you? Useful phrase, I admit, but in this case it's true. We need statements before people can forget details—or change their stories.

"I did gather Morrison isn't very happy with Pettifer. Apparently Pettifer admits to closing the eyes whilst you and Mrs. Finch were fortifying yourselves. He says he couldn't bear to be stared at by a dead man. Very well, but he had no business to do it, and he probably destroyed valuable evidence. There are also one or two fingerprints that look like friend Archie's, but then, there would be, wouldn't there? He's still in and out of the building rather a lot.

"The problem, of course, is that there are damned few prints, or fibers, or what have you, about the place at all. Mrs. Finch is too efficient, bless her misguided heart. They'll have to talk to the old dear later, ask exactly where she wreaked her havoc."

"They've already asked, and believe me, she won't appreciate repeating it. Alan, what can I tell Clarice? I don't want to break the news that her husband is a murder suspect if I don't have to. She's frantic, and she wants him home. When do you think . . . ?"

"That's up to Morrison, of course, but it may be quite a time yet. They want to grill Pettifer about his alibi. It looks as though our man died before midnight, and Pettifer says he had a dinner meeting with the Lord Mayor and some others early on, and then went drinking with a builder friend, one Herbert Benson. It'll have to be checked."

"Alan, how—do they know how the poor man died?"

"They're theorizing he took a sharp right to the jaw—I don't know if you noticed the bruise—and was knocked into the newel post. It's iron hard after four hundred–odd years; it would have done for him. That doesn't explain, of course, why he was found several yards away behind a closed door. However, Pettifer has no apparent injuries to either hand—and he would have if he'd delivered a blow like that. Which is another good reason to let him go.

"At any rate, he'll be released presently, I suspect in rather a foul mood. I gather we haven't treated him with quite the deference he seems to feel is his due." Alan's voice held a hint of a chuckle.

I was not amused. "Oh, fine, an irate husband is just what Clarice needs. That man mustn't be allowed to bully her when he gets home, and I certainly can't referee between them. He and I get along like two strange cats; I'd be worse than no help at all."

I heard a faint sigh. Alan needed to get back to his own affairs, but his manners held. "What about Mrs. Finch?"

"What about her?"

"Why don't you ring her up? She strikes me as the motherly type when she's not having hysterics. Would she, perhaps, enjoy ministering to Clarice?"

"Alan, you're a genius! Ada Finch is the very person. Pettifer's used to having her around, and she'll adore being in the middle of things. I'll call her right now, and you can get back to worrying about the Prince."

After three tries I hit the right Mrs. Finch, and she was there in ten minutes, talking a blue streak. We went upstairs to find Clarice still awake and fretting.

"Clarice, do you know Mrs. Finch? She works for the city and knows Mr. Pettifer, and she's come to stay with you for a while, at least until he gets home. I wasn't able to speak to him, but I gather he'll be out for a bit longer, and I didn't like to leave you alone." I was rather pleased with my little speech and its careful omissions, but Mrs. Finch opened her mouth and nearly spoiled everything.

"And 'oo better than me to look after you, as can understand wot you're goin' through, me 'avin' a 'usband as was never 'ome when I needed 'im, though with 'im it was the drink, not bein' mixed up with—"

I shook my head frantically and Mrs. Finch went on without missing a beat, "—with important affairs like your man. But there, a man's a man when all's said an' done and the best of 'em can't 'old a candle to a woman when things 'as come crashin' down about our 'eads. Now, dearie, just you stay right there an' 'ave yourself a nice lie down. It'll do you a power o' good, an' you're not to worry about a thing, I'll see to it all."

The tide of words flowed over Clarice like syrup, completing the work the pill had begun. She relaxed back into her pillows with a little sigh, like a child. Probably, I thought, she'd had a nanny just like Mrs. Finch.

"Thank you so much, Mrs. Finch." Her voice was weak, but she almost smiled. "I'm quite all right, really, but it's very kind of you to stay if you can spare the time. It was clever of you to think of this, Dorothy."

I would pass on the thanks; now was not the time to give credit where credit was due. Clarice's eyes were closing; her hands lay trustingly half open. She looked very young; for the first time I wondered just how much older her husband was. Mrs. Finch put a finger to her lips and, tiptoeing heavily, drew me out of the room.

It was getting on toward suppertime, but if I wanted to talk to Mrs. Finch, I knew I was doomed to a nice cup of tea. We headed for the kitchen, where she put the kettle on and found another teapot while I sat and appraised the room.

Mr. Pettifer had certainly done well for himself. After all the window-shopping I'd been slogging through, planning the improvements I wanted to make to my own house, I had a pretty good idea just how many thousands of pounds a kitchen like this would cost. Everything was the very best, though the decor was peculiarly mixed. White cabinets, white tile countertops, white appliances made for a hospital-like sterility, but the bright curtains and canisters, the hooked rugs, the lovely old Welsh dresser with flowery china displayed on its shelves looked like a very different personality at work. Perhaps Clarice did have some say in her household, after all.

"Naow, then!" Mrs. Finch plunked the tea tray in the middle of the kitchen table, sat down, and got right to the point. "'Oo do you think done it?"

I recalled my thoughts abruptly. "Well, actually, I—"

"I think it was 'im." Her eyes rolled upward, presumably to the bedroom above. "'Er 'usband. Mr. Bleedin' Muckety-Muck."

"He has an alibi," I said before I remembered that the information was probably confidential.

Mrs. Finch shrugged away an alibi with fine disdain. "'Ee would 'ave, wouldn't 'ee? They always do."

I realized I was dealing with a fellow lover of detective fiction. "Well, there is that," I admitted. "But, Mrs. Finch, why do you think he did it? I mean, not just why do you think so, but what motive would he have had? We don't even know who the victim is, yet."

"So 'ow would I know why 'ee done it?" She waved her hand airily. "'Ee got in 'is way."

The pronouns were a little ambiguous, but I understood that she meant the victim somehow inconvenienced Pettifer.

"But wot I mean to say is, 'oo else would it be?

'Ee was in and out o' the place every time you turned around, doin' 'oo knows wot. *And* 'ee still had a key, and wot for, I'd like to know?"

"You know, I wondered that myself. Was he planning his new project, measuring and so on?" It sounded thin, even to me, and Mrs. Finch gave me her best pitying look.

"'Ee don't do that 'imself, dearie," she said, as to a not too bright child. "'Ee's got architects and 'oo knows wot to do all the work. And they've been traipsin' through as well, trackin' mud all over me clean floors and talkin' about 'ow they was gonner pull down this and build over that till I could've 'it 'em over the 'ead wiv me mop.

"Wot I think," she said, lowering her voice and gesturing once more toward the ceiling, "I think 'ee was meetin' some woman there. And the more shame to 'im, with 'is pore wife sittin' at 'ome, cryin' 'er 'eart out—"

"You don't have to whisper; I gave Mrs. Pettifer a sleeping pill and I think she's out for the count. But, Mrs. Finch, think what you're saying! Not that I'd put it past him, but in the Town Hall? There's not a stick of furniture in the place. Where would they—I mean—?"

She laughed richly. "It don't want thinkin' about, do it? Ah, well, there you 'as me. But this I do know, an' I'll 'old to, as 'ee was plottin' some-thin', wot I don't know, sneakin' about an' jumpin' a foot if I comes near. Asks me wot I was doin' there. Wot *I* was doin' there, if you please, when I was only doin' me job wot I get paid for, same as I've always done, and no thanks for it, neither. Wot was '*ee* doin' there, I'd like to know?"

That seemed to get us back to where we'd started.

"What *I'd* like to know, Mrs. Finch—" I began, when she put her finger to her lips with an exaggerated gesture. A car door slammed. A key turned in the front door.

With a conspiratorial grin, Mrs. Finch gestured frantically toward the back door.

"I'll call you!" I mouthed, gathered up my belongings, and got out before my dignity got caught in the door.

The first order of business, when I'd managed the long walk home, was, of course, to feed the cats—cats have a way of making sure they always come first. Once they'd settled down happily to a dish of liver and bacon, I was free to think about my own belated meal.

The knock at the back door came while I was still standing in front of the open refrigerator.

"Come in, Jane." I closed the fridge and opened the cupboard. "I'm just trying to find something to eat in this house. All I seem to have is cat food and noodles, and I'm not sure a Seafood Treat casserole sounds appealing."

"Thought you'd be in no mood to cook, after the day you've had. Does cold roast beef sound good?"

"Heavenly! You're a lifesaver. I wanted to talk to you anyway."

I didn't question how she knew about my day. It had taken me only a few weeks of living in Sherebury to understand that there is very little privacy in a cathedral town. Some mysterious equivalent of jungle drums ensures that everyone will know everyone else's business, at least within cathedral circles. Jane, a retired teacher with friends all over town, knows everything that happens in Sherebury, including what is likely to happen and what is reputed to have happened but didn't. It makes her a marvelous source of information for an outsider like me.

I trailed happily after her across the backyard.

She waited with commendable patience until we were established in her kitchen with lovely thin slices of rare beef, fragrant crusty bread, and a horseradish sauce guaranteed to clear up any sinus condition. Along with mugs of beer, mine frosty-cold for my peculiar American taste. Jane is truly a paragon.

"Tell me about Clarice Pettifer," I said finally, after I'd taken a couple of bites of my superb sandwich and shooed away three amiably slobbering bulldogs whose eyes were alight with hope.

"Worm," said Jane. "Spineless. Wouldn't say boo to a goose. Not," she added, "that I've ever known what good it would do a person to say boo to a goose. However. Lived in Sherebury all her life, pretty when she was young, chocolate-box type. Enough, dogs! Go!"

They retreated a few inches and I pursued the subject. "Really! I would never have guessed. I can see it now that you mention it, though, the fair skin and china-blue eyes and so on. I suppose that's what attracted Pettifer."

Jane snorted and went on with her story. "Father well-off, owned ironmongers' shops all over the county. Started converting them to DIY shops just before the craze for do-it-yourself set in, made a fortune."

"Oh, she isn't from a—an old family—that is . . ." I floundered.

Jane barked one of her disconcerting laughs. "What you mean is, Is she upper class? Never know why Americans get so embarrassed about it. No, she isn't. Common as good English dirt, her family was, and not ashamed of it. She'd have turned out sensible if they'd lived."

"What happened?"

"Killed in an accident when Clarice was only seventeen, both her father and mother. She was left a rich orphan."

"Oh, dear. And Pettifer?" I asked, guessing the rest of the scenario.

"He was working for her father, or with him. Twelve years older than she is, you know. Involved in building the new shops. Saw a chance to rake in a fortune and a pretty wife at one go. Swept her off her feet." Jane's tone was dry enough to dehumidify a swamp. "They married when she was eighteen."

"So the money in the family is hers."

"Not all of it. Give the devil his due, he's worked hard, made a fortune of his own. Best builder in town."

"You keep surprising me. I thought he was just a developer, a—a monument-gobbling monster."

"Now, perhaps. Not back then, before he fell in love with money and power."

There was a dismal little silence.

"What a depressing story," I said finally, finishing my beer. "So that was how long ago, when they were married, I mean? Thirty years or so?"

"Twenty, more like." At the look on my face, Jane laughed, without amusement. "They're both younger than they look. He cultivates the pompous role. That's why you thought she was a nob. He's bullied her into the proper accent and the proper clothes and the proper charities till she's washed out and dried up before her time. Bloody bastard."

I raised my eyebrows. Jane is plainspoken, but seldom coarse. A horrid thought crossed my mind.

"Is he—you don't think he actually beats her? I've never seen any bruises, but . . ."

"Not that kind of bastard. Browbeats her, ignores her, sucks all the life out of her and then despises her for being dull and dead. More beer?"

"Thanks." I held out my pewter mug. "You know, though, I've always thought that people who act like doormats positively invite other people to walk on them."

"Something in that," Jane acknowledged. "Adoration brings out the worst in some men. No excuse, though."

"No." I laughed, a little bitterly. "I thought, today, that she responded so well to Mrs. Finch because she'd had a nanny like her. And all the time—"

"She *is* Mrs. Finch, that's the answer. Only without the sense. Now, Dorothy, tell me. All I know is, Ada Finch found a murdered man."

"Well—a body anyway," I said, and proceeded to tell her all I knew. "And I was just getting around to asking Mrs. Finch exactly what she'd seen this morning, when Pettifer—I cannot bring myself to call that man 'Archie'—came home and I beat it out of there. Do you suppose she's right about him being a womanizer?"

"There are rumors," Jane said. "But not at the Town Hall, not even for a meeting place."

"No," I agreed with a yawn. "Too cautious." I yawned again and put my plate on the floor to be snuffled over by the dogs, who had crept back to the table. "So if I want to soothe Clarice's fears, what do you think I ought to do next?"

"Go home to bed," said Jane promptly. "You were up with the lark. Tomorrow's soon enough to start asking awkward questions. And Alan will have some ideas of his own."

"He's going to be too busy with the royal visit to do much about this one, I think. Which is fine with me—it means I can poke around with no interference."

"Except possibly from the murderer," said Jane.

4

THAT EVENTFUL DAY was a Monday. The next day, Tuesday, normal English summer weather reasserted itself. The soothing, steady patter of rain on my roof kept me in bed until the cats decided breakfast had been delayed long enough.

I'm ashamed to say that, when my bare foot encountered a puddle on my way to the bathroom, my first reaction was to glare at the cats, who were twining themselves eagerly around my ankles. "All right, which of you was it?" They looked offended (an expression that comes naturally to any cat), and then I felt the drop of water on my head. Outside wasn't the only place it was raining.

So that, by the time I had fed my tyrants and myself, dressed in proper summer clothing (wool sweater and skirt), and put a bucket under the leak, I was in no sweet mood. I'd called my landlord's answering machine with little hope of a prompt response. Though keeping the roof in repair was clearly his responsibility, he'd been dodging my calls for some time, hoping I'd take the house off his hands soon. Well, I was doing all I could, dammit! Muttering to myself, I splashed across the Close to the bookshop.

Mrs. Williamson was puttering about the shop, replacing stock, dusting a shelf of poetry that was seldom touched. "Good morning, Dorothy. Frightful morning, actually, isn't it? We shan't have many customers today, I shouldn't think. Now tell me, how is poor Clarice? I couldn't quite make out just what sent her into such a tizz."

"I'm not sure myself, but I think she was afraid her husband was going to get into trouble. I left her in Mrs. Finch's capable hands—d'you know Mrs. Finch?" She nodded. "Anyway, Clarice was very shaky when I last saw her. Have you heard from her this morning?"

"Mr. Pettifer rang up last evening to say she wouldn't be in, so I arranged for a substitute, though with the weather what it is, I doubt she'll be needed."

"Well, I'd better hang these things up before I drip all over the stock, and then we'll see what there is to do."

As I put my yellow slicker and hat on the peg in the staff room, Barbara Dean sailed in and my heart sank.

I don't know if Mrs. Dean (she's another one I don't dare call by her first name) set out deliberately to imitate Margaret Thatcher, or if they're just naturally sisters under the skin, but I do know that if Lady Thatcher ever wants a double she need look no farther than Sherebury. The resemblance extends far beyond the helmet of gray-blond hair, the rigid carriage, the steely eye; I haven't the slightest doubt Barbara Dean could run the country quite as efficiently as she runs the Sherebury

Preservation Society and several other worthy organizations. She can be utterly charming when she wants to, but her ruthless capability reduces me to quivering jelly.

"Good gracious, Mrs. Martin, you are wet, aren't you?" She looked pointedly at the puddle forming under my slicker.

"Oh, dear, I suppose I should mop that up." And why couldn't I say that being wet is a normal consequence of being out in the rain? Perhaps it was because she appeared to be only a bit damp around the edges. Typical.

"And how is your planning application coming along?" she inquired, shooting her perfectly furled umbrella into the stand. "I assume you are nearly ready to submit it?" She sits on the City Council, naturally, and its Planning Committee.

"Well, no, actually, I can't seem to get anyone to come and talk about what I want to do. And now the roof is leaking, and—"

"Oh, but that can't be allowed." I knew she'd blame me. "You must deal with that at once, mustn't you, or there will be structural damage." It was her best headmistress tone.

"Yes, but I *can't* deal with it." Frustration bubbled over and I dared argue. "I don't own the house yet, so it's still the landlord's responsibility—and he's avoiding me because he hopes I'll be taking over soon. But until I get planning permission—*and* listed building permission—"

"No, no." She waved her hands impatiently. "Simply to repair a roof you need neither, so long as the appearance isn't altered, of course. And you needn't consider your landlord. He is obliged to maintain a listed building; if he avoids his obligations, he can be made to comply. No, your real difficulty lies with the contractors, apparently, who refuse to provide you with plans and an estimate."

"Well, it isn't exactly that they refuse, they just haven't gotten around to—"

"Quite. Obviously you must find someone else."

"There isn't anyone else. I've checked with every—"

"Nonsense. There's always someone, if one looks in the right place. I shall ask the secretary of Planning Aid to phone you this afternoon; I'm sure she'll be of help."

Planning Aid, the voluntary bureau that is supposed to help steer applicants through the maze of the planning system, had been of remarkably little help so far. Of course, Barbara Dean hadn't been the one asking.

"Thank you. I hope—"

"You must move quickly, of course, with respect to the roof, but as for the major renovations, as soon as you have plans I shall present them personally to the committee, and I think I can promise you will have your permission in short order." Another small frown appeared. "The committee has been rather taken up with other matters, to be sure. Mr. Pettifer must be stopped from despoiling the Town Hall. I was rather in despair about it two days ago, I don't mind admitting. However," she coughed delicately, "er—current events have rather rendered the issue moot, for the moment."

I was visited by sudden inspiration. "Things went Mr. Pettifer's way at the Lord Mayor's meeting, then?"

She looked at me sharply, but didn't ask how I knew about the meeting. "Certainly the prevailing wind seemed to be blowing his way, discounting a few—er—personalities that were exchanged. However, that was only a small and hardly a disinterested group of people. If you are at all concerned about the Town Hall, I suggest you attend the public meeting this evening, where the matter will be thoroughly aired. Seven o'clock, in the Victoria Hall."

The Victoria Hall, designed for concerts, was the largest meeting place in Sherebury outside the cathedral. They must be expecting a crowd.

"I'm very interested in the fate of the Town Hall. I'll be there."

I'd actually been allowed to complete a few sentences, I reflected as we went into the shop to deal with an unexpected busload of Japanese tourists. I was making progress.

I was also intrigued about what manner of "personalities" might have been exchanged Sunday night. In the mouth of a Barbara Dean, the phrase might mean anything from a nasty glare to fisticuffs. She allowed me no opening to ask, however, and, in fact, spoke to me only once more, just before lunch.

"I assume that you will be at home early this afternoon, Mrs. Martin? So that Planning Aid can ring you?"

It was obviously a royal command. I nodded humbly; it was all I could do not to tug my forelock.

The Planning Aid secretary, when she called about two-thirty, was much more approachable.

"Mrs. Dean asked me to ring you first thing this afternoon; I'm sorry I'm a bit late, but it took a little time to find the information you need. I did manage to reach Mr. Peabody—he's the local chairman for listed building permission. He said you don't need an architect just for the roof; roof repairs aren't tricky so long as the proper materials are used. Any good builder will do, and there's a new one in town you might try. He says he knows nothing about the man at all, but as he's new, he might not be booked up. Do you have a pencil? Right, then his name is Herbert Benson and his number is Sherebury 43527. I do hope it'll work out."

Her warm concern was an agreeable change. If I owed it to Barbara Dean, I was duly grateful.

Now. Herbert Benson. The name sounded vaguely familiar, with some slightly unpleasant association. I teased my brain for a moment, but whatever it was just buried itself deeper, so I made the phone call. I didn't have a lot of choice.

The man sounded nice enough and promised to come look at the roof on Thursday. I enjoyed leaving another message for the invisible landlord, informing him of his obligation in the matter of roof repairs, and set off for the Town Hall meeting a few hours later with a spring in my step.

I'd decided to walk, even though it was a stiffish pull to the university. The rain had let up a little, and I told myself parking would be impossible to find. My hat, quite a modest affair this time in pale pink straw with a simple white ribbon, would be amply protected by my umbrella, and my shoes didn't matter. I refused to admit, even to myself, my fear of driving in a country where they use the wrong side of the road and consider roundabouts to be the ideal intersection control. Myself, I find them indistinguishable from Dante's circles of hell.

Cowardice or not, walking turned out to be a smart move. The parking lots really were jammed by the time I got there, and hardly any seats were left in the Victoria Hall, even though extra chairs had been set up in the back. I secured one of them, glad to sit down even on a folding wooden chair, settled my hat, and studied with interest the people milling around the great, uncomfortable box of a room. The floor sloped sharply toward the stage, so from my position behind the last row of theater-style seats I could see everyone, the backs of their heads if nothing else.

It was a strangely mixed crowd. The chattering classes were prominent. The women, dressed with what looked like an almost deliberate lack of chic, fiddled with their pearls and conversed in throttled, well-bred voices. Mine, as usual, was the only hat in evidence. The men, in rumpled tweed suits, looked as though they wished they could smoke the pipes that bulged in their pockets.

The other distinct element, sitting in a solid block and looking somewhat formidable, consisted of working-class men and a few women. Some of the men on the other side of the hall, the ones in suits, were eying the workers uneasily, and I, too, hoped that feelings wouldn't run too high for civilized discussion. I settled back into my chair with some apprehension as the Lord Mayor walked onto the stage, chain of office and all, and everyone took their seats. This meeting was going to be interesting, at the very least.

The Lord Mayor was followed by Barbara Dean and Archibald Pettifer, who sat down, avoiding each other's eyes, as the Lord Mayor moved up to the lectern.

He cleared his throat. "Ladies and gentlemen, if I may have your attention, please . . . ah, thank you. I think we are ready to begin.

"As you all know, we in Sherebury have for some time been quite concerned about the fate of our Town Hall. It has, most regrettably, been allowed to fall into a state of disrepair owing to the lack of funds to restore it. Although grants have been sought, some of you may know that the final resort to English Heritage was unsuccessful; the cost of necessary repairs is estimated to run to millions of pounds, and since the Council simply cannot provide the city's share, English Heritage have declined their help.

"This decision, rendered only in the past few days, has been a major blow to preservation efforts. However, as you may also know, an alternative proposal has been on the table for some time. This proposal, put forward by Mr. Pettifer—" the mayor nodded gravely to Pettifer, who nodded back "—is, briefly, that he use his own funds to restore the Town Hall, in several stages, in return for which he would be granted a ninety-nine-year lease on the building. There is, of course, a quid pro quo: The proposal is contingent upon his being allowed to effect certain nonstructural changes to the interior of the building so that he could put it to commercial use."

There was a murmur at that, soft but menacing, and I saw Barbara Dean's hands, clasped in her lap, make a convulsive little movement before she controlled them.

"Ah, I see that many of you are familiar with Mr. Pettifer's plans," said the mayor with just the hint of a smile. It was exactly the right touch; a chuckle

passed lightly through the room and the tension
dissipated—for the moment.

"Because the Town Hall decision is a matter so
controversial, and so fundamental to the city, the
chairman of the Planning Committee has invited
me as your Lord Mayor to take the chair of this
meeting. I have invited Mr. Pettifer, and Mrs.
Dean, chairman of the Sherebury Preservation
Society, to present their views on the matter. I
think I may safely say that those views have points
of difference."

Again the crowd chuckled. I began to see why
this man was such a successful politician.

"After their formal remarks, I shall open the
floor for discussion. I ask those who wish to speak
to come to one of the microphones, identify themselves, and keep their remarks brief, so that we may
allow everyone a chance.

"Mr. Pettifer, will you begin?"

Pettifer, as he took the Mayor's place at the lectern, cut rather a poor figure by contrast. Although
the Mayor's suit was older and his hair thinner, his
tall, spare figure and ascetic face held a dignity that
made his elaborate chain of office seem a natural
part of his ensemble. Pettifer's tailoring was impec-
cable, his shoes were polished to a high gloss, but
there was nothing he could do about a florid com-
plexion or a tendency to embonpoint. I was
reminded of a Kewpie doll trying to be impressive,
and suddenly, most unexpectedly, I felt a little sorry
for him.

"My friends," he said in the unctuous tones that
had doubtless won him votes over the years, "I see
no need to belabor the points our esteemed Lord
Mayor has made so eloquently. The facts are very

clear indeed. Our Town Hall is falling down. Although the exterior walls remain sound, the roof and the interior are in sorry condition. I am fully prepared to present the reports of the inspectors should you wish to take the time, but there is no disagreement about their verdict. If the necessary repairs are not made, and made soon, this precious monument to Sherebury's illustrious history will be lost forever.

"You will note that I have referred to the exalted status of the building in order to take the words out of the mouth of my distinguished opponent." He bowed and smiled at Barbara Dean as the crowd tittered; her smile in return was a mere baring of teeth.

"My friends, I am a builder by trade. I would venture to say that no one—I repeat, no one—in Sherebury is more aware than I of the great beauty and exemplary workmanship represented by the Town Hall. I revere its builders as the geniuses they were. *But!*" He raised an admonitory finger. "As I venerate the building, so I am convinced that it is a living building, deserving, and indeed requiring, to be of use. Did its builders intend it to be an object of worship? No! They constructed it for use, use by the journeymen of the town of Sherebury, by ordinary people like you and me."

He looked directly at the group of workmen, who responded with nods and nudgings and one muted cry of "'Ear, 'ear!" from a walrus-mustached man standing against the wall.

Encouraged, Pettifer leaned forward and rested his forearms on the lectern. "Now, we all know that Sherebury is in economic trouble. Hundreds of able-bodied men in our small community are unable to find work; hundreds more have left with their wives and families to seek a better life elsewhere. Can we afford to let this situation continue? Can we afford to allow our strongest and best workers remain in despair, or depart in disgust? My friends, I say we cannot, and I have a solution. Put them to work on the Town Hall! Bring new business to town, new commerce in my Town Hall Mall. Rescue, not just a fine building, but the spirit of Sherebury!"

The rising murmurs of approval from the workmen erupted in a little chorus of cheers. The rest of the room sat in chilly silence as Pettifer sat down and Barbara Dean stepped forward, every silver hair lacquered into place, every line of her powder blue suit firmly under control.

"You're quite a powerful speaker, sir," she said with a ferocious smile. "I wonder you don't go into Parliament." The quote from Dickens was a nasty little dig at Pettifer's political ambitions. His face turned puce as he bowed coldly.

"I am sure, however, that your audience is too intelligent to be swayed by political posturings. Let us return to our senses, ladies and gentlemen, from which we have been invited to take leave, and consider. Mr. Pettifer pretends that he has two motives, both philanthropic: He wishes to preserve the fabric of the Town Hall and he wishes to assume the role of Father Christmas to the working men of Sherebury. I submit that, although he does bear some physical resemblance—" she stared meaningfully at Pettifer's little paunch and raised a giggle or two "—his essential characteristic is more Scrooge-like.

"We are all heartily sick and tired of militaristic governments throughout the world who for so many years have insisted that the way to preserve the peace is by making war. I submit that Mr. Pettifer's plan to preserve the Town Hall by despoiling it falls into the same category of logic. I submit that those workmen whom he is so anxious to protect could be as fully employed in the proper restoration of the Town Hall as in its desecration.

"Can anyone doubt that Mr. Pettifer's real motives are much simpler? Profit and personal aggrandizement are far more likely to drive such a man than philanthropy. I would ask you to consider Mr. Pettifer's plans, of which most of you are aware, to build what he refers to as 'University Housing.' He has sought planning permission to pull down a row of perfectly sound houses which rent cheaply—to students, for the most part—and put up cracker boxes in their stead. Can we doubt that the rents will be far higher? Can we doubt that the profits will be far higher than if the existing houses were simply renovated?

"This is the man who asks you to give the Town Hall into his hands. I ask you all: Is there anyone here who can point to any action in Mr. Pettifer's past that shows his concern for the public good? Is he a notable contributor to any charity? Has he, in fact, ever given a shilling to the poor or even rescued a stray dog?"

The murmurs had been growing, and now one workman spoke loudly enough to be heard. "Sacked me once, 'ee did, for nothin' at all!" The mood of the crowd had changed, as is the fickle way of crowds. As the level of sound in the room rose and took on an ugly undertone, I felt a moment of panic. Was this meeting going to degenerate into a riot?

5

"NOW, LADIES AND gentlemen." Mrs. Dean raised her hands in placatory fashion, and spoke in tones that were honeyed, clear, and low enough that people were forced to hush in order to hear her. Clever, I thought. The workmen sat down again.

"You must not think that I wish to assassinate Mr. Pettifer's character." Chuckles and a couple of jeers. "No, indeed. If that were my purpose, I have more serviceable weapons at my command." More laughter, with a mean-tempered edge to it. I thought for a moment that she was going to refer to the murder, and Pettifer looked up sharply, but Dean was apparently not prepared to stoop so low. Or maybe she thought the insinuation was sufficient.

She went on. "I am simply trying to impress upon you that he is not the man we need for the job at hand, which is to save the Town Hall. I have a plan, ladies and gentlemen, and I ask you to listen carefully and—without prejudice—decide whether it is not a better plan for the purpose."

The languid majority sat up and perked their ears.

"Until now we have put our faith in grants from outside Sherebury. As the Lord Mayor has told you, all these appeals have come to naught. It is time to look to our own community, time to take our fate into our own hands. I have, therefore, in the past several days, had conversations with the leaders of Sherebury: political, religious, commercial, and educational. Everyone was most eager to cooperate in a massive fund drive for the preservation of one of Sherebury's most important pieces of history. To be specific: Our Lord Mayor, Councillor Daniel Clarke, has agreed to open his home for a fête in aid of the cause. The Very Reverend Mr. Kenneth Allenby, Dean of the Cathedral, proposed that one night of the forthcoming Cathedral Music Festival be dedicated to the Town Hall, with all proceeds being donated to the fund. A number of businessmen and -women have agreed to allow solicitation of funds at their places of business, and many have promised personal or corporate donations, as well. And finally, the vice chancellor of Sherebury University has agreed to enlist the aid of a number of students, not only as solicitors, but in the planning of benefit projects.

"Ladies and gentlemen, if this much support can be generated in a few days, is there any question that we can raise our share of the necessary funds? We must prove to English Heritage that Sherebury has the will to save the Town Hall. We must do it, and we shall!"

The crowd was with her now. Cheers and shouts of "Hear, hear!" sounded from all sides. As the Lord Mayor began to restore order, rapping on the lectern, and the people resumed their seats, one

woman rose from her seat on the aisle and marched
to the nearest microphone. I recognized her after a
moment as the owner of a gift shop in the High
Street. She was dressed in a bright yellow suit,
somewhat too tight, and her fiercely red hair positively bristled. She raised her voice.

"Lord Mayor, may I speak?"

"Certainly, certainly, everyone must have a
chance to be heard—if you will please be seated—
your attention, please!"

The woman at the microphone began to speak
before all the noise had abated, but her angry tones
cut through.

"And what about me, I'd like to know? Me and
all the other shopkeepers in town? Where do we fit
into this lovely scheme? It's all very well to save a
building, but what's the point if there's nobody to
use it?"

The Mayor interrupted her. "For the record, will
you identify yourself, please?"

"Mavis Underwood, as you know. I keep the gift
shop in the High Street, and three more in Seldon,
Watsford, and King's Abbot, and you all know that,
too. *And* you know how business is in Sherebury
High Street. Or if you don't, I'll tell you. It scarcely
exists. This month my receipts won't meet my
rent, and not for the first time, and the other mer-
chants will tell you the same. How much longer
can we operate at a loss?" There was a little murmur of agreement from various quarters of the
room.

"At the end of the day, the Sherebury shop is an
albatross, dragging the rest down. I need—we all
need—new clientele, and a new mall will bring
them. The Town Hall Mall—that's different than

the rest; it'll draw the punters. What'll an empty building draw? Flies!"

She took a deep breath, audible over the sound system, and was clearly prepared to go on in the same vein, but the Lord Mayor cut her off neatly.

"Thank you so much, Mrs. Underwood. Your point of view is a valuable one, which I'm sure represents the thoughts of many here." He turned toward a microphone on the other side of the room. "Mr. Farrell, have you something to say?"

"William Farrell, contractor." He spoke in a deep growl that boomed out over the loudspeakers and set up an excruciating shriek of feedback. While someone tried to adjust the volume, I studied the man with interest. He was standing at a microphone near the back of the room, and although I couldn't see most of his face, I could see the tension in his prominent jaw. He was altogether a formidable-looking person, tall and powerfully built, with dark hair and a hulking sort of squareness to his shoulders that reminded me uncomfortably of Boris Karloff.

"I'm so sorry, Mr. Farrell," said the Lord Mayor. "Would you like to try again?"

"What I've got to say is soon said. There's no need for all this talk. I've had a proposal on the table for nearly a year now to build a proper mall, with proper parking and access, at the old hop farm on the A28. There's your new clientele, Mavis. There's your traffic; you all know how much traffic the A28 carries every day of the week. No need to put the Town Hall to a silly use that was never intended. Preserve it; take the shopping out of town, where people want it nowadays. Everyone's pleased."

Mr. Pettifer didn't look pleased at all, and jumped up to reply, but the Lord Mayor motioned to him with a frown, and he sat down, folding his arms across his chest, the alarming color rising again in his face.

There was a stirring in the group of workmen and then a middle-aged man with sparse gray hair, evidently chosen as their spokesman, forced his way out of a tightly packed row of seats and moved to the microphone.

"I'm Jem 'Iggins, Yer Worship," he said, grasping the mike stand uneasily in gnarled hands. "And like a lot of us 'ere tonight, I'm out of work. And what me mates and me got ter say is, we don't none of us care where they builds whatever they're goin' to build, so long as we 'as a part in it. But it 'pears to us as if the work would be double, like, if they was to do them repairs to the Town Hall *and* build their shoppin' mall someplace else. And it stands to reason, don't it, that if we 'as more money, we'll spend more money, and that's good for trade, too. And—that's all."

He turned away abruptly to an approving chorus from his mates, and now everyone was eager to speak. A few malcontents grumbled about various aspects of the problem, and a few more wandered far from the issue at hand, arguing about everything from civic government in general to environmental issues to animal rights, but most of the comments reiterated support for Mrs. Dean's preservation efforts, and the audience grew restive.

I stopped listening and concentrated on watching Pettifer. His color had returned to its normal hue, but his expression had set in a hard half smile.

He had lost this battle, and he knew it, but he hadn't given up the war. Too good a politician to try to sway a crowd that had so obviously turned against him, he nevertheless sat erect in his chair, looking each speaker defiantly in the eye. Some of them faltered in mid-speech, and Pettifer looked grimly satisfied each time.

Finally the Lord Mayor decided to call a halt. "Thank you, ladies and gentlemen. I think we have been able to air this matter thoroughly, and I thank you for your time and patience, and for your courtesy in listening to other points of view. You understand, of course, that as the Town Hall is a Grade One listed building, the Secretary of State will make the ultimate decision about its fate, but you may be sure he will have a report of this meeting. I notice, Mr. Thorpe, that you have made no contribution, and wonder if there is anything you would like to say to close the meeting."

A bulky sort of man got up and moved back a row or two to the nearest mike, a used-car salesman smile on his face. "I have nothing to add, Lord Mayor. My name, for the record, is John Thorpe, and I am an estate agent." He said it as John Gielgud might have said "I am an actor."

"I feel it would be inappropriate for me to comment, since I am likely to be an interested party in dealing with leases for any new mall. I'm sure that all plans put forward today have merit, and simply wish to say, may the best man—or woman—" he sketched a little bow to Mrs. Dean "—win!" He turned away without looking at Pettifer, who was glaring balefully.

"Very well, then, ladies and gentlemen, I thank you all again and declare this meeting adjourned."

I creaked to my feet, stumbling a little. A steadying hand caught my elbow.

"Alan! Bless you, I thought my joints were going to give out on me altogether. My bones do not appreciate two hours of this kind of chair. What are you doing here? I didn't see you when I came in."

"No, I drifted in late. I like to keep my finger on the community pulse, you know, especially when it's getting a trifle feverish—to mix a metaphor. What did you think of the meeting?"

I shivered a little. "It's very different from this sort of thing in America, of course. We'd have everybody yelling at each other. This was all very polite, but it was that terrible English politeness that can feel like being slammed into a meat locker. To tell the truth, it scared me a little. I can see why you're worried. Those workmen were ready to do something drastic, if Barbara Dean hadn't handled them so well—did you get here in time for that?"

Alan nodded. "Played them like a violin, didn't she? Stirring them up to a nice crescendo and then calming them down. A remarkable lady, our Barbara."

I shivered again. "And that Mr. Farrell scares me."

Alan hugged my shoulders. "You've been watching too many old horror videos, is your trouble. How about a drink to take the bogeyman away?"

"And a sandwich—I feel in need of sustenance. Alan, Mr. Pettifer isn't going to take this sitting down, I could tell. He was ready to kill that man Thorpe."

Alan just looked at me and I grimaced.

"Sorry—poor choice of words. But honestly, if looks could kill, I should think you'd have another corpse on your hands. I suppose Thorpe's been in Pettifer's camp and now Pettifer thinks he's a Judas."

"Probably. Where's your car? I didn't ask my driver to wait."

"Then we're out of luck. I walked. For the exercise," I added defiantly.

"One of these days I'm going to make you a present of driving lessons," said Alan cheerfully, looking around. "Ah, constable!"

The uniformed man just leaving the hall stopped in his tracks, trotted over, and saluted smartly, looking anxious. "Yes, sir!"

"It's all right, Wilkins," Alan said, reading the name tag without missing a beat. "I simply need a favor, if you have your car."

Wilkins nodded, mute in the presence of his Big Boss.

"The lady and I need a ride over to the Cathedral Close, if it's not too much trouble."

"Yes, sir. That is, no, sir, no trouble at all, sir. This way, sir—madam."

So we ended the evening peaceably at the Rose and Crown discussing leaky roofs and other domestic disasters, with not a word about murders or civic passions.

Over breakfast the next day my mind reverted to the meeting of the night before. I wished I understood a little more about all the crosscurrents. Why, for example, had Thorpe done what looked like such an abrupt about-face? Why hadn't Farrell's proposal—which sounded so reasonable—gained approval, or even discussion, over the past year?

And most of all, what had gone on at that meeting the Lord Mayor had held Sunday night? The tensions at the public meeting had been only thinly veiled; I could well believe in those heated private exchanges Barbara Dean had hinted at.

I considered my sources of information. Jane, of course, but Jane wasn't available at the moment; she volunteered at the animal shelter on Wednesdays. Margaret Allenby, wife of the dean of the cathedral, could sometimes be persuaded to talk about personalities in ecclesiastical circles, and Jeremy Sayers, the organist, was always open to gossip, the bitchier the better—but this wasn't a church matter. It wasn't a university matter, either, which left out dear old Dr. Temple, who knew everything about everyone academic but wasn't interested in general gossip.

That just about exhausted the possibilities in my limited group of friends, which meant I'd have to wait till Jane got home. Meanwhile, there were other worries to deal with, the foremost being Clarice. Archie couldn't have been feeling very pleasant when he got home last night after the meeting. In her present jellylike state, was Clarice in any condition to cope with him?

I groaned aloud and Samantha, in the corner of the kitchen by the Aga, interrupted her ablutions to stare at me through her huge blue eyes.

"It's all very well for you," I said glumly. "You can sit there by a nice, warm stove. I've got to go out in the rain. Aren't you glad you're a cat?"

Sam yawned; of course she was glad. No cat would even consider the infinitely inferior status of human.

So I emptied the buckets in the upstairs hall—

they were filling faster today, I noted with a mental curse for my landlord—and headed for the Pettifers' new, watertight, sterile house.

I drove. The long walk in the rain last night had caused arthritic twinges in several joints I'd never noticed before, and I was also smarting from Alan's crack about driving lessons. I got insignificantly lost twice and, in desperation, drove the wrong way down a deserted one-way street to get to where I needed to be, but on the whole I thought I did rather well, though my knees were shaking as I got out of the car.

They shook even more on the front step as I considered the awful possibility that Archie might be home, but I was in luck. The door opened promptly to my ring and there, sturdy and blessedly sane and normal, was Mrs. Finch.

"'Ere, now, 'ere's a treat for you, luv," she called in to the hall. "'Ere's Mrs. Martin come to see you."

She stage-whispered at me behind her hand. "Wobbly on 'er pins still, she is, but comin' along. Company'll do 'er no end o' good."

"I'm glad you're still here, Mrs. Finch," I whispered back as I followed her into the kitchen, marveling a little. Here was a woman who had found a body, ministering calmly to the vapors of one who had only heard about it. Truly the Cockney is a rare and precious breed.

Clarice was looking better. What color she ever had was back in her cheeks and her soft, fair hair was neatly combed, if a bit discouraged-looking. She was sitting at the breakfast table in a becoming pink-flowered housecoat, with a teacup in front of her.

"Oh, Dorothy, I'm so glad to see you." Her voice was almost back to normal, too. "Won't you have some tea? Ada makes the most lovely tea, and frightfully good biscuits."

She sounded like a little girl inviting me to a dolls' tea party. I sat, and Mrs. Finch happily assumed her role of nanny, seizing the tea tray and making for the stove.

"I can't imagine what you must be thinking of me, Dorothy," Clarice went on shyly. "So silly of me to go to pieces like that."

"Don't worry about it. You had a shock."

"But I do wish I were more like you. You never turn a hair at frightful things, and nor does Ada."

I thought of Mrs. Finch's hysterics, but I didn't want to mention the murder scene. "It's easier for me. I'm still an outlander here, so terrible things aren't so—immediate, I guess. Besides, I've gotten good at hiding my feelings. Don't forget, I've got more than twenty years on you. Anyway, I'm glad you're feeling more like yourself."

"You're very kind, Dorothy." There was a tear on her cheek; she brushed it away and pulled herself together. "But I mustn't be cosseted when I'm being foolish. I was afraid that Archie would be in trouble, you see, since it was the Town Hall. But the police have had the sense to realize he couldn't have had anything to do with it, so it's quite all right."

What a fragile bubble of hope! From what Alan had told me, neither Archie nor anyone else was out of the running at the moment. But let Clarice play with her pretty bubble while she could.

Mrs. Finch set a tray in front of us and waited, hands on hips, for applause. She certainly deserved it. The tray was beautifully arranged with a lace cloth, flowered china, and a mouthwatering plateful of scones and homemade cookies. I took a bite of one and rolled my eyes skyward, grateful not only for the goodies but for a reason not to reply to Clarice.

"This is sublime, Mrs. Finch. Do you ever give people your recipes?"

"We-ell. That almond biscuit's me granny's own receipt, and I said I'd never part with it but to me own flesh and blood. But seein' as 'ow me son ain't got 'imself a wife no more, nor yet no children—"

I caught my breath. "No children" was a phrase to be avoided around Clarice. One of our bonds was our childlessness, but whereas I'd learned over the years to deal with the pain, for Clarice it was fresh and new every single month, as her hopes were dashed again. I've seen her cry helplessly during a baptism at the cathedral.

This morning, thank goodness, her thoughts were otherwise occupied. "Ada's been telling me about the meeting last night," she said. "Do sit down and go on, Ada."

I breathed again. "Oh, were you there, Mrs. Finch? I didn't see you."

"I didn't like to leave 'ere, but me son went, an' come an' told me about it after. I was just sayin' as 'ow it don't look too good for Mr. Pettifer bein' allowed to build 'is mall."

"Yes, but Ada," Clarice said eagerly, "last night was only a public discussion. Archie will talk them round, the Council and the people who matter. He's such a powerful speaker. And the important thing is that no one said a word about him being accused—involved in the—accident. I'm sure it was an accident, it must have been. Don't you think so, Dorothy?"

I was very glad I had a mouthful of biscuit, even if I nearly choked. "Certainly the police haven't made up their minds yet about the circumstances," I said after I'd taken as long as possible to chew and swallow. "At least according to the little I know. Could I have a little more tea? And Clarice, not to change the subject, but when do you think you might be able to get back to work? Mrs. Williamson really needs you."

It was rude, but it worked; Clarice is easily led. We talked about the bookshop for a few minutes, and then Clarice excused herself. "I'm having my hair done," she confided. "Ada thought it would brace me up."

"Good for you. Make sure they really pamper you."

I lingered in the hall after she had gone upstairs to dress. "What did your son really think of the meeting? I didn't want to talk about it in front of Clarice."

Mrs. Finch snickered. "'Ee said it were a tea party compared to the one on Sunday."

"You mean the Lord Mayor's meeting?" I was all ears. "How does he know about that?"

"'Ee didn't. I told 'im."

She looked at me, a cheeky grin on her weather-beaten face.

"All right, all right! How did you know, then? You know perfectly well I'm dying to hear all about it."

She sat down on the elegant Directoire chaise longue in the hall, an incongruous figure in a too tight nylon housedress, work boots, and white socks, and told me.

"See, the meetin', it was at the private room in the Feathers, seein' as 'ow the Mayor's parlor is bein' done up. You know the Feathers?"

I nodded. It was the biggest pub in the High Street, a good place for food and drink.

"Well, Tom 'Arris, 'im as keeps the Feathers, is by way o' bein' a friend of mine." She looked up coyly, and I nodded and obliged with the wink that seemed to be expected. "So when we was 'avin' a friendly drop o' gin, like, 'ee told me all about it. There was just the six of 'em: 'is Worship, an' Mr. Pettifer, 'an Mrs. Dean as runs everything, an' then them as spoke at the big meetin'. That John Thorpe—" She sniffed disdainfully. "An' Mr. Farrell and Mavis Underwood, 'oo 'as got entirely above 'erself. An' the Mayor thought 'ee could keep it all civilized, like." She affected a genteel accent. "'See if we carn't all come to a meetin' of minds,' 'ee said. Wanted to see which way the cat would jump, if you arsk me, so's 'ee'd know which side to come down on 'imself.

"So for a bit it was all la-di-da and properlike. Then after dinner, when they'd all 'ad one or two, Mr. Pettifer started in. Talkin' big, like it was all settled, and lordin' it over Mr. Farrell.

"Well, Mr. Farrell, 'ee just blew up. The *language,* Tom said—such as you wouldn't 'ardly believe. A right down shindy, it were! An' Tom said Mr. Farrell just crashed out of there, like to took the door off the 'inges—an' 'ee said 'ee'd stop Archie if it was the last thing 'ee did, an' left lookin' fit to kill somebody!"

6

WHEN I GOT home, self and car amazingly still in one piece, I picked up the nearest cat and sat down on the couch to mull over Mrs. Finch's news.

Her sensational style made the most of the story, of course. When you got right down to it, all it amounted to was that the Lord Mayor's meeting had been less than cordial, and I'd already known that. Still, I now had the full personnel list and information about one specific run-in. What I didn't know was whether any of it was relevant.

I stretched to reach the end table (Emmy, who had purred herself almost to sleep on my lap, commented crossly) and got a pad and pen. Time to make some lists.

First I listed everyone who had been at the meeting Sunday night. Of course, there was no assurance that one of them was the murderer. But when six people get together and quarrel fiercely, and shortly thereafter a murder is committed that affects them all, in a site close to the meeting, my common sense refuses to dismiss the possibility of a connection. Very well:

Daniel Clarke, the Lord Mayor
Archibald Pettifer
Barbara Dean
John Thorpe
Mavis Underwood
William Farrell

Now, one of the first principles of criminal investigation, at least as practiced in my favorite form of fiction, is to establish who benefits. Or, as Hercule Poirot used to put it, to see what the real effect of the crime is and then determine who is better off because of it. And the most important result of this crime, to my mind, was that Pettifer's plans for the Town Hall were at least deferred, if not doomed. I studied my list of names. I'd lived in Sherebury long enough to know a little about most of them. Who was a likely murderer?

It was hard to imagine any personal benefit to the Mayor. Aside from the sheer effrontery of suspecting such an important personage, I honestly didn't see that he had any ax to grind one way or the other. He had appeared, last night, to come down on the preservation side, but his motives seemed truly disinterested, with the welfare of the town foremost.

Pettifer was undoubtedly a loser at this point. True, he had access to the Town Hall, and he had acted peculiarly in the matter of tampering with the body. But I couldn't see any reason why he'd want to scuttle his own project.

Barbara Dean, I thought almost guiltily, looked like a front-runner. She had said that Pettifer had been in the ascendant Sunday night—and now she had the upper hand. Preservation was more than a preference with her, it was a religion. And she was a determined woman. To the point of ruthlessness? To the point of murder? I didn't know, but somehow I couldn't quite dismiss the idea. Her Eminence didn't let obstacles stand in her way, and she was used to getting what she wanted—somehow.

John Thorpe. Wealthy, the leading real-estate dealer in Sherebury, with a reputation as a sharp dealer, a hustler. I could imagine that ethics might play very little part in his actions, so he was attractive as a murder suspect. Unfortunately, he seemed to have no motive. He had shown last night that he was ready to throw Pettifer to the wolves if it was expedient. What a pity I couldn't figure out a private motive, so to speak. Could he have some grudge, a quarrel with Pettifer, so that he wanted to see him fail?

Mavis Underwood was an enigma. Unless she was a fine actress, she'd been genuinely furious about the prospect of the failure of the Town Hall Mall. But if her only interests were business-related, I couldn't see why another location wouldn't do just as well. And why would she want to cause trouble for Pettifer?

Which left me with William Farrell. I'd deliberately saved the best for last, and now I let myself take a good, long look. There was a lot against him. He wanted his own project to prevail. He'd quarreled, violently and publicly, with Pettifer the night of the murder. He was a powerful man with a hot temper. Yes, I liked Farrell a lot.

The problem was that I didn't have a single iota of evidence to support any of this theorizing. Until I had some answers about motive, and means, and opportunity—all the police-court questions—I was playing Blind Man's Buff.

I moved Emmy's tail off the pad and made another list of things I wanted badly to know.

QUESTIONS
Access to the scene of the crime: Who had a key to the Town Hall? Where are the keys now?
Who is the victim? (That was one for the police, though.)
Is there another motive besides ruining Pettifer's plans?

And there was another way to look at those ruined plans, I suddenly realized. If this murder—and it was murder, I was sure—were never solved, it would still stop Pettifer in his tracks. Suspicion is just as bad as proof for a politician, and Pettifer was nothing if not a politician. His position on the City Council was, in his mind, only a stepping-stone to greater things. If someone wanted to stop his political career badly enough to murder some unfortunate vagrant and plant the body . . .

Far-fetched? Perhaps. At any rate it was an unproductive train of thought at the moment. Until the body was identified, I reminded myself again, what I was doing was mere speculation.

And when had that ever stopped me?

Emmy grunted irritably in her sleep and moved her tail back where she wanted it, covering most of the page. I retrieved my pad, studied my meager notes, and sighed.

There certainly wasn't much inspiration there. As usual, list-making had made me feel busy while accomplishing exactly nothing. What I needed to do was talk to people.

Right, said the internal killjoy who gives me trouble every now and then. *You're going to go see a lot of people you don't know, any of whom might be a murderer, and ask them a lot of very snoopy questions. Have you lost your mind completely this time?*

I'll be subtle about it, I argued with myself.

Hmmph! You're about as subtle as a Mack truck.

Shut up. I'm American. They think talking to me doesn't count.

You can't get by with that one anymore. You've lived here a year, they know you're here to stay. If you don't get yourself killed first.

SHUT UP! This is only a game, anyway. Probably the kid fell downstairs or something and none of these highly respectable people had anything to do with it.

Then how did he get in the closet?

That, I answered triumphantly, is what I intend to find out by talking to people!

The killjoy shrugged its figurative shoulders, murmuring something about geriatric Nancy Drews, but I ignored it.

I concentrated on how to approach the people on my list. I knew two of them, of course, which didn't make it any easier. Barbara Dean would ignore any questions she didn't want to answer, and freeze me out in the process. And Pettifer—I just plain didn't want to talk to Pettifer. We'd been slightly acquainted for six months; it hadn't been a pleasure. Neither of us had found any reason to modify the mutual dislike that had crystallized at first sight. I didn't approve of his ambitions, and he thought me a reactionary, interfering busybody.

He had a point, in a way. Mind you, I'm not one of those people who are automatically against progress, but I have no time for the attitude that change and progress are necessarily the same thing. Something new is not guaranteed to be better than something old; it is, in fact, very often much worse.

Look at my house. (I stretched and did so, lovingly; Emmy protested.) After four centuries it needed work, true. Wood changes its shape through the years and adjustments must be made. But there was no problem with the structure itself. The craftsmen who put this house together knew what they were doing, and they took pride in their work. Joints were designed to bear the load they were given. Materials were chosen carefully for the job they had to do, especially the oak, so achingly difficult to work with but so strong and tough and durable—and so beautiful.

Perhaps that was at the heart of it. They cared about beauty then, those long-dead carpenters, and the glaziers who joyously let in the light. Those tiny diamond panes spoke not only of glassmaking techniques in the seventeenth century, but of the artisans' love of grace and proportion.

Whereas men like Pettifer—

Emmy, sensing my tension even in her sleep, sat up with a low growl and blinked at me, her claws pricking my leg.

"It's all right, cat. I won't hurt you. I don't think I'd hurt anybody, but it's sure a temptation with some people."

Better safe than sorry, Emmy decided, and leapt from my lap, landing with a heavy thud. That woke Samantha, who exploded from a featureless lump on the hearth into a lean bundle of energetic mischief.

The two streaked into the kitchen, hissing and spitting. I climbed off my mental soapbox, put another log on the fire, and reconsidered my list.

Save Pettifer for last, anyway. How to tackle the others, then?

I hadn't the slightest idea how I was to arrange an informal conversation with the Lord Mayor, whom I had never met. Leave him for the moment. Of the others, the easiest was undoubtedly Mavis Underwood. If you keep a shop, you must expect people to come into it. I'd probably have to buy something, but information might be cheap at the price.

John Thorpe wasn't hard, either. I didn't look forward to a conversation with him, but he was an estate agent, and, like Mavis, had to expect the public to appear at his door from time to time. I even had an almost legitimate excuse: I was going to have to do something about my housing problem soon, either buy this house or continue to rent it, or find someplace else. Very well, call on him after Mavis.

Again I saved Farrell for last. He made me nervous. (The killjoy gave a little cackle at that thought.) Not, I insisted defiantly, because he was a murderer. Of course, I didn't really think that. He was just—scary.

And all right, so I'm not always perfectly logical, I told the killjoy as I struggled to my feet and prepared to go shopping. So sue me.

I chose one of my favorite hats, a crimson straw cloche decorated with a single huge poppy. It's extremely becoming, and the white silk dress piped in red that goes with it takes off at least ten pounds. I didn't care if my attire was more suitable for a

Buckingham Palace garden party than a small-town shopping (and snooping) expedition. I knew I looked good, and I needed the self-confidence.

Besides, when you're overdressed, people tend to patronize you, and patronizing means underestimating. I could use that advantage, too.

I enjoyed the walk. The rain seemed to be over. It had made the paving stones slick and I had to watch my step, but it had also brought out heavenly smells as only a summer rain can. The freshness of growing things and the earthy aroma of wet stone and the elusive scent of water itself made me feel as if I were breathing in nourishment.

The sun came out just as I turned into the High Street, and a rainbow arched itself across the sky, so lovely that I stopped in my tracks and blocked the sidewalk. The beautiful jumble of buildings—Tudor, Jacobean, Queen Anne, Georgian—sparkled in the sun, their roofs and chimney stacks and small-paned windows all at irregular angles that caught the light and threw it back in generous sprays. Color sprang up out of grayness: the pink and red of small, handmade bricks, the subtle blues and greens and rusts of lichen-covered slate and tile roofs, the sharp black and white of half-timbering, all set off by the bright arc curving against retreating clouds. I don't know how long I would have stood there stock-still, tears in my eyes, but a small man ran into me, muttered a reproachful "Sorry," and then turned to look where I was looking. He grinned then, said, "Nice, innit?" and tipped his hat before hurrying off.

Underwood's occupies a central position on the High Street, across the street from the Town Hall and down a few doors. I'd been inside only once, trying to find something that would do for a niece's wedding. I hadn't found it.

The shop (the gaudy sign over the door spelled it "Shoppe") was deserted. Scarcely had the bell over the door stopped tinkling before Mavis bore down upon me, steely determination in her eye. Aha, the look said, a live one. I was grateful for the morale-stiffening hat.

"Mrs. Underwood?" I smiled brightly. "You won't remember me, I haven't lived here very long—"

"Mrs. Martin, isn't it?" Her smile showed even more teeth than mine. "How nice to see you again. Are you looking for a gift, or treating yourself?"

"Actually I'm just window-shopping," I said firmly.

Mavis was not to be deterred. "Well, then, let me show you something I know you'll love. They're just in, and they'd be lovely in your *exquisite* house. Brass occasional tables, genuine Indian work, and practical, as well—they nest, you see. Aren't they charming? Or perhaps you need something for your kitchen . . ."

I let her adamantly genteel tones wash over me, nodded and smiled until my face hurt, and waited for an opportunity to ask questions. It wasn't going to come soon. She didn't intend to let a customer escape her brightly varnished talons. I studied her inventory for something that might conceivably be of use, if only for a gift, and wouldn't cost an arm and a leg. The stuffed chintz cats and rabbits were attractive, but what would you do with them? Ashtrays—pretty, but nobody smokes anymore. Finally, desperately, I picked up the smallest china cottage I could find and interrupted her lavish praise of a wildly expensive brass bed stead.

"How much is this?"

Her face fell for only an instant. Never irritate a customer; she might buy something worthwhile next time. "You do have an eye for a bargain, Mrs. Martin! It's a lovely little cottage, isn't it, and only sixty pounds, including VAT."

I swallowed hard. The thing fitted nicely into the palm of my hand. "I am tempted," I lied gamely. How many plants for my garden would sixty pounds have bought? However— "I like it, you see, because it's so beautiful and old-fashioned. I just love your old English buildings! That *gorgeous* Town Hall, for instance. I understand it's going to be renovated, now that the offices have moved out?"

Her eyes narrowed a bit; I noticed the right eyelash was about to fall off. "Why, yes. As a matter of fact, my new shop is to be in the Town Hall Shopping Mall. Far larger and more convenient; you'll like it, I'm sure."

"Is that a fact!" My voice dripped innocent admiration, but her face was shrewdly speculative and I thought I'd better play it safe. "Actually, I did go to the meeting last night—maybe you saw me there—but I couldn't follow everything that was said. It's so hard for a foreigner, you know, the various accents and all. There seemed to be some opposition, though—or did I misunderstand?"

Was I laying it on too thick? No, apparently my hat was doing its trick. Mavis shrugged; the very short skirt of her bright green linen suit hiked yet higher, and her voice became confidential, her accent more like the one she'd been born with.

"There are always a few old bas—a few fuddy-duddies who want to stand in the way of progress. Just between you and me, if something isn't done, I'm closing this shop. I tell you, most days I could stand in here in me knickers and there'd be nobody to notice! Archie Pettifer has the right idea, but that man Farrell—not, I suppose, that it makes all that difference to me at the end of the day. If William Farrell wants to put up a mall at the edge of town where there's no foot traffic at all, I daresay the punters—uh, buyers—will come in cars, and my shop will fare just as well there."

"Oh, yes, Mr. Farrell. Frightening sort of man, I thought."

Mavis allowed herself a throaty chuckle entirely unlike the bright, tinkly laugh she had been affecting. "You ought to've seen him Sunday, if you were frightened last night."

"Oh?" Such a useful little word.

"The mayor had a few of us to dinner, you see, to talk out the project before the public meeting. Just those who were most involved." She preened a little, smoothing her hair with one beringed hand. "And Farrell was a trifle upset, as you might say. Those big hands of his—I thought he was going to strangle Archie, I really did. Of course he'd been drinking a bit, but I didn't know where to look, I really didn't. And he stormed out looking like murder."

I could, myself, have murdered the mother who came in at that moment with her noisy and obstreperous five-year-old. Mavis's attention was instantly transferred to the little boy, who represented a hazard to her stock approximately equal to a freight train, and I was forced to stand around fiddling with china dogs and tin boxes with pictures of Sherebury Cathedral on them. I was sure Mavis had more to say.

When the mother finally dragged her son away—without buying anything—Mavis turned back to me.

"Honestly!" she said. "The nerve of some people!"

I shook my head in hypocritical sympathy. "I was sure that child was going to break something. I guess some people have nothing better to do than take up a shopkeeper's time." I managed that line unblushingly, too. "You were saying about Mr. Farrell? This is *so* interesting," I added in a coo that would have startled my friends considerably. And where I dredged up the Atlanta accent I have no idea; I'm from Indiana.

But the moment had passed. "Oh, old Farrell has a hot temper. I reckon he cooled off soon enough. He really wouldn't harm a fly."

"It's an interesting coincidence, though, that someone actually did die that night, and in the Town Hall, too. I suppose Mr. Farrell has a key?"

I had no reason to suppose anything of the sort, but Mavis took the bait.

"Well, as a matter of fact, he does. I happen to know. It was his wife's. She worked there, you know, when I did, years ago. She's been gone now for over a year, but he kept the key. I know, because he told me so. Wondered who he should give it back to, now that the building's closed up."

"Oh, his wife—er—left him?"

Mavis stared at me. "You could say that. She died."

"Oh, dear. Did you know her well?"

She shrugged. "Not bl—not likely. I was just a

typist, she was in the Planning Office. Of course, I was never meant to work in an office—too stifling. It wasn't until I got a job at a gift shop that I discovered my real mission in life. Not that it was as nice as this one." Her eyes swiveled, surveying her domain lovingly, possessively.

"You do have some lovely things. You must be very proud of your achievement."

"Yes." Her mind was firmly back to business. "Now, about that cottage. Or would you prefer this one? It's a bit more expensive, but it's Anne Hathaway's, you see."

I bought the smaller cottage in the interests of continued goodwill; maybe I knew someone who'd like it for Christmas. I was on my way out of the shop, the bell tinkling over my head, when I stopped and turned as if I'd had a sudden idea.

"Oh, by the way, I don't suppose you still have your key to the Town Hall? I dropped an earring when—well, the last time I was in there, and I don't like to bother the police about such a little thing."

The thick makeup couldn't conceal the hard lines that suddenly set in Mavis's face. "No. No, I don't. I turned it in when I left my job. I'd report that earring to the police if I was you, or they might think— I mean, you finding the body and all—"

She left the thought unfinished, but it was clear enough.

"Actually, Mrs. Finch found the body, but I see what you mean. Thank you so much—good afternoon."

Snooping was expensive, I thought indignantly, plodding down the street. Sixty pounds, and what did I have to show for it?

Well, I knew a little more about keys. Farrell had one and Mavis didn't. Or at least that was Mavis's version. Come to think of it, why had a mere typist had one in the first place? But if Farrell really did still have a key—he had a terrible temper—he left the meeting wanting to kill somebody.

That was the second time somebody had used that expression about Farrell. But the somebody he wanted to kill was Pettifer, and Pettifer was still alive.

No, at the price, my information was no bargain. Onward, Dorothy.

7

THORPE AND SMYTHE occupied an ugly, modern building on the High Street, next to the Tudor black-and-white that housed a number of offices, including William Farrell's. In my hurry to get past the ogre's den, I nearly missed the estate agency; the only noticeable thing about it was the window display of house pictures with descriptions and breathtaking prices. I opened the door, a bored clerk pointed me in the direction of Thorpe's office, and I knocked and went in.

John Thorpe was a stocky man who looked a lot like Michael Caine, and talked like him, too, his nasal accent grating on the ear. His suit, though impeccably cut and obviously expensive, was just a shade too blue; so were his eyes. I tried not to wince when he shook my hand with a bone-crushing grip. "Delighted to meet you, Mrs. Martin. And how may I be of service to your good self?"

"Well—" I launched into the almost true story about my waning lease and the planning permission delays. "And I thought it would be just as well to look at some other houses, because I really don't know when the Planning Committee's going to get its mind off the Town Hall long enough to consider my house."

If I hoped that would give me a lead-in to my real agenda, I was wrong. John Thorpe hadn't gotten to be a highly successful businessman by going off on tangents. "Quite right, madam. I can see you're as astute as you are charming!" A good many very white teeth flashed in a very sincere smile. "Now, I happen to have an especially fine property on my books at the moment, made for you, I assure you. Only two years old, in perfect condition, no need to worry about any repairs for years to come—and no fuss with the regulations when repairs do enter the picture!"

He showed me a picture of the ghastly place, all pebble-dashed concrete and shiny new brick, and followed with several others almost as awful. I finally stemmed the flow.

"These are all lovely, Mr. Thorpe, but I really prefer old houses. I know they're a lot of trouble, but—oh, what I really want is to stay where I am. After the meeting last night, do you have any idea when the Town Hall question might be settled?"

"Well, as to that, we all thought it was settled, didn't we, until—however. If you were at the meeting, you do understand I can take no sides, no sides at all. John Farrell has a good case, a very good case indeed."

"He seemed to be an angry sort of man. Someone told me he had a fight with Mr. Pettifer?"

Thorpe spread his hands deprecatingly. "Bit of a slanging match, that's all. Farrell has a temper, right enough, but no stomach for a good fight. Oh, there were words, words I couldn't repeat to a lady, I don't mind saying. But Farrell's got no stamina for the long pull, y'see. Got to be ready to get your teeth in and hold on, in this business." He laughed heartily at his mixed metaphors, his own excellent teeth showing to full advantage.

"Oh, my, it sounds—exhausting."

"No, no, just business. A lady like you wouldn't understand, of course. And no need!" He patted my shoulder.

I hoped he didn't hear my teeth gritting. When I could unclench my jaw, I opened it to ask more questions, but Thorpe suddenly realized we had strayed far from my ostensible purpose. "But enough of unpleasantness. Now, about your house—"

My supply of insincerities exhausted, I stood. "Unfortunately I have an appointment, Mr. Thorpe. I wish you'd keep me in mind, though, if a nice old house in good condition comes on the market." I gave him my address and telephone number, and turned to go. "Oh, there is one thing you might be able to do for me."

"Anything at all, of course." He expanded visibly.

Mavis Underwood had been suspicious, and Thorpe certainly knew just as well as she did when I'd last been in the Town Hall, but it was worth a try. "You see, what with the—unpleasantness—the other day, I managed to lose an earring in the Town Hall. I haven't liked to ask the police about it—such a little thing—anyway, would it be too much trouble for you to lend me your key so I could look for it? It's a pair I particularly like." I smiled winningly, my head to one side in a nauseating Shirley Temple imitation.

Which didn't work. Thorpe's smile froze into place.

"Ah, well now, what a pity. I regard that key as a solemn trust, Mrs. Martin. I never let it out of my possession. Never. Of course, I shall be more than happy to search for your earring the next time I am in the building. Though I should have thought the police would have found it. I'd report it if I were you." He shook my hand, and showed me out the door with more enthusiasm over my departure than he had displayed a few moments before.

Excellent advice, I thought as I walked slowly down the street, if my ridiculous story were true. Not that either Mavis or John Thorpe had believed a word of it. Oh, well. At least I'd confirmed that Thorpe had a key, too. Or said he still had it. And that he doubted Farrell had enough backbone to murder anyone. And he had, I was afraid, begun to develop some suspicions about me.

Did that matter? Perhaps not, unless he was the murderer. Then it might matter very much indeed. Alan would not be pleased if I got myself into a dangerous situation he then had to get me out of.

I shook my head impatiently. I could take care of myself. I'd just have to be a little more subtle from now on, that was all. At any rate Thorpe obviously thought me a "lady," and therefore negligible. Much as his attitude grated, it was useful under the circumstances. Dismissing him and Alan from my mind, I went on to the next thing.

It was time I met Mr. Farrell.

By this time I had walked to the end of the High Street. I stopped and stood for a few minutes staring sightlessly into a window displaying orthopedic appliances. There was plenty of afternoon left, and it had turned into a beautiful day. There wasn't the slightest reason why I shouldn't call on Farrell.

Except that I was scared.

And why? I demanded of myself. Just because he looks like every movie monster you've ever seen? Be your age.

I sighed rebelliously. Why does being one's age always involve doing things one doesn't want to do? Surely I'd earned the right to be irrationally scared if I wanted to. And why was I involving myself in something that was none of my business anyway? I could go have a lovely cup of tea and some sinful pastries somewhere and forget all about murders.

And call myself a coward for the rest of my life.

I turned around and walked back to the gorgeous black-and-white.

It was one of Sherebury's finest buildings, pure Tudor, with both beams and plaster carved wherever decoration could be applied. I'd wanted to see the inside of it for a long time.

WILLIAM FARRELL, BUILDER, was listed with a room number on a sign by the massive front door. I took a deep breath and pushed the door open with a dentist's-office feeling in my stomach.

The English don't use a standardized numbering system by floor, the way American buildings do, so room seven could be anywhere. As I stood in the dim hallway, delaying, I drank in the linen fold paneling, the heavily carved plaster rose on the ceiling with its accompanying crystal chandelier—much later period, that, but it fit— the gorgeous brass hardware on the heavy oak doors—

"May I help you, madam?"

I turned so suddenly I nearly lost my balance. He'd approached silently, on rubber-soled shoes, and stood towering over me, looking annoyed and bored.

Boris Karloff, in person.

I gulped and tried to get my breathing back in order. "No, thank you—well, actually—yes, I was looking for you."

"Yes?"

Never had the monosyllable been more intimidating. I took a deep breath, and some guardian angel supplied my barren brain with an idea. "Yes," I said firmly. "To talk to you about my house. Do you suppose we could go to your office? I'm getting a crick in my neck, looking up at you."

The atmosphere lightened a little. The jutting jaws moved slightly in what might have been meant for a smile as he gestured wordlessly toward the door to the right.

He seated me in the visitor's chair, sat down himself, and raised formidable eyebrows. I took a moment to study him and collect myself.

I hadn't been mistaken about the Frankenstein's monster face: cheekbones sharp enough to cut yourself on, with great hollows underneath, incredible shoulders, great awkward red hands dangling from too short coat sleeves. A man of about forty, he wasn't ugly, really, just craggy and very, very determined-looking.

He cleared his throat, but I didn't let him remind me what a busy man he was.

"Mr. Farrell, what was this building originally?" I wanted to get him talking.

To my great surprise, when he relaxed his face fell into lines more reminiscent of Gregory Peck— still craggy, but without the menace. "It was built to be a wool merchant's house, in 1562. His name was Thomas Lynley, and he was probably the wealthiest man in Sherebury at the time. There are records that the house cost one thousand pounds, which was an enormous sum then; the average workman earned about six shillings a week, if he was lucky."

He leaned forward as he spoke, his huge, ugly hands waving with enthusiasm.

"Was that the Lynley who endowed the hospital?"

"His son. You know some local history, then? You are Mrs. Martin, aren't you—the American lady?"

"Oh, dear, I'm always forgetting to introduce myself. Yes, I'm Dorothy Martin, and no, I don't know much Sherebury history, really, but Lynley's Hospital is one of the sights. You certainly have it all down pat; are you a Sherebury native?"

"No, I've settled here only in the past year, but there's been the odd job in the area now and again, and architectural history interests me. A hospital back then, you know, was an almshouse, a place of shelter, for the old or needy rather than the sick. Lynley's Hospital was endowed to provide a place for twenty old, indigent men to live out their days in comfort and decency. Their clothing was provided, as well as food and a daily ration of ale, and even a tiny income, enough to give them some self-respect."

"And it's still functioning, isn't it?"

"Not only functioning, but thriving—and on the original endowment, at that! That money has grown to a trust so formidable that additional charities have had to be added in order to try to fulfill the donor's original intent. A corresponding institution for old women was built in the eighteenth century, and early in the nineteen hundreds the whole lot were modernized, electricity and plumbing and so on."

"Oh, dear! They haven't spoiled it, I hope?"

"My dear madam," he said impatiently, "if ancient buildings are to be used, they must be made to meet modern needs—if it can be done. This building, admittedly lovely, is badly suited for offices."

"I admit I was surprised to see you in this setting. From what you said at the meeting the other night, I'd have thought you'd prefer something starkly modern."

"I should, if something suitable were available." He looked at his watch and frowned. "Now, Mrs. Martin, what can I do for you?"

"I shouldn't have come without an appointment, I know, and I've been wasting your time. But I was hoping you might be able to help me with my house." I gave him a brief version of my housing woes. "I know historic work isn't your specialty, but I'd hoped you might make an exception."

Boris Karloff returned, forcefully. "Even though you've hired Herbert Benson to do your roof. And you thought I despised old buildings."

I should have known—the Sherebury grapevine at work again. "I haven't hired him!" I said, stung. "He hasn't even looked at it yet. And I—I've tried everyone who—"

"Mrs. Martin, why are you here?" His voice could have etched glass, and it scared the truth out of me.

"I wanted to meet you."

The eyebrows looked incredulous. I floundered on. "I was next door, talking to Mr. Thorpe, and thought I'd see if you were in. I'm snooping, if you really want to know. It's about the Town Hall, you see."

His jaw muscles tightened, and so did my nerves. I swallowed hard. "You can throw me out if you want to. You'd have a perfect right. But I think I have a right to ask questions, too. Not only did I find the body, but I'm worried about Clarice Pettifer. She's a friend, and she's extremely upset over the Town Hall murder. Do you think her husband had anything to do with it?"

He looked down at his desk for a very long moment, those big hands clenched. When he finally spoke, his voice was quiet enough, but taut. "I'm not the right person to ask about Archibald Pettifer, Mrs. Martin. If you've been speaking to Thorpe, you know I've no time for Pettifer, nor he for me. I'd be sorry to learn he was a murderer, but not entirely surprised. And now, if you'll excuse me, I am late for a meeting."

He stood and opened the door, and if his tone was just short of rude, I could hardly blame him.

I made one last, feeble try.

"I don't suppose you'd have time to let me in the Town Hall on your way? I've lost an earring, and—"

"No." The monosyllable was unequivocal, and uninformative. He nodded curtly as he showed me out the door and shut it firmly behind me.

And I'd learned nothing about a key, nothing about a motive. All the same, it hadn't been a total waste of time.

Those hands of his, those frightening hands, didn't quite match. The right one was bruised and swollen and scratched, all across the knuckles.

•   •   •

The minute I got home, I put in a call to Alan.

"I'm sorry, Mrs. Martin," said his pleasant-voiced secretary. "Mr. Nesbitt is in London today, and I don't expect him back until quite late. May I give him a message?"

"No, that's all right. Or—you might just ask him to call me when he gets a chance. Nothing important."

I felt as if my lollipop had been snatched away. Here I was with all sorts of lovely new ideas and no one to tell.

As I mulled over my information, though, it seemed to lose a lot of its vitality. Pettifer and Farrell had quarreled bitterly on the night of the death. Everyone at the Lord Mayor's meeting apparently possessed a key to the Town Hall, or had at one time (though Barbara Dean was still an unknown quantity). And Farrell's right hand was a bloody mess.

I grinned as I imagined Alan's response to that still (in England) very improper adjective. It was true enough, though, and my best piece of news—if the police didn't already know about it. Did I dare call Inspector Morrison and ask? Probably not. My unofficial position was too precarious. No, until Alan got back there was really nothing to do but mind my own business.

You could call on the Lord Mayor. Or how about your friend Mr. Pettifer? Since you're so determined to play girl detective.

If I must keep telling myself what to do, I thought bitterly, I do wish I could manage to keep from being so blasted sarcastic about it.

•   •   •

When I woke up Thursday morning, I lay wondering why I felt pleased, and then remembered. My roof! Mr. Benson was coming to fix my roof! And maybe we could start on plans for the rest of the alterations.

"Well, girls," I said to the cats after I finished breakfast, "we may actually know, soon, whether we're going to keep on living here. You don't want to move, do you?"

They lay blinking at me sleepily, each in her own patch of the sunshine that streamed in the windows. Summer was once more acting like summer, the sky a gorgeous blue with decorative little puffy clouds. Samantha was stretched out full-length on the window seat whose blue cushion went so well with her blue eyes. Esmeralda's green ones were mere slits that closed again as she snuggled luxuriously into the corner of the couch. No, they didn't want to move. Cats are territorial animals. And so am I.

I couldn't settle to anything with Mr. Benson coming. He hadn't said when he'd be there, and it was a perfect day for gardening, but the minute I got good and muddy, he'd turn up. I'd spent the preceding afternoon in a self-righteous fit of house-cleaning, so the house was spic and span, and I'd promised myself no more sleuthing until I could consult Alan. So I fidgeted around, annoyed the cats, picked up a couple of books and put them down, and wrote two entirely unnecessary letters, growing more and more impatient.

Part of my agitation was due to a change in barometric pressure, I realized as I looked out the front window for the twentieth time. England's weather can change between breaths; those puffy little clouds I'd admired earlier were beginning to mass and build, and the temperature was dropping. A thunderstorm was coming before the day was out, and there would go a little more of my roof.

Mr. Benson and the rain arrived at almost the same moment, in midafternoon. A large, cheerful-looking man with a ruddy face that spoke of long hours in pubs, he was at the moment somewhat bedraggled. The rain was the cold, mean-spirited sort that veered with the wind from moment to moment, now flinging itself at the parlor windows, now beating against the front door and soaking the poor man thoroughly. As I let him in, a thunder-clap followed a lightning flash so quickly that we both jumped, and Sam and Emmy streaked up the stairs.

"What the—?"

"Oh, sorry, just my cats. They're terrified of thunder. I'm *very* grateful to you for coming out in this weather, but goodness, you're wet! Would you like a towel?"

He peeled off his raincoat and dropped his umbrella into the stand. "No, no, not to worry. Not sweet enough to melt, am I, now?" A massive hand squeezed mine; I tried not to wince from the pressure of his rings. "Herbert Benson, at your ser-vice." He smiled genially, patting his bright brown hair. Nature never made it that color, I thought with amusement. He was probably afraid the dye would rub off.

"Come and have some tea, then. The roof can wait a few more minutes, and I've laid a fire in the parlor."

The storm increased in fury as we sat over cinnamon toast and tea (Mr. Benson's laced with a little bourbon to keep out the cold). He had excellent opportunity to observe the drafts eddying through my house. As the fire leapt and danced to the caprices of the wind, he waved a bit of toast toward the curtains rippling gaily at the closed windows.

"You could do with new windows, couldn't you?"

"I certainly could. Much as I love those tiny old diamond panes, they don't keep the weather out anymore. But new ones would have to look just like the old ones. This is a listed building, you see."

He rolled his eyes skyward. "Oh, yes, endless regulations, and a positive prejudice against nice, weather tight, plastic windows. Can't be helped, but it's a pity, all the same. However. Shall we see if there's anything left of that roof of yours, eh?"

I led him to the upstairs hall, where generous new leaks had appeared. We spent a few minutes racing between kitchen and landing with most of my collection of pots and pans, the extent of my problem having made itself dramatically apparent.

When we'd taken care of the immediate emergency, Mr. Benson asked me to show him the attic access, and disappeared. I listened apprehensively to bumps and thumps for a good half hour before he climbed down, as dirty as a chimney sweep and almost as wet as if he'd been outside.

Once he'd cleaned up a bit and settled back in the parlor, Mr. Benson shook his head mournfully.

"Bad news, I'm afraid. You need a new roof, from the timbers out. Oh, ta, don't mind if I do—no, no, that's quite enough. There's no point in repairing it, the whole lot is going to go soon.

Now, I can put down a tarpaulin for you as soon as the rain stops, and order in the tiles—"

"Slates," I said. "You may not have had the chance to look when you came in—the rain started just then. But it's a slate roof. And of course—"

"—it must remain slate to please the nosy-parker authorities," he finished, and sighed. "Cost you a packet, that will; take longer, too. Blasted nuisance, these regulations. But I'll keep a sharp eye on costs for you, Mrs. Martin. You may trust me for that." He rose.

"Actually, it's my landlord who'll be paying for it, but I'm sure he'll appreciate your care. How soon do you think you could get me an estimate?"

"Now, don't you worry about a thing, my dear," he said expansively. "I'll have it for you just as soon as the rain stops and I can get my men up top to measure. We'll do you a good job. And then we can take a look at those windows."

"Yes, and the other things I want done as well. Mr. Benson, you've taken a load off my mind."

We shook hands on it (carefully, on my part), and I spent the evening happily planning the details of my kitchen.

8

ALAN CALLED JUST as I was ready for bed.

"Sorry, did I wake you? I've been in town all day, but I've only just got back to the office and found your message, and I'm off again tomorrow for the next few days."

"No, I'm glad you called, though it wasn't all that important." The rain pattered against the windows cozily, and plinked into various pots and buckets, not so cozily. "I do have some news, though. I've found someone to work on my roof! And maybe draw up plans for the rest of the work as well."

"That *is* good news, indeed!" His weary voice relaxed into warmth. "What shall we do to celebrate?"

"Come for dinner," I said promptly. "We can roam all over the house and gloat about how nice it's going to be. When will you be back?"

"Late Sunday. Would Monday be convenient for you?"

"Fine. Sevenish—or whenever you can make it."

"I'll put you on the schedule for seven on the dot as an unbreakable obligation," he said firmly. "Rank ought to carry *some* privileges."

I fell into a peaceful sleep despite the ragged percussion section still operating in the upstairs hall.

The next couple of days, however, were disappointing. On Friday I awoke to brilliant sunshine and went off to the bookshop confidently expecting to see a tarp on my roof when I got home. All morning I glanced out the window whenever I got a chance, which wasn't often. Clarice still wasn't back, and this time Mrs. Williamson hadn't been able to find a replacement, so I was left to cope alone with the crowds of tourists brought out by the beautiful weather.

There was still no tarp when I got home, so I called Benson and got his answering machine. It was nearly six when he called back, sounding harried.

"*So* sorry, Mrs. Martin. Three of my men didn't turn up for work today, and I was hard put to finish a job we had in hand. They're an unreliable lot, some of these local lads. But the weather is expected to hold fine now for a few days, and we'll be out straightaway on Monday morning. And I promise you, if it rains, I'll lay your tarpaulin myself!"

I had to be satisfied with that, and it was true that the weather stayed beautiful—which actually added to my troubles, since my weeds reacted to sun and warmth by growing several inches a day. The cats, for whatever reason, had a two-day attack of the crazies, that unexplainable burst of hyperactivity known and feared by cat owners everywhere. And to top it all off, Jane, who would have commiserated with me, was down with a summer cold.

So I made chicken soup, left it (by gruff command) on her back doorstep, and fretted alone. By Sunday I was more than ready for the calming influence of the Church.

Shérebury Cathedral is a marvel of late-medieval architecture, designed in the fifteenth century for but one purpose: to lift the spirit to God. Five hundred years later it still works its miracles. Even my worst moods can't stand up to the soaring arches of carved stone, the brilliant stained glass, the quiet but intense drama of the Eucharist, and some of the finest liturgical music in England. At the end of the service, feeling exalted, I joined the line for coffee and buns in the parish hall, still humming the last hymn under my breath.

"You sound cheerful, Dorothy." Margaret Allenby, the dean's wife, stood at my elbow.

"I am—now. It hasn't been a very good week, but the service this morning was a great restorative."

"I'll tell Kenneth, he'll be pleased. Are you really feeling yourself again, after such a frightful shock?"

Jungle drums again. "Oh, I'm fine. The one who worries me is Clarice Pettifer. I saw they were both in church this morning, but she looked like death—did you notice? White and shaking, and her eyes all red. She hasn't been to work at the bookshop since it happened, you know. I wonder if the dean should have someone call on her?"

"Call on whom?" The dean came up to us, beaming, a tray in his hands. "I saw you two languishing back there and fetched us all some sustenance. Shall we try to find a place to sit?"

The parish hall has been adapted from the old scriptorium, the lone survivor, besides the church itself and the chapter house, of the medieval monastery that flourished on the site until the days of Henry VIII. The building, filled with the light

the monks needed for their exacting work of copy-
ing and illuminating sacred texts, is otherwise
ill-adapted to the needs of a large and busy twentieth-
century parish, being full of stone pillars that
obstruct traffic and interfere with furniture arrangement. We squeezed with difficulty into a corner, negotiating treacherous folding chairs, and the
dean warily set the tray of coffee and buns down on
the tippy table.

"Call on whom, Mrs. Martin?" he asked again,
raising his voice. All those pillars and the stone sur-
faces of walls and arched roof create echoes that
make normal speech impossible.

"Clarice Pettifer." I repeated my story. "I'm very
concerned about her, but I hesitate to go over
there again. If I happened to run into Mr. Pettifer,
it'd probably make things worse—we hiss and
spit at each other. Figuratively speaking," I added
hastily, and the dean found it necessary to cough
into his handkerchief.

"Anyway, Mrs. Finch—do you know Mrs.
Finch?"

"Since we were children," said Margaret, who
was Sherebury born and bred. "She's chapel, all
her family always were, but her mother was one
of the cathedral cleaners and used to bring little
Ada along. I was a bit older, and we used to play
together. Now she's taken over the family stand,
comes in one day a week to do the brass. She does
a lovely job, but I do try not to get talking with
her, at least if I'm in a hurry—"

"Because you'd be listening till Christmas," I
said, laughing with her. "I know. Anyway, she's
been looking after Clarice from time to time, but I
think Clarice needs to talk to someone who'll let

her get a word in edgewise. Something's bothering her, and I can't figure out what."

"I'm glad you told me," said the dean. "I can't do it myself; I've no time. Sometimes I wish I'd never taken on an administrative post; it leaves me so little energy for any real pastoral work. But I'll speak to Canon Richards; he knows her quite well, I believe. The Pettifers are not at all regular church-goers, of course, but she's a very loyal volunteer."

"I know. I think Mr. Pettifer comes mostly to be seen and do a little politicking, and brings her along for window dressing. It didn't work very well this morning, I shouldn't think. They were barely speaking to each other, from the way it looked."

Someone was trying to get the dean's attention, waving and inching toward us, smiling as he excused his way through the crowd.

"Mr. Dean—" I gestured and he turned, trying without success to push his chair back.

"Ah, Lord Mayor! I'm sorry, I don't seem able to stand up at the moment. However—do you know Mrs. Martin?"

"Daniel Clarke," he said in reply, shaking my hand. "Delighted to meet you, Mrs. Martin."

I'd never seen the Lord Mayor up close before. Without the trappings of his office, it was somehow even more obvious that he was a man to be reck-oned with. I noticed the very keen eye, the alert tilt to the head—oh, yes, this man had earned his office.

"I'm so sorry, Kenneth, I know this isn't the time or place, but with the festival less than a week off there are a few details I do need to check, and I'll be away for a few days, so if you don't mind—"

"Yes, of course," said the dean. "We'll have to go

elsewhere, if we're to hear ourselves think. If you'll excuse us, ladies—oh, I'm so sorry, Mr. Wellington, I didn't mean to back right into you—"

The dean finally pushed himself out of the tight corner and led the Lord Mayor away, while Margaret and I finished our coffee.

"They're two of a kind, those two," she said with a fondly exasperated sigh. "Kenneth should leave the details of the music festival to the canons responsible, but he can never feel that anything is really properly done unless he's seen to it himself. And Daniel Clarke is exactly like him. Small wonder neither of them ever finds time for a holiday."

"He's a conscientious mayor, then?"

"Oh, yes, I should think so. Of course Kenneth and I try to stay away from town politics, but one can't help hearing things."

Indeed. I suppressed a grin.

"And people do say he's hardworking, and incorruptible. Which of course makes him unpopular in some quarters."

"I didn't think there was such a thing anymore as an incorruptible politician."

"We-ell, Daniel isn't exactly a politician. At least, he is in a sense, of course. He's been on the City Council for a donkey's age, and they finally elected him head—which gives him the title Lord Mayor, you know. But his primary interest, I think, really is the welfare of the town, rather than his own ambitions. His people have lived here for generations, time out of mind—he's actually connected with the Lynleys, through his great-great-grandmother, or something like that. You know the Lynleys?"

"Not personally," I said with an attempt at a

straight face. "They've all been dead for a hundred years or so, haven't they? But of course I know who they were, more or less. Richest people in town, endowed everything in sight, and so on."

"There's more to it than that, actually." As people were beginning to go home, the noise level was dropping so that Margaret and I could talk in some comfort. "In a sense, the Lynleys and their extended family built Sherebury. They put up a lot of the money for the abbey—the first abbey, the one that burned down in the fifteenth century, you know, and then again the present one."

I nodded. The cathedral in use today had been begun in 1415 to replace the eleventh-century Cistercian abbey, destroyed by fire in 1402. With blinding speed, in abbey-building terms, the church was completed in 1504. One short transept leading from the choir to the cloisters had survived the fire, and the monks had been just about ready to tear it down and rebuild it to match the rest, when the dissolution of the abbeys intervened. For over a hundred years the abbey buildings had languished, houses had been built on the grounds (mine among them), and decay had set in, until the political climate changed and the old abbey was repaired and designated a cathedral.

Margaret was still talking about the Lynleys. "Several of them were abbots over the centuries, and later, deans, when it was made a cathedral. One was even a bishop, not a very effective one, early in Victoria's reign, I think that was. And, of course, the family laid out the street plan as the city began to outgrow its walls. I could go on, but the point is the Lynleys have been a power in Sherebury for—oh, nearly a thousand years, I suppose. Daniel actually lives in Lynley Hall, though he had to buy it; it had been out of the family for a generation or two. So one can see why he has a protective interest in the town."

"Indeed," I said thoughtfully. One could also see why he might be distressed about Pettifer's plans for the Town Hall. A man who liked to take matters into his own hands—I wished I'd noticed his hands while he stood next to me. I was going to have to find an excuse, somehow, to get better acquainted with the Lord Mayor.

Alan's driver delivered him right on time Monday evening.

"Good, you're being driven, that means you can have a drink or two. When's he coming back to take you home?"

"I'm not going home," he said with a grimace that turned to a laugh when he saw my face. "No, I don't mean what you think I mean. I have to go back to the office to clear a huge stack of paperwork. So I can't drink much, or I'll fall asleep at my desk."

"Well, we'll start with something good, then," I murmured, very busy pouring Jack Daniel's into brandy snifters. I was glad I could excuse myself to the kitchen for a little last-minute soufflé preparation; it gave me time to recover from the ridiculous blush.

Alan and I had agreed, without ever saying a word, that we were not of the generation that fall into bed before knowing each other's full name. The circles we move in actually tend to the old-fashioned practice of waiting until marriage vows have been exchanged. Still, there was enough

serious attraction between us that we'd given the
matter some thought. At least I had, which was
the reason for the blush. But, unsure as I was
about the nature of our relationship, I wasn't
anything like ready for it to take that kind of
turn, so I was profoundly glad, when I got back
to the parlor, that Alan had forgotten the subject.

"Do you want to tell me about your house first,
or shall I make my report?" he asked, settling himself in my squashiest chair with Emmy on his lap.

"Report?"

"On the Town Hall body."

"Oh, yes, please!"

He smiled. "You sound exactly like a well-
brought-up child about to be given a present."

"It's the way I feel. You're not always so forthcoming about crime, when I'm involved. I'm
thrilled!"

"I'm not sure I've anything very thrilling to tell
you, but for a start, we've identified the body.
HOLMES tracked him down for us."

I giggled, as I always do when the acronym for
the police computer system is mentioned. Who
would ever suspect the British police of a sense of
humor? Emmy looked up, offended until she
decided I wasn't laughing at her.

"And what did Sherlock discover?"

"Not a lot more than a name, actually. The
man's finger-prints were easy to identify, because
he had a minor criminal record—joyriding, assault,
petty larceny, that sort of thing. His name is Jack
Jenkins, he was twenty-three years old, and he lived
in Sheffield."

"Sheffield! That's a long way away. What was he
doing in a little backwater like Sherebury?"

"That, of course, is one of the things Morrison is eager to discover." He scratched under the cat's chin and her purr filled the room with organ music. "There's the obvious connection, of course."

I shook my head. "I may be dense, but . . ."

"Pettifer. He's from Sheffield, you know."

"No, I didn't. I didn't even know he wasn't a Sherebury native. But Alan, that sounds serious!"

"Not really. It may mean nothing at all. Sheffield is a very large city indeed. Just because two people were born there doesn't mean they know one another. The crew are working on Jenkins's connections in Sheffield, but his associates don't like talking to the police, and apparently he had very little family. Just his mother, so far as anyone has said, and she seems to be out of town. Something may turn up there, in time. The curious thing, though, is that Pettifer isn't the only one in the case with a Sheffield background."

"You're going to make me ask, aren't you?"

He lifted his glass and drained it. "I'm not being coy, really. It's only that it seems like *lèse-majesté* even to mention the name of Barbara Dean in connection with a suspected murder."

I choked on my bourbon. When I had finished snorting and could speak again, I shook my head and croaked, "Oh, Alan! Surely not. I admit I'd thought of her, but only because she was at that meeting and is opposed to Pettifer. Really, I'd almost as soon believe the Queen had something to do with all this. You don't actually think—"

"I don't think anything at this stage, and neither does Morrison. He's gathering information, that's all. Do you want to hear the results of the autopsy?"

I thought of my lovely dinner, nearly ready in the kitchen. "How gory is it?"

"Not bad at all."

"Come in the kitchen and tell me, then, while I put together a salad. I'm sorry I can't offer you another drink," I added, pointing at his glass. "We've drunk it all—I keep forgetting to stock up."

"Just as well. Now, I've already told you," he said, gathering up Sam, who was trying to trip him, "about the head injury. That was the cause of death, as Morrison thought. The medical examiner found another one, just a bad bump, really, that he thinks happened some little time before death, so there may have been a quarrel that went on for a bit. Quite a wide range for time of death, because so many variables are unknown—they say from nine P.M. to two A.M. And then there's the bruise on the chin. Some scratches there, so the M.E. has guessed the murderer may have worn knuckle-dusters. It would explain why the blow was so effective; it actually broke the jaw, though it was the crashing of the head into whatever it hit that did the job. I gather you don't want all the medical details."

"Not really," I agreed. "I notice you've stopped qualifying yourself every time you say 'murder,' though."

"The injuries couldn't have been self-inflicted, and no one delivers a punch like that to the jaw by accident. The inquest hasn't been held yet, and all sorts of routine inquiries are still grinding along—tracing Jenkins's movements, and everyone else's, that sort of thing—but murder does seem the only reasonable possibility at this point."

"Then all we have to do is figure out what a

petty crook from Sheffield was doing in the Town Hall, and why someone wanted to murder him," I said, taking the smoked salmon from the fridge. "Here, guard it with your life. That and a spinach soufflé are most of dinner—catch her!"

Sam managed to make off with only a little of the salmon, and my house is solid enough that the chase didn't damage the soufflé much. We put the cats out and sat down to our meal in peace.

"You haven't told me anything about your house yet," said Alan. "I didn't notice any signs of roofing."

"There aren't any. And my enthusiasm has dimmed considerably. The man I asked to do something about my roof isn't keeping his promises."

Alan raised his eyebrows. "Who is he?"

"His name is Herbert Benson."

The eyebrows rose still further. "Pettifer's friend?"

I smacked my hand on the table. "That's it! I knew I'd heard the name somewhere. He's the one Pettifer was drinking with, the night of the murder—the alibi. Good grief, and I thought I could trust him!"

Alan chuckled. "Having a pint or two with Pettifer surely isn't enough to make a man untrustworthy."

"Maybe not, but add his failure to show up when he said he would—twice, now—"

"Did he give you a reason?"

"The first time he said he was shorthanded—some of his men didn't show up for work," I admitted grudgingly. "Today I couldn't reach him."

"Unreliable workmen can happen to anyone.

Give the man a chance. But if he doesn't work out, what about Pettifer himself?"

I put my fork down. "Alan, are you out of your mind? He'd never stoop to such a plebeian task as a new roof. And I wouldn't let him even if he wanted to. The man who's going to desecrate the Town Hall, working on *my house*? The man who's driving his wife into a nervous breakdown? And probably a murderer, to boot?"

"You do love jumping to conclusions, don't you?" said Alan calmly. "Have some more of this excellent wine of yours and listen for a moment. First, Pettifer has done nothing to the Town Hall thus far, and he won't unless and until planning permission is given. Second, I don't know what the matter with Mrs. Pettifer is, and neither do you. It may have nothing to do with her husband. Third, a man is innocent until proven guilty in this country. I believe you've heard of the system."

I glared at him. He appeared not to notice.

"Finally, whatever else he may be, Archibald Pettifer is an excellent builder, and I doubt his men have a great deal of work just now. Dorothy, I don't like the man myself. He's arrogant and pretentious and a social climber and all the rest of it, I freely admit. But he doesn't feel to me like a murderer, and I confess I have some sympathy for him just now. This Town Hall project is an abomination, of course, but it was the dream of his life and his chances of completing it grow dimmer every day that this murder is left unsolved. Morrison says he saw him in church yesterday, and the man is disintegrating before one's eyes. You must have noticed, yourself."

Well, no, I hadn't. I'd had eyes only for Clarice. I

pushed some salmon around my plate and avoided Alan's eye. We sat in silence for a moment.

"Alan," I said finally, "you have a talent for making me feel ashamed of myself. I think I've been childish about a number of things."

"Dorothy, I—"

"No, let me finish. I've been running around poking my nose into things, even knowing you wouldn't like it much. And you've made me see I've been unfair to Pettifer. I'd like to start over on a better footing. If Benson doesn't show up tomorrow, I'll call Pettifer. And I promise—"

"No," said Alan, putting his big, warm hand over mine. "Stop punishing yourself. You're not childish, just curious and independent and impulsive and very, very human. Don't make me any promises. Or—no, on second thought, I'll accept one. Promise me you'll look after yourself. I do care a great deal about what happens to you, you know."

He leaned over and kissed me on the cheek, so gently and tenderly that there were tears in my eyes when I tried to smile at him.

"Now," he said, pushing back his chair. "What delectable sweet have you concocted to finish off this marvelous meal?"

It wasn't until the middle of the night that I swam up out of insidiously pleasant dreams and realized I'd never told him about Mr. Farrell's injured hand.

9

TUESDAY MORNING CLARICE finally turned up at work.

"I sure am glad to see *you*! How are you feeling?" She looked awful, a lot worse than when I'd seen her last. Her sweater and skirt hung limply on a body that seemed at least ten pounds thinner, though she could hardly have lost that much weight in a week. She was making a brave attempt to keep the flags flying, however. Her hair looked all right, and careful makeup tried to hide her pallor and the purple circles under her eyes. Looking at those eyes, I wondered for the first time if she were really physically ill, not just upset. "Are you sure you're well enough to be here?"

She tried to smile. "I'm fine, truly. Canon Richards came to see me yesterday, and made me see how foolish I was to give way to my nerves over such a little thing. He says I'll be better out of the house, keeping my mind occupied. I hope we're busy today."

"Speaking of busy, I have a job that needs doing," I said, a little nervously. Might as well get it over with. "I know your husband is an important contractor, of course, and probably doesn't take on small jobs, but—"

The change of subject was a great success. Clarice's face took on some animation. "Oh, I'm sure he'd be happy to help you! He's just waiting, you know, for a decision to be made about the new mall, and now that . . ." Her voice trailed off, and I hurried into the breach.

"Yes, well, it's my roof, you see. It's leaking badly. I'm embarrassed even to mention it, and I wouldn't dream of bothering him ordinarily, but the people who usually do this sort of thing all seem to be booked up, and unless I get it repaired or replaced soon I may have serious problems. I did talk to Mr. Benson, and I don't suppose he'll be very happy if I give the job to someone else, but he hasn't done anything about it, and Alan thought—"

Clarice's chin lifted. "Herbert Benson?"

"Yes. Oh, that's right, you must know him, he's a friend of Mr. Pettifer's."

"A business acquaintance." There was no mistaking the frost in her voice. "You'd be *much* better off having Archie do the work. Shall I speak to him this afternoon?"

"I wish you would. Have him call me—ring me up, I mean." What on earth was Clarice's problem with Herbert Benson? Clarice gave me no chance to pursue that thought.

"I'm sure he'd like to work on your house," she went on with some vigor. "It's a very interesting period, you know—architecturally, I mean. I shouldn't be at all surprised to find a hidden passage or a secret room—a priest's hole or something like that, you know. There's a book here—if I can find it—" She rummaged around in the architecture section of the shelves, and finally pulled out a little volume with a cry of triumph.

"Here it is! *The Architecture of Dissent*. It's all about the Reformation and the Civil War and times like that, and the way buildings were altered to help people escape persecution. Archie has a copy; he's always been fascinated with that sort of thing."

"I'm sure there's nothing like that in my house; it's too small," I objected, but I took the book. It *was* intriguing. The secret passages that sound so fairy tale–like to an American were indeed a way of life in England's history, and I've always been interested myself, but I was startled to hear of Pettifer's fascination. It began to look as though Alan might be right about the man.

I was a little unnerved by the way Alan kept working his way into my thoughts. I was too old, I told myself, to go around mooning like a teenager over a kiss—a brotherly one, at that. And if I gave in, I'd get nothing else done.

I managed to close the mental door, but the hinges were a lot stiffer than I'd expected.

Clarice and I were as busy as she'd hoped, and as the morning wore on, it seemed that the canon's advice had been good. She went about her duties with a lighter step and her voice grew stronger and more assured. The crowd of teenagers that arrived just before noon, though, did her in. A school group from Birmingham, doing a tour of cathedrals just before their holidays began, they were noisy and demanding.

"You look ready to drop," I said as we were leaving for lunch. "What did those miserable kids do to you?"

"Nothing, really. They were only—being kids." Her voice was back to virtually inaudible.

"Well, I think you did too much. You'd better go straight home to bed. Or can I buy you some lunch first?"

"No, I'll have something at home, but thank you very much all the same. And I shan't forget to tell Archie to ring you."

There was that stubbornness again. Well, one couldn't hold the woman's hand forever, after all. She had to learn sometime to deal with life's vicissitudes. She hadn't even seen the body, for heaven's sake. There was no real reason why she shouldn't pull herself together. And if she was so eager to get home to Archie, let her. No accounting for taste, I thought with great originality as I waved good-bye and headed for home.

Pettifer phoned me before I'd finished my sandwich lunch. I was profusely apologetic about bothering him with such a small matter, and he was at least civil—a major step forward in our relationship. Furthermore, he was at my house an hour later, with two men to measure the roof, and when he sent them away and the two of us sat down to talk about the project, I began to think humble pie was going to be my dessert du jour.

"We'll have to tear off the whole lot and start fresh; repair any structural damage first, though from what I can see there's very little so far," Pettifer said authoritatively. "Now, what you want is slates that match the originals, and they're not going to come cheap if we have to buy them new. The best thing would be old ones that have already weathered. I'll ask about, see if I can lay my hands on some. There's a redundant church being pulled down over Bradford way with a slate roof; I might—"

"Yes, but Mr. Pettifer," I interrupted, "will old slate keep out the rain?"

He looked at me pityingly. "So long as they're not broken. They're used because they're durable, you know. And we'll reuse any of yours that we can remove in one piece. That way we'll still have the lichens, and you'll want them—nice, soft, old look they give the place."

I could hardly believe this was the same man who was so pompous in public, the man who wanted to do unspeakable things to the Town Hall.

"It's very nice of you to deal with this for me. You do realize the roof will have to be identical in appearance to the old one?"

"Yes," he said, reverting to his old manner, "I am familiar with the requirements of a listed building."

Well, it *had* been a stupid question, hadn't it? I studied the pattern on the carpet. "I'm sorry, silly of me. Of course you are. When do you think . . . ?"

"The men will be back with a tarpaulin within an hour or two, so you'll not have to worry the next time it rains. I'll have a cost estimate by Thursday at the latest. You understand it depends on what we find when we get to the timbers, but I can give you a range. The men can proceed as soon as you wish. Now, if there's nothing else—"

I stood. "Mr. Pettifer, you can't imagine how grateful I am to deal with someone who obviously knows what he's doing. My only problem now is to tell Mr. Benson I've given the job to someone else, and I'm not looking forward to it."

"My wife mentioned that. I shall be seeing him later this afternoon; I'll tell him if you like."

There was a look in his eye that told me he would be delighted to pass bad news along to his colleague, and again I wondered why, but lacked the nerve to ask.

"Yes, thank you again." I shook his hand. "Mr. Pettifer, I—we haven't always gotten along too well, and I—er—apologize if I was ever rude, or—"

"Not at all." With the all-purpose English non-response and a curt nod, he was out the door and I was left shaking my head and wondering if I would ever understand the man.

At any rate, he kept his promises. An enormous sheet of blue plastic arrived in short order and was firmly fastened down. Let it rain!

Not that it showed any signs of doing so. The English summer was still behaving the way the tourist brochures make you think it always does, with blue skies and enough heat to seem almost like real summer. Too much of the afternoon was left to fritter it away; my conscience drove me into the garden, trowel in hand.

An hour later, hot, dirty, and thoroughly fed up, I was knocking on Jane's back door.

"Is your cold better?" I asked when she appeared. "I sure hope so, for my sake as well as yours."

"Nearly gone," she said. "Soup did the trick. *Down*, sir!" (This to the friendliest of the bulldogs, Winston, who was eagerly raising his head to be patted.) "Beer?" she added, noting the sweat pouring down my face.

She produced it, cold and ambrosial, along with a couple of damp paper towels that removed the worst of the grime.

"I've had it," I announced after a life-giving

swig or two. "That garden is defeating me and enjoying it. The only things that are thriving are the weeds. It needs someone to tell it who's boss. Do you know of a good gardener looking for work?"

"Thought you'd never ask. Bob Finch," she said promptly.

"Finch? Is he—?"

Jane nodded. "Her son. Likes his drink now and again, but works hard in between. Knows his business."

"Well, if he's anything at all like his mother, he's the man for me. He lives with her?" I downed several more cold swallows.

"Does now. Wife left him a few years ago; he moved back in with mum. Seems to suit both of them. He's company for her and she chivvies him back to work when he's on the drink."

I finished my beer and pushed my chair back. "Jane, you've come to my rescue so many times I'll never be able to repay you. There is no one else's kitchen in the world that I'd dare invade looking like this and asking a favor. And that's a dubious honor if there ever was one. I'd give you a hug if I were fit to touch anybody." Embarrassed, she muttered something and turned away to scold a dog, and I made off home to call Bob Finch.

Fortune was smiling on me today; maybe it had something to do with the sunshine. Bob was at home and sober, and would be 'appy to come over and 'ave a look at my problem.

He turned up a few minutes later in an amazing vehicle that had once been a pickup truck. A short, compact, wiry man of indeterminate age, he wore earth-brown garments that looked older than he did and gave him a distinct resemblance to a gnome. The watery blue eyes and ruddy nose trumpeted his alcohol problem, but his hands, today, were steady and as strong as pieces of oak, and his weather-beaten face was honest, the rosy-apple cheeks good-humored.

"Dear, oh dear, madam, let the place go somethin' shockin', 'aven't you?" He clucked accusingly and picked up a handful of dirt, letting it sift through his fingers. "Good soil, that, too—you could make a picture o' this 'ere place. Delphiniums along the wall, see, with 'olly'ocks in the corners to 'old it all up, like. Not too many roses, they'd be too fancy, except for some of the old-fashioned ramblers on this 'ere fence. Daffs in the spring, o' course, and snow drops, and you want some lavender for the smell, and then wallflowers in summer. Some cuttin' flowers, you'll want, snapdragons and mebbe some asters and chrysanths . . ."

As he went on, gesturing broadly, it all materialized before my eyes. Gone were the weeds; in their place a perfect English cottage garden nodded drowsily in the soft breeze, birds sang, butterflies skipped from blossom to blossom . . . I blinked, and there were only weeds, with a little brown gnome standing in the middle of them, pointing.

"That there mint, you got to dig it all out. Take the place, mint will; put it in a pot if you 'ave to 'ave it."

"How long will it take?" I asked abruptly.

Bob blinked. "To get that mint out? I'd say—"

"To do it all. What you said—hollyhocks and snapdragons—all that."

"Given a free 'and, madam?"

"Absolutely."

"Four, five years." He saw the look on my face and went on reassuringly. "Gardens takes time to grow proper. But I can 'ave it lookin' tidy in a month or two, and get a start with bedding plants, then we can add on, like."

"When can you start?"

The brown face split in a grin. The gnome spat on his hands and rubbed them together. "I'll get me spade and barrow."

Three hours later my garden was transformed. Oh, it looked awful, but progress was being made. Great piles of dirt and weeds punctuated an expanse of mud that overflowed onto the grass, with only a few isolated plants surviving; I was well satisfied.

"I'll be 'ere first thing tomorrer," he said as he climbed into his battered truck. "Cheerio!"

As I waved good-bye to my gnome I suddenly remembered we hadn't even discussed wages. Oh, well. Live dangerously. Whatever he charged, he was worth it.

The next morning the doorbell roused me at what felt like dawn.

"'Ullo, madam, I 'ope as I 'aven't got you out of bed," said Bob, studiously ignoring my slippered feet and robed figure. "'Ere's a list o' the flahs I thought we might put in, fer a start, like. Fer you to approve."

It was a matter of form, of course. Bob was going to plant whatever he wanted, with my heart-felt blessing. But I took the list, gravely thanked him, and got started on my own day while he went whistling about his work.

I had a good deal to do, but while I was trying to organize tasks Samantha jumped into my lap. Of course, once a cat has honored you with her presence, you can't insult her by getting up. I reached for reading material, and my hand lit on the book I had brought home from the bookshop the day before: *The Architecture of Dissent*.

I was absorbed in two minutes. The book was full of references to passages and priest's holes and secret meeting rooms, many of them in famous buildings I'd visited. Most, of course, were in the great country houses or public buildings, where thick walls could easily accommodate a passageway, and elaborate paneling was convenient to hide an entrance. Some of the priest's holes, especially, were made from perfectly ordinary back stairs or cupboards that had fallen into disuse, a concealed door being all that was required to convert them for devious use.

Great Scott!

My sudden movement startled Sam awake; she jumped down in alarm, but I scarcely noticed. I'd had an *idea*.

What if there were some hidden place in the Town Hall?

It would explain such a lot. Maybe the dead man had discovered something he shouldn't, and that's why he was killed. And his body was moved because it was too close to the secret whatever. And if there was some kind of treasure hidden in the place, it would explain why Archie was so anxious to get hold of the Town Hall at whatever price!

Some people never grow up. Blissfully refusing to let common sense intervene, I sprang up, grabbed the first hat I laid hands on in the dark hall closet, and took the shortcut through the cathedral to the Town Hall.

I was so full of my wonderful idea when I set out that it never occurred to me to wonder how I was to get into the place—nor what I would do if I found Mr. Pettifer in sole occupation. If I'd stopped to think at all I suppose I'd have assumed the police seal was still on the doors. But Providence is said to look after fools. When I came to a breathless halt at the massive front doors, they stood wide open and I could see Mrs. Finch toiling her way up the stairs with a mop.

"Yoo-hoo! Mrs. Finch! May I come in?"

She turned and beamed at me. "Mornin', dearie. You're a sight for sore eyes—specially in that 'at."

"What's the matter with my hat? I just—oh, dear."

I pulled it off my head, looked back at Mrs. Finch, and succumbed to a fit of the giggles.

The hat I had clapped on my head without a glance revealed itself in all its glory as the patriotic tricorn I had decorated for the Fourth of July, complete with white ribbon and one rakish red ostrich feather.

"Well, that'll teach me to look in the mirror before I go out, anyway. Come to think of it, though," I said in growing indignation, "Bob saw me when I left. He waved. Why on earth didn't he say something?"

"'Ee's nearsighted, dearie, an' 'ee never wears 'is glasses when 'ee's workin'. Men 'as no eye for a 'at, anyway."

"He certainly has an eye for flowers, though. Yesterday he showed me a few things I had no idea were there—just puny little plants I would have pulled up as weeds. I'm so glad he's agreed to do my garden for me."

"Hmmph!" Mrs. Finch snorted. Not for worlds would she have admitted she was proud of her son's talents. "Mind you keep 'im up to the mark, now. 'Ee takes a drop now and again, there's no denyin', but not when 'ee's workin' proper. 'Ee'll do a good job for you, but you 'as to keep 'im to it."

There was an awkward little pause. Now that I was there, I felt a little shy about introducing my subject. In the face of Mrs. Finch's solid common sense, secret passages seemed awfully far-fetched.

"So you're back to work," I finally said inanely.

She snorted again. "Come to give the place a good dustin' an' airin' out one more time. 'Ee's told me I needn't come back." Her sniff left no doubt about who " 'ee" was. "Until they makes up their minds what's to be done with the place, I've lost me job 'ere. Not but what it was only the two days a week, an' there's plenty as want me to work in their 'ouses, but it's a comedown, and no mistake."

"Oh, I *am* sorry, Mrs. Finch. You're right, it's a slap in the face, after all you've done here over the years. But I'm glad you're here today, anyway, because—well—"

She looked at me inquiringly and I took the plunge.

"Well, it's probably silly of me, but I wondered if you'd ever heard any talk of any secret rooms or passages in the Town Hall, or—or anything like that," I ended lamely.

To my great relief she took me seriously and scratched her head in thought.

"Not in the Town 'All," she said finally, a thoughtful frown on her face. "There's the underground passages, under the streets, o' course—medieval, those are, for drains and the like. An' Lynley 'All 'as a priest's 'ole or two, an' there's 'oo knows wot all over the cathedral—but I never 'eard tell of anything 'ere. Barrin' the room in the attic, that is to say."

I scarcely dared breathe. "There's a secret room in the attic?"

"Don't know 'ow secret it is. It 'as a sort of 'idden door, but everybody knows about it. Everybody as knows the building, anyway. I can show you, if you likes."

It was better than nothing. My balloon was deflating rapidly, but I trooped up the stairs behind Mrs. Finch, the two of us wheezing and puffing in a geriatric chorus.

10

"MIND WHERE YOU step, dearie," said Mrs.
Finch. "There ain't no real floor up 'ere, just them
boards laid across the beams. One slip and you'd
go straight through."

We were in the biggest of the attics, the central
one with the gable windows. There was quite
enough light on that sun-drenched day to show me
the perils of my footing. The light showed, too,
just how serious the Town Hall's condition was.
Huge oak roof timbers were riddled with beetle
damage; the dust we kicked up as we picked our
cautious way across the floor was more than half
sawdust left behind by the busy destroyers.
Cobwebs hung everywhere in great, dirty festoons,
and the smell of dry rot was overpowering.

"Mind your 'ead!"

The warning came too late. Watching the floor,
I'd ignored what was above me, and fetched up
against a hammer beam—this one still sound and
extremely solid. I yelped and put up one hand to
steady myself, the other, cautiously, to examine the
damage to my temple—and then stood staring,
openmouthed.

In the wall facing me, a door was slowly creaking open.

"It's that there beam," said Mrs. Finch stolidly. "You pushes on it to make the door open. Most people," she added, "uses their 'ands."

"I'll remember that next time," I said just as dryly. "It's a good thing I was wearing this silly thing, or I'd be laid out on the floor." I picked up the thick felt hat, brushed it off ineffectually, and, balancing on the unsteady floorboards, walked into the secret room.

It was a vast disappointment. There was nothing much there, just a small room with one dusty gable window and no door except the one by which we'd entered.

"Do they know what it was used for?" I asked my guide. I doubted it had been a priest's hole or anything so romantic.

"Papers," she said briefly. "Important dockyments, as they didn't want to get lost. They cleared 'em out an' took 'em to that new buildin' when they moved, though wot they wants with papers 'undreds of years old, as is crumblin' to bits besides, is more than wot I can tell you."

I took one more look around. Shelves lined the walls, empty except for thick dust and, in one corner, a forgotten piece of paper. I picked it up gingerly and shook off some of the fuzz; it seemed, so far as I could make out the faded, spidery handwriting, to be a tax roll of some kind for 1737, of interest possibly to historians but not to me.

Well, of such disappointments are the lives of superannuated girl detectives made. There was nothing in this room except decay. I tucked the paper into my purse to give to somebody who might want it and went back into the main attic, carefully avoiding the hammer beam. Mrs. Finch manipulated the beam to close the door, and we plodded back down the stairs in silence.

Perhaps, I thought dismally, the Pettifers of this world were right and this building needed a new purpose, a new life before it moldered to ruin. Signs of decay were all about me, now that I actually looked. Water-damaged plaster ceilings were stained and moldy; in places they had fallen. Paneling was beginning to crack and warp; floorboards were coming up; window frames were rotting. Only on the main floor had Mrs. Finch's efforts kept the wood shining and smooth, the ceilings and staircase intact.

"Well, thank you, Mrs. Finch," I said as we reached the front hall. "I thought we might find something important, but I suppose it was silly of me."

"Do call me Ada, luv," she said comfortably. "And don't you fret about nothin'. It'll all come out in the wash, you'll see. Wot was you goin' to do with that there paper?" she added. "On account of, it didn't ought to be taken away, like."

"Oh. I'd forgotten about it. Take it to the Civic Centre, I suppose, where the rest of them are. Although I do hate to drive out there."

"Or the museum, mebbe," Mrs. Finch—Ada—proposed. "It's just round the corner, and they'd know what to do with it."

"Good idea. Thanks again."

I stood in the brilliant sunshine of the High Street, my dusty hat dangling from my hand. I couldn't put it back on; the bump on my head was swelling fast. Besides, it looked ridiculous, and while I usually don't mind looking ridiculous, today I wasn't in the mood.

I was, in fact, both depressed and cross. I had been so sure I'd had a brilliant idea, and not only had it been exposed for the silliness it was, but I'd finally realized the desperate state of the Town Hall. I would have enjoyed having a temper tantrum on the spot, out of sheer frustration, but the influence of civilization was too strong.

Oh, well, I might as well take the stupid paper to the stupid museum and have done with it. Then I could go home and kick the cat, or something equally unfair and unproductive.

I stumped crossly down the street.

Sherebury Museum, tucked away in a dark little building on a narrow side street, was a drab-looking place with a drab little curator, and very few exhibits of any real interest. The bell over the door tinkled as I entered.

"Good afternoon, madam. May I help you find something in particular, or would you just like to look about?"

His tone made it clear that he found either eventuality unlikely. He was a Mr. Chips–type with the enthusiasm left out, a gray little man of about eighty in tired tweeds, who had obviously decided there was nothing in the museum worth looking at—or maintaining.

Oh, well, presumably he would know what to do with a stray piece of Sherebury history, and frankly, I didn't care much. I pulled the piece of paper out of my purse, trying not to tear off any more of the fragile edges.

"I happened to find this in the Town Hall just now. It's old and I thought the museum should have it. I don't suppose it's important, but anyway, here it is."

Mr. Chips took the paper from me, frowning in bewilderment over the tops of his granny glasses, as the doorbell behind us tinkled. A red-letter day, indeed—two visitors at once.

"Good morning, Mr. Pym."

The deep voice startled me, and I turned to see a large, looming form.

"Mrs. Martin." He nodded slightly.

"Good morning, Mr. Farrell," I said, and turned back to Mr. Chips—or Pym, I supposed.

"As I said, the paper may be of no importance, but it certainly doesn't belong to me, and I thought someone should have it who knows what to do with it. Do you suppose you could give me a receipt or whatever, just so there won't be any question?"

Mr. Pym looked at Mr. Farrell helplessly. "The lady found this, she says—I can't make out what it is or what she wants me to do with it."

Farrell shot a sharp glance at me. "Let me see."

The gray little man complied.

"Hmm. Part of an electoral roll, it seems. Where's the rest of it?"

The question was addressed to me. I shrugged.

"Search me. I found this in the Town Hall. I—er—went to see Mrs. Finch and she was—showing me some of the damage up in the attics. This was on a dusty shelf; there was nothing with it."

"I see. And did you find your earring?"

"What earring?"

The question was out before I had time to think, and Farrell's sarcastic smile was ample punishment for my witlessness.

"The one you lost the other day. Or had you forgotten?"

"I found it. Under my bed. So kind of you to ask." I smiled, showing as many teeth as possible, and gathered myself to return the attack. "I must say I'm surprised to find you here, Mr. Farrell. Given your modernist views, I wouldn't have thought history was your cup of tea."

Perhaps someday I'll learn not to let my mouth run away with me. Too late, I remembered that Farrell had displayed considerable knowledge and interest in Sherebury history.

"History is a fine thing in its place, Mrs. Martin. Its place is here, in museums, not trying to ruin lives in the twentieth century. And if you've been snooping about the Town Hall, I should think you'd have seen for yourself that such a ruin is no place for a shopping mall."

I was so upset at finding myself in agreement with him that I lost my head completely. "My snooping, as you call it, has to do with trying to find out who committed murder, not with civic disputes. I suppose you'd rather the question remained unresolved?" My tone was as nasty as I could make it, and little Mr. Pym shrank back nervously.

"As a matter of fact, I should!" Farrell shouted, pounding his fist on the counter. "So far as I'm concerned, doubt about that murder is perfectly splendid. Uncertainty is just as good as guilt any day for putting spokes in Archie Pettifer's wheels. I would suggest, Mrs. Martin, that you consider minding your own business from now on. An excellent policy, especially for foreigners! Good day, Mr. Pym."

He slammed my miserable electoral roll down on the counter, breaking off a corner in the process, and banged the door so hard behind him that one bell shook loose, fell to the floor, and rolled into the corner, tinkling madly all the way.

I went home with an ache in my head and determination in my soul, and picked up the phone.

"Alan, I need to talk to you. Would you be free for a few minutes if I drove out there?" Central police headquarters for the county are located in a sprawling complex just outside Sherebury, accessible by a busy highway and a terrifying double roundabout. I must have let some apprehension show, because Alan's voice developed a hint of a chuckle.

"Longing for a drive in the country, are you? I've an appointment at the cathedral at three to pin down security arrangements for the concert for our royal guest." The sigh was only a small one. "Supposing I call for you when I've finished with that, and we'll go to tea somewhere."

"Fine." It wasn't, actually. I wanted privacy to express my suspicions, and I wanted to talk *now*. But I could have tea ready for him, and preparing it would give me time to sort out my thoughts.

So I made sandwiches and cut them into crustless triangles, whipped up a batch of cookies, and tidied away some of the cat hair that settles on every surface of my house. Alan was ringing my doorbell as I put away the vacuum cleaner.

"I see your roof work is under way," he said as he came in. "Benson or Pettifer?"

"Pettifer, much as I hate to admit it. At least he's

covered it—we'll see whether he comes through with the rest."

Alan sniffed and changed the subject. "Is that peanut butter cookies I smell?"

"That's right, they're your favorite, aren't they?" I said brightly—as if I didn't know! "I thought we'd have tea here, if you don't mind. The cookies aren't proper tea fare, I know, too American, but the sandwiches are all right. How did your session go at the cathedral?"

Alan followed me into the kitchen and munched on a cookie as I heated water and arranged the tray.

"All serene there, I think," he said between bites. "We've all been through this so many times before, it was just a matter of going over the drill once more, with a few added touches to try to meet whatever additional threat there may be. Frustrating not to know what that might be, but—" he waved his hand in the air and scattered crumbs "—one does one's best. The dean is being perfectly cooperative, of course, as usual."

"That's nice." Alan looked up sharply, and I pulled myself together. "I'm sorry, I was thinking of something else. Alan, I may be making mountains out of molehills. I've had time to think about it since I called you, and I think I probably am. But I'll feel better if you tell me that. Shall we take this into the parlor?"

Prevailing English usage for the principal room of the house is "lounge." I think it sounds like a hotel or a bar and refuse to use it. On the other hand, "living room" is far too American for a house as old and English as mine. I've compromised on "parlor," and my friends accept it amiably as another American eccentricity. We settled down on either side of the fireplace, unlit on this warm and beautiful day, and I poured out the tea before I drew a deep breath and launched into it.

"You won't think I'm silly?"

Alan just looked at me. I've learned to recognize that look. It means something like, *Don't you know me well enough by now to know I take you seriously?*

"All right, then. Alan, I think William Farrell may have killed that boy."

He took a sandwich and bit into it thoughtfully. "Why do you think so? Any evidence, or just a feeling?"

"When you're as old as I am, feelings about people are perfectly legitimate evidence in themselves," I retorted. "They're always based on experience. But I know what you mean—police-court evidence. And I do have some. Has anyone working on the case noticed Farrell's right hand?"

He relaxed and took another sandwich. "Ah, his hand. So you saw that, too—and drew the perfectly logical conclusion. Yes, Morrison interviewed him personally, and got an explanation.

"It seems that our Farrell has quite a temper. He says that after the Lord Mayor's famous dinner party the night of the murder, he was extremely upset. He went home fuming about Pettifer and his plans, and by the time he got home, he'd worked himself up to the point of slamming his fist into the wall."

"He could be lying."

"Of course. But our people checked; the wall next to the door had marks of blood and skin on it, at about the right height. And the M.E., who took a look at Farrell's hand, doesn't think the injuries could have been caused by contact with Jenkins's

jaw. He's quite sure a bare fist couldn't have done
so much damage to the jaw, either, not unless the
fist belonged to a trained boxer—which Farrell certainly is not."

I was both relieved and disappointed. "Well.
Then it looks as though he's out of it. But—Alan,
his temper *is* awful! Two people, on separate occasions, told me he left that dinner meeting looking
as if he wanted to kill someone—those were their
very words. And this morning when I saw him, he
certainly looked ready to kill me!"

"And when was that?" Alan's tone was mild, but
his eyes narrowed and he put down a cookie.

"Oh, a perfectly innocent encounter in the
Shferebury Museum. I went in to take—um, that is,
I found something old, and . . ."

I floundered to a stop and Alan picked up the
cookie again, and simply waited.

"Oh, all right, if you must know. Did you rise to
your exalted rank by exploiting the power of silence
in an interview?"

He said nothing to that, either. I rolled my eyes
heavenward. "You are the most exasperating man!
I had no intention of telling you I was poking
around the Town Hall looking for secret passages."

"Ah. So that's it. And I presume you found the
room in the attic?"

It was so deflating to have everyone at least one
step ahead of me.

"Mrs. Finch showed it to me. I thought—oh, I
suppose you might as well have all of it. I was off
on a Nancy Drew tangent again. I thought maybe
there was something hidden close to where Jenkins
was actually killed. And maybe the murderer
moved him to keep whatever it was secret. And if

Pettifer knew about it—well, anyway, it seemed to hang together when it first occurred to me. But Mrs. Finch—Ada, I mean, I keep forgetting—she says the attic room is the only one in the Town Hall. And she ought to know."

"Have a sandwich; you're not eating anything," said Alan kindly. "It's a perfectly plausible theory, actually. We—that is, Morrison—thought of it, too."

"You did? I wasn't being totally ridiculous? I even thought Jenkins might have gotten his head injury on one of those beams—they're pretty low."

"Dorothy, you really must stop underestimating yourself, you know. The idea is sound, and we've investigated it thoroughly. Unfortunately, it looks as though Ada Finch is right. The plans for the Town Hall—the original plans, and drawings of alterations down through the years—have been kept. It's a remarkable piece of cultural history, actually, all in the Sherebury Museum. But when our people studied them they found no sign of anything except the attic strong room, and that's shown quite clearly. Of course, an addition that was really meant to be a secret would have been kept out of documents, so the men went over the building itself with a fine-tooth comb, measuring the depth of walls and so forth. They came up with absolutely nothing. So I'm afraid we know no more than we did about why the man was moved."

"Or by whom," I said, and sighed. "So that's that. As a detective I think I make a great—"

"Cook," Alan supplied, polishing off the last cookie on the plate. "So was it interesting, that 'something old' you found in the Town Hall?"

"No. Just a piece of old town records. I don't

think Mr. Pym has the slightest idea of what to do with it; not that it matters. That museum is a disaster, Alan!"

"Another victim of a strained municipal budget. It needs more space and a proper curator, is all. The collection is actually quite good."

"Well, it doesn't look like it! Somebody needs to take it in hand."

He grinned at me as he heaved himself out of the overstuffed chair. "There's a project for you, my dear—just mind you keep out of the way of our bad-tempered Farrell. I must go. Splendid tea, Dorothy. By the way, what have you done to your hair?"

"Oh, just got tired of it and decided to experiment." I'd rearranged it to cover up the lump I had no intention of telling him about.

"Oh, I thought you might have bumped your head on one of those wicked beams." He grinned at my scowl, gathered me up in a brief but very efficient bear hug, and was gone; my musings for the rest of the day had nothing whatever to do with museums or murder.

11

BY THURSDAY MORNING Bob was ready to start planting one small part of my garden, so I spent a few hours in the delightful occupation of watching someone else work, now and then offering a suggestion, praise, or even a little help. And early in the afternoon Mr. Pettifer, true to his word, telephoned to say that the plans and estimate for my roof were ready, and could he drop them off straightaway?

He was there in ten minutes. I showed him into the parlor and he got down to business at once. "Now," he said, "here's the estimate. It's high, but not so bad as it might be because I was able to pick up those old slates. And of course you'll get some help from English Heritage, and/or the council."

He handed it to me. It took my breath away; I certainly hoped a great deal of financial help would be forthcoming from somewhere or my landlord was in danger of cardiac arrest.

"We'll match the original techniques and materials as nearly as possible," he went on, "and the appearance will be identical."

"I must confess I had a few qualms about that

when I talked to Mr. Benson. He didn't seem to realize that I *wanted* the house kept the same; it wasn't just a question of complying with the authorities. By the way—uh—have you talked to him?"

"Yes. He wasn't best pleased, but he must learn to keep his promises. Nothing drives off trade faster than breaking appointments. I told him so." He smiled grimly.

"Yes, well—thank you for dealing with him. Now, once the financing is worked out, how long do you think the job will take?"

"No more than three weeks, given reasonable weather. There's nothing much on our plate at the moment." He grimaced and then shut his mouth firmly and looked the other way.

There was something about his unspoken comment that made me suddenly see him as a human being instead of a cardboard villain, and (as I often do and almost always live to regret) I said the first thing that came into my head. "Mr. Pettifer. You're obviously a good craftsman, with respect for fine old work. Why do you want to destroy the Town Hall?"

Mr. Pettifer gave me a look that would peel paint and stood, drawing himself up to his full five and a half feet. "Destroy it! I don't want to destroy it! I want to save it, make it of some use to the town! Where's the crime in taking a fine old building and using it for something different, putting people to work, getting new money flowing? I am fed to the teeth with all the do-gooders acting as if I was proposing to commit murder!"

I glared right back at him as anger stripped off what few restraints were left on my tongue. "Well, if that's the way you answer a civil question, I don't blame them! I asked because I wanted to hear your point of view, instead of just believing what everyone says. If you don't want to talk about it rationally, fine!"

"And what," he asked, purple in the face, "does everyone say?"

"That you used to be a fine builder before you fell in love with money and power. That all you care about now is your own advancement, no matter who or what stands in your way. That you've got enough influence to push through this Town Hall plan even though it's an absolute sacrilege, and the university housing project, too." I paused and then threw the last shred of caution to the winds. "That you bully your wife, and you probably killed the man in the Town Hall because he might have ruined your plans somehow."

There was a long pause. The house was very quiet. As I watched Pettifer's face, wondering if I should reach for the poker, I could hear the *chink* of Bob's tools in the garden, and even the lapping of Emmy's tongue as she drank some water out of her bowl in the kitchen.

"You speak your mind, don't you?" he said, finally, his color closer to normal. "I wonder you care to employ me if that's what you believe."

"I didn't say I believed it all. You asked what was being said. I told you."

"Yes. In reply, then, A: I am still an extremely good builder, with high standards. B: I do not find either the Town Hall Mall or the university housing project to be detrimental to Sherebury. My mall will save a magnificent building from destruction, and the Victorian houses I propose to replace with new flats are insanitary, ugly, and poorly built. I sincerely hope my influence is still sufficient to see that both proposals are approved. C: My relationship with my wife is no one's business but ours. D: I did not murder anyone. Good day, Mrs. Martin."

Whew! After he slammed the front door, I stood for a moment shaking my head just to make sure it was still on my shoulders. My record of winning friends and influencing people was growing more and more dismal. And all I'd done was ask a few honest questions. A few more and I wouldn't have a friend left in Sherebury.

It was just as well that I had an urgent errand to keep me from brooding about that nasty little encounter. Now that I actually had a cost estimate for my roof, I intended to ginger up my dilatory landlord by presenting him with the proper grant applications, all filled out and ready for his signature. I'd seen the forms, which weren't impossibly complicated; I could get them from the planning office this afternoon, complete them, and mail them to him tomorrow.

There were, I had learned, various legal recourses open to me if the landlord didn't act quickly. I was mulling them over, hoping very much I wouldn't have to use them, as I pulled into the Civic Centre parking lot and congratulated myself on still being alive after the drive.

I was in no way mentally ready for an encounter with John Thorpe, who was coming out the door as I went in.

He saw me, of course, and his eyes lit up. There was no escape; civility forced me to respond, if coolly, to his greeting and handshake.

"Ah, Mrs. Martin!" he boomed, bouncing on

the balls of his feet. "I believe I may have some good news for you. We have a new house on our books—at least, an old house, ha, ha—that may be just what you're looking for. The moment I saw it, I thought of you. A Victorian rectory, marvelous old place, all sorts of charming woodwork and so on. In need of some tender, loving care, but I think it's just up your street. When may I show it to you?"

"Well—actually—I don't like Victorian architecture much, not the English variety anyway. And I think I've decided to go ahead and fix up my own house. I have the estimate for the roof here, as a matter of fact, just ready to submit with the grant applications. So you see . . ."

He saw, unfortunately, a good deal more than I intended him to. His geniality vanished. "Yes, indeed. Quick decision, wasn't it? Looking for a new house last week, staying in the old one this week? Just what *are* you planning to do, Mrs. Martin? Or don't you know?"

I stood my ground. I was tired of being bullied. Surely I could do as I liked about my housing problem.

"I'm staying in my house. Definitely. I'm so sorry to have taken up your time before I made up my mind. If you'll excuse me—"

"Yes, well, there's no accounting for tastes, is there? I wouldn't stay in that house myself, the condition it's in. Who knows what might happen? But it's your funeral."

He nodded curtly and strode away. I picked up my forms and drove home, where I painstakingly filled in blanks for a couple of hours, posted the letter to the landlord whose existence I was beginning to question, and spent the evening with a nice, familiar Agatha Christie. I found it comforting to deal with something I knew the ending to.

I woke to a fine drizzle on Friday morning. As I plodded across the Close to work, the murky light washed the color out of the world, and the cathedral seemed to brood, its great gray bulk hugging the earth.

Inside, though, the atmosphere was entirely different. The staff were arranging chairs and music stands at the east end of the nave, and marking rows of seats with numbers. Armies of volunteers scurried about with masses of flowers in their arms. Screeches and the voices of invisible technicians issued raucously from the sound system.

The cathedral was *en fête*. I had completely forgotten that the Sherebury Cathedral Music Festival began tonight. And I was going to the gala opening, a performance of Beethoven's Ninth Symphony by an extremely exalted orchestra.

With Alan.

My step was light as I walked into the bookshop.

Clarice evaded my inquiries about her health. "I'm fine," she said persistently. "Truly."

And not another word could I get out of her. Well, she looked more or less all right, if a bit droopy—but she was often droopy. And we were too busy to talk, anyway. The hundreds of music lovers who had come to town for the festival all seemed to be whiling away the time in the cathedral. They raised a brisk trade in postcards and guidebooks.

At about eleven Barbara Dean blew in and came straight over to me.

"I've been hoping to speak to you," she said, "and this is the first moment I've had. Some of those volunteers!" She threw up her hands and rolled her eyes, and I remembered that she was (of course!) in charge of the front of the house arrangements for the music festival.

"If you're too busy, we can make it another time," I said hastily, but she was not to be deflected.

"No, no, I simply wished to know about your house. I see that you have a tarpaulin in place. I trust that means you have been successful in finding a contractor for the work?"

"Yes, thank you. The man recommended by Planning Aid, a new man in town named Herbert Benson, wasn't getting anything done, so I called in Mr. Pettifer, and he's given me an estimate for the work. I—er—I know you and he aren't exactly friends, but he does seem to be quite professional." She said nothing at all, and I hurried nervously on. "I mailed—posted the grant applications to my landlord yesterday."

"Good," she said briskly. "And you'll let me know if he doesn't respond?"

"Well—"

"Splendid. Good morning!"

The breeze as she swept out wafted three sheets of poetry off the counter.

When my shift was over and I'd had some lunch at home, I lay down for a nap. I wanted to be fresh and rested for the concert, and at my age, the way to be fresh in the evening is to sleep in the afternoon.

I had just settled myself comfortably, with a cat

curled up on each side and the rain beating a nice
lullaby on the plastic covered roof, when the phone
rang.

"Afternoon, Mrs. Martin, Herbert Benson
here."

"Oh, Mr. Benson, I—"

"Sorry about the little misunderstanding over
your roof. No hard feelings, of course, but you
might have let me know. *But* still, no use crying
over spilt milk, eh? I have a quote for you on those
windows we talked about. Shall I bring it over
straight, away?"

"No! No, Mr. Benson, I don't want—"

"Ah, well, if this is a bad time I'll ring up again.
Ta-ta!"

He had hung up before I could make some
excuse. He reminded me of one of those hard rubber balls. The harder you throw it away, the faster
it bounces back to you. Would I never be able to
get rid of him? It was a good half hour before I
could stop fretting and get to sleep. Even then, my
dreams wrapped me in blue tarps and buried me
under tiles and slates, and I woke with the sheets
wound around me and the cats long fled.

It was an effort to work up any enthusiasm for
getting dressed and going out, but I put lots of car-
nation bath oil in the tub and soaked for a long
time in the bubbles, and when I'd applied careful
makeup and gotten into my laciest, most feminine
undies, I was myself again.

I hesitated for quite a while about the outer
layer. I tend to overdress. If I'd been going by
myself I wouldn't have cared, but I didn't want to
embarrass Alan. I finally chose a slimming black
silk sheath, topped off with a very chic scarlet

jacket I'd bought for almost nothing in the Portobello Road. Pearls were always correct, and I put on and then regretfully took off a little black satin evening hat that I loved. I was cramming necessities into a small black beaded bag when the doorbell rang.

Alan didn't whistle; that wasn't his style. He didn't say anything, either. He just stood there in his immaculate black suit and regimental tie and looked me over with his careful policeman's eye, a smile slowly broadening on his mobile face.

When he spoke at last I could have kissed him. "Smashing. Absolutely top marks, except—where's your hat? You're not really you without a hat."

"I'll be the only woman in the place wearing one."

"What does that matter?"

"Alan, I do love you," I said gratefully, and flew upstairs to get it.

"It's stopped raining," he said as he held my raincoat for me, "but it may start again at any moment. And will you ruin your shoes if you walk on the wet path?"

"Yes," I said. "That's why I'm wearing wellies." I slipped out of my black patent heels and into a pair of yellow rubber boots, and we set off across the Close, arm in arm and well pleased with ourselves despite the glances that greeted my eccentric ensemble and the shoes dangling from one hand.

"How is your roof holding up in the rain?" asked Alan as we made our way up the nave looking for our seats.

"Fine, and Pettifer's come through with the plans and cost figures." We'd reached our row, second from the front, and had begun to excuse our way past the knees. "Now if my landlord will get a move on, and the grant applications can actually make it through the planning bureaucracy—oh, heavens! I'm *so* sorry!"

For in scrambling past a very large, pillowy woman I had slipped, and grabbed the first thing that came to hand to keep from falling.

It happened to be the head of the man in the front row.

And the man in the front row happened to be Daniel Clarke, Lord Mayor of Shrewsbury.

If I could have vaporized I gladly would have. Or better yet, been beamed up to the *Enterprise,* to return in a time warp a few seconds ago with the sense to be more careful.

Somehow one survives these things. I apologized profusely to everyone in sight, was established by Alan's firm hand on my elbow in the seat directly behind my victim, and hid behind my program until a shaking of my chair caught my attention. I peeked out to see who was moving it, and why, and saw that Alan had nearly reached the point of apoplexy with suppressed laughter.

I could have killed him, but when he caught my eye he snorted loudly and had to reach for his handkerchief to cover more unseemly demonstrations, and I began to giggle myself. It was perhaps fortunate for all concerned that the conductor came out just then and we had to behave. I wasn't sure I would make it through the politenesses at the beginning, with all the dignitaries welcoming everyone, but when the music began I forgot everything else.

Beethoven's Ninth Symphony isn't easy to program. It's too short to make up an evening by itself, really too long for a second half, and too spectacular for anything to follow it. Tonight's conductor had chosen the conventional route, beginning with a short Haydn symphony and giving us a long intermission to prepare for the master. It was at the intermission, just as I was feeling calm and comfortable, that the Lord Mayor turned to speak to me.

"It's Mrs. Martin, isn't it? I believe we were introduced last Sunday."

A politician needs a good memory for names and faces, but I would have been much happier to remain his anonymous assailant. However, I acknowledged my identity while Alan, infuriatingly, stood smiling and silent by my side.

The Lord Mayor went on. "Did I hear you say you're having some difficulty with grant applications, or something of the sort? Is it possible that I might be of some help? Mrs. Dean mentioned something to me a day or two ago."

I was awed. So La Dean could talk even the Lord Mayor into dealing with a peon. I muttered something inarticulate and Alan, at last, came to my rescue.

"Mrs. Martin is eager to get the roof question settled quickly, since her lease will expire soon and there is a good deal of further work to be done on the house, as well." He explained about my conditional purchase offer.

"Oh, dear, dear. Well, I shall certainly do all I can. Your house is quite lovely, Mrs. Martin, and essential to the character, not only of your street, but of the Close, since it can be seen from the cathedral. We cannot allow our finest buildings to perish from neglect, can we?"

Here he was interrupted by the dean.

"I'm so sorry, I must go and attend to some details, but I shall speak to you again, Mrs. Martin. I shan't forget."

Well, no, he probably wouldn't forget the woman who had nearly snatched him bald.

"That color is very becoming," murmured Alan.

I hoped he was talking about my jacket, not my face, but my blush ebbed as I mulled over what the Lord Mayor had said. He was concerned enough about Shrewsbury's architectural heritage to go out of his way for a stranger.

Was he concerned enough to commit murder?

That one so distracted me that I surfaced again only when the baritone launched into his fourth-movement solo, and then I tried to dismiss everything but the music from my mind. But a niggling thought kept insisting that the brotherhood of man espoused by the "Ode to Joy" was a lovely idea, all right, but even the first pair of brothers didn't get along any too well.

In fact, one of them had killed the other.

12

DEARLY AS I love England, every now and then I reach a stage of acute frustration with its pace of life, and with the relentless politenesses and restraints. By Saturday, having gotten exactly nowhere with a solution to the murder, and chafing under the delay with my housing problem, I was more than ready to spend the weekend with American friends in London, celebrating the Fourth of July.

It did me good. The Andersons are two of my favorite people, and the party was marvelous. Tom is some sort of exalted vice president of a multinational with a lot of American employees in London, and every July 4 they throw a big shindig at the company headquarters, a country estate on the Thames. A picnic, brass bands, fireworks—the whole bit, including a tour of the mansion. I hadn't liked the idea of a big manor house being turned into offices, but after I saw how tastefully it had been done, I came back to Shccbury on Monday morning thoughtfully considering a new aspect of the preservation question. Surely it was better to put a glorious old house to a new use than to let it decay because no family could afford to live there anymore.

Much as I detested Pettifer's plan, it was sounding more and more logical.

The cats pointedly ignored me, as punishment for my absence. When I sat down at the dining-room table, however, and began to open my mail, the rustle of paper was too much for Samantha. She dived onto the table, claws extended.

"Ouch! *Bad* cat! You know you're not allowed up here—and you've been told before about those claws. Scat!"

I had to crumple an envelope for her to chase before I could get rid of her. Sucking on a scratched knuckle, I turned over the letter she'd attacked. It had survived pretty well, with just two neat punctures where she'd grabbed it between her teeth.

It was nothing very interesting, just a note from friends asking how I was and saying they missed me. Not important at all, except that the Davises live in Sheffield.

"Sam, it's a sign," I informed her. She stopped in mid-chase, all four legs stiff, brown tail quirked into a question mark. "I hadn't been sure whether I ought to pursue this thing anymore, but here's an excuse to go right to the heart of the mystery. Now, I certainly can't turn it down, can I?"

I waved the letter, which was a mistake. Sam leapt into the air, neatly seized it from my hand, and killed it.

After a hasty lunch, I poked my head out the back door to check the weather. It had been deteriorating all morning; the air hung still, hot, and heavy under a sullen sky.

"Is it going to rain, Bob?" He was hard at work on my back flower bed, seemingly impervious to the heat.

He sat back on his heels and studied the sky. "Not today." He spoke with authority. "Just get 'otter. Tonight, mebbe. Tomorrow, sure. Got to get these 'ere chrysanths in 'afore it comes; they're good and sturdy to stand up to a storm, but they don't like bein' planted in mud."

I trusted his forecast. My umbrella stayed in the stand and I strolled across the Close with no raincoat.

"Aren't you going to get wet, Dorothy?"

Clarice was in the staff room ahead of me, hanging her yellow slicker on her peg and setting her umbrella quietly in the stand.

"Bob Finch says it won't rain until tonight at the earliest. I should think you'd boil in that oilskin thing, or plastic, or whatever it is."

"Oh. Yes, I suppose it is warm, but Archie thought I should wear it." She smiled a little, and there was something in her tone that made me look up.

"You're looking very nice today, Clarice. That pink blouse suits you. You must be feeling better."

"I'm quite all right. I told you I was. I—had a headache on Friday, that's all. Did you have a pleasant weekend?"

I told her all about the party, and she smiled again.

"It sounds rather exhausting in this heat. Archie and I enjoyed a quiet weekend at home." There was that tone of voice again. Satisfied? Happy? I couldn't quite put my finger on it, but at any rate, she didn't seem likely to throw a fit of the vapors this afternoon.

Which was just as well. We were worked off our feet; for once I was glad Barbara Dean was also helping. We found ourselves side by side straightening the stock in one of the few slack moments.

"I had occasion to call on Mr. Benson this weekend, Dorothy; he does not seem to be an entirely satisfactory person, so perhaps you were wise to consult Mr. Pettifer. I trust your tarpaulin is properly fixed in place; a storm is coming, and we don't want further damage before the repairs can be completed."

"It seems secure, thank you, Mrs.—er—Barbara." Lightning didn't strike me down, so I ventured further conversation. "By the way, I'm thinking of a little visit to your old haunts. Some friends from Sheffield want me to come see them; you're from there originally, aren't you?"

"Yes."

The monosyllable was not encouraging, but I persisted. "I don't suppose you know them—Colin and Gillian Davis? They're both at Hallam University; he teaches sculpture and she's in drama."

"I have very few contacts in Sheffield now. My family are all gone, and I have lived in Sherebury since I married, many years ago. Yes, sir, may I help you?"

And she turned to a customer, almost, I thought, with relief. But probably she was simply discouraging familiarity on the part of her inferior. And I'd thought we were beginning to be on equal terms. The nuances of English social relations still elude me.

Business slacked off at the end of the day, and Willie shooed me away a bit early. True to Bob's prediction, the storm hadn't broken by the time I got home, but it was nearer and I was as restless as the cats. I ate an unsatisfactory supper of leftovers and decided to call Alan. I wanted to tell him I was probably leaving town again for a few days, and he might also have some updated information. He wasn't home, though; I finally reached him at his office.

"No, nothing new. So far as I know." He sounded tired and distracted, and I could hear conversation in the background. "The trail's pretty cold by now, you know. Two weeks—Morrison reports to me only when there's some promising development. And we've had two serious drugs cases break over the weekend, and an armed robbery, and a smash-and-grab raid on the jewelers in the High Street. And of course The Visit." I could hear the capital letters even on the phone. "How was your weekend?"

"Fun. A little hectic. Alan, I won't keep you, but I'm thinking of paying a short visit to some friends in Sheffield. They've written, and I thought I might take it as an invitation. I just might find out something."

"It's a big place, Dorothy. I very much doubt that you'll learn anything to the purpose. In any case—damn, there's the other phone, and my secretary's gone home."

"I'll let you know when I'm leaving."

"Fine."

He'd hung up before he'd even finished the word.

Well! This was apparently my day for being rebuffed. He was busy, of course, and tired, but surely he could have been a little friendlier? Or had

I just been imagining that his feelings for me were—
I didn't want to pin down exactly what I'd thought
about our relationship, but I was certainly confused.
My restless energy suddenly collapsed in on itself
like a dying star, leaving the same sort of black hole.
Turning for comfort to a cat, I found that both of
them had disappeared, probably under my bed, to
wait out the approach of the storm. The sky was
growing very dark, with an ominous greenish cast.

I turned on the lights and tried to think positively. I had other friends, after all. Friends who
enjoyed my company. They'd said so. I picked up
the phone again and punched in the lengthy series
of numbers to reach Sheffield.

Colin answered on the second ring.

"Hello, Colin? It's Dorothy Martin."

"Well, hullo, love! Gill, it's Dorothy—pick up
the other phone." He came back to me. "I can't
hear you very well. Are you here in Sheffield?"

"No, I'm at home, and we're going to have a
thunderstorm any minute. You're not very clear,
either." I raised my voice and pressed the receiver
to my ear. "Gillian, I got your note, and I really
have been meaning to come up and see you. It's
awfully short notice, but how would this coming
weekend do?"

"Oh, but what a pity!" It was Gillian's voice, but
it faded in and out. "We're just off to . . . tomorrow, for a fortnight. Colin . . . some sketches for a
big bronze he's planning, and I'm . . . a play."

"Sorry, I missed some of that. You're off to
where?"

"Portugal!" Colin's voice came through loud and
clear for a moment. "Why don't you come along
with us, and we could have a good, long holiday?"

I tried to hide my disappointment. "It sounds delightful, and it's very kind of you to ask, but I can't. I've got too many irons in the fire here to be gone for more than a few days. Actually—oh, I might as well admit it. I was hoping to pick your brains about a—well, something puzzling that's happened here in Sh'erebury."

"About *what*?" said Gill. The line was getting worse.

"A murder," I shouted. We might be cut off at any moment; there wasn't time for circumlocution.

"There's a man here, a builder named Pettifer, who's from Sheffield originally. He's been trying to develop the Town Hall into a shopping mall, and there's a lot of controversy about it. Anyway, a couple of weeks ago a young man was found murdered in the Town Hall. His name was Jack Jenkins, and he was from Sheffield, too. And there's a third person involved, also from Sheffield —Pettifer's chief opposition, a formidable lady named Barbara Dean, head of the local preservation society. So you see, your part of the world plays rather a prominent role, and I wondered if any of those names rang a bell."

There was a crackly silence at the other end of the line, and thunder began to rumble close by.

"Did you get all that?" I asked anxiously.

"Most of it." Colin's voice sounded faint. "I can't say it raised any instant recognition in my mind. What about you, Gill?"

"None of the names, no," she said, and I thought I could hear doubt in her voice. "I do recall a scandal here a few years ago about a building controversy, if that might have a connection, but I don't think any of your people were involved."

It sounded awfully tenuous. "What was it about?"

The static began again in earnest as Colin and Gillian talked at once. "Council housing . . . blocks of flats . . . pensioners . . . fire . . . faulty wiring . . . three people died."

"Who was the contractor?" I shouted, afraid of the answer, but straining to hear. The rain had begun pelting down, and thunder boomed almost continuously. "Was it Archibald Pettifer?"

"No," said Colin, decisively, and for a moment clearly. "I'd remember a damn-fool name like that. No, it was about three years ago, and the names have vanished from my mind. I do remember the preservation faction was led by a woman, but then they nearly always are, aren't they? That's probably why Gill remembered at all—parallel with your case—but I've lost her name as well."

"Me, too," said Gillian, "but I do recall one rather poignant detail, now that I think of it. One of the people killed in the fire was her old auntie. The newspapers—"

There was a blinding flash of lightning and a doomsday crack of thunder. All my lights went out, and I was holding a dead telephone in my shaking hand.

The house hadn't been struck, I realized after a quick, terrified tour of inspection. It was the magnificent old oak tree between my house and Jane's. A large limb lay in my backyard, crushing all Bob's work in the flower beds, and incidentally burying electrical and phone wires. As the tempest raged and lightning flashed, I could see other trees straining before the wind.

It was a terrifying storm, but like most of its

kind, it didn't last long. As soon as the rain slowed to a drizzle, I ran over to check on Jane—the front way. She popped out of her front door the same moment I did.

"Stay out of your back garden, Dorothy!" she shouted. "The cables are down!"

"I know. I was coming to tell you the same thing. I'm off to the nearest working telephone to report it."

I awoke late to a clear, balmy morning denying all connection with storm and tempest, and began to assess the damage. Destruction was everywhere. Limbs had fallen from venerable old trees all over the neighborhood, in one case through a roof. My tarp had miraculously held, but the wind had driven rain under it and into my upstairs hall.

As I set out for my job, Bob stood mutely by my gate, unable to work with live wires everywhere, but shaking his head at the flood of mud and all the young plants that lay with roots miserably exposed, dying in the brilliant, crisp sunshine.

13

I WAS GREETED at the bookshop by a notice on
the door announcing that, due to power failure,
the shop was closed until further notice. As the
only window in the place was so small as to admit
almost no light anyway, the decision was practical,
but I was annoyed that no one had let me know.
Unreasonable, of course—how was anyone to
phone me?—but I wasn't feeling reasonable. Upset
with Alan, my nerves frayed by the storm and my
abortive conversation with the Davises, I badly
needed to talk to someone sensible. As usual, Jane
was the chosen victim.

I dumped my purse in my kitchen and was heading out the door when I happened to glance at the
calendar. It had a red ring around Tuesday, July 6.
Today was Jane's birthday.

Oh, dear. I couldn't go over there without
an offering of some sort. Jane might snort over
whatever I brought and say it was all nonsense, one
didn't have birthdays at her age, I should have had
better sense—but she would be deeply hurt if I
forgot. I picked up my purse and headed out again.

Almost without conscious volition, I found

myself walking into Underwood's. A silly choice of shops, really; I'd never seen anything in Mavis's emporium to appeal to Jane's practical, earthy taste, and I knew from past experience that I'd almost certainly end up buying something. Perhaps my subconscious wanted to see how Mavis was doing.

Once I had seen, I had plenty of material for thought.

For Mavis was doing very well indeed. The shop, deserted the last time I'd been in, had five or six customers. A pretty young assistant was manning the cash register, while Mavis was showing the brass bedstead to a couple that looked likely to buy it.

I lurked in the back of the shop, fiddling with a pile of hearth rugs until Mavis had triumphantly negotiated the sale and noticed me.

"Good morning, Mrs. Martin," she trilled. "Lovely morning after the storm, isn't it?"

"A good day for cleaning up, and there's a lot of it to do. At least you have electricity, which is more than I can say. Did you have any damage at home?"

"I hadn't the time to notice, did I? Rushed myself off just to look in at the other shops before I fetched up here."

"You seem to be very busy today."

"My dear! I haven't had a moment to so much as sneeze these past few days. It's quite incredible."

The color in her cheeks today looked natural, and her hair had been toned up to an even brighter auburn. She glowed.

"It looks as though murder's been good for business, then, doesn't it? One can't always rely on how the public will react, I suppose."

Her eyes hardened. "I can't imagine what you

mean, dear. Were you interested in those rugs? Lovely and thick, you see, they'll wear forever."

They weren't actually impossible. The roses were a trifle too large and a trifle too pink, but for keeping sparks off the carpet, they'd do. I picked one up, paid the exorbitant price, and walked out wondering with half my mind what on earth Jane was going to do with it, while the other half was busy considering the benefit Mavis had, unexpectedly, derived from the death of a twenty-three-year-old boy.

I found a ribbon in a crowded drawer in my kitchen, tied it around the rug, and marched next door, avoiding the workmen who were cautiously dealing with live wires in my erstwhile flower beds.

"Happy birthday," I said, thrusting the rug into Jane's arms as I stepped around a rush of eager, curious dogs. "If you hate it, take it to the next jumble sale or use it on the floor of one of the kennels. And for pity's sake, make me a cup of tea and let me talk to you."

Jane, being Jane, accepted that ungracious speech with no more than a raised eyebrow and established me at the kitchen table with tea and biscuits before she even untied the ribbon. Then she growled an utterly characteristic, deprecating thanks and sat down opposite me, head cocked inquiringly. "Problems?"

"Oh, I don't know! It's just—that was a really bad storm; it scared me. And I'm being snubbed by Barbara Dean—though that's hardly news—and Alan doesn't have time for me and some friends I wanted to visit are going away. In short, I'm feeling thoroughly sorry for myself. And I'm not getting any-where with the murder, either."

Jane's eyes were calm, searching. "Why do you have to?"

"Well, of all the—do you want a murderer to go free? I thought the English cared more about justice than that!" My voice had risen; my hands waved in the air, and the nearest dog growled a small warning.

Jane's voice remained level. "We do. Why you?"

"What—oh." I felt suddenly very warm. "Sorry. I get carried away. It's a reasonable question, and I don't really know the answer. Except that this whole business seems to be connected with the question of preserving old buildings and—and good workmanship in general—and those are things I care about. And Alan is so busy—oh, I know he doesn't really have anything to do with day-to-day police work, but his men are all tied up with the royal visit, too, and they just don't seem to be doing anything. And besides—you didn't see him, Jane. That young kid, spread out there on the floor. I can't forget how pathetic he looked."

Jane looked at me searchingly over her teacup. "Can't leave well enough alone, can you?"

"I could," I retorted. "If anything were well enough. It isn't."

"Ah, well. You have a talent for landing on your feet. And as for Alan—he'll come round." She looked out the kitchen window. "Phone's probably working now—they've done with the wires."

I put my cup down. "Oh, then I'll get out of your way. I have a phone call to make."

I couldn't help it if she thought I was about to phone Alan.

In fact, he was not even on my list for today. I was definitely annoyed with Alan Nesbitt. If he wasn't interested in what I had to say, fine. No doubt he could get along perfectly well without my help, and I had no wish to intrude where I wasn't wanted. He obviously had better things to do with his precious time.

Which just goes to show how silly and spiteful a middle-aged woman can be.

My phone call was to Sheffield, or it was intended to be. I couldn't get through. Even though my phone was working fine, lines were evidently down all over the place, and circuits weren't available.

Well, I wasn't going to let that stop me. Probably the Davises were already on their way to Portugal, anyway. If I wanted more details about that building scandal that had begun to intrigue me, I'd have to look closer to home.

In the year I had lived in Sherebury, I'd become well acquainted with its excellent public library. I wasn't quite sure how to go about looking up an old news story, when I didn't know the date or the papers that might have covered it, but assuming the lights were on and the library open, someone, I was confident, would help me.

It was the reference librarian who showed me the microfilm machines and gave me a whole drawer full of the *Times,* as well as an index. I'd have to rely on the national papers; Sherebury, in the southeast, wasn't particularly interested in the affairs of a big city far to the northwest of it, and the library didn't carry their regional publication.

The search was less tedious than I'd supposed. In less than an hour I had my information, but I wasn't sure I knew much more than I had before. The fire that had destroyed a Sheffield apartment complex (a "block of flats"), built to house the elderly, had happened over three years ago, in March. It had been a late-breaking story; names of the victims were withheld pending notification of their families. The *Times* said there would be an investigation into the possibility that faulty wiring was to blame, but I couldn't find a follow-up article on the results of the investigation, nor did I see the names of the victims, presumably published later. The only other mention of the affair at all was a very brief news item a couple of years earlier, about the proposed project to be built by the firm of Mr. George Crenshawe & Co., which was arousing some opposition on the part of preservationists who felt the Victorian terrace and redundant church on the site should not be demolished. No members of the opposition were named. There was a picture of Mr. Crenshawe and a member of the county council, shaking hands and beaming.

I sighed. Really there seemed to be no connection with Sherebury at all. Peering again at the picture, squinting through the bottom of my bifocals, I could see that Mr. Crenshawe was a man, had the usual number of arms, legs, and eyes, and was bald. The photograph had never been especially good; microfilm reproduction hadn't improved it.

I decided to be thorough about the search while I was at it. Knowing the dates helped. I worked my way through the *Telegraph,* the *Guardian,* and the *Evening Standard* before deciding enough was enough. My neck had what felt like a permanent crick in it from the angle required to read a screen through bifocals, and I'd learned nothing really relevant. The *Standard,* given the benefit of a later deadline, did give the names and ages of those killed in the fire, and I dutifully copied them down.

Miss Hattie Bulstrode, 83, Mrs. Janet MacLeod, a mere 76, and Mr. James Wyatt, 99. The last was particularly pathetic, since Mr. Wyatt's 100th birthday would have been in three days, and he was said to have been vigorous, active, and looking forward to the celebration.

Well, the *Standard* would have said that even if he'd been a feeble old man with little mind left. All girls are pretty in newspapers, all women at least striking, all victims pitiable. It makes better copy. Still, I left the library full of fury.

If I ever encountered Mr. George Crenshawe, he'd better watch out.

I spent the afternoon trying to help Bob restore some order to my desolate wreck of a garden. Working on my knees, getting mud on my hands and very nearly everywhere else, had the usual effect of restoring balance to my mind. Gardening is a steadying occupation; it's so very real.

So, after I'd scrubbed off the worst of the mud, I decided to relent and try to call Alan. I had no idea whether the pitiful little bits of information I'd gathered would be of interest, but he deserved to have them. It was simply silly to carry a pique, like a teenager.

He was, as I expected, at the office, and my high-minded mood didn't last long.

"Hello, Dorothy, I'm up to—hold on a moment." I could hear a brief, muted conversation at the other end of the line before he turned his attention back to me. "Sorry. As I started to say, things are a trifle frantic here. What can I do for you?"

"Well, there are some things I wanted to talk to you about, and I was hoping you might have time for a quick meal, but I don't suppose . . ." I trailed off disconsolately, but Alan, usually sensitive to my moods, didn't pick up on my tone of voice.

"Sorry, it's sandwiches from the canteen for me this evening. What's on your mind?"

His impatience was fully justified. He was plainly juggling a great many problems at once and didn't have time to deal with a dithering female.

Which didn't make me feel one bit better.

"It's nothing I can talk about on the phone. And probably not important, anyway. You're busy; I'll let you go."

This time he did catch it. "Dorothy, I—"

I hung up, gently.

14

THE TROUBLE WITH assertions of independence is that they often feel fine at the time, but the warm self-righteousness cools all too soon to a hard lump of misery. I spent the rest of the evening wishing I hadn't hung up on Alan, or hadn't called him at all, and forcing myself not to call again, and went to bed missing Frank so fiercely I cried myself to sleep. For once, two warm, friendly cats were no help at all.

Weary, red-eyed, and late, I dragged myself out of bed in the morning and decided to go to the bookshop. Wednesday isn't one of my regular days, but they might be deluged with tourists after being closed for a day, and I felt I needed something productive to do. My moods were becoming entirely too dependent on one Alan Nesbitt.

When I got there I found everyone as edgy as I was. It was another British Tourist Authority kind of day, warm and sunny, so the place was full of customers clamoring for service, and Mrs. Williamson—I *had* to remember to call her Willie—and Barbara Dean were trying to cope by themselves with a bus load of camera-laden

Japanese and another of earnest-looking Germans. I hurled myself into the fray, wishing I had some proficiency in some language other than English (or, as the English would insist, American).

"Where's Clarice?" I hissed at Willie as I rang up seventeen postcards and she finished explaining that she really could not take traveler's checks written in yen, they'd have to be changed at a bank. "We need her."

"Don't know," she said, pawing frantically through a pile of illustrated cathedral guidebooks for the German-language version. "Home, I suppose. She hasn't phoned and I haven't had a moment to ring her or talk to Barbara. She might know, if you can catch her; it was late Monday afternoon, after you left, when Clarice collapsed again and had to be taken home. Here you are, sir, that's one pound fifty."

"*Bitte?*" said the elderly man, studying his handful of heavy English coins with a puzzled frown.

Willie managed a smile, though it was a little frayed around the edges, and began to sort through the coins for the ones she needed. "See, this thick one is a pound, and this is ten pence . . ."

But Clarice had been in such a good mood Monday! I didn't understand at all, but there was no time to think about it until a lull hit a couple of hours later, and I made a pot of tea. Barbara Dean came into the staff room to join me, looking more human than I'd ever seen her. Her hair wasn't perfect and there was actually a smudge on her lapel. She sat down heavily in the squashy old armchair and accepted a cup of tea with murmured thanks.

"You look tired, Barbara," I ventured, settling

gingerly on the couch, which was easier to get into than out of.

She sighed, and then pulled herself together. "So do you," she said, "and we've both earned it. We should all have been a great deal better off this morning with more help."

That gave me my opening. "Yes, what's the matter with Clarice, do you know? Mrs.—Willie said she caved in again on Monday."

"I'm afraid I haven't the slightest idea," Barbara said crisply. "We were simply talking when she turned white as paper and crumpled. Canon Richards took her home."

"Good heavens. Was it something about the murder again, do you think? She's awfully sensitive about that, for some reason. I think she's still worried that her husband might be—suspected."

"If that is the case, she ought to have been reassured. Yes, we were discussing the matter, but quite calmly. I told her I was quite certain that the roots of the matter lay with the boy's background, in Sheffield. And she fainted dead away."

"But that makes no sense at all. Do you think she's ill?"

Barbara shrugged, and I took a different tack.

"I'm curious, though. There was a building scandal in Sheffield not too long ago—well, you probably know all about it. Do you think it could possibly have anything to do with our murder?"

"I'm afraid I prefer not to talk about Sheffield. There are some rather painful memories . . ." There was a surge of noise, and Barbara put down her teacup and stood up. "There seems to be quite a crowd coming in again. Perhaps we should get back to work."

Well, that was a clear "No Trespassing" sign. But she'd talked about Sheffield to Clarice. Was it because I was a foreigner, or had I said something wrong somehow? I was going to have to be very careful with future questions, at any rate. Not sure of an approach, I wasn't really sorry I had no more chance to speak to Barbara until the end of the morning, which was when the really odd thing happened.

Lunchtime had thinned out the crowd, and all three of us, Barbara, Willie, and I, had seized the chance to tidy up. Barbara and I were working together at a shelf of poetry that had been wildly disarranged, and I was making conversation, trying to work my way back to Sheffield, when she suddenly stood stock-still, staring at the book in her hand. I had never seen such a look on anyone's face. She might have been a Greek goddess, or one of the Fates—cold, implacable marble.

"Barbara, is something wrong? Are you okay?"

"What?" Her voice came from a great distance. "Oh. Yes. Please excuse me." And she put the book on the shelf, precisely where it belonged, and walked out of the shop, stopping only to pick up her handbag.

I stared after her, and then picked up the book she had been holding.

What on earth was there about the poems of George Herbert to turn anyone to stone?

I stayed most of the afternoon. Even with the two women of the afternoon shift, we were frantically busy until after four, when the weather changed and the flood of tourists diminished to a trickle, and Willie shooed me out. "You've done a yeoman's job, and I'm truly grateful, but it's time you put your feet up. You look tired."

I was, in fact, exhausted after a restless night and hours of standing, and nothing sounded better than putting my feet up and having a cup of tea. Or perhaps something stronger. However, duty called, and resentfully I listened. I should stop at Clarice's to see how she was. The woman could be infuriating, but she was a friend, and friendship shouldn't be taken lightly.

The gray sky and gentle sound of the rain were most conducive to a nap. I knew if I once relaxed, I was out for the count. So I hurried home, getting wet in the process, greeted the cats, had a cup of tea, and climbed into the car. Maybe I could find out what was bothering the wretched woman, anyway.

Once I got to her house, with no more than the usual number of wrong turns, I thought I might have saved myself the trouble. Clarice wasn't talking and didn't appreciate my solicitude. She let me in with a reluctance that was downright insulting, though she tried to disguise it, and sat nervously on the very edge of one of the blocky modern couches in the living room.

"It's very good of you to come, I'm sure, but Archie will be home in a moment and I really must—"

She tried to think what she really must do while I assessed her. Her hair was in strings, her face, blotchy from crying, was innocent of makeup, and her frilly blue blouse and brown-and-orange tweed skirt didn't go together. Balled up in one hand was a damp handkerchief which the other hand picked at.

"You're very kind, but I—I have a bit of a headache, and—"

I could stand it no longer. "Clarice, I can well believe you have a headache, but there's a lot more to it than that. You're a wreck. I've never seen you like this. Is it Archie?"

She looked terrified. "No! No, of course not! There's nothing wrong with Archie—he—I have a headache, that's all."

"You're on the verge of a nervous breakdown," I said flatly. I had lost my patience. "When will your husband be home?"

"Soon. You mustn't—"

"I intend to see to it that you're looked after, since he doesn't seem to be doing a very good job. Clarice, you must see that you need help. You've been falling apart ever since that wretched murder—"

She went even whiter than before and slid off the couch to the floor as Mr. Pettifer walked into the room.

"May I ask," he said with cold fury, "precisely why you are bullying my wife?"

"Bullying! I'm trying to—we can't stand here arguing, she's fainted, she needs—"

"I believe I am the best judge of what she needs. You will have the goodness to leave my house, Mrs. Martin!" He turned his back on me, picked up Clarice with a strength I hadn't known he possessed, laid her on the couch, and began chafing her wrists.

"But—she needs a doctor, I could—"

"Get out!" It was a stage whisper, with the effect of a roar.

I got out.

And just what, I thought as I drove slowly down the wrong side of the fortunately deserted street, was that all about? Was she afraid of Archie? Did he beat her, after all? If so, he was careful to make sure it didn't show; her face was a mess, but it wasn't bruised. He certainly had a temper, but he had treated her gently when he'd picked her up, and only two days ago she had acted—well, to tell the truth, she'd acted like a teenager in love, mooning about Archie, making excuses to bring his name into the conversation.

Was she afraid *for* him? I was sure she'd had suspicions all along that he was involved in the Town Hall murder. That could explain her behavior. Suppose Archie had managed somehow to convince her that he was in the clear, and then—yes! And then Barbara Dean said something to her that awakened her suspicions with more force than ever! Hence her collapse. It would have to be something to do with Sheffield. Was Archie the crooked contractor after all? And why wouldn't Barbara talk to me about Sheffield?

The blare of a horn shocked me back onto my side of the road, where I promptly stalled the engine and sat for a moment, quivering. When my mind began to function again, I realized the Archie-as-criminal-contractor theory wouldn't fly. He'd left Sheffield far too long ago. But logically, Barbara Dean must have said *something* to send Clarice into a tailspin. Well, why not ask her again?

I peered out the car windows; I'd been driving more or less aimlessly for a few minutes while my thoughts were racing after an explanation. Sherebury isn't a big town, but it can be confusing, and I wasn't sure quite where I was. The Pettifers live in an exclusive development, all cul-de-sacs and curves, which adjoins a lovely old neighborhood with even more narrow, curvy streets and complicated hills.

There was something familiar about the area, though. Surely I'd been here before? These houses looked familiar. The big stone one, especially—

The big stone one was Barbara Dean's house. I'd been there only once, to a genteel sort of tea party for the bookshop volunteers, but I was certain.

Almost certain, at least. I got out of the car. There was no harm in ringing the bell. If it was the wrong house, I could apologize, go home, and phone the blasted woman. If I was right, she could hardly refuse to let me in, and it was just possible I could extract some information.

I rang.

And rang once more.

And waited.

The rain was setting in hard now, and obviously no one was home. Of course, Barbara was a widow and lived alone. If this was even her house. I gave up, splashed back to my car, and drove off, peering anxiously past the monotonous swish of the windshield wipers. After three random turns, I had no idea at all where I was. It wasn't yet six, but the clouds were so dark and the rain so heavy I could see very little. There wouldn't be a soul on the street in this downpour; asking directions was out.

Maybe if I tried to head downhill? That at least would bring me to the main body of the town, and with luck to a street I recognized. How lost could one get, for heaven's sake, in a town the size of Sherebury?

Very lost.

The last straw was when I slithered down a steep, nasty little cobbled lane, took the sharp turn at the bottom too fast, and came to a shuddering stop a couple of feet from the edge of the river-bank.

That scared some sense into me. There was no point in my continuing to drive aimlessly in this weather. If I had to, I could walk home. At least I knew where the river was, though I wasn't familiar with this part of it. I must be on the very edge of town, even if I wasn't certain whether it was the east or the west edge. I abandoned the car to its wildly unsuitable and probably illegal parking spot and set out, umbrella-less, to seek help.

And there, looming out of the rain and put there by all the saints, was a pub, a large, well-known riverside pub that was supposed to have good food. Then this was the Lanterngate area, to the west, and only five minutes from the High Street. Well, no matter that I now knew where I was and where home was; I was tired and wet and hungry, and I made for the sign of the King's Head like a homing pigeon.

"'Struth, madam, been out for a dip in the river, have you, then?"

I dripped copiously on the flagstone floor as I walked into the bar and cast bitter glances at the stone-cold hearth. "No," I answered the barman through chattering teeth. "Just a dip in your lovely English climate. Is there someplace where I could dry off a bit, do you think?"

"Sarah!" he bellowed through a doorway, and a comfortable-looking woman bustled in, a white apron around her ample waist. "Sarah, love, take the lady upstairs and get her dry. Here you are, dear." This was to me, as he handed me a balloon glass with something amber in it. "Keep the cold out. On the house."

"Oh, dear, dear, dear," murmured Sarah. "You look like a drowned kitten, you poor thing. You come right through with me."

The King's Head, it seemed, was an inn as well. Sarah, presumably the innkeeper's wife, led me up steep, narrow stairs to a small room with a sloping floor and chintz curtains, and switched on the electric space heater that stood forlornly in a large fireplace.

"Now just you get out of those wet things, dear, and here are towels and a bathrobe. I'll have to bring you something of my own to wear whilst we dry your clothes in the kitchen."

"But—I'm not spending the night, you know. I just came in for a meal—"

"That'll be all right, dear. Don't worry. You're American, aren't you?"

I admitted it.

"Well, we can't have a visitor getting pneumonia, can we? Whatever would you think of us? Now you just drink your brandy and warm yourself at that nice electric fire and I'll be back in a tick."

"No, I do appreciate this, but I actually live in town, just at the other end, near the Cathedral. I should go home, really, I can't—"

Sarah put her hands on her hips and studied me. "Of course, dear! You're Mrs. Martin, aren't you? I didn't recognize you, with your hair all streaming. Now, you're not getting any younger, dear, if you don't mind my saying so. I couldn't rest easy, letting you go back out in the wet, cold through as you are. You'll have a nice meal, won't you, and your own things will dry and you'll go home feeling much better. You just leave things to me."

I gave in gratefully. Sarah bustled out, and I was glad to strip to my underwear, dry myself on the rough towels, and slip into the thick terry-cloth robe. I was warming my hands in front of the heater when she came back with an armful of clothes.

"Here you are, dear. The dress'll be big on you, but it has a belt, and I've brought you a nice cardi to keep you warm."

I slipped into the navy blue dress and white cardigan sweater.

"There now!" said my rescuer delightedly. "That isn't so bad, after all!"

"It's wonderful," I said sincerely. "This is so very kind of you, and I don't even know your name—except Sarah."

"Sarah Hawkins. My husband and I own this place; he's Derek, down in the bar." She shook hands, the formal gesture seeming a little odd from someone who had seen me in my skivvies a moment before.

"Well, Mrs. Hawkins, I certainly owe you a great favor. Now about that meal—do you really have room for one more for dinner? I'm sure you're busy."

"We are that," she said with satisfaction. "If you wouldn't mind sharing a table? There's one of our residents dining alone, and he never minds a bit of company. You'll find him a very pleasant gentleman, friendly, but not—you know." She cocked her eyebrows to indicate that I was safe from molestation, and I grinned.

"Sounds fine to me."

I was settled at a table for two, my brandy had been topped up, and I had ordered a substantial meal before I had cause to change my mind. I was scrabbling in my purse for a tissue when a familiar voice made me look up.

"Well, well, what a pleasant surprise! Our good hostess told me I was to have a dinner companion, but she didn't mention your name. Doing well, are you, Mrs. Martin, eh?"

Herbert Benson clapped me on the shoulder with a heavy, ringed hand, scraped back his chair, put down his large glass of gin, and sat down, beaming all the way to the edge of his bright-brown hair.

15

THERE WAS NO help for it. Mr. Benson might not be my favorite person, but I could scarcely stalk out of the King's Head in a downpour, wearing someone else's clothes. I was stuck.

"Why, Mr. Benson," I said with as much charm as I could muster, "I had no idea you were staying here. I would have thought you'd have found a house. How long have you been living in Sherebury, then?"

"Few months. To tell the truth, I've been too busy to look for a place of my own, and the Hawkinses do me very well here." He waved the matter away and went straight to the issue I wanted to avoid. "How're you getting on with your roof?"

My soup was served just then, which gave me an excuse for a brief reply. "Well, the tarp keeps the house more or less dry, and I have hopes the grant applications may be approved soon."

"Ah, well." He made a large gesture. "You'd have done better to leave it to me, you know. But—" He waved his right hand airily again and one of his rings slipped from his finger, clattering to the table. He put it back on and continued without missing a beat. "No harm done, and no offense taken, I'm sure. No need for you to worry about that!"

What chutzpah! He'd neatly turned his irresponsibility into my transgression—and then forgiven me for it! Torn between irritation and admiration, I concentrated on my soup.

"I'm afraid I won't have the time to take on those windows we talked about," he went on.

Well, thank goodness for that, anyway. Clearly I was no match for this man. If he'd decided he wanted to oversee the rest of my renovations, I'd not only have ended up with plastic windows, but been convinced they were what I wanted.

"I'm on to quite a good thing, actually," he went on. "Set to build those new blocks of flats for Pettifer. You've heard about them, I'm sure, going to pull down the old Victorian terraces near the university, not that they'll need much pulling down, ready to fall down by themselves, and put up nice new flats, modern, convenient . . ."

Ugly, I thought. But, looked at with the dispassionate eye I was trying to cultivate, the old ones weren't all that beautiful, either. Old and quaint, but dilapidated. Perhaps Pettifer was right, and they should be replaced. At any rate, Benson, with his love of modernity, was probably more safely employed on new buildings. However . . .

"Oh, yes? I'm surprised you're involved in that project, Mr. Benson." It was catty, but I felt I had the right to a lick or two. "Somehow I got the impression you and Mr. Pettifer were—not on very good terms. And surely his own men don't have enough to do right now. Why would he hire someone else to take over the job for him?"

My soup bowl was replaced by a plate of sausage, lamb chop, steak, bacon, liver, mushrooms, tomato—loaded with fat and cholesterol, and smelling wonderful.

"Oh, Archie and I are good friends, you know," Benson said, finishing his gin. "Here, waiter, I'll have the mixed grill as well, and we'll share a bottle of Australian claret, eh, Mrs. Martin?" He beamed at me. "No, we may quarrel from time to time, as old friends do, but when we can see it in our way to do the other a favor, we do it. There's too much between us for us not to be friends, you see."

The last remark made me look up sharply. There was more than a hint of a nudge-and-wink in Benson's voice, and an unmistakable leer on his face.

"What *do* you mean?"

My tone would have frozen an unruly fourth-grader back in my teaching days, but Benson was beginning to feel his gin, and took no notice.

"Ah, well, no need to spell it out to a clever lady like yourself, is there? We've all got our little secrets, haven't we? I dare say Archie has one or two things up his sleeve that he'd just as soon didn't get known, eh? An indiscretion or two in his past? That boy in the Town Hall, now. I fancied he had quite a look of—but least said soonest mended, eh? Here, now, you're not drinking your wine!"

"I don't care very much for red wine," I lied. Actually I didn't care very much for Benson's increasing inebriation, nor for his innuendos.

"What a pity—you ought to've told me. Would you prefer white? Or a nice glass of beer, or—"

"No, thank you." Probably he meant well, I

thought, trying to be charitable. "It's very kind of you, but I really don't want anything more to drink. I didn't get a lot of sleep last night, and I don't like to drink much when I'm driving anyway. The English laws—" I stopped. Why was I explaining so elaborately?

Benson leaned forward earnestly. "Ah, now, y'see, that's your trouble. You let the law intimidate you. Planning laws, traffic laws. The way I look at it is, see, the law's your servant. Who had the idea of laws to protect us in the first place? The common people, that's who. Magna Carta and all that, the common people against the king. It's even called common law, isn't it? But now they have their laws here and their laws there and they're all to put you under, keep you in your place. If a man's to look out for himself, he has to find the way to get round them, thass all." He burped. "'Scuse me."

Taking out a cigarette, he put it between his lips, struck a match, and paused, fractionally. "Don't mind if I smoke, do you?"

"Yes, I do mind, as a matter of fact."

He had already taken a long drag. He looked at me in astonishment and choked on the lungful of smoke that was seeping out of his open mouth. I looked pointedly at the cigarette; he extinguished it, carefully, and slipped it back into the packet in his shirt pocket.

"Always happy t'oblige a lady," he said cheerfully, and I was hard put not to roll my eyes to the ceiling. Just once I would like to catch the man out, put him in the wrong so firmly that he would be forced to apologize, but he seemed unable even to recognize his own sins, much less repent them. I hoped his shirt caught fire.

"You're sure you won't have a li'l wine?"

"I'm sure." I was crisp. It had no effect whatever.

"Making a mistake, you know. 'S'nothing like a nice glass of wine, and this stuff's very nice indeed."

He poured the rest of the bottle into his glass and his left hand caressed it, fat little fingers looking like sausages with rings tightly embedded in the flesh. His sibilants were beginning to hiss a trifle more than he intended.

"'S'matter of fact, this was what I was drinking the night—the night of that meeting, you know. Good old Derek's got quite a lot of it laid down, 's good stuff . . ."

He was more than a little tight, and I didn't like the way he was leaning toward me. "That would have been the night of the murder, wouldn't it?" I said hurriedly. "When Mr. Pettifer was with you, after the meeting?"

He looked at me with owlish solemnity. "Couldn' deceive a lady, now could I? Don't like to let down a pal, but mush—mussen lie to a lady. Lie to the police. Don' like the poleesh. Laws, intid—timin—out to get you." He finished his wine in one large gulp and began to sing. "All alone—I'm so all alone—" He broke off. "Can't remember resh of wordsh. Alone. All alone. 'Scuse me."

He got up with careful dignity and walked in the direction of the stairway, wavering only slightly, but causing raised eyebrows as he passed. Mrs. Hawkins, drawn by the singing, came over to me, flustered.

"Oh, dear, I'm so sorry, Mrs. Martin! I've never seen the poor man like that before. I suppose he was being convivial and lost count. Are you quite all right?"

"Yes, thank you. It's certainly not your fault. It's been a long day, though, and I'm ready to drop. Are my clothes dry, do you think?"

"I'm afraid they're still quite damp. Why don't you just wear that dress home? It's too tight for me, you know, so I shan't be wanting it till I can slim a bit." She sighed, running her hands down her hips. "But our cook is so good—did you enjoy your dinner? You'll have your sweet, won't you, and some coffee to buck you up? It's still raining."

I was too tired to resist, even if I'd wanted to. I did as she suggested, left when the rain finally stopped, and managed to find my way home before sleep caught up with me and blotted everything out.

The next morning the world was soft and foggy, with sounds and sights muffled and misty, a perfect day to roll over and go back to sleep. I wasn't allowed to, of course. Last night I'd heartlessly closed the bedroom door against my four-legged alarm clocks, but the instant they heard me move they'd bounded up the stairs to my door and stayed, creating various sound effects designed to speed up breakfast. Esmeralda has perfected a door-pounding method, standing on her hind legs and battering very quickly with alternate front paws. It's similar to a scratching-post routine except with retracted claws, and with her considerable weight behind those powerful legs, it's extremely effective on the loose-fitting old door. *Bam bam bam bam bam* . . . endlessly.

Samantha, of course, has her Siamese wail.

I endured half an hour of it before dragging

myself out of bed in martyrly fashion, afflicted with a headache and what my grandmother used to call "the rheumatics," my reward for getting soaked to the skin the day before.

My brain wasn't working very well either, I realized as I brooded over a cup of coffee. A confused mass of ideas thrashed about, refusing to form a coherent whole or even settle down long enough to be looked at intelligently. Sheffield, Barbara Dean, William Farrell, Archie Pettifer, the Town Hall, Clarice, Benson's nasty hints—I reached for a pad and put it down again drearily. I didn't have the energy to make a list.

What I needed was to talk to someone who knew all the details of the murder and could help me sort it out, see if some pattern would emerge.

What I needed was Alan.

I looked at the phone, and then looked away. I'd gotten over my temper, but common sense told me there was no point in trying to reach the chief constable three days before a royal visit. Even if he was in, he was likely to be barricaded behind a wall of secretaries, and in no mood to talk. I might be able to reach him this evening, talk him into a late dessert, but that was hours from now.

So, failing Alan, I was on my own. Even Jane hadn't been all that sympathetic; she clearly thought I should mind my own business.

Three aspirin and two cups of coffee later I reached for the phone. As my headache faded (replaced by heartburn), I'd remembered I wanted to talk to Barbara Dean. This time I intended to be direct. I couldn't spend the rest of my life in terrified awe of the woman, and I needed some answers. Why did she think Sheffield was at the heart of a

ShCrebury murder? Did it have anything to do with the Sheffield building scandal? I was sorry if she didn't want to talk about it, but I was tired of playing games by other people's rules. I intended to ask about Pettifer's past, too. Much as I hated to put any stock in Benson's hints, they might be relevant.

I punched in the number briskly and let the phone ring at least twenty times before I dropped the receiver back on the cradle.

So that, too, would have to wait. Frustrated, but doggedly stubborn, I reached again for the pad and pencil.

A half hour of intense concentration produced only a brief list of not very brilliant questions in no particular order.

THINGS I WANT TO FIND OUT

1. What, if anything, does Sheffield have to do with our murder?
2. Who were the preservationists in that battle?
3. Why doesn't Barbara want to talk about it?
4. What on earth is the matter with Clarice?
5. Is there anything to Benson's hint about Jack Jenkins being Archie's son?
6. Was Benson really with Archie the night of the murder?

And I couldn't think of a single answer.

After trying Barbara again, I gave it up and headed next door, praying Jane would be home. If she didn't want to talk, she might at least have some idea where I could find Barbara. (I was beginning to be able to think of her by her first name, I congratulated myself. Another year or two and I might get comfortable with it.)

I negotiated Jane's slippery back path, but before I could knock, a confusion of dogs leapt out the door, whining and barking and turning themselves inside out in their eagerness for a walk. They approached me for a ritual snuffle, but immediately turned their attention back to Jane, following with three leashes in hand.

"Uh-oh!" I shouted over the commotion. "Bad timing! I was coming to see you, but I don't dare delay the troops, do I?"

"Come along with us," Jane roared. "*Quiet*, dogs!" The clamor decreased by a decibel or two and she shrugged. "They'll shut up once we're on our way."

We made for a vacant lot a few streets away, covered with rank grass and weeds, and much favored by dog owners. There Jane turned the dogs loose to run as they wished, and we sank onto a wooden bench whose surface was beaded with water.

"Jane, I must confess I have an agenda. Do you have any idea where I might reach Barbara Dean? I really need to talk to her, and she doesn't seem to be home."

She sat up a little straighter and looked at me. "Second person today to ask me that. Don't know why everyone thinks I'm the information bureau." But it was said without rancor. She knew perfectly well why, really; she almost always had the answers.

"Mayor rang up this morning," she went on. "Or his secretary did. Dean missed a meeting last night. Preservation Society. Didn't send word. Mayor was speaking, everyone upset she wasn't there."

My eyes widened. "But, Jane, she's chairman of the Preservation Society!"

"Mmm." Her eyes turned back to the dogs.

"And she wasn't home yesterday, either, at least early in the evening, because I knocked on her door about—oh, six, probably. I thought she'd gone out to dinner. I could have been mistaken about the house, but I don't think I was. And I've been calling all morning, on the phone, I mean, and there's been no answer. Do you think we should check on her? She—I suppose she could have fallen . . . or something . . ." My voice trailed away doubtfully. Somehow, the vision of Barbara Dean as the helpless victim of an accident wasn't easy to conjure up; she was so totally competent, so utterly in control.

But Jane was frowning. "Not like her to be irresponsible. Never missed a meeting that I know of."

And Jane would know.

I looked at Jane, unease beginning to stir, and Jane looked at me and came to a decision. She stood and whistled for the dogs.

"Probably nothing wrong, but can't hurt to find out. Come along, dogs, better walkies later." They came, slowly, and allowed their leashes to be clipped on, voicing their disappointment and bewilderment all the way home.

Jane made one more attempt on the phone, letting it ring until it disconnected itself, and we sat there looking at each other.

"Jane, do you think . . . ?"

"Yes. I'll drive."

"Thank God," I said fervently.

I had driven around, lost, for at least half an hour last night; Jane found the house in five minutes. It was the right house, the house I'd tried, but there was still no sign of life. No lights were on, though the day was dull enough to need them. No one answered the door.

"Do you suppose the neighbors—?" I asked very tentatively. If Barbara had simply gone away on short notice, she would not appreciate our making a fuss about it.

Jane was made of sterner stuff, and had the bit between her teeth. "Not like her at all," she said stubbornly. "Something wrong. You take that side."

She set out for the houses to the right while I went to the left. Some of the neighbors weren't home, but the ones immediately to either side, interrupted in the middle of their lunches, had no knowledge of Dean's being away, and expressed astonishment that she had failed to show up for a scheduled appointment. "But she'd never do such a thing!" was the universal opinion.

It was the man who lived directly across the street who was helpful. "You could check her car," he suggested. "She garages it just round the corner, where I put mine, as well." Certainly he would show us the way. He'd just tell his wife he'd be a moment—

"Each door has its own padlock, you see," he explained as we walked to the corner. "But it's one big building, and the individual bays are divided only by partitions, half height, rather like horse stalls, eh? Mrs. Dean keeps her car just next to mine, so we can easily see—ah, here we are."

The building was little more than a shed, flimsily built of wood, probably designed for some other purpose originally. But the enterprising owner, see-ing profit in the ever-growing, desperate need for a place to park, had turned it into a five-bay garage with just enough space for the owner of each car to park it and squeeze out. The obliging neighbor pulled open the double doors of his bay and stepped inside. We didn't have to follow him; from the doorway we could see the car in the next bay.

Spotless, smug, uncommunicative, it sat there. Jane did manage to slide her bulk between the neighbor's car and the partition wall long enough to peer into Dean's car and then slide out again.

"Nothing," she said briefly.

There, behind firmly padlocked doors, was Barbara Dean's car, cold and empty. Where, then, was Barbara Dean?

16

"ALAN, I HAVE to see you."

I'd been doing a lot of serious worrying. It was clear that Barbara knew a lot more about the Sheffield end of this story than she had told anyone. What if she knew too much—knew for certain that the builder of those council flats was responsible for the fire? If the preservation people in Sheffield were her friends, as seemed likely, she'd be bitter about the deaths, particularly of the "old auntie."

Or, the thought had suddenly hit me, what if she'd been involved herself, and it was *her* aunt who had been killed? She'd said something about painful memories. And suppose, just suppose, that the builder in question, George Crenshawe, was in Sherebury?

It had taken me ages to reach Alan. His regular secretary wasn't in, and the substitute answering his calls was new and extremely protective. When she finally gave him my message and he finally called me back, I'd been pacing the floor for nearly an hour.

"What is it?" he asked, his voice sharp. "Sergeant Rogers didn't say your message was urgent—are you in trouble? Why didn't you ring my private number?"

"Samantha ate it," I said sourly. "She chewed off the whole bottom corner of my little address book. Look, there are a lot of things I don't want to discuss on the phone. Barbara Dean, and Clarice Pettifer, and the murder. And I do realize you're frantically busy, but this is important, Alan. Can't you take a break for tea?"

"Impossible. I'm off to London in an hour, with two hours' work to do before I go. If this is about the murder, I'll put you through to Morrison." Without giving me a chance to reply, he put the phone down. There was a series of clicks and buzzes and then the officious secretary came on the line.

"I'm sorry, Mrs. Martin, Inspector Morrison is not in the office. He'll ring you as soon as we can reach him."

"Oh, no, that's too much trouble, I don't want—"

"No trouble at all, Mrs. Martin." She hung up.

The tears in my eyes were due entirely to frustration. I was still trying to convince myself of that when the phone rang. Well, apologies weren't going to get him anywhere this time. I'd teach him to toy with my affections, I'd—I picked up the phone.

"Yes?" I hissed, trying to sound like Judith Anderson's Mrs. Danvers.

"Mrs. Martin? This is Inspector Morrison. The chief constable just rang me up, said you had some important information for me. He's frightfully sorry he can't deal with it himself, of course, but he asked if I'd pop round to see you. Would now be convenient?"

"Oh." I sounded as deflated as I felt. "Oh—uh—yes, that's fine. I live right next to the Cathedral Close, you know, at the end of Monkswell Street, you have to go up the High Street and turn left, and then—"

"I think I can find it, Mrs. Martin." His tone was carefully not amused. "I'll be there in ten minutes, then."

The interval was exactly long enough for me to set out tea, while feeling fifteen kinds of a fool. For calling a busy policeman out on what might well be a wild-goose chase, for venturing to give him directions, I, an American who had lived here for less than a year . . .

He was very nice about it.

"I hope you really don't mind my coming round on such short notice," he began when I had established him in a comfortable chair, "but the chief was quite insistent. He said if you thought something was important, it was, and we must sort it out immediately. He did ask me to send his apologies, by the way." He grinned in a friendly sort of way, becoming instantly much more human. "I was to tell you he's ready to do murder himself, either to a certain royal personage or to his staff—I quote verbatim—and he hopes you'll forgive him for being a trifle—er—preoccupied."

Preoccupied wasn't quite the way I would have put it, but I wasn't going to carry on my quarrel with Alan through an intermediary. "It just means you'll get his tea, though perhaps he isn't missing much; it's all out of tins. I haven't had much time to bake."

"I'm quite fond of chocolate biscuits, actually," said the inspector, helping himself to four. "However,

I mustn't waste your time. The chief said you mentioned Barbara Dean and Pettifer. Is there a connection there we've missed?"

"I don't know." I poured him a cup of tea and adjusted my mind back to business, and suddenly felt much less apologetic. There really was something odd going on. "What I do know is this: There was a very messy affair in Sheffield some years ago." I told him the story I had pieced together from what the Davises had told me and my own researches, including my suppositions about Barbara Dean.

"Now, obviously, there's no proven connection with Sherebury there, but I'm convinced Mrs. Dean knows quite a lot about it. She's been saying the oddest things. In fact, she said something to Clarice Pettifer on Monday that upset her almost to the point of a nervous breakdown. She—Mrs. Dean, I mean—said she told Clarice the key to the murder must lie in Sheffield. And that brings me to the real point. I'm sure you wondered if I was eventually going to have one."

Morrison merely smiled.

"I've been trying for the best part of twenty-four hours now to reach Barbara Dean and ask her about all this. And—this is going to sound melodramatic, but I can't help it—she seems to be missing."

The inspector put down his teacup and gave me his full attention. "Exactly what do you mean by 'missing'?"

"Oh, not what the police mean officially, I suppose," I said a little impatiently. "I know there's something about forty-eight hours before they—you—will do anything."

"It depends upon the circumstances," Morrison said grimly. "Please go on."

"Well, she hasn't been seen, apparently, since yesterday around noon. There was a meeting of the Preservation Society—the *Preservation Society*, Inspector, she's the chairman, for heaven's sake—last night, and she neither showed up nor canceled. And she wasn't home sick, either, at least not around six, because I was at her house trying to find her. Anyway she was perfectly well when she left the bookshop just before lunch. A bit strange in manner, but in good health. And today she doesn't answer her phone, or her doorbell, but—and this is the worst part—her car is in the garage. Jane Langland and I checked. Now, doesn't that all sound to you like she's missing?"

"It warrants following up." Morrison swallowed the last bite of biscuit and and took out his notebook. "Now, what do you mean exactly by saying Dean was 'strange in manner' yesterday?"

"Well—preoccupied. She got that look on her face, as if she'd suddenly seen something in her mind. In cartoons they put a light bulb over the head. You know, 'Eureka'?"

He nodded, with a small grin.

"Only this didn't seem to be a very pleasant thing, because I remember thinking she looked for a moment as if she'd been turned to stone. And then she put the book back on the shelf and just left, without a word of explanation or good-bye or anything."

"What book?"

"Oh, sorry. Just a book of poems. By George Herbert. I remember that because it seemed so dull and harmless."

The inspector stood up. "I'm very much obliged to you, Mrs. Martin, for letting us know about this right away. I'll set the machinery in motion, and let you know what progress we make in locating Mrs. Dean."

"Wait, there's more! I'll try not to take any more time than I have to, but you should know what Mr. Benson said to me last night about Mr. Pettifer."

"Ah, yes, Pettifer." The inspector sat down again.

"I had dinner with Benson last night, you see. Quite by accident; the King's Head was crowded and we had to share a table. I was tired, so he did most of the talking—and he said a lot, one way and another.

"I wish I could remember his exact words, because none of this was what you could call a definite statement; it was all in the way he looked and sounded. Innuendo, you know, nudges and winks and knowing looks. I hate that sort of thing, and I may have inferred all the wrong meanings. And to be honest, he'd had quite a lot too much to drink, so none of it may be very reliable. But what it boiled down to, if not in so many words, was a strong hint that Jack Jenkins was Mr. Pettifer's illegitimate son. He as much as said that the two of them looked alike, and that Mr. Pettifer had some dire secrets in his past."

"Really." The inspector tilted his head to one side and pursed his lips.

"I thought that might interest you. And what may be of even more interest, although this was when he was really under the weather, was that he almost admitted he was lying about Pettifer being with him the night of the murder."

The inspector whistled softly.

"Now I could be all wet, as I said. And you

won't forget he was drunk, will you? I don't pretend I have any fondness for Benson, but I'd hate for a man's ramblings to be held against him. I just thought you might want to talk to Benson yourself. You see, I can't help wondering if Pettifer might have had something to do with the fire in the Sheffield council flats."

"Perhaps. At any rate, yes, we'd like a little chat with Mr. Benson. If you're even close to the right interpretation, he has some explaining to do. Why didn't he come to us with all this?"

"He said he didn't like the police. He seems to be something of a—free spirit, wants to be unfettered by the law—that sort of thing."

"There are fetters," said the inspector darkly, "and then there are fetters. He'd best go carefully, or he may get a taste of the real thing. But go on."

"That really is all, I think, Inspector. I'm sorry if it turns out to be nothing, but I thought someone should know. I'm really concerned about Barbara Dean."

"I'll see to it that someone lets you know as soon as we learn anything, Mrs. Martin, and thank you."

I fell into a troubled nap that afternoon, full of the kind of dream you'd rather not remember when you wake. This time I was driving my car down a steep hill into the river, over and over, jerking partly awake just as the water threatened to close over my face, and then starting the whole terrifying sequence over again. It was a relief when the phone by the bed roused me.

"Mrs. Martin? Morrison here. I've only negative news, I'm afraid, but I thought you'd want to know. We searched Mrs. Dean's house—a neighbor had a key—and there's no sign of her, nor clue to her whereabouts. Her handbag is gone, but her clothing and luggage seem to be in place, so far as we can tell. There's no convenient telephone number scribbled on a pad, no lovely railway guide left open to a particular page—nothing. It seems she simply left on a normal errand—though how, with her car in the garage?—and didn't return. We're trying to trace her earlier movements, where her car was seen, that sort of thing."

I absorbed that for a moment. "You might check with Mrs. Williamson at the bookshop," I offered. "I didn't see her speak to Barbara when she left so abruptly yesterday, but I suppose they might have talked earlier in the morning about Barbara's plans for the rest of the day." Actually, I doubted it; Barbara wasn't the type to confide in anyone else. But I was trying desperately to be useful.

"That's certainly a possibility," said the inspector politely. He didn't think much of the idea, either. "At any rate, it's a place to start. We'll be in touch."

So much for being useful. I went downstairs in search of friendly, purry company, but the cats led me straight to the door and stood there expectantly, tails erect. The mist had cleared.

I let them out, wandered miserably into my parlor, and sank down on the couch, wishing my own fog would clear. I felt dragged out and depressed, and my headache had returned. I couldn't seem to think. My mind was stuck on a treadmill, repeating itself over and over, like my dream.

Where was Barbara Dean? Her car was in the garage, where was she? She'd gone out and not come back, where was she? If she'd left town, she would have packed a bag. She would have canceled her engagements. She would have told someone. And if she hadn't left town, *where was she?*

I presume I fed the cats and myself and read or something until it was time to go to bed. I know I tossed and turned for hours, finally falling into a fitful doze shortly before dawn, only to be jolted out of it by the phone. I picked it up, my blood racing fast enough to make my aching head much worse.

"Yes?"

"Mrs. Martin, Morrison here. I do apologize for ringing you so early, but I've been on the blower with the chief in London, and he was sure you'd want to know. He said to tell you he'd try to phone later." He cleared his throat, sounding as weary as I felt. "I'm afraid it's bad news. We've found Mrs. Dean."

I lay silent. His words could mean only one thing.

"Where?" I said at last.

"In the river. She'd been there for at least twenty-four hours, but she didn't drown—no water in the lungs. I'm afraid it's unquestionably murder."

17

"I SEE." It was no surprise, but the confirmation was still a terrible shock. I'd hoped I was wrong. There were so many questions, but I was numb. The inspector cleared his throat.

"The chief asked me to stress what I would have said in any case. You must be very careful, Mrs. Martin. Not all the connections between this murder and the Town Hall case are yet apparent, but it seems evident that they exist. We think, and this is conjecture at this point, and confidential, that Mrs. Dean was killed because she knew something in connection with the Town Hall murder. Our villain could very well decide you know too much, as well."

"I don't know anything," I said bitterly.

"You inferred a connection between Mrs. Dean and an old scandal. And now Mrs. Dean is dead. If the murderer thinks you know more than you do . . . well, the chief specifically said I was not to forbid you to look into matters, but he and I would both appreciate your—er—discretion. To be quite candid, I don't need any more on my plate at the moment, especially not the murder of my chief's—er—"

My mind was sluggishly coming to life. "Why the river? I mean, why did you look there?"

There was the faint hint of a sigh on the line. "The last place we were able to trace Mrs. Dean's car to was a car park hard by Lanterngate bridge. There is an attendant who patrols several car parks to make sure the cars are displaying the slips that show they've paid. Hers was the only car there shortly after five, and it was gone—in fact, the car park was empty—the next time the attendant came round, about seven. We don't know when it arrived back at her garage, or who drove it there. Except that it was quite evidently not Mrs. Dean."

"Evidently. Look, Inspector, there's a lot more I want to know, but you sound dead on your feet. I'll call you later. And please don't worry about me. I promise I'll look after myself."

In fact all I wanted to do was turn over and sleep and sleep. But even in the face of sudden death, cats want to be fed. I went about the chore mechanically, and of course they noticed. My cats are very fond of their housekeeper/cook, and when something is wrong with me, they know. I dragged back up to bed after they'd had their breakfast, and they trotted right after me, Emmy settling on my chest and Sam on my feet, and purred themselves to sleep. Their presence was so comforting I actually slept myself, and for nearly two hours enjoyed the blessing of dreamless oblivion.

When I woke for good I was in fighting trim—rested, angry, and ready to do battle.

And the first battle was with the Pettifers.

It was time Clarice answered some questions,

and Archie as well. I was through with fencing. Barbara Dean was dead. I'd wished ever since I met her that I could really get to know that cool, detached woman. I admired her executive ability and agreed with her about many things, and lately she'd unbent enough to let me hope that someday we could become friends.

Now that could never happen. Someone had taken the chance away from us, and I couldn't help blaming myself. If I had just been quicker on the uptake, I might have learned what Barbara knew, and the two of us . . .

The two of you might have been killed together, said a voice in my head that sounded remarkably like Alan's.

Well, at any rate, what was past was past and I couldn't undo it, but I could take some action now. I heaved myself out of bed and headed for the shower.

Bob Finch was hard at work when I was ready to leave.

"I suppose you've heard about Mrs. Dean?" I called out the back door.

"Wot abaht 'er?"

"Oh, dear." I went out and lowered my voice. "I thought you would have heard, or I wouldn't have brought it up. She's dead. She was found in the river, murdered."

It takes a lot to shock a Cockney. Bob processed the information stolidly as he plied his spade.

"Pore lady," he said finally. "Nice enough, under all 'er lah-di-dah ways. I 'ope as 'ow Mr. Archibald Bleedin' Pettifer 'as 'imself a better alibi for this one than 'ee 'as for the first."

"Bob!" I raised my voice, and he looked up at

me in mild surprise. "Sorry, I didn't mean to shout. But what do you know about Mr. Pettifer's alibi for the first murder?"

"'Ee 'asn't got one, that's wot." He resumed his digging. "I never said nothin', not wantin' to get a man in trouble. But if 'ee's done for a lady . . . madam, 'ee was never with that Benson, that night. I was in the King's 'Ead the 'ole time, and Benson, 'ee were drinkin' by 'isself."

My heart was beating very uncomfortably, but I had to be sure. "But Bob, if you were drinking yourself, were you—I mean, could you—"

"I weren't pissed," he said with dignity. "Not that night. Just mellow like. An' I saw Benson come in, just after me, an' I saw 'im go up to 'is room abaht nine-thirty, lookin' like 'ee weren't feelin' so good. An' 'ee come back down in 'arf an hour an' drank 'isself silly. Wine, 'ee were drinkin'. 'Ee were still at it come closin' time, 'im bein' a resident in the pub and not 'avin' to observe licensin' hours. An' 'ee were alone the 'ole evenin'."

He turned his back decisively and I went back into the kitchen, stunned.

That seemed to settle it. Pettifer had no alibi, and had been lying about it. I hadn't been eager to believe Benson, but I trusted Bob.

I stalked to the garage for my car.

I'd forgotten how early it still was. Archie answered the door in his pajamas and bathrobe, red-faced and plainly furious. "And may I ask to what I owe this intrusion? Is a man to have no peace in his own home?" He stood in the doorway, his hand on the door, ready to slam it in my face.

"I must come in, Mr. Pettifer. You don't want to discuss this on your doorstep."

"I've nothing whatever to discuss with you, Mrs. Martin, whether on my doorstep or elsewhere."

"I see." I was as angry as he. "I suppose you'd rather I went to the police to talk about where you were the night Jack Jenkins was murdered."

He took a step backward and his face paled. "I was at the King's Head. The police know that."

"No, you weren't. May I come in, or do you really want to have this conversation in front of your neighbors?"

He might have bluffed it out, even then, but a weak, frightened voice came from the stairway. "What is it, Archie? What's the matter? Who are you shouting at?"

Archie raised his hands in exasperation and turned his back, leaving me to walk in and close the door behind me. Clarice, clutching a filmy peignoir with one hand and the stair rail with the other, did not look glad to see me.

I would have preferred to talk to Archie alone, but there was no backing out now. "I'm sorry, but I think we'd better sit down, all three of us. Are you all right, Clarice? Do you need help?" The shadows under her eyes looked like bruises, and her skin and hair were dull and not very clean. She looked very ill indeed, but she shrank away from my touch and clung to Archie, who deposited her on an overstuffed white sofa in the front room and stood guard over her.

"Very well, Mrs. Martin. You've succeeded in invading our home and frightening my wife. Now state your business and go."

Clarice made a little squeak, of nerves or protest.

"It isn't quite that simple," I said, sitting without invitation in the nearest chair. "I need some answers, and I intend to get them or turn the questions over to the police. You see, I've been talking to Bob Finch. I believe him to be a reliable witness, at least as long as he's sober, which he says he was, more or less, on the Sunday night when Jack Jenkins was killed."

Clarice sobbed and buried her head against Archie's chest; he reached a protective arm around her but never moved his gaze from my face.

"He says, Mr. Pettifer, that Herbert Benson was drinking alone all that evening, except for a little time when he went up to his room. He says you were never with him, nor was anyone else.

"Now that, of course, was presumably the time Jenkins was killed. And if—" I faltered, looking at Clarice, but I had to go on with it. "If what I've heard is true, that you—knew Jack very well—you might have had reason to kill him. I've told the police some of this, but not all of it, not what Bob said. I thought it would be only fair to see if you had some explanation before I went to them."

Archie sat down heavily next to Clarice and put his head in his hands. Clarice sobbed quietly. The only other sound in the room was the ticking of the clock.

"Yes," he finally said, raising his head and taking one of Clarice's hands firmly in his. His bluster was gone, replaced by a kind of desperate dignity. "Yes, you're quite right. I'm sorry this had to come up in front of you, my dear," he said to Clarice, "but the truth is, I killed Jack. He was my son, you see. There was a barmaid, years ago—at any rate, he'd come to town to make a scandal just when the Town Hall deal was at a critical point. I'd paid support for him, all the years when he was growing up and turning into a young lout, and worse. But now that wasn't enough; he wanted more. He planned to tell lies about how badly I'd treated him unless I paid him a great deal of money.

"I didn't intend to kill him. I went to the Town Hall after the Lord Mayor's meeting; we'd agreed on that spot as private. He—he taunted me and I pushed him, and—"

He couldn't go on. He shook his head and made a repudiating, pushing-away movement of his hands, and then turned to gather Clarice into his arms, but she struggled free.

"No." Tears were streaming down her face, but she struggled to control her sobs. "No, I won't let you. It was me, Dorothy. It was me, all the time."

"My dear—"

"*No*, Archie, I have to tell it. Don't look at me like that. Go away, over there—" she pointed to the other side of the room "—and don't look at me at all. Then maybe I can say it."

She drew a shuddering breath, gathered herself together with a kind of threadbare courage, and fixed her eyes on me. "I thought Archie was meeting a woman, you see. He'd been so—odd, lately. Angry, and wouldn't talk to me. I know now he was worried about—that boy—but I thought—anyway, I decided they'd meet at the Town Hall after Archie had finished with his dinner meeting, and I went there to wait for them. You do see, don't you?"

Archie started to speak, but I turned so fierce a glare on him that he stopped and looked away.

"I went to the side door, of course. I was sure I was too early—I knew the meeting would go on for hours and it was only about nine—but after a bit, when nothing happened, I began to think they were already inside, and I couldn't bear it. So I tried the door and it was unlocked. I crept inside, trying not to make any noise, and he nearly frightened me to death."

"Archie?"

"No—that—that boy. It wasn't dark outside yet, of course, but it was like midnight in that back hall. And he laughed, out of the darkness, and then switched a torch on my face. I was blinded, and so frightened, but he only laughed some more. And then he switched the torch off, and he said, 'So this must be the little wifey. Well, well. Let's go someplace where we can get to know each other.' And he grabbed my arm—I nearly screamed, then, but my throat was all closed up and I couldn't—and he held the torch to the floor and pulled me through the front of the building to some frightful sort of cupboard and shut the door and turned on the light."

"And told you who he was?"

"Yes, presently, but he didn't have to. I knew. He looked so like Archie when he was younger. Of course, Archie never dressed like that—he cares about his appearance, and he's always clean. But— oh, I can't explain, the eyes, the cheekbones—I knew.

"And then he started saying how much he needed money, and how upset Archie would be if he thought I knew about him, and perhaps we could work something out—oh, I can't remember everything he said, because I was so frightened, and I kept thinking about the son I'd always wanted to have and never could, and here was this— this—hooligan claiming to be Archie's son, and I didn't want it to be true, but I knew it was. And I tried to get away, but he ran after me out into the hallway and grabbed my arm, and I turned around and pushed as hard as I could—but we were standing next to the stairs, and he fell, and—and then he just lay there, so still, on the landing, and I thought I heard something, and I turned and ran, and ran . . ."

She took out a handkerchief and blew her nose.

I cleared my throat. "Clarice, dear, don't you think you'd better—"

"No. I have to finish it. I went home and waited for hours, but when Archie finally came home I couldn't talk to him after all. I pretended to be asleep. I thought we could talk later, when I wasn't so upset. I—I didn't know the boy was dead, you see. And then when you found the body, I nearly lost my mind, but I realized they might blame Archie, and I would have to be clever. If I just kept on saying nothing about it, with a bit of luck no one would connect the dead boy with us. And when things seemed to calm down, I thought it would be all right. But you wouldn't leave it alone."

"I couldn't—I didn't know—"

"It wasn't your fault. It wasn't anybody's fault. And I think I'm glad you know, now. I couldn't let Archie take the blame for what I did. I'm tired, Archie."

She looked up at him and he strode across the room to her, and the doorbell rang.

I knew it would be Inspector Morrison even before I looked out the window and saw the police car. I walked to the door and opened it; Archie and Clarice were oblivious, lost in their own world of sorrow and grief.

"I think you'd better come in, Inspector." I had to clear my throat before I could go on. "There's been—Clarice has confessed to the murder. But give them a moment, if you can. They need to forgive each other before the law steps in."

18

THE MORNING WAS nearly spent before I was able, very shakily, to drive home. I'd had to repeat everything I'd been told. Then Clarice had been asked to make her statement all over again, with a sergeant taking it down, and after she was taken away, Archie, still sitting limply on the beautiful, sterile white couch, had to explain his part in the confusing events of the evening.

"It was about ten when I finally left the meeting and went to the Town Hall to meet Jack. When I saw the side door standing wide open, I was angry; I'd given Jack the key against my better judgment and told him to keep the door shut and locked until I got there. I went in intending to give him a piece of my mind, but I couldn't find him. I didn't dare call out very loudly or switch on a light; it wasn't yet really dark outside and there were still people on the streets. I stumbled about and finally risked the light in the broom cupboard."

"And he was in there, I suppose," said the inspector. "Head injuries affect people oddly; they can sometimes walk about for a bit before they collapse."

"No, he wasn't there. The room was empty. I

left the light on with the door almost shut, and it gave me enough light to see—on the landing—"

He couldn't go on for a moment, and the inspector waited patiently enough.

Archie blew his nose and continued. "He was my son, Inspector. I'd never known him very well, and he was no good, and he was making my life a misery to me, but he was my only son, and he was dead. Inspector, when can I see my wife?"

"Presently, sir. Go on with your story."

Gray and weary, Archie pulled himself together with visible effort. "Where was I?"

"You'd just seen Jack, on the landing."

"Yes, well, it was a terrible shock. I went down to him, of course, but—well, it only took a moment to know that—that there was nothing I could do. And after a bit I started to think about my position. I ought to have called the police right then, but—you would have wanted to know why I was there, and the whole story would have come out. I thought, if I could move him—hide him until I could think what to do—I knew I shouldn't, but I wanted some time.

"So I carried him up the stairs, just half a flight to the ground floor, and put him in the cupboard. It would have been better to get him out of the Hall altogether, but with people about, and the twilight, I didn't dare. And it was—it was dreadful." He shuddered strongly. "He was still warm and limp; he couldn't have been dead very long. I thought I could deal with the nightmare better after I'd had some sleep. I did search his pockets as best I could in the dark, because I wanted to get my key back—I knew that would lead straight to me—but I couldn't find it.

"That was why I came back Monday morning, to find the key and take away any identification. I'd quite forgotten it was Mrs. Finch's day, and the sound of her scream put the wind up me so badly I very nearly turned tail and ran. But there was nothing for it but to bluff it out. I searched the body while she and Mrs. Martin were having their tea, but the key was gone. There was nothing in his pockets at all. Inspector, I really must be allowed to see my wife."

It was a feeble imitation of Archie's usual bluster, and it didn't impress the inspector at all.

"After you have completed your statement, Mr. Pettifer," he said grimly. "Now tell me, sir, just when did you strike Jenkins on the jaw?"

Archie looked at him without comprehension. "Strike him? I didn't strike him. I tried to be as careful as I could, moving him. It was almost—I couldn't help feeling I ought not to hurt him. Silly, I knew that—but I told you, he was my son."

"And why did you lie about where you were that night?"

"I—it was stupid. I don't know. I couldn't say where I really was, but that weak story—it was Benson's idea. He said he'd vouch for me, and no one could prove I wasn't there, and at the time it seemed reasonable. I—I'm almost glad it's all out—lately he's been hinting that he'd have to tell the truth, and I didn't know what to do—it's been hell." He dropped his head into his hands, but the inspector took no notice.

"And what can you tell us about Mrs. Dean?" he asked in the same level, implacable tone.

Archie just blinked, looking as if he couldn't quite remember who Mrs. Dean was. "What about

Mrs. Dean? What does she have to do with any of it?" He brushed his hand across his eyes, but the tears welled up again. "Inspector, I implore you—"

His voice broke, and Morrison rose. "Very well, we'll talk again later. Sergeant Tanner will transcribe your statement for you to sign at the station. If you'll come with me, we'll see if you can be allowed to speak with Mrs. Pettifer for a few moments."

I had to turn away; it was indecent to look at the naked longing in Archie's face. Whatever had caused him to bully his wife, I thought, shaken, it hadn't been a lack of love. It was there, raw, powerful, frightening.

When I got home I wanted two things quite desperately, and couldn't get either of them. I needed to talk things out with Alan so badly it was a physical longing, and I needed a very large, very powerful drink. It's a bad idea to drink out of necessity, but there are exceptions to every rule.

Of course, Alan was still in London. Presumably. I called his office with no hope at all, and my pessimism was fully justified. "Very late this evening" was the best guess about his return. I left a message that he was to call, no matter how late, and sat considering my second problem.

I'd been meaning for some time to stock up on liquor, but I hadn't been planning a party, so there was no hurry. Now there was literally not a drop of anything alcoholic in the house, barring the vanilla. Jane wasn't home, apparently—there was no movement visible in the windows on the side of her house I could see from mine.

I was so tired I could barely move, but I couldn't nap. The thoughts in my head wouldn't cease their squirrel-cage chase.

Furthermore, I knew I needed to eat, even though I was too upset to be hungry, and I still hadn't bought groceries. And there was that dress I needed to return to Mrs. Hawkins at the King's Head. I got out the car.

My mind was working so badly, I was actually inside the door of the pub before I remembered that I might well run into Benson, and I nearly turned and left. But I could always snub him, I reasoned. And I truly needed something to eat, and yes, all right, at least a moderate something to drink.

Mrs. Hawkins, when she came bustling to greet me at the bar, reassured me. "Thank you, dearie, you didn't need to worry about the dress, but ta all the same. And you needn't think you may be bothered with Mr. Benson; he's away for the weekend, left early this morning. Now, it's a bit early for lunch, but can we do you a sandwich? There's cold ham and cold beef, or salmon if you'd like, or a salad, or a ploughman's, of course—"

"A cold beef sandwich would be lovely," I said hastily, before she could list the entire contents of her larder. "And do you stock bourbon whiskey?"

I was settled with a large bourbon—neat—and a huge, crusty sandwich with salad and pickles, in what seemed like a few seconds. I prudently ate some of the food first and then sipped the drink with appreciation. It tasted good, but I didn't want it as much as I'd thought. Mrs. Hawkins's conversation flowed over me soothingly, calming my troubled thoughts as she moved about the bar, polishing the beer handles, wiping the glasses.

"And you could've knocked me over with a

feather when they told us, me and Derek." I realized she was talking, not about the Pettifers, but about the discovery of Barbara Dean's body, and tried to concentrate. Somehow it didn't seem as important as it had earlier. I couldn't stop thinking about meek little Clarice and bullying Archie, now cast in roles befitting neither of them.

". . . and just outside our door, too, would you believe it?"

She was waiting for me to answer a question. "I'm sorry, what? I was—distracted." I'd drunk more of the bourbon than I'd intended. I pushed the glass away.

"It's all right, dear, you look tired to death. I just said, who'd have thought it, a lovely lady like her, to jump in the river? Why would she go and do a thing like that?"

I wasn't going to debate the manner of Barbara's death with Mrs. Hawkins. "It's very sad," I said, shaking my head. "And that was lovely, but I'd better be getting home." I was taking no chances about Benson. "Oh, and could I buy a bottle of Jack Daniel's to take with me?"

"There, now, just you take this." She thrust a bottle into my hands. "We don't have an off-license, but you bring us a fresh bottle one day. You look as though you could do with the stuff now."

I went home and slept like a baby for most of the afternoon. Kindness was the real cure.

With waking, though, came memory, and with memory came pain. I went downstairs, fed the cats, and then walked restlessly in my garden, where Bob had made some impressive progress, though it was still a disaster area. Picking up a leaf or a twig here and there, I tried to wipe out the pictures that kept replaying across my mind. The look on Clarice's face as she talked about the son she'd never had—and on Archie's, talking about the son he did have, who died trying to blackmail him. It was no use. Nothing would ever erase those images from my memory.

There was the image, too, of Archie with his arms around his wife as she sobbed against him. Those two had begun to understand each other this morning.

Yes, and what good was that going to do them? England doesn't execute murderers anymore—and Clarice would probably be charged with something short of murder, in any case—but she'd be away for a very long time. And would Archie begin to brood about her killing his son, for whatever reason, however accidentally? Would he end by hating her—or she him, for giving another woman the child she wanted?

The bells from the cathedral tower had been sounding over my head for quite a while, I suddenly realized. Evensong was about to begin. I didn't even bother to wash my hands or tidy my hair, just walked straight across the Close and slipped into an obscure place as the choir was beginning the first psalm. Here, at least, was peace and respite.

And in the calm and quiet of the great cathedral, with timeless chant washing over me and light from the altar candles gently touching the incomparable beauty of carved stone and wood, my mind slowed and hushed and began to work properly again. Through the familiar words, one layer of my mind replayed the morning's scene yet once again, but analytically this time.

And I realized I didn't believe it.

Very well, why not? They weren't lying. No one lies that convincingly. They both meant every word they said. Well, at least Archie was lying at first, but that was to protect Clarice. He must have guessed the truth by then. But later, in his statement to the police, he was telling the truth.

Yes, that felt right. And Clarice's statement, tearful, wrenched out of her by her fear for Archie—she was telling the truth, too, surely. I knelt for the General Confession, and its words intertwined with mental protests: . . . *the devices and desires of our own hearts. We have left undone those things which we ought to have done* . . . Yes, there's too much left unanswered. How did Jack's jaw get broken? Clarice couldn't possibly have done it, and Archie claimed he'd never touched him, except to drag him upstairs. And he was telling the truth. And what happened to the key?

The rest of the prayers droned on, unheard, as I considered other questions. Who killed Barbara Dean, and why? It certainly wasn't Clarice. Archie hadn't even seemed to know she was dead. And what was the Sheffield connection? I was sure there was one, but had the police looked into the matter of one George Crenshawe?

It was an anonymous-sounding name. Of course! I made some small noise that I had to turn into a cough to reassure the woman kneeling next to me. Why hadn't I realized until now that the man could be operating under another name? Nothing was easier. Assume that the Sheffield investigation had uncovered criminal culpability in the building of those council flats. George Crenshawe was long gone by that time. Why shouldn't he be here, in Sherebury as—well, why not as a nasty-tempered builder named Farrell?

I surfaced for the benediction, and accepted it gratefully, but as I walked home through the brilliant sunshine of a July evening my mind was wholly occupied with my new theory. I thought about it as I made myself supper of toast and tea, with a little whiskey thrown in. I thought about it as I curled up on the couch with two contented cats.

I was still thinking about it when the doorbell rang, a little after eleven. I sat up in alarm, and the cats scattered. What new, terrible thing, at this hour—?

"Dorothy, it's me."

The voice came through the open window, deep and low. I was at the door in two seconds, and in Alan's arms, crying in sheer relief.

Bless the man, he let me cry, holding me and making soothing, meaningless noises. And when I'd slowed down a little, he handed me a box of tissues and sat me down on the couch, and disappeared into the kitchen. The marvelous smell of coffee floated into the parlor. When Alan came back, he was carrying a tray with steaming cups and a large plate of cookies.

"Where on earth did you find those?" I said with a last, shaky sniffle. "I would have sworn the cupboard was as bare as Mother Hubbard's."

"Fortnum's best biscuits. I bought them as a peace offering." He put the tray on the coffee table and sat down beside me. "Just as well I did. You need some sugar, woman. Eat."

I ate, and drank. Alan makes marvelous coffee,

much better than mine, and the cookies were rich and delicious.

"I'm sorry I made such a fool of myself," I said finally.

"Not to worry. You've had rather a trying day."

That made me giggle, as perhaps he had intended. Talk about the English gift for understatement! But I sobered quickly. He'd obviously talked to Morrison.

"Alan, it isn't true. I'm sure it isn't, but I'm not sure what's wrong with it. They're both telling the truth, but there are too many things that don't fit."

He nodded. "I've had a quick briefing from Morrison, and he agrees. We've had to charge Clarice, of course; she's confessed to manslaughter. But—" He spread his hands wearily. "She'll be out on bail tomorrow, I expect."

"Oh, Alan, that's wonderful! I'd forgotten about bail. I was picturing her—" I had to reach for the tissues again, but I mopped up hastily. "No, I'm all right. I'm not going to come apart on you again. Alan, I'm so glad you're here."

"I must leave soon. Tomorrow is a frantic day, and, of course, Sunday will be even worse. Then it'll be over."

"Over? How can you be so sure—oh, yes, the royal visit. I'd forgotten."

He gave a great guffaw. "Here I've been working myself to a shadow over nothing else, and you've forgotten that the Prince of Wales is coming to town."

"Well, I hadn't actually forgotten. I mean, that's why you've been away so much. But compared to what happened this morning, it just didn't seem very important, somehow, and it slipped my mind. I'm so worried about the Pettifers, Alan."

He put his arm around my shoulders and hugged me close. "You have a greater capacity for worrying about people you don't even care for than anyone else I know. I think that's one reason I love you so much."

He turned my face toward his, and this time the kiss was not on the cheek. It went on a long time, and when he stood up to leave, we were both a little shaky.

"Good night, my dear. Get some sleep. I'll ring you tomorrow."

19

ONE OF LIFE'S great blessings is that death and tragedy are never allowed to take full possession. Life goes on. People say it bitterly, as if one ought to be occupied solely with the current disaster. In fact we couldn't cope if, in the midst of crisis, people didn't eat and drink and relax a bit and comfort one another.

Alan had comforted me. I slept very late the next morning, waking only at the insistence of the cats (who also make sure I take a balanced view of life's problems—their needs coming high on the list). After coffee I felt ready to deal rationally with serious problems. What was left of Saturday morning was spent waiting for Alan to call, and making lists of what I knew (or felt I could safely conjecture), and what I wanted to know.

KNOWN
1. Jack Jenkins was blackmailing Archie, and tried to blackmail Clarice.
2. If he recognized George Crenshawe under some other name in Shrerebury, Jack would probably have tried to blackmail him, too.

3. Barbara Dean might also have recognized Crenshawe.
4. Jack's jaw was broken. Not by Clarice or Archie.
5. Somebody took Archie's key from Jack, or from his body.

NEED TO KNOW
1. Where's the key?
2. Who hit Jack hard enough to break his jaw, and when?
3. Is Crenshawe in Sherebury, and if so, WHO IS HE?
4. Who killed Barbara?

A meager harvest, but concentrating on the puzzle kept me from thinking, over and over, about yesterday's horrors. I studied the piece of paper and then added a sixth point to the first list.

6. Crenshawe is bald in the newspaper picture.

The point that interested me the most, of course, was the identity of Crenshawe. If I was right, he was at the center of these crimes, which would seem to take Mavis Underwood, the Lord Mayor, and John Thorpe right out of the picture. None of them, by the remotest stretch of the imagination, could be Crenshawe. Only Farrell seemed to fit the bill, and he was emphatically not bald.

But the others could have some connection with Crenshawe.

My mind had just dredged up that unhelpful suggestion when the phone rang.

"Morning, love. I have exactly five minutes before I must meet the Prince's advance guard."

"I thought he didn't get to town until tomorrow."

"Nor does he. His people arrive today. Now don't interrupt; there isn't time. I called, first, to tell you that Clarice is home, still insisting she's a killer. Second, how are you holding up?"

I hadn't thought about it. "I'm fine. How's Clarice feeling?"

"Bloody, I gather from Morrison. Look, my time is fully occupied until about nine tomorrow evening, when we thankfully pack His Royal Highness back to Kensington Palace. I can't go to the concert with you—I've got to do the official— but after the reception is over and he's gone, we're going on a carouse, just the two of us, and I shall brook no interference. Understood?"

"Yes, sir," I said demurely. "Orders received and understood, sir."

He chuckled. "Carry on, Lieutenant!" He pronounced it "leftenant," and I saluted smartly as I hung up the phone.

Amazing how a few words on the phone could make the sky brighter, the air sweeter. I thought I'd outgrown that sort of thing years ago.

How nice that I hadn't!

Abandoning for the moment my unproductive speculations, I ate a few of Alan's biscuits as a stand-in for lunch and decided to go to the book shop. Although I dreaded questions about the Pettifers, work was good therapy. Perhaps it would jump-start my stalled mind.

Fortunately, the cathedral grapevine had been operating at full roar, with the result that every detail of the Pettifer drama was already known by the time I showed up. Willie, bless her heart, had the sense to see I didn't want to talk about it, and the two rather scared new volunteers who were trying to take the place of Barbara and Clarice treated me like a leper. I wanted to tell them tragedy wasn't catching, but after all, I was just as pleased to be left alone to do my job.

The work did keep my mind from dwelling on the two women who should have been there, but by late afternoon I still hadn't made any mental connections that would help Clarice. This one, I thought grimly, is going to take a miracle.

One was waiting in the wings.

I volunteered to straighten up the shop after closing time. The others had worked all day, and were eager to get home; with Alan occupied, I had nothing to do for the evening but go to the supermarket, a chore I can put off indefinitely. And I felt I wanted to be alone there, anyway. Perhaps, with half the shop lights out and no one else around, I'd have the chance to tell Barbara Dean I was sorry.

A person gets odd notions in a medieval cathedral.

Or maybe not so odd, after all. For as I worked my way down the shelves, tidying, I found myself drawn to the poetry section, where no work needed to be done. And I'll swear to my dying day that it was Barbara Dean who made me take that volume of George Herbert from the shelf again and stare at it.

The cover design was rather ornate, suitable for a poet who died in 1633. A little typographical ornament separated the words George and Herbert, and as I looked at it in the half-light, slightly out of focus, it transformed itself into an equals sign.

George = Herbert.

George Crenshawe equals Herbert Benson.

That was what Barbara had seen. It was all so obvious once I saw it myself that I sagged, open mouthed, against the bookshelves. That bright-brown hair—not a dye job, a wig. And all those rings would have made a perfectly acceptable substitute for brass knuckles. And—I slapped myself on the forehead—surely he was from Sheffield! He'd as much as said so: "Archie and I are good friends, old friends."

Now that, I thought, was an exaggeration. He was a good deal younger than Archie. He probably knew him slightly, being in the same trade. But it certainly seemed to put him in Sheffield many years ago, when Archie lived there. So why not three years ago, when a building burned down?

But wait a minute. Bob Finch had said Benson had been drinking alone all that Sunday night, when Jack was killed. I stood up straight and walked back to the staff room. Forget tidying up, I needed to sit and think about this.

He hadn't said quite that, had he? I collapsed in the armchair and played back Bob's words. He'd said Benson had come in a little after he, Bob, had. And then he was drinking alone until—until—yes! Until he went up to his room for half an hour!

How did Bob know where Benson went when he left the bar? Even if he saw him start up the stairs—and you could see the main stairs from one corner of the bar—there were back stairs.

Now, exactly what might have happened? Suppose Jack had recognized Benson/Crenshawe, maybe a day or two before, and decided to try another spot of blackmail while he was at it. Very well. He already had an appointment with his father in the Town Hall, and he'd wangled the key out of him. He could have made an earlier appointment with Benson.

All right. So Sunday night comes. Clarice—oh, yes, this was working out perfectly! Clarice goes to spy on Archie and finds Jack instead. He upsets her so much she pushes him down the stairs and runs away, terrified because she hears a noise!

And that noise is Benson. He's sneaked away from the King's Head to keep his appointment. He must have already had some idea of murder in his mind, or he wouldn't have been so careful to cover his tracks. Anyway, he finds Clarice there and hides until she leaves, and then sees Jack, who's staggered up the stairs, just beginning to recover. It's too good an opportunity to waste. He pastes him one on the jaw hard enough to break the jaw-bone, hard enough to crush Jack's head against the cruel carved oak. He satisfies himself that Jack is dead, takes everything out of his pockets, and is about to get out of there, locking the door behind him with the key he found, when the third of Jack's victims enters the scene. Benson sneaks out through the open door, leaving Archie to his terrible discovery, and goes back to the pub, where he checks to make sure there's no blood on his clothes and "comes back down from his room." And drinks enough to float a battleship, according to Bob.

The very thought made my mouth dry, and I got up to make a pot of tea. That all seemed to make sense, I thought as I sank into the chair again, the tray beside me on the rickety table. Benson could drink quite a lot, as I was in a position to know.

He'd drunk himself nearly blotto the night I'd been forced to have dinner with him.

The night—oh, dear God! I spilled my tea before I carefully released the cup from my suddenly shaking hand.

He'd been drinking hard that night for the same reason he'd been drinking hard the night Bob saw him. He'd just committed murder. While we were sitting at the table, Barbara Dean was floating in the river a few yards away. I had dined with a murderer, his victim barely cold.

I made it to the sink before I was sick.

I cleaned up the mess myself, too. Fortunately I'd eaten very little all day. My mind kept repeating that phrase: Fortunately I've eaten very little . . . I went into the kind of autopilot that serves us so well in shock, doing what needs to be done, thinking of trivial practicalities. Let's see, I'd better shut up the shop properly and then have someone walk me home, I'm pretty shaky.

After I'd carefully checked the till—empty—and the teakettle and lights—off—one of the vergers was happy to see me to my door. They were all working frantically to cope with tonight's festival concert, and then get the cathedral brushed and polished for the Prince, who was to attend the concert tomorrow night, after he'd dedicated the hospital. My man was ready for a little break, but very excited about the royal visit; he talked nonstop for the short walk across the Close to my house. I responded politely and thanked him at my door, and then walked the few more steps to Jane's house.

"No, I won't come in, thanks. I'm not feeling very well. I think reaction's set in, from yesterday.

But I need to eat something, and I've absolutely no food in the house. Could I borrow some bread and eggs, or maybe something frozen? No, really, it's very kind of you, but I'd rather be alone."

I didn't dare be with Jane. I'd talk if I were with Jane, and the coldly rational part of my brain, the only part functioning, told me silence was much safer.

For there was absolutely nothing I could do with my new information. Indeed, it wasn't information at all, but guesswork. I refused to go over it all again, but I knew there wasn't one single verifiable piece of evidence in the whole scenario. Everything needed to be checked, confirmed, nailed down by the police before there was any kind of case.

And every senior policeman who could deal properly with it was occupied for the next twenty-seven hours with His Royal Highness, the Prince of Wales.

I'll never know how I managed to stay inside my skin for those next few hours. I ate something Jane supplied, without tasting it, and then sat with a book in my lap and the TV turned on, paying attention to neither, until it was time to go to bed.

That was possibly the worst part. I'd never been afraid of the dark, and after sleeping alone for over a year, I'd gotten over jumpiness. Now, every slight creak of the old house, every tap of tree branch against window, brought me wide awake, muscles tense, heart pounding. About two o'clock, I began to wonder whether I had really locked all the doors and windows downstairs. I was afraid to get up and check, and afraid not to. I finally tiptoed downstairs in the dark and checked everything—locked, of course—and scurried back up to bed with my heart beating so painfully fast I lay and worried about having a heart attack. I'd just made myself relax a little when I heard footsteps on the stairs.

I very nearly *did* have a heart attack before I realized the intruder was Emmy.

That did it; enough was enough. I rummaged in my medicine cabinet and found two antihistamine tablets, which always knock me out. I woke only when church bells roused me, dry-mouthed from the cold tablets but in my right mind.

I was in no danger. I never had been. Benson—it was easier to go on thinking of him as Benson—had no idea I suspected anything. And this was Sunday, a beautiful summer Sunday in the most civilized, law-abiding country on earth. As long as I acted normal, pursued my usual activities and kept my mouth shut, I would come to no harm. And in a few hours—I glanced at my watch—in thirteen hours or so, I could turn the whole terrible business over to Alan and retire from the field.

The amateur sleuths who got into trouble, I reminded myself, were the ones who went off on their own, performing silly heroics. Obviously, an intelligent person who minded her own business was perfectly safe.

I had reckoned without the influence of the Church.

Since I would normally attend Matins and the Eucharist on a Sunday morning, I fed the cats, got dressed, and made my way across the Close. I did try to be a little late, so I wouldn't have to talk to anyone. Then I would leave early, for the same reason, stick close to home until time for the concert, and tell Alan my whole story as soon as I possibly could.

All went according to plan until we got to the psalm appointed for the day. I was enjoying the harmonies of the male choir until the words began to get through to me. ". . . It is God that girdeth me with strength . . . He teacheth mine hands to fight . . . I will follow upon mine enemies and overtake them; neither will I turn again till I have destroyed them . . ."

The rest of the lessons were a call to action, as well, the sermon followed suit, and to top it off, the final hymn was "Onward, Christian Soldiers!"

Now, I'm not the superstitious type. I don't try to solve problems by opening the Bible at random and reading a verse, and I think it's downright presumptuous to go around asking for a sign from above.

On the other hand, when I'm bombarded with messages all saying the same thing, I do begin to wonder.

Jane caught up with me as I hurried home. "No coffee this morning, Dorothy?" She was panting; my legs are longer than hers.

"Not this morning," I said, smiling but not slacking my pace. "I'll talk to you later; there's something I have to do."

If only I were sure what!

There was no point in pretending, I thought to myself over coffee in the kitchen, that I was fired solely by zeal to do what might possibly be my Christian duty. The truth was, inaction had never suited me. Common sense be damned; I wanted to charge off in some direction or other. My problem, as usual, was to decide which direction.

Very well. I dug in a drawer for my lists and consulted them. They were no help at all. I now knew the answers to all my questions. The trouble was proving the story, and that was police work.

Yes, but was it?

The police couldn't take action for several hours yet, and meanwhile, what was Benson up to? Mrs. Hawkins had said he was away for the weekend. What if he was escaping at this very moment? What if someone else knew too much, and he was busy disposing of another body? What if . . . ?

What if I could uncover some proof of Benson's guilt while he was away? That would force the police, busy as they were, to take action—to find him, arrest him.

But where to look? He would have thrown the key to the Town Hall in the river long ago, surely. And the Hall itself could hold no clue; the police had searched it thoroughly, and they simply don't miss anything these days, even the most micro-scopic evidence.

But they hadn't, so far as I knew, searched Benson's room at the King's Head. Why would they? They had no reason to suspect him.

But I had.

20

THERE'S VIRTUALLY NO traffic in Sherebury on a Sunday morning, so I drove to the King's Head unscathed, parked my car, and went in to find Mrs. Hawkins busy setting tables for the lunchtime rush that would arrive in about an hour. I was the only customer in the place, and she served me my coffee with a preoccupied smile and immediately went back to her work. Good.

I paid my bill and drank two cups of excellent coffee as fast as I could, to provide myself with an excuse to go upstairs to the ladies' loo. I needn't have bothered; no one was paying the slightest attention.

After a genuinely necessary stop at the facilities, I turned the other way, toward the guest rooms. I didn't know which one was Benson's, of course, but for a long-term guest it would probably be one of the biggest and best the house had to offer. And in an old inn like this, that would mean a center room, looking out over either the river or the garden. With a guilty glance over my shoulder, I chose a likely door, knocked twice, and then took out my Swiss Army knife.

I've been teased about my extra-large, all-inclusive Swiss Army knife, lying heavily at the bottom of my purse at all times. The fact remains that nothing comes in quite so handy in quite so many situations. I had even used mine for a spot or two of burglary before, but in every case on doors for which I possessed a legitimate key, somewhere. This door, loose-fitting, with an old lock, would have been easy if my hands hadn't been shaking and slippery with sweat. I dropped the knife with a clatter that sounded like the entire percussion section of a brass band—but no one came, and I doggedly carried on until the bolt slipped back and I was in.

It was a pleasant room with a little balcony. More to the point, it was the right one. I could see that at a glance. Even if I hadn't recognized the sport coat hanging over the back of a chair, the room bore signs of long occupancy—a half-empty box of cigars, a pile of well-thumbed magazines, no luggage in sight.

Very well. I was here. Now what?

It would have been easier if I'd known what I was looking for, but I was determined to be as thorough as possible, under the circumstances. I knew Alan would have my head if I disturbed evidence for the police, but I could look, so long as I was careful. I locked the door behind me and began.

A search of the clothes hanging in the wardrobe revealed nothing. Nothing in the pockets except what one would expect—train tickets, dirty handkerchiefs, shreds of tobacco. No stains I could see on any article of clothing.

The drawers were no more helpful. Besides the usual underwear and socks there was only a pornographic novel, lying offensively in the bedside drawer on top of the Gideon Bible. It was certainly nasty, but probably not illegal, and if there was anything hidden in it, I wasn't going to find it. I couldn't bring myself to pick the thing up, even with a tissue over my hand.

It was as I was about to check the bathroom that I heard footsteps. The wide old floorboards creaked as the steps drew nearer, and for a moment I couldn't think at all. The balcony? Too small, no place to hide. The bathroom? I'd be discovered at once. In total panic I dropped to the floor and rolled under the bed.

Of course the steps went on past. "The wicked flee when no man pursueth." I lay and listened while whoever it was stopped at the end of the hall and a door opened and closed. My heart was pounding so loudly in my ears I had trouble hearing further movement, but when a toilet flushed, I was pretty sure I had heard a resident of the hotel, not an employee who might enter other rooms in turn. I could get up.

Sure, I could. Getting into that tight space with adrenaline pushing me all the way had been one thing. Forcing arthritic joints to get me out was another. I wiggled and grunted, and finally hooked my fingers into the bedsprings to give me some leverage.

But my left hand couldn't find a purchase. There was something in the way—not a bed slat, but something smooth that, as my fingers poked blindly at it, gave way and dropped onto my stomach.

Fingers and toes shoving against the springs, I managed finally to wriggle out from under, sit up, and look at my find.

It was a wallet, or at least a small black leather

folder intended to carry papers of some sort. It bulged slightly in the middle.

It held two things. One was a ring, a heavily carved man's ring with small gold prongs bent slightly back where the stone had been.

The other was a key.

I managed to stand up, every joint protesting, and then sneezed six times in a row. The standard of housekeeping was very high at the King's Head, but even they did not dust the underside of the bedsprings very often.

Which created a dilemma. I had done exactly what I had warned myself not to do—tampered with evidence. I held in my hands the missing key to the Town Hall, and one of the rings Benson had been wearing when he had delivered a death blow to Jack Jenkins.

They should have been left exactly where they were, with the dust on the springs but not on the wallet showing that they hadn't been there very long. But there was no point in putting them back now, not with my fingerprints all over them. Besides, Benson might realize they'd been disturbed and throw them out.

Why on earth hadn't he disposed of them? The answer, I supposed, lay in the setting that was missing from the ring. He'd kept the key to search for the stone in the Town Hall, where it must have fallen when he hit Jack. Some hope—the police would have found it long ago.

And maybe he'd kept the ring, stupidly, because it was valuable and he didn't think anyone would notice.

Well, no one had. I'd even seen that he wore one ring that didn't fit, that fell off, and thought nothing about what it might be replacing. I'd heard nothing about any gem being found—

Wait a minute! The police hadn't found it! Alan would have told me. And if they hadn't found it, it wasn't there. They use a vacuum at crime scenes these days, with a very fine filter, and sift through absolutely everything.

They hadn't found it. Pettifer said he hadn't found anything. Benson hadn't found it or he wouldn't have kept the key. That meant—

Mrs. Finch.

Dear Mrs. Finch, going around with her rags and her polish and her mop the next morning, scrubbing conscientiously in all the corners. Picking up something small and shiny, perhaps, and dropping it in her capacious handbag—and forgetting all about it when she discovered the body.

How long was it going to take Benson to make that same connection?

I peeked out the door before scuttling down the back stairs and out the back door. I hadn't been able to lock Benson's door behind me, but that was the least of my worries just now.

Bob was still setting out wallflowers in my flower beds.

"Is your mother busy this afternoon, Bob?" I would have her over for tea, and casually bring up odd things I had found while cleaning, and—

"She's in Brighton, 'avin' a nice day out. Be 'ome by teatime, she said, so as to dress proper for the concert. Ever such a one for royalty, she is, and no end pleased at the chance to see 'Is 'Ighness."

It was time to turn this all over to the police. I picked up the phone.

"Inspector Morrison? I'm so sorry, Mrs. Martin,

he's following up a lead in Sheffield. Shall I try to reach him, or would you like to talk to someone else? We're a bit shorthanded, what with the visit and all, but I could try—"

"No, it's all right. Nothing that can't wait." At any rate, it would have to. Now there was nothing for it but to wait for Mrs. Finch.

The first one in the cathedral when it opened for the concert, I waited by the door in an agony of apprehension until a hat appeared that even I found amazing.

"Mrs. Finch! Ada, I mean, sorry. I'm so glad I saw you. You look splendid."

She preened herself. The bright blue silk dress was a trifle tight, and the hat had probably been worn to weddings since the fifties.

"Ta, dearie." Her hand brushed one of the ostrich feathers and set it trembling, shedding a tri-fle in the process. "Wot I say is, 'ee may not've been quite the gent to 'is wife, but 'ee 'ad a lot to put up with, dint 'ee? An' still an' all, 'ee's the next king, an' we owes 'im respect."

I stayed by her side as we walked up the aisle, not trying to deal with her views on royal infidelity. "Do you have anyone to sit with? Would you mind if I keep you company?"

She looked gratified at that, but doubtful. "I'd like that, I'm sure, dearie, but the seats is reserved, you know. Mine is—" she looked at her ticket again "—is down this row 'ere. Where's yours?"

"Oh, it's up front somewhere. I'll bet whoever is sitting next to you wouldn't mind trading with me." And if they did, I wasn't above a bribe. Of course, if there were two people together, on both sides of her, we'd have trouble. But I'd manage it somehow. I intended to stick to Ada Finch like glue, if I had to sit on the floor.

I didn't have to. The scholarly-looking man who had the seat to Ada's left was delighted to move up twenty or so rows. We settled ourselves, and I encouraged Ada to tell me about her day in Brighton. More important matters would have to wait until later, preferably with Alan present.

And then it was "God Save the Queen," not the shortened version that sometimes precedes or follows a performance, but a full rendition in Charles's honor, and Ada, full of bliss, finally saw him. I felt better, too—I'd spotted Alan just behind him in the VIP section.

I imagine the concert was superb. The orchestra, the choir, the soprano, the violinist all were of the very first rank. I didn't hear a note. The wallet was burning a hole in my pocketbook. What was Alan going to say? How were we going to prove the case against Benson now that I'd messed up the chain of evidence? Did Ada really have the missing stone from his ring, and had he figured that out yet? If this blasted concert would just end so I could get to Alan! I looked at my watch for the tenth time: seven forty-five.

They were playing the last selection, a Mozart thing I should have enjoyed, when I saw him. He was sitting on the other side of the aisle, two rows ahead, and he wasn't paying attention to the music either. His eyes scanned the crowd, and as I watched, he glanced over his shoulder and spotted Ada's hat.

Benson. Back in town and loaded for bear.

I looked away as fast as I could, but not before he'd seen me see him.

His look was three parts malice and one part sheer satisfaction.

Oh, dear God. He knew I had his wallet. He'd talked to Mrs. Hawkins.

And he knew Ada had the rest of the evidence that would help convict him of two murders.

I looked around frantically for help, but there was no help. Only the crowd, the blessed, slow-to-move crowd that surrounded us. And the social conventions that decree one does not make a scene in the middle of a concert.

Especially not when royalty is present. There was that. All those unobtrusive policemen around—we stood a very good chance, after all!

"I will follow upon mine enemies and overtake them . . ." Or, in this case, I would escape mine enemy, and Ada with me, until I could get the proper authorities to overtake him. We'd get out of there the very moment the music ended, and we'd sit locked up in my house until Alan came knocking at the door.

Would they never stop playing?

They did, of course, and there was a standing ovation, joined in enthusiastically by Ada, who hadn't followed a note, either, but would go along with anything her prince enjoyed. Then the VIPs were ushered out and we were free to leave.

But all the south doors into the Close were open, and everyone was heading that way, for the reception. I'd forgotten the reception. Damn the reception! We'd edge out along the side of the crowd, my eyes open all the time for Benson, and just go through the Close to my house.

I hadn't counted on the obsession of Ada Finch.

She grasped me by the hand. "'Urry along, luv! No seats out there. We can get up as close to 'im as we like. Come on, shake a leg there, dearie!" I was towed behind as she elbowed her way through the throng. They were pressing so close, I couldn't see anyone except the people whose feet I was stepping on as we passed.

When she finally panted to a satisfied stop, we were just in front of the dais that had been set up on the grass. On the dais sat Charles, the dean, the bishop, the Lord Mayor, and Alan. Behind us was a mass of humanity that made escape impossible.

And just on the edge of the crowd, at the front and to our right, stood Herbert Benson, pointing toward us and speaking urgently to the constable standing guard.

"Ada, I'm not feeling very well," I stage-whispered. It was true enough. "Let's go home. This way." I tugged to the left.

She remained firmly planted. "Not me, dearie. You go ahead if you've a mind. I'm staying right 'ere."

"No, you have to come, too. It's—please, Ada! Come *now*!"

She just stared at me.

"Oh, all right! It's Benson. I think he thinks you have something he lost in the Town Hall, and I don't think he's going to be very nice about it. Do come before he—"

I finally got through. "The Town 'All?" she said slowly. "Would this be it?"

She opened her handbag and pulled out something very small, laying it in the palm of her other hand. It was black and shiny, like a tiny pool of black water.

It was the onyx from Benson's ring.

I've never fully believed in thought transference, but that night I think Ada read my mind, or part of it.

"Oh, my Gawd!" she said, her voice beginning to rise. "'Ee musta lost it that night—and that means 'ee—"

She looked at him and screamed.

21

IT WAS ALMOST three in the morning.

"I must go home," said Alan, yawning.

"You'll have to see yourself to the door. I can't move." I was in the biggest chair in my parlor, looking and feeling like a rag doll, dropped there by a careless child. Sam, on the window seat, and Emmy, on the hearth rug, had long since settled themselves for the night.

"Nor can I." He yawned again from the couch and propped one long leg over the other.

"Will they ever let you supervise a royal visit again, do you think? I mean, to say that all hell broke loose is an understatement." Mrs. Finch's scream had brought Benson and the police guards to our side simultaneously, and Benson's furious shouts during the struggle were enough to convict him of a number of things. Prince Charles, of course, had been unceremoniously removed from the scene the moment the fracas began.

He grinned, a little wryly. "At least we caught the villain, and we've got the evidence, and no harm came to the Prince, even if he did have to be hustled out of there rather more quickly than we'd planned."

"We'd have gotten the villain a long time ago if Mrs. Finch hadn't held out on us."

"Morrison did point that out to her." The grin was pure pleasure this time. "She said she was just doing her job and what harm did it do to pick up something pretty for her locket as her son gave her for her birthday, and were we accusing an honest woman of stealing—words to that effect, and lots more. Morrison was totally vanquished."

"All the same, if she'd given it to the police, Barbara Dean might not have died."

"There's never any point in 'if only,' love. And you're not to apologize again for stealing evidence. I'm happy we have him now. He has a lot to answer for."

I accepted Alan's dictum and changed the subject. "I wonder what'll become of the Town Hall."

He shrugged and yawned, his jaws cracking, and struggled out of the couch. The cats twitched their ears and opened sleepy eyes.

"Who knows? Something useful, I hope."

"I know! How about moving the Sherebury Museum there? It would be a perfect place—"

Alan yawned again. "Your next project. I'm for home. Come here."

He held out both his hands, and I managed, after all, to get out of the embrace of the chair and into Alan's.

When he could speak again, he said, "By the way, to answer your question, No, I'll never supervise a royal visit again."

"Alan! Do you mean you're retiring?"

"Not quite yet. I'm being posted away for a few months, starting in September."

"Away where?" I moved out of his arms, disturbed.

"I'm to take over temporarily as commandant of the Police Staff College at Bramshill. Have you heard of it?"

"Heavens, yes! That's where they send the senior officers for special courses. But Alan that's a really important job! Congratulations! Only—"

I stopped.

"Only what?"

"Nothing. I'm really happy for you. That's a wonderful promotion." Emmy and Sam caught my tone of voice and woke fully.

"Only what?" He pulled me back into his embrace.

"I'll—miss you."

"Why?"

"Because I like having you around! Because I—"

"No, I'm not trying to make you say it!" He chuckled. "What I meant was, why need you miss me? Why not come along? It's a Jacobean house, you know, same period as this one but rather larger—about fifty bedrooms, originally. And there's an extremely nice apartment for the commandant and his wife."

"His—wife?" There was something wrong with my breathing.

"Well, we're going to have to do something, aren't we? Because if we see much more of each other, one evening neither of us is going to want me to leave, and it would never do for a chief constable and a respectable American lady . . ."

"No, it wouldn't, would it?"

There was an interval.

"Alan, I—"

"It's all right. Don't answer me now. I really am going home, because my driver's waiting and I daren't shock him." He gave me one more very proficient kiss and Emmy, jealous, twined herself around his ankles. "I'll ring you in the morning—well, afternoon, perhaps, when you've had a chance for some sleep. We never had that carouse, did we?"

"No, Mrs. Finch and Benson between them canceled those plans. And I'd enjoy a really wild evening with you. But, Alan, what I was about to say is, I—I'm not sure I'm ready for marriage quite yet. But—well, even the cats seem to approve of the general idea."

Half an hour later, as his car drove decorously up a sleeping Monkswell Street, the first hint of dawn's gray appeared in the eastern sky, and somewhere, tentatively, a lark began to sing.

My Purpose Holds:

Reactions and Experiences in Retirement of TIAA-CREF Annuitants

By **Mark H. Ingraham**
with the collaboration of
James M. Mulanaphy

Teachers Insurance and Annuity Association
College Retirement Equities Fund

Published by
Educational Research Division
Teachers Insurance and Annuity Association
College Retirement Equities Fund
730 Third Avenue, New York, N.Y. 10017

Printed by
The Winchell Company
Philadelphia, Pennsylvania 19107

Library of Congress Catalog Card Number 74-83623

To the unknown, but oldest respondent,
who at the age of 99 answered the questionnaire
with the aid of his son.

Foreword

My Purpose Holds comes as a result of a TIAA-CREF survey in which we asked our retired annuitants to write down their comments and observations about retirement—viewpoints, personal experiences, and advice to others.

The response to our request was extraordinary. We received hundreds of thoughtful statements on retirement and its meaning. Some were actually essays. Admittedly, we had tapped articulate persons, but their willingness to share experiences went beyond our expectations.

To prepare a book in which these thoughts and observations could be organized and made available to persons recently retired or not yet retired, we turned to Dr. Mark H. Ingraham, Dean Emeritus of the College of Arts and Sciences, University of Wisconsin. No one could be better qualified than Dr. Ingraham to prepare for educators a book on retirement from materials provided by people who had devoted their lives to educational service.

Dr. Ingraham is a former trustee of both TIAA and CREF and of the Wisconsin Teachers' Retirement System. He is the author of two previous works sponsored by TIAA-CREF, *The Outer Fringe: Faculty Benefits Other Than Insurance and Annuities*, published in 1965, and *The Mirror of Brass: Compensation of College Administrators*, published in 1968. Readers familiar with either of these books, or with Dr. Ingraham's other writings, are well aware of his delightful style and sense of humor. Dr. Ingraham is also a distin-

v

guished mathematician and is the only person to have received from TIAA-CREF the certificate award of Honorary Actuary.

It is a pleasure to offer this readable and, we believe, rewarding essay, and we are indebted to Dr. Ingraham and to the many retired annuitants who took the time to express their thoughts on the experience of retirement.

William C. Greenough
Chairman, TIAA-CREF

New York, N.Y.
August, 1974

Preface

It was a pleasure to again work with the staff of TIAA, especially with my colleague in other ventures, Francis P. King, and with James M. Mulanaphy who furnished most of the statistical material of this report.

I wish to thank Helen M. Guzman and Alice E. Schroeder of the University of Wisconsin. Mrs. Guzman has again given me invaluable editorial advice and Mrs. Schroeder's typing of the manuscript involved the deciphering of many elderly, and sometimes difficult, handwritings.

Acknowledgment is also due the contributions of those who assisted TIAA-CREF in developing and successfully completing the survey on which this report is based. I am informed they were as follows. From the Survey Research Center at the University of Michigan, Robert L. Kahn, Director, John C. Scott, Head of the Field Section, and Charles F. Cannell, Program Director—Interviewing Methodology provided helpful comments and suggestions during construction of the survey questionnaire. Juanita M. Kreps, James B. Duke Professor of Economics at Duke University, and Leo A. Haak, retired Professor of Social Sciences at Michigan State University, supplied useful ideas for the questionnaire design and gave expert counsel throughout the formative stages of the survey. Likewise deserving of gratitude are Patricia F. St. Pierre who diligently edited all returned questionnaires and Mary Toulis and Roy Hardiman of the data processing firm Trewhella/Cohen/

vii

Arbuckle, Inc., for their patient and proficient guidance in the world of computers and print-outs.

My affectionate gratitude goes to my wife, Katherine. During the course of this study each of us has seen the other through a serious illness.

As to the title, my first choice was "The Druids of Eld." The unretired officers of TIAA, having learned about druids from the encyclopedia rather than from Longfellow, dissuaded me, making more poignant the lines near the end of *Evangeline*: "Still stands the forest primeval, but under the shade of its branches / Dwells another race, with other customs and language."

The title finally chosen comes from that magnificent description of resolute old-age, Tennyson's *Ulysses*, which concludes with:

> . . .for my purpose holds
> To sail beyond the sunset, and the baths
> Of all the western stars, until I die.
> It may be that the gulfs will wash us down;
> It may be we shall touch the Happy Isles,
> And see the great Achilles, whom we knew.
> Tho' much is taken, much abides; and tho'
> We are not now that strength which in old days
> Moved earth and heaven, that which we are, we are,—
> One equal temper of heroic hearts,
> Made weak by time and fate, but strong in will
> To strive, to seek, to find, and not to yield.

Mark H. Ingraham

Madison, Wis.
May, 1974

Table of Contents

Chapter 1: Introduction

In the fall of 1972 TIAA-CREF undertook a sample survey by mail questionnaire of the status of TIAA-CREF annuitants. The questionnaire is reproduced in the appendix. The survey asked for data of two types. The first covered specific items of information about such matters as age, sex, health, housing, finances, and present activities. The second area of inquiry was an open-ended section asking for comments on problems faced in retirement, evaluation of retirement experiences, and for any "do's and don'ts" that might be suggested for persons about to retire.

This book is a resumé of the answers to the open-ended questions. It attempts not only to extract the respondents' useful suggestions, but also to give some idea of both the experiences and the thinking of the annuitants, for most of us learn more from experience—even the experience of others—than from advice.

There are a few ground rules which the reader should know:

1) Quotations in the main text which are not attributed to anybody either are from one of the respondents or are so well-known as not to be mistaken.

2) Almost every chapter includes, under the heading "Voices of Experience," a set of quotations from those who answered the questionnaire. These have been edited with every effort to preserve their meaning and character. However, they are mostly mere extracts from a longer statement and in general this fact is not indicated. Moreover, since questionnaires were often answered in a hurry (I

1

myself either don't answer them or do so rapidly), misspellings and grammatical slips frequently crept in. These usually have been corrected. Quotations from a single person may be scattered in several chapters.

3) The problem of tense has at times been sticky. The present tense has frequently been used to describe continuing situations even if the reports of them were written in 1972. It should also be noted that many quotes reflect the timing of the survey. With respect to investments, common stock prices were at a relatively high level in the fall of 1972. Furthermore, income purchasing power since 1972 has been affected by upward thrusts in the cost of living.

4) We have tried to depict the diversity of the elderly as well as their patterns, for instance, one lawyer who had practiced his profession until the year of retirement tapered off by teaching law, and one professor of law found practicing an easy way to slide into retirement.

5) We have attempted to write a text which can be read as a whole without listening to the "Voices of Experience" except in connection with subjects of special interest to the individual reader. I expect there will be some who will read only the quotes without bothering about the text; this alone could well be worthwhile, for from them one can get the flavor of the lives led by the respondents.

6) Short statistical notes follow Chapters 1-7 and Chapter 12. The information was furnished by TIAA-CREF from a separate statistical report based on responses to the closed-end survey questions, and enables the reader to gain a perspective on the subject matter of a chapter. Of necessity these notes contain in amplified form some material given in the text.

Who Answered. The survey questionnaire was sent out to 2269 TIAA-CREF annuitants over 60 years old, chosen at random from primary annuitants rather than from annuitants receiving payments as survivors. These included not only those from the academic but also those from the nonacademic staff of many institutions. At the time the file was closed in order to make statistical analyses there had been 1571 questionnaires returned, some of which were from persons who had never retired, leaving 1507 questionnaires which were used for statistical purposes, about two-thirds of the survey group. In addition there were 159 replies explaining why the questionnaires were not filled out—so that some sort of reply had been received from 1730 annuitants; a dozen or so additional answers were received later and

used for this portion of the study. This response was larger than is general with questionnaires sent out by mail and greater than had been expected.

We thought that perhaps most of those who answered the statistical questions would not fill out the open-ended questions. That notion was a mistake. Of the respondents, 85 percent answered at least some part of these questions, and a number found inadequate the three-and-a-half blank pages provided for this purpose and added others. In spite of what will shortly be said concerning those who did not answer, it is obvious that a substantial portion of those who received the questionnaire were more than merely willing to fill it out, discovering that it afforded them a helpful guide for reviewing their affairs and a welcome opportunity for self-expression. The chance to give advice was taken. Good advice is an amalgam of experience, temperament, and pleasure in the use of words; without the first, it is foolish; without the second, lifeless; and without the third, dull. There was much good advice given.

Several persons indignantly pointed out that, in spite of the anonymity of the questionnaire, it would be possible to identify the respondents from the replies given concerning such matters as sex, age, and the amount of the TIAA-CREF annuities. Theoretically, perhaps, they were correct, but there has been no attempt in any case to do so. There were a few who signed their returns either from habit or on principle, and others told of positions they held which would completely identify them without use of TIAA records.

Clearly a sample to whom a questionnaire is sent can be random, and still the replies have strong biases. Since in this case the replies are anonymous, the extent of the biases, if any, is hard to measure.

It was possible to make some comparisons of characteristics of the respondents with known characteristics of the group to whom the questionnaire was sent, e.g., age and sex distribution. In these respects the variations between the replying group and the whole group were small. The sex distribution of those to whom the questionnaire was sent was 42 percent women and 58 percent men; among those who replied, 39 percent were women and 61 percent men. The age distribution of the respondents was almost a perfect match with that of the sample. There was also close agreement between the median income from TIAA annuities for the sample and for the respondents. It may be concluded that for most statistical purposes the study yields a reliable picture of TIAA-CREF annuitants.

There are two areas, health and viewpoint toward the question-naire, where there were probably rather strong statistical biases. This is to be expected and is borne out by the evidence furnished by the letters which explained why the questionnaire was not filled out. Some had died. Relatives, friends, or guardians of others explained that the annuitants were in such bad health that they could not re-ply—although in some cases the questionnaires were filled out for such persons. For instance, by the devoted wife who had power of attorney and was happy to have her husband home again. It is evident that the proportion of those in nursing homes was much higher for those who did not fill out the questionnaire than for those who did. Some strenuously objected to questionnaires in general and to this one in particular. Several felt that the financial questions were too personal and others that the questionnaire asked for information which they could not readily find. One had resolved for his "peace of mind" upon retirement not to fill out questionnaires, and another declared "Frankly, I am sick and tired of being researched and surveyed!" As has been mentioned above many were delighted to participate, but others believed that their connections with TIAA-CREF were so brief or their situations so atypical that a reply would be useless—not realizing that atypical replies are valuable and also typical. Besides the ill and the displeased, there were some too busy to reply. It seems probable that many among the over 500 who made no reply had similar reasons for not doing so.

Therefore, the replies tended to come in greater proportion from the comparatively healthy and perhaps the more happy. With only a few warnings here and there, the rest of this book is based solely on the replies to the questionnaire.

STATISTICAL NOTE

• Seventy-nine percent of the respondents were retired faculty or educational administrators, 15 percent were retired clerical-service personnel from educational institutions, and 6 percent were retired "non-educationals," i.e., had spent some time employed by an edu-cational institution (and were thus able to join and participate in TIAA-CREF) but worked mostly outside the education sector.

• Forty-nine percent of the respondents were between ages 60-70 (the younger retired), 34 percent were between ages 71-77 (the mid-period retired), and 17 percent were age 78 or older (the older retired).

• Eighty-six percent of the men and 21 percent of the women were currently married, 8 percent of the men and 23 percent of the women were widowed, and 6 percent of the men and 56 percent of the women were single (including separated or divorced).

• Seventy-three percent of the respondents had retired from a university or college, 10 percent had retired from an independent primary or secondary school or academy, 8 percent had retired from another type of educational organization, and 8 percent had retired from a non-educational organization such as Red Cross, the Federal government, etc., and 1 percent did not specify what type of organization their last full-time employer was.

Chapter 2: General Attitude towards Retirement

The variety of points of view brought to retirement is fascinating. Even if one's attitudes are in large part internally generated, they often also reflect circumstances of finances, health, family, activity, etc. No part of the book is irrelevant to the subject of this chapter, yet there should be some attempt to depict in one place (here) the range of satisfaction and dissatisfaction that the respondents found in their lives. There were those who totally rejected retirement, even condemning those who enjoy it. "I do not know of any aspect of retirement that is likeable, if one has enjoyed his work and has been busy for years. Those who enjoy retirement are the ones who have never liked to work in any case." By contrast, "retirement is the best thing to happen since the invention of the wheel," or, in the same vein, "I would rank retirement second only to the wheel." The writers of these last two statements were very different, one describing herself as "a semi-administrative female employee who was bumping her head on the promotion ceiling"; while the other liked the fact that he was "Free to be one's self; free from the pressure of maintaining the image of 'The Dean' and 'The Institution'; free to say 'no'; free to say 'To hell with it' (or 'with you') and walk away; free from the telephone; free to be as selfish or as selfless as I like."

Of course most of the respondents were neither resentful nor ecstatic, but registered milder degrees of discontent or, much more often, of pleasure with their current lives. The usual picture given by more detailed analysis was of a person with at least adequate means but fearing inflation or overwhelming medical expenses; active, but

6

wondering how long he can keep up the pace; healthy, but realizing that a period of poor health may be in store; pleased with the persons he knows, especially children and grandchildren, but rather put out with those under sixty—and even more with those under thirty—whom he does not know.

For many, contentment with retirement derives from satisfaction with new or continued activities, under less-pressured conditions than formerly, as in the case of the woman, who, though no longer rising at 5:30 a.m. declared, "I really love retirement although I have become involved in so many different activities that I am attending meetings all the time." Others care more for the life of appreciation, delightfully typified by the woman of 70 years who quoted Stevenson's *A Child's Garden of Verses*, "The world is so full of a number of things, / I'm sure we should all be as happy as kings."

There were a number who welcomed a new and stimulating period of life, sometimes even termed "career." But one man in a more ironic mood welcomed "the transition from organized confusion to disorganized chaos."

My rather extensive acquaintance with the elderly should have, but had not, prepared me for the general euphoria of the replies. Depending on your temperament and momentary mood, you might say that the spirit of the retirees was an inspiration or that they were "disgustingly cheerful." The attitudes of a few may have been bravado and lack of realism, but I believe that far more frequently the elderly had acquired serenity based upon a mature philosophy of life, and courage often strengthened by religious faith. They knew that their energy was lessening and that the major portion of their work was done, yet they had tasted life and the sweetness of its savour had not departed. Sometimes, however, the courage and philosophy were being severely tested.

Most of those who had lost their husbands or wives had made, if the losses were not recent, reasonably good adjustments, but still lived with an undercurrent of sadness—more with resignation than with zest.

For some perhaps the greatest struggle had been to attain a more relaxed conscience which could tolerate unused moments and the receipt of unreciprocated kindnesses.

Of course there were some who were unhappy because of ill health or because they found retirement an emotional catastrophe, but the latter were exceptions.

The following quotations (in this first chapter containing "Voices of Experience") indicate how much more variety and flavor are in the individual replies than can be summarized. Read them.

VOICES OF EXPERIENCE

I found retirement no problem. My wife and I had practiced thrift and economy down through the years and at retirement we had sufficient income to provide for us during our remaining years. Also we had contacts with clubs and organizations that provided sufficient social contacts and activities to supply such needs. I was active in two historical societies, church, Lions Club. She was active in several clubs, church, book-club, home-making, etc. As we see it retirement should be easy for anyone if they have lived sensibly in their active years. We are now each 84 years old. I retired at 69. She at 65. So we have had considerable experience.—*Male, married, age 84.*

. . . We began retirement planning twenty years before the event and are most happy with the results.—*Male, married, age 69.*

I know I'm one of the lucky ones—endowed by my ancestors with an adequate income and a sturdy physique, and having simple tastes and an optimistic disposition.—*Female, single, age 69.*

. . . So far there is nothing about retirement we do not like but we are fortunate in having four active children, all married with homes of their own and children of their own, financially independent of us (so far!). In this way we have family ties and interests here in this area. Without such close ties I think we would both be dissatisfied with retirement.—*Male, married, age 69.*

No problems—but then I have been so fortunate that my situation is, I fear, altogether atypical. Freedom from institutional responsibility is a boon for both my wife and me; it equates itself with freedom at long last to do the kind of research and writing we have wanted to do for a long time. This kind of freedom, with the means to live where we want to live—in the country and with every comfort—seems almost too good to be true.—*Male, married, age 71.*

Get outdoors every day and really look at the out-of-doors. Enjoy the fall colors, the wind in your face and on your arms, enjoy the snow, or the new green on the trees, and the birds and squirrels. It will do you no good if you merely look at your feet as you walk.—*Female, single, age 73.*

I think I am enjoying retirement more than any other period of my life. Of course I cannot but miss the moments of ecstasy that are far rarer now than in my youth. On the other hand, I have discovered that, as I find myself face to face with the realization that my life on this earth is actually finite, that I have only a very limited number of years to spend here, every aspect of existence acquires a deeper meaning, greater value, a new brilliance; the sun shines brighter, the autumn leaves on the maples are more golden, on the oaks more piercingly red, every human contact is a little more meaningful, and, best of all, friends are dearer. In other words I am learning the glory of the transitory. . . .

Take time to develop some philosophy of existence, religious faith if that meets your need, if not, some belief that can give meaning to both life and death.

On a lower level don't neglect your physical appearance; the better you look, the better you feel and act.

I made the mistake of not having several lost teeth replaced, result bad wrinkles! Don't make that mistake!

Finally, don't forget to laugh as often as possible.—*Female, single, age 82.*

Free time, time to relax, the removal of pressure to meet deadlines, the joy of watching a blizzard and knowing you do not have to go out in it—all this is wonderful. But one should remember that there is still much to do in this world, and what "the retired" can do to help is a tremendous amount.—*Female, married, age 68.*

The world is so full of beauty and wonder that it really seems pitiful to shut it all out in favor of the one narrow line of work in which one happened to make his living.—*Male, married, age 66.*

Do not dread, fight, or resent retirement. I have seen many people who did, including some in my own family, and it spoiled their last years. Retirement is as natural (and as inevitable) as night following day—and night is in many ways a pleasant relief.

Perhaps people should start to rationalize this, many years before retirement. One difficulty, I think is that they tend to blame retirement for all sorts of things that would have happened even if they had continued on their jobs: diminishing physical powers, disappearance of contemporaries, diminishing status, changes in their environment ("the good old days have gone forever"), weaker appetites, less sex appeal, and all the rest. Retirement has not caused these. A man who holds his job beyond the usual retirement years does not escape them. He is a lame duck; he is still losing his friends by death, or migration; he still has to face changing conditions; he is not particularly fortunate.

This is not hard to grasp; and it make the difference, in some cases, between contentment and unhappiness.—*Male, married, age 71.*

When one retires he decides to break with his past, in a sense, and he prepares to write new and exciting chapters to his book of life. Retirement isn't an ending, but a beginning of something new and different. Retirement isn't a cessation of activity nor a rocking-chair experience. It is alive, dynamic, active, different, relaxing!—*Male, married, age 65.*

Aspects we like the most:
Being able to spend our summers in Maine and our winters in Florida.
Having time to pursue pleasurable activities that we did not have time for before retirement.
Aspects we like the least:
Growing older and having to watch our diets.—*Male, married, age 71.*

. . . While I regretted terribly having to give up my work, I think that two very serious illnesses that followed almost at once (one involving eye surgery) helped to make the transition easier. By the time I was convalescent, I had moved into retirement without any trauma. . . .
I think all professional people who are serious about their work should also take their communities seriously, also their pleasures.—*Female, single, age 67.*

. . . I have no comment on what I like or dislike about retirement. I am only trying to survive my trials and tribulations [illness and death of husband and stroke of youngest sister], so as to have an opportunity to find this out.—*Female, widow, age 68.*

Dislike facing end of productive life and less time to live.—*Male, married, age 72.*

I expected the adjustment to be difficult and have accepted the changes but don't like them.—*Female, single, age 72.*

[Like Most]
Chance to know my wife, son and grandson better.
Escape from the bustle of commitments, demands, pressures, and disappointments of an active career that met headlong the frustrations produced by segments of society that put personal gain ahead of general welfare.—*Male, married, age 66.*

After you retire:
Don't let people make you feel guilty or uncomfortable about having retired completely. If you don't want another job, part-time or otherwise,

don't let anyone make you feel you are useless, not contributing anything to society, etc. There is plenty of volunteer work to be done, which will give you a sense of accomplishment and usefulness and will not tie you down like a regular job.

Do keep up with what's going on in the world even though you don't really have to anymore.—*Female, widow, age 65.*

. . . Keep your mind free from worry, for peace of mind is perhaps the best tonic that any man may possess. Do not for a moment think that you have reached the end of your productive life simply because you have retired. Frankly, the word retired is a badly chosen word, for no man who has an active mind can retire. As Shakespeare wrote: "My mind to me, a kingdom is."—*Male, married, age 75.*

. . . Do a piece of work so that someone will say "thank you" and you can keep your entity as "somebody."—*Female, single, age 65.*

. . . When you move you take yourself with you. If you found it easy in the past to adjust you can expect to find it easy to adjust to your retirement home. We have found no do's and don'ts in retirement that are not applicable to otherwise ordinary daily living. Courage is still the greatest virtue.—*Male, married, age 75.*

If you can't face the awakening day cheerfully, take stock again immediately.—*Male, married, age 74.*

. . . Anyone who can't keep busy, physically and mentally, just hasn't done his homework properly before retirement. . . .

Don't retire feeling that you're not going to like it. Approach it as you would a new and challenging job—but don't make work of it. Anticipate and savor it as though you were just about to go on your annual vacation.—*Male, married, age 63.*

Increasingly the retirement years form a significant portion of adult life. Plan it according to its probable importance and don't drift into it.—*Male, married, age 69.*

If the retiree is an extrovert he should by all means get some other work or position when he retires. If he is an introvert—as I am—he will have no particular problem.—*Male, married, age 71.*

. . . Increasingly I have become occupied with reflections on the meaning of life and its rounding out in death.—*Male, married, age 76.* .

Don't expect retirement to be great or not great. Just let it happen.—*Male, married, age 66.*

STATISTICAL NOTE

• As a group, the respondents were well-off in many important respects: the median of their reported total monthly incomes was $862; the median of their reported holdings in cash accounts, securities, and real estate (excluding a main residence) exceeded $30,000; almost three-quarters of the respondents said their health was very good or good; 90 percent of the respondents said they were very satisfied or satisfied with their housing; and, they were an active group—about half continued or resumed working for salary or wages following retirement and about half performed some voluntary service during retirement.

• With this background, three-quarters of the respondents reported they were very satisfied or satisfied with the preparation they had made for retirement and only 8 percent indicated they were dissatisfied.

Chapter 3: When to Retire

When They Retired.

Before discussing the opinions of annuitants as to when people should retire, we give a few facts as to the ages of the respondents when they did retire, which with many exceptions are likely to seem to them to have been satisfactory. The median age at retirement was slightly over 65, and 53 percent retired because of reaching mandatory retirement age.

There is a marked difference between men and women. Sixty percent of the men retired because of reaching the mandatory age while nearly the same percentage of women did not do so. This is reflected in the fact that 18 percent of the men and 30 percent of the women retired before the age of 65. The leading reason given for retirement before the mandatory age was health (19 percent of this group), a slightly larger proportion of the women giving this reason than of the men, and the largest proportion being in the group of women over 78 years old when they answered the question. (If my memory serves me correctly, Oliver Wendell Holmes declared that the surest guarantee of longevity was an incurable ailment.) The greatest disparity between men and women was that whereas only about 1 percent of all the men had retired to fulfill a domestic obligation, over 11 percent of the women had (20 percent of those who retired early). A somewhat larger percentage of the men who retired early did so because of discontent with working conditions: "arro-

13

gance of superior," "a corrupt administration," or the milder objection to a "proposed reorganization." Another was skipped when promotions came around. There was a great scattering of reasons: from a group who felt ready to move aside to the man who retired in 1940 to enlist in de Gaulle's army. A few succeeded in serving beyond the "mandatory" age. Those who had been faced with a sudden lowering of the retirement age felt particularly bitter as did those who expected to be retained beyond the "normal" retirement age and were not.

When to Retire.

"Among my former colleagues, those who retired as early as possible seem to regret not having worked longer before retirement, while those who continued their regular employment to the latest possible time regret not having retired much earlier."

As the above quotation indicates, one of the matters on which there is greater diversity of opinion than consensus is "when to retire." This diversity is shown in institutional policies and also in personal opinions. Some institutions have a single mandatory retirement age; others have a normal retirement age, a later mandatory age and between, a limbo subject to administrative decisions. Individual beliefs as to what is desirable vary greatly. For instance, one woman advises "retire as soon as possible" (she retired at 63), while one man, age 76, said "being in good health and in good teaching performance, my retirement, even at the age of 72, was too early."

The optimum retirement age is a subject often discussed by administrators, and it is notable how much their perceptions of human abilities conform to institutional stresses. In a time of expansion, maturity, judgment, experience, even mellowness (which in fruit foreruns decay) is praised, while currently, with limited budgets and stable or shrinking student bodies, it is time for the old fogies to move along and young men with new ideas (and lower salaries) to come in. Changing circumstances can justify altered decisions but a certain continuity of viewpoint concerning one's fellowmen is desirable.

There are many persons who believe that retirement should be gradual, with perhaps part-time work for a number of years. In fact, it often is gradual, considering how frequently committee assignments and administrative chores become lighter as a man nears retirement. Sometimes I wonder if our system is not one of overtime on part pay

for younger men, and part time on overpay for elders. Sometimes special part-time appointments are given. Of course there are those whose post-retirement activities form a buffer that provides for a gradual slowdown. This is described in more detail in a later chapter.

There were many statements as to the undesirability of a mandatory retirement age, especially one as low as 65. Some of these deal with the variability in persons, declaring that retirement should be based on "capacity and ability"; others with the waste of talent; and still others with the impact of formal retirement on an active individual. Moreover, some people resented being told that they must retire, even to such an extent that they chose to retire a year early in order that it might be voluntary.

A few spoke with pleasure of the fact that their retirement occurred before the then recent campus disturbances. One dean was almost jubilant. Another man retired earlier than planned because of being upset by violence in Washington, D.C.

VOICES OF EXPERIENCE

Plan to retire while you can make the decision.
Do not wait until:
a. The employer decides you should go. (The long-range personal happiness and satisfaction will be a pleasant, rather than an unpleasant, memory.)
or
b. The doctor says you must quit. Leave sufficient time and strength for some happy activity.—*Male, married, age 66.*

Retire at 65 and enjoy life before you get too feeble.—*Female, single, age 67.*

Don't retire early unless you are ready to enjoy your home and live more quietly. But if you are ready and can get along without your salary, retire and enjoy it while you're still young enough to get around and do things.— *Female, married, age 60.*

Retire before you have to. It makes you more popular with your younger colleagues, and obviates the necessity of having to keep up with them professionally!—*Male, married, age 64.*

. . . retirement at 65 is almost a "must" with most people, because of today's emphasis on youth, although I believe that most (like myself) would prefer to go on until 70, as it is easy enough to keep ahead of these so-called "advances" of our present era. . . .—*Male, widower, age 70.*

I retired at age 75 because I wished to have freedom while still in good health to enjoy theater, music, museums and travel.—*Female, single, age 80.*

People have said to me, "Aren't you sorry you didn't retire long ago?" I can honestly say, "No, I am not sorry." Had I taken Social Security at 62, it would have been considerably lower. My TIAA-CREF would have been negligible. I was still much too active and well to feel that stopping would be a necessity or even desirable.—*Female, married, age 65.*

Upon my initial retirement at age 65, the financial situation did not look good. My TIAA-CREF take would have been about $333 per month—very inadequate. Fortunately, I was able to take a five-year appointment at another university at a better salary than I had been getting. Not only did this cushion the financial problem (postponing for 5½ years the beginning of TIAA-CREF annuity), it also provided needed continuing activity. [TIAA-CREF annuity $817 per month.]—*Male, married, age 72.*

I also believe that compulsory retirement affects the attitudes of staff throughout their period of service, some beginning to adopt the attitude of the retiree years in advance.—*Male, married, age 81.*

. . . I believe the normal age of retirement at 65 to be quite absurd for a man who is able and well to carry out his duties. [Another said "stupid."]—*Male married, age 67.*

I did not like being told I had to retire because I was 65. No firm should be allowed to have a compulsory policy. It only holds for the average worker, they find loopholes for the higher-ups.—*Male, married, age 70.*

I resigned from my position in the University prior to mandatory retirement because I did not want that University to have the dubious pleasure of reminding me of my age.—*Female, married, age 66.*

. . . the foreseeable result of earlier retirement would be a glut on the employment market of aging professors wandering about and this would become a real cause for friction between generations.—*Male, married, age 76.*

. . . I've known a few teachers who wanted to go on teaching until they dropped dead, and long after their students wished they would.—*Male, married, age 78.*

Don't continue to rail against a society where mandatory retirement practices exist in so many professions and businesses. If you are a victim of mandatory retirement, and don't like it, thumb your nose at the Establishment and start a new career.—*Male, married, age 73.*

I hope I never really retire.—*Male, married, age 72.*

STATISTICAL NOTE

• Twenty-four percent of the respondents had retired at the traditionally prescribed age of 65, 23 percent had retired before age 65, and 51 percent had retired after age 65, including 14 percent who had retired in their 70's. Two percent of the respondents did not report their age at retirement. Women had retired at generally younger ages than men (30 percent of the women and 18 percent of the men retired before age 65), and there was a high correlation for women between retiring early and being married: 53 percent of the married women had retired before age 65, 24 percent before age 60.

• Fifty-three percent of the respondents had retired because they reached a mandatory retirement age set by their last employer, 9 percent because of poor health, 8 percent because they wanted to change their life style, 7 percent because they were dissatisfied with their work or work environment, 5 percent because they had to fulfill a domestic obligation, 2 percent because they were financially secure, and 15 percent because of other, less specific reasons. One percent did not give a reason for their retirement. Men were much more likely than women to have retired because of reaching a mandatory retirement age, whereas women were much more likely than men to have retired for a domestic reason, especially the married women, 36 percent of whom retired to raise a family, care for an ill husband, etc.

Chapter 4: Where to Live

As throughout the rest of life, the possibility of moving is usually present during retirement. Two very different types of moves occur: changes in the general place of residence, such as going from Wisconsin to Arizona; and changes in the type of home, for instance, from a one-family house to an apartment or from either of these to a nursing home. Of course, a change of general location often is accompanied by a change of the type or of the size of the residence.

There are three occasions during retirement when the question of moving arises with considerable frequency: first, immediately upon retirement; second, when one of the married couple dies, or when the housekeeping becomes such a burden that a smaller or more convenient place, often an apartment, seems desirable; and finally, when living in a nursing home, or a retirement center with nursing facilities, becomes necessary. In the latter two cases the decision is usually dictated by circumstances. This often occurs in the first case, but here opinions and decisions frequently differ when outwardly the circumstances appear to be similar.

Change of Location. This section deals chiefly, but not exclusively, with a change of general location.

The annuitants were not asked to state where they were living, only how far they had moved; and no record of the postmarks on the return envelopes was made. Moreover, no question was asked as to why the moves were made. A good deal of information on these matters was volunteered in answering the open-ended questions. Hence we

18

know, as we would expect, that more moved to mild climates than away from them, and more moved to the country or to small towns than to the cities. It is also clear that a major reason for moves made long after retirement and sometimes upon retirement, is the health of the respondent or of the respondent's spouse.

There are those, especially if they have held responsible administrative posts, who feel there is an obligation to get out of the way of their successors. To quote one man, aged 66, "Some problems were no doubt created by my own decision to retire and move to another place to grant my successor complete freedom and avoid certain problems friends of mine encountered by retiring to live in the same community—often at the edge of the campus. This was a wise decision from the standpoint of the general welfare of the university." There are a few who have become alienated from their colleagues and do not wish to live near the campus. The desire to immediately move to a warmer area induces some to pick up and go. The call of rural life, of childhood surroundings, of relatives (especially children), is answered by a considerable number. In spite of all these reasons for moving only about one-third of the annuitants moved immediately upon retirement. Nearly two-thirds of those who are 78 years of age or over have moved at or since retirement, but even among this older group nearly half are living in their former residence or within ten miles of it.

The proportion of women who move upon retirement is about the same as that of men. The proportion of women over 78 who have moved at or since retirement is considerably greater than the proportion of men who have done so. The widowed are more apt to have moved than either the single or those whose spouses are still living.

Much stress is placed on giving plenty of thought and time to the consideration of any move. The time may be prior to retirement. There are those who advise that if one does move, much should be discarded or perhaps sold through a garage sale or an auction.

Some people are a problem to themselves, being chronically restless. "They continually look for 'greener pastures' and fail to realize that the difficulty is theirs, not location or environment." But there are also those who enjoy staying put for its own sake; staying "in my own home and on the college campus where I taught for 41 years." Or the man of 74 who likes to "live in the country in the home where I was born." Or the woman of 75 who maintains "the 100+ year appearance" of the old family home where she lives with her brother.

People are thoroughly happy with extremely diverse decisions —also unhappy. Very few of those who have stayed where they were say that they are sorry that they did so. This is natural since most of them were happy with their location before retirement, or else they would have moved, and they have not found it unpleasant thereafter. One gives the following advice: "Stay where your friends are. It is very difficult to make new, real friends when older. Stay in your own house with its 'lares and penates'; have all your own things around; avoid apartments—no place to put anything."

It is expected that those who made long moves would have mixed experiences and they did. Some people write with the greatest of enthusiasm from Florida, Arizona, Hawaii, Texas, Mexico, Spain, an island in the Mediterranean, or even from California. But there are also those who, after going away, have come home and love home better than ever. I judge that more of those who have moved to a warm climate are glad they did so than are sorry, but this reaction is far from universal.

Not all who have moved have sought the sun. There are those who report on the joys and problems of rural life in many parts of the country. Another group, who are on the whole having less pleasant experiences, have moved to childhood neighborhoods or to places where they lived happily years before; nostalgia is not satisfied in a changed, especially a deteriorating, environment. Some have moved to another country, often their native land or that of their wife. The experiences of those who have moved to be near relatives are mixed, and certainly quite a number have found such situations disappointing.

There is an additional problem if husband and wife have different opinions concerning the move, and this may easily be accentuated when the difference is not discovered until the move has been made.

One wife is homesick for her house and garden while another who lived in large cities became "apathetic and uninterested" in a small town.

Although a considerable amount of advice is given concerning whether or not to move, some of the most emphatic advice concerns the necessity of being careful and not too trusting in locating in the new place or even in a new residence in a familiar location. Obviously, some have been "taken" by real estate dealers and reported their bitterness. Major points listed as needing examination are:

1) Desirability of the climate at all seasons.
2) The availability of medical help.
3) The availability of a church.
4) The congeniality of the people and their age mix.
5) The cultural opportunities and the availability of a good library.
6) The problem of transportation.
7) The quality and sale value of a house and real estate if purchased and whether the neighborhood is deteriorating or not.
8) The tax situation, and the price level.
9) In the case of an apartment or other rental facilities, the standard of its upkeep.

Most of these merit added discussion and there is also further amplification in the "Voices of Experience."

1) Climate. It is said to be possible to find in Hawaii and some other spots an almost even climate throughout the year if such monotony is desired. However, some people who have moved to avoid northern winters find southern summers hot and perhaps humid. One may have to choose between a furnace and an air conditioner. Sage advice is given to sample the various seasons ("bad seasons") in a place before committing oneself to the extent of buying a new home or selling an old one.

2) Health Care. The establishing of satisfactory relations with doctors, hospitals, and various medical services including ambulances, in new surroundings when not in a nursing home, has sometimes proved difficult. (Security guards are mentioned in the same breath.) Some have found that busy doctors do not wish to take on new regular patients, especially elderly ones, and that hospitals are reluctant, except in emergency, to admit persons not referred to them by physicians with whom they are affiliated. One woman says it may take up to six months to make proper health arrangements. Of course even without a move, if one's regular doctor retires, finding a new one can be a problem—at least emotionally.

4) Associations. Clearly there are many old people who wish to associate with persons other than those of the same age. Some of these perhaps, and certainly others, find children a trial. One woman enjoys retirement in a converted garage of a friend who "has six children, three dogs, two cats, six guitars, three Hifi, two T.V., bagpipes, drums, piano, shrill voices." She wishes to live alone, but clearly a lively neighborhood is congenial, and we might guess that

the conversion of the garage included soundproofing. The same widow who warns us to "beware of salesmen" and that "there are many plans to entice old people to give up their savings," places first among her "don'ts": "Do not go to a retirement home where only teachers live, or associate only with people of your age." In fact, there are few more recurrent themes, whether connected with "where to live" or "what to do," than the wisdom of associating with persons of all ages, even with children—but perhaps not to an excessive extent.

It is not only the "age-mix" that is important; some have found they cannot overcome barriers of prejudice: "Neighbors—people who live in area; a clique by nationality and age; or those who never speak or wave."

It was suggested that one live with a congenial friend who is financially in similar circumstances. Successful solutions of the problem of where to live have been made by single women living together in retirement complexes. Another suggestion was that two elderly couples share a home, thus facilitating caring for the house when one pair travels.

5) Cultural Opportunities. The happiness of some is much more dependent on cultural opportunities than that of others who find satisfactions in nature or physical activities. Those who have stayed in cities declare "the theater, the symphony, the art museums are things we love and we would feel lost without them." For many, the availability of a scholarly library is a major concern. Those who have remained in the city or continue to live in, or have moved to, a college town frequently mention their pleasure in having a satisfactory library.

6) Transportation. The present or future problems of transportation are recognized by those who no longer drive or those who expect soon to stop doing so. The desire not to rely on friends is almost universal, and bus lines must be close to supply any real solution. Taxis are expensive and often involve delays. For those who live in the country or in small towns the trips beyond the immediate locality are increasingly difficult by public transportation. Transportation can be vertical as well as horizontal and we were warned against elevators without attendants and against escalators. Annuitants stressed the need to look into the adequacy of transportation services before settling in a new home.

8) Tax Rates. It is not wise to assume that the tax situation in

another state is the same as where one currently lives. Some people have found real advantages in moving either because of lower state income tax rates or because of lesser real estate taxes, especially for the elderly with moderate means. This deserves careful scrutiny and accurate information not always provided by those with something to sell.

The above and other matters need special attention in the case of retirement homes, but that will be taken up in a separate section.

VOICES OF EXPERIENCE

To Move or Not to Move. The following quotations form a discussion as to whether to move at, or shortly after, retirement, or not to do so. They express opinions or relate experiences relevant to this subject. I found the opinions extremely interesting as expressions of human diversity. They will bolster anyone in concluding that other persons of sense have made the same decisions he is inclined to make—often with fortunate results. However, as advice, they are less useful than the concrete suggestions given in a later section of this chapter as to what to check if one does move. The quotes are arranged to proceed from those of pure advice to those that describe experiences, but this rule is not adhered to strictly.

If conditions of health and finance permit, never, never, NEVER permanently leave the university or college community with which you have been associated before retirement.—*Male, married, age 71.*

Don't show yourself at your former place of employment except on special (invited) occasions.—*Male, married, age 74.*

If possible when you retire continue to live in the community where you lived before retirement. Do not move to a new and strange place and especially don't move to a foreign land with an unfamiliar language.—*Male, married, age 70.*

Decided I could live better for less money in Mexico. . . .
Don't retire until you investigate the many locations near Guadalajara.—*Male, widower, age 75.*

Loss of status, both functional and social. People in the new community don't know what a great guy I am, and I'm not the kind who can tell them. (They don't care, which is maybe worse!)—*Male, married, age 71.*

I think that leaving your home for some faraway spot in Florida has grave risks—unless your reputation at home is so poor that you wish to make a fresh start.—*Female, married, age 79.*

. . .places with nice climates the year round are cultural deserts.—*Male, married, age 75.*

I enjoy living in a large city (NYC) where there are so many interesting things to do each day, more than I can possibly do.—*Female, single, age 79.*

We are living in Spain, associating with all ages—young teenagers and oldsters who do not have the oldster look nor attitude. We read much of the time, enjoy our "siesta," go out every day, sit at a sidewalk café and meet fascinating people from all over the world. Their different viewpoints, cultures, attitudes are exhilarating and exciting. If this is retirement, and it is in Spain, we recommend it!—*Female, married, age 64.*

And if we moved permanently to a warm climate, we would be far away from at least one of our two children, most of close personal friends (we have lived in this community 37 years) and our Friends Meeting which we helped to establish in 1935.—*Male, married, age 79.*

We solved the problem by finding a place in the Tucson foothills and buying acre lots on each side of us. On the other hand, the doctor and the dentist are still about ten miles away; there is no grocery store within easy walking distance; and the air is not very clean.—*Male, married, age 70.*

[This couple moved to San Francisco in summer and for some months were completely happy.] Presently, the days shortened, the morning fogs in the city lingered longer, the evening fogs rolled in over the hills earlier and stayed later, our apartment grew chilly and chillier, our coughing grew deeper, the doctors we consulted seemed as hurried and distant and perfunctory as emergency room interns, the streets on rainy nights seemed darker and more menacing and became windier and colder; we took to phoning nearby markets and having our food sent to our apartment C.O.D., we spent more and more of our days and nights holed up there, swathed in blankets and yearning to be home again.

When, at long last, we got back here, we reveled in our old familiar surroundings and for months had a marvelous time matching rueful stories with old familiar friends who had sojourned in Florida or Southern California or Colorado or Mexico or that place in Arizona where a London bridge has been moved stone by stone. And with them we chorused, "Never again."—*Male, married, age 72.*

What I like most is being able to be in Vermont instead of New Jersey and during six months of the [year] in the place I own and think most beautiful of any I have seen. I've been able to do a lot to the place that before there was no time for.—*Female, single, age 70.*

We lived on the college campus, owning no home when we retired. Without established roots, we have moved frequently, often to be close to one or another of our four children, and partly to be in various areas we have enjoyed on vacation trips. Adding this up, we have found pleasure in the experiences involved. There have been no particular problems, since we had not planned beyond being near our family members. And they are scattered!—*Male, married, age 82.*

I like being in a new community where we have all had to be friendly and outgoing if we are to have friends. I like the fact that [it] is a "mixed age" group community but with the retirees predominating. We have so many activities run by retirees that we never feel left out. In fact, I think it is the young married group and teenagers who are made to feel less important. Not so good for them, but good for us!—*Female, married, age 65.*

I doubt if many people can figure on being completely happy in retirement after making a move for from two years to three years. It just takes a period of time to wean yourself away from former surroundings.

Most of we retired people make a move for two main reasons. First to locate in a warm climate. Second to locate in a place where our retirement income can give us the most pleasure.—*Male, married, age 66.*

City, Town, and Country.

I enjoyed tremendously continuing to live in New York City with all it had to offer in opportunities, and now that I have moved to a town with two colleges, and many persons who are a joy to know and with whom to talk and work, I am very content.—*Female, single, age 80.*

In our case the move to a small college town where we already had friends was ideal for us. The college provides us with library, lectures, musicals, sports, etc. We are active in church work, garden club, Audubon Society, etc.—*Female, married, age 71.*

If one lives alone, a small place is much the best, in my opinion, both for the ease of neighborliness and the safety of movement. A woman alone in a city in this day of increased crime is often unable to take advantage of the cultural opportunities it offers, and so in that respect is no better off than if she lived where these things are not offered.—*Female, single, age 78.*

I chose a small coastal village because I have always been unhappy away from salt water. I have many congenial friends here, but I find that I miss associations with people in my former profession of astronomy. This is partly made up for by reading many scientific magazines and partly by visiting colleges in my state, but nothing takes the place of frequent stimulating discussions with colleagues.

I like most being able to give unlimited time to my hobbies—sailing (racing and cruising) in summer, and sometimes in warmer climes in winter; and working in my basement carpenter shop, refinishing furniture, making wooden articles, etc. I have entirely refinished my old (1790) house inside and out, doing the work myself, and enjoying every minute of it.—*Male, married, age 71.*

Husband's and Wife's Reactions to Moving.

Before moving to a new locale it's my opinion that both parties involved—man and wife—should both be sold completely on the idea. We have met several retirees where one or the other was completely happy with the new environment, whereas, the other was equally unhappy. In my opinion, much of it is psychological—either one expects to find a Shangri-la or their mind is made up in advance that they are not going to like it—this is fatal.—*Male, married, age 66.*

If one's spouse is not enthusiastic about the change, it may prove to have been a costly mistake.—*Male, married, age 69.*

Living with Relatives.

Retire close enough to your children so you can contact them easily, but do not retire in their homes or so near to them that constant association with them becomes a problem.—*Male, married, age 74.*

But I feel that we (when my wife was alive) made the right decision not to live too close to our children and grandchildren. They have to live their lives and we had to live ours.—*Male, widower, age 67.*

Returning to Earlier Surroundings.

I moved from the city in which I had been teaching for 35 years, back to the city in which I had grown up. It turned out to be a greater change than I had expected due to the development of the city. Old landmarks had gone and various monstrosities had taken their place. Old friends were no longer there and to a certain degree it was like moving into a strange city. The period of adjustment was especially difficult because I made an unfortunate choice of residence and after having signed a 2-year lease I found that my landlord was less than satisfactory and the place was badly run and unsafe—not poor

maintenance, but none. I moved as soon as possible, even sacrificing a couple of months' rent.—*Female, single, age 68.*

Haste Makes Waste.

Retiring in Florida was easy for us since we had lived in the State for 18 years. We had made many friends and there was no sudden wrench or break. We are still close to our old friends, and, as well, to the beach and the Gulf. An ideal situation.

We do feel sorry for some retirees coming into the State and changing their whole way of life suddenly. Some are lonely; some go back to the old home area again; some stick to it. This plan of moving to Florida should be tried out several times before retirement.—*Male, married, age 78.*

Do not pick up and move your residence before moving to the new or anticipated location for a trial period of time. We had planned moving to Florida but after taking a temporary home for three months we decided to maintain our residence in the University community we had enjoyed for 25 years. We continue to spend three to four of the cold months in Florida or a warm climate.—*Male, married, age 69.*

Be sure you are close to good medical care—dentist, doctor and hospital. The people I know who have to go miles and miles for such care have a really tough time—and neglect their health, and live in fear of a real emergency.—*Female, single, age 69.*

We bought our new home too quickly and discovered it was not right for us in retirement, so sold if after two years.

Unless you are absolutely certain of where and how you want to live in retirement, don't buy immediately. Try it out first. Preferably rent for awhile.—*Male, married, age 71.*

When and if you decide to make a move check various states thoroughly to find one where taxes are lowest and your money will go farthest.

If a move is planned check carefully the financial set up regarding any condominium or co-op you may be interested in. Also check carefully the type of people in that area to be sure, if possible, they are the type of people you can be happy living with.—*Male, married, age 66.*

Try to get away from high tax districts or states. But don't settle in the proverbial boondocks to get away from it all. You will need increasingly the services of doctors, dentists, opthalmologists.—*Male, widower, age 67.*

Adjusting to living in and caring for a house which we had not been accustomed to. We found this to be a great care that we wished to discon-

tinue, and so moved into an apartment. This involved less worries and in the end doesn't cost much more than a homestead.—*Female, single, age 75.*

My own experience: . . . we decided to sell our home and to risk the chances and changes of living in an apartment in some smaller city with a good university library.

Shortage of adequate housing has forced us to live in an expensive apartment that is comfortable within, but like a ghetto outside and totally unsuited to a person in retirement, who likes to walk for his health but can no longer drive, and would willingly run errands unendangered by traffic, dogs and lack of sidewalks. This confinement and lack of outdoor living space, except for a narrow balcony, makes me feel increasingly dependent and I fear accelerates the aging process.—*Male, married, age 76.*

Don't retire to too confining living quarters. (Have retired friends who talk about "climbing walls" because they moved into efficiency luxury apartments.)—*Female, single, age 68.*

My one suggestion is that if possible the house chosen early in life (if possible) should be correct for living in when older—for instance a bathroom and bedroom downstairs and not too big a house.—*Female, married, age 66.*

Moreover, if changes in residence are necessary, one must or should always rent or lease first for a year at least, before buying a new house or apartment. Moving into an apartment can be exasperating if children are allowed. If they are above you, they irritate you constantly, they run around shouting, riding their bicycles or what have you, they also play ball and scream and shout under your window. Rent first is my advice.—*Male, married, age 78.*

My main problem, I think, was having housing that was adequate and that I could afford. I had a good equity in a house. I sold the house and bought a mobile home, paying cash for it. I have been very well satisfied, though spaces to rent for mobile homes are much higher now than eight years ago, and there is a move in this state to tax mobile homes on the same basis as a house. I think this is a sad situation; there will soon be no place for retired people on limited incomes to live. . . .

I think it is possible that the life of a mobile home might not be what one would need, depending on how long one lived and how well he stayed. It is a good way for one to remain independent.—*Female, single, age 73.*

The following single quote involves several items which were voiced separately above.

We were in rural Connecticut five miles from the nearest store. This was our home, although we were usually overseas working for the U.S. Govern-

ment. In the winter the snow outside our home was sometimes four or five feet deep. After looking around we decided on Virginia, near Washington where we had many friends whom we had met overseas. We found a retirement residence which suited us.

The next problem was getting rid of the accumulations of fifty years. This we finally managed by the help of our children.

Selling our place. We first put it on the market with one agent on an exclusive basis for a month's trial. Nothing happened, so at the end of the month we listed it with five agents. The next day three prospective buyers arrived and the following day the deal was closed. Competition did it . . . .

Start early to locate the place you want to retire to. Be careful as to availability of friends, climate, shopping facilities, medical facilities, cost, retirement communities versus separate quarters.

Don't accumulate too many possessions in later life.—*Male, married, age 76.*

Retirement Facilities. In old age decreased vitality or poor health may make living in some sort of retirement facility appropriate. These facilities range from those which are hardly distinguishable from ordinary apartments to nursing homes which come close to being hospitals. There are retirement centers which are clusters of apartments specially planned for old people. They may contain dining places where the residents may (or must) eat, provisions for recreation, planned cultural activities, rooms for social gatherings, and libraries, probably not adequate for scholarly work. Some or all of these special provisions may be absent. Some centers have infirmaries and have doctors regularly associated with them. The financial arrangements at some retirement centers are cared for by rental and at others by the ownership of apartments with payments for maintenance. Less pretentious, but in many cases comfortable and well-run, are the retirement homes providing meals both in a common dining room and through room service when necessary. Some of these have nursing facilities. Finally, there are nursing homes where all persons served (or perhaps one out of each couple) need nursing care. Of course there are many variations between those prototypes.

Although many centers have good infirmaries, few—if any —contain hospitals which provide for those needing surgery and intensive care.

One annuitant described the various stages of living in what must be one of the most complete retirement complexes: "Preparation for decline in health, to be expected. I moved into a Retirement Village which has three stages: (1) As long as I am able, I will continue in my

apartment; (2) When I can no longer keep house, alone, Senior Residency, living in small suite in large building, no kitchen, eat in dining room; (3) If seriously ill, I would move into two-patient bedroom in the Convalescent Hospital; (4) In case surgery necessary use Medicare, in Memorial Hospital; and for convalescence, move into Convalescent Hospital."

The warnings concerning care in choosing a new home, especially in a strange locality, apply, perhaps with added emphasis, to retirement centers. At the more advanced age of many of those entering these facilities it is especially important to seek reliable legal advice.

Annuitants were requested to state the type of residence in which they lived and also whether or not they lived in a "planned retirement community." Slightly over 8 percent of those who replied lived in such a community, but of those over 78 years of age about 12 percent of the males and 24 percent of the females did so. Only about 1 percent of the respondents were in nursing homes, so that we can assume that most of those in planned communities lived in apartments. It is probable that a considerably larger portion of those who did not fill out the questionnaire were in places which provided extensive care. In fact the explanations (sometimes given by others) of why the questionnaires were not completed often indicate this to be the reason.

We now give some of the testimony, both advice and recounting of experiences.

VOICES OF EXPERIENCE

Attitudes toward Retirement Centers. [not all voices of experience]

God forbid!! [As to living in a "planned" retirement community]—*Male, married, age 73.*

Do expect that independence grows more dear and necessary as some of its former supports (physical, familial, social, economic) begin to fade out.

Otherwise you'll find you've surrendered your independence to the nurse in a nursing home, to the matron in an old age home, to the politician who offers you "dignity" as a senior citizen.—*Male, married, age 76.*

Don't "hole up" in a "senior citizen" enclave or retirement home until you must. Stay where you can get mad at the school kids cutting across your lawn.—*Male, married, age 69.*

Those who moved into a retirement home to die have emotional problems. Rather they should have felt that ahead of them were still many good years, many opportunities to do things of interest to them: Like dances, study groups; recreation like shuffleboard, pool, hikes, bridge; hobbies like woodworking, gardening, photography, sewing, swimming, T.V., visiting, singing groups . . . . An unexpected pleasure was finding so many friends of like age and interests. There was no need to be bored if one were interested in living. Attitude of mind is a prime factor at any age.—*Female, widow, age 80.*

I had expressed interest in a retirement home. When my children told their friends of my decision, the reactions were varied. One would say, "Lucky you. A good way to be rid of them." The next one would say, "Those terrible institutions. How can you condemn your parents to such a life. It is your duty to care for your parents."

I settled the question. I said, "I love you too much to live with you. We are all strong minded and have many good years ahead of us in which we should be able to enjoy, to the highest, the interests of that particular stage of our development. We are a generation apart; so are our interests. So I am going into a retirement home where there is an infirmary. This will eliminate worry for both the children and myself."

After living in a retirement home for twelve years I think this is the smartest decision I have ever made.—*Female, widow, age 80.*

Living with Old People.

Main problem: Living in retirement center: finding people you can associate with significantly. Most people here are either senile, hard of hearing, unable to speak above a whisper, slow "on the trigger. . . ."—*Male, single, age 79.*

[Like the most:] The comfort of growing old in a place where "age" is still considered to be an achievement rather than an affliction. [Respondent resides in France.]—*Male, married, age 64.*

Financial Warnings.

Leisure villages are good for real estate operators, but it means segregating old age.—*Female, single, age 79.*

We surveyed possible shelter, meals and care provided. Our first experiment proved costly (a long story—double dealings—we had to employ an attorney—settled out of court—we lost about $800, but pulled out). Our second experiment looks excellent.—*Male, married, age 73*

Complaints about Management.

Investigate very thoroughly the retirement place you have your eye on. Get legal advice before you sign any contract. Be skeptical of oral promises. Avoid the first year or two of a new community: there are sure to be mistakes, often corrected later. This whole business of retirement communities for the elderly is still new and experimental.—*Female, single, age 87.*

Odds and Ends of Advice and Experiences.

Choose a church-sponsored, financially-sound retirement home (200 or less) close to shopping district and not too far from relatives and friends.

Don't be satisfied with anything less than complete medical and nursing care—at no additional expense.—*Male, widower, age 86.*

Visit several times if possible a number of Retirement Homes of different sorts. Talk with Residents as well as Administrators. Investigate financial condition of the home. Relative number of men and women. Always more women than men.—*Female, single, age 73.*

The happiest people in a retirement complex are those who can move in with one close congenial companion—spouse or relative or good friend of long standing. Easier to make new friends "as a pair." Good to always have someone to do things with.—*Female, single, age 80.*

I wondered when coming here if I would make new friends at my age. But I need not have worried. Some of my new friends are the best and closest I've ever had.

. . . Most good retirement communities have long waiting lists of applicants and it is well to make plans ahead with this in mind. Do make your plans before you become disabled as many places are reluctant to admit those with serious health problems.—*Female, widow, age 75.*

Life in a retirement home is very pleasant. One replaces former activities by committee and service work in the Members Council, and there is no abrupt break or the boredom that I had feared might result in going from a busy life to retirement.—*Male, married, age 77.*

Retirement homes provide desirable living conditions for the aged in many ways: (a) Protection; (b) Diets planned to provide good nutrition; (c) Care for minor or major illnesses; (d) Companionship if desired; (e) Privacy as desired; (f) Entrance to a retirement home early enough to make new associations; (g) Adjustments will have to be made psychologically for group living—if this is a new mode of living for the individual; (h) The feeling of

independence rather than dependence on friends or relatives for care makes for better mental health. . . . —*Female, single, age 78.*

A Fine General Statement. This essay of a single woman, age 81, is so excellent that it is included in its entirety.

Where to live. Unmarried and with no relatives nearer than cousins, this decision was less of a problem for me than for many. I did have to choose between staying in a northern state, where I had grown up and did have friends and a place with a more equable climate. I chose the latter. The factors I considered important in choosing exact location were: (1) climate; (2) non-industrial area; (3) water supply; (4) availability of hospital and physician; (5) type of stores and market—fresh produce—milk supply; (6) cost of living in comparison with other areas; (7) scenic attractions; (8) transportation, both local and long distance; (9) churches; (10) cultural advantages.

Financial. I chose a southern state partly because cost of living, including housing, was less there, but my problem was much less of a one than I had expected it to be because of social security and, even more, because a friend and I decided to share a home together, which halved the capital expenditures involved in purchasing, improving and maintaining a home (which we did for 13 years before coming to this Retirement Home). In this connection I might add that this was a successful and happy "joining of forces," but two friends—or relatives, for that matter—should be very sure that their needs, tastes, likes and dislikes are compatible before making more or less permanent arrangements. I have known sisters who, though fond of each other, could not stand living together in adult life. We talked everything that we could think of as being important—particularly finances—over beforehand. My friend has had a larger income than I. We have shared capital expenditures—as I said—half and half, but she proposed that for running expenses we set up a joint checking account into which we should put the first of each month an amount proportionate to our incomes—which I accepted. This made it possible for her to enjoy more comforts and luxuries than if we had tailored our budget to conform to the share I could contribute, and to share them with me, as she wished to do, in a sensible, fair and frictionless way. We each had our own personal checking account for our own personal expenses—everything except for food, electricity, household and yard help, and such household expenses.

With companionship assured and an adequate income I have found retirement very pleasant. I enjoyed cooking and gardening and more free time for travel and all sorts of cultural and recreational activities. Even now, 18 years from retirement and less vigorous, I find plenty to interest me and more to do than I have time for. The physical disabilities which are something of a trial are the result of aging and can't be blamed on retirement!! I think companion-

ship is a sine qua non for almost everyone. Old people can be very lonely. They need the security—as much as children do—of being loved, of being of importance to some one.

First of all: Do not permit yourself to be rushed into making decisions —particularly if recently bereaved.

I should like to confine my comments to Retirement Home living. When we were trying to decide whether or not to go to a Retirement Home, we found little information available to help us in making the decision. This seems to me to be an area in which the TIAA could be helpful—in collecting data, interpreting it, etc.

We accumulated a good deal of information about Homes and visited several before choosing this one—and this every one should do to some extent. At least some of the factors we thought important are:

1. Home provides for life care, i.e., medical, nursing and personal care, as necessary, to the end of life (except for psychopathic cases where physical restraint becomes necessary) without extra charge. Some homes provide this but monthly fee is increased on admission to Nursing Home facility; some make all medical expenses chargeable to the individuals for whom they were incurred. In this case the regular monthly fee is much smaller. A study to learn which of these methods works out best for the residents would be helpful. Perhaps it is nothing but a gamble. Our choice was for the first which is, obviously, a kind of group insurance. The per capita cost above what was recovered from Medicare in this Home (235 residents) in 1971 was $637! Covered are minimal "Home Care," clinic visits to nurse and/or Staff doctor, referrals as deemed necessary by staff doctor, diagnostic tests, etc., nursing home care, and hospitalization including surgery. Prescription drugs are not included. Whatever the method of providing for it, Life Care provisions are important—for this is the usual primary reason for coming to a Retirement Home. Those who are alone want to know that they will be taken care of; those with children do not want to be a "burden" to them.

2. Costs. Living in a modern type Retirement Home is not inexpensive, and usually requires an unrecoverable capital expenditure in the form of an entrance fee. Some people feel it is impossible or undesirable to reduce their estate by such an amount—or at least must consider that as a factor in making a decision. It is necessary that expected income, estimated conservatively, should be sufficient not only to cover monthly fees and increases which may be made in fees, but also continuing personal expenses such as clothes, eye glasses, books and magazines, travel, gifts and contributions, with some allowance here too for increases. There is considerable variation both in entrance and in monthly fees among Homes. Comparison is difficult because of variation in coverages (one may provide for all meals, another for dinner only, for example), location, type—whether high-rise or "garden" apartments, etc., so it is best to make a decision on the basis of other factors and take second or third best only if the first is too expensive.

3. Contract. Cost and services will be described in brochures and amplified in interview with administrator, but every applicant should read the contract, which is the binding agreement and, probably, have his lawyer read it. Some contracts limit the increases that can be made in fees. If the cost of living goes up beyond this, it may result in a reduction in the quality of food and services; no limit makes it difficult for applicant to plan ahead with any degree of security, and also provides no incentive to economy in administration. Homes which tie increases to increases in cost of living probably offer the best solution. It should be noted that under stress some Homes have renegotiated contracts. Homes of current type have evidently had little to go on in determining what these costs will be and what, therefore, fees should be charged.

4. Advantage of Retirement Home. Life care provision has been mentioned. Medical clinics at the Home. Registered nurse—and doctor if necessary—available for emergencies around the clock. If the Nursing Home [is] one [that] is not isolated, spouse and/or friends can call easily, and, depending upon physical condition, one can participate in some of the many activities of the Home—even go by wheel chair to concerts, religious services, movies and so on. A great variety of recreational, educational and cultural activities are available with little effort and, usually, with little or no expense involved. Arts and crafts available. There are sewing groups and study groups and prayer groups; there is unlimited opportunity for service in small and larger ways to others. For those who find housework difficult (including bachelors and widowers) meals in the dining room and maid service are boons. For those who cannot drive any longer there is a limousine service to shopping centers and to church on Sundays. There is companionship and a certain camaraderie that makes one's increasing age and disabilities easier. A limp or a cane, a hearing-aid or a lapse of memory does not make one conspicuous and one is ashamed to complain when so many others have as much or more to bear—yet finds sympathetic understanding too. Persons who are upset by having people around with canes and crutches or seeing people "fail," however, may find adjustment difficult.

5. Disadvantages. Residents should have a great deal of control over their own pursuits and their life at the Home, as they do here through a Residents Association, Council and Committees, and be able to make suggestions and criticisms to the Administrator. Even so, it must be recognized that the Home is an Institution. There may be policies established which one does not like and to which one must adjust. Some few people find it difficult to adjust to small living quarters. Our apartments vary in size and seem adequate to me.

6. Miscellaneous. (1) Homes require that entrants be ambulatory, so it is a gamble to postpone entrance, but I feel 70 is young enough if one is in reasonable health.

(2) A home of 200 or so residents will provide more chances for congenial companionship and a greater diversity of activities than one of a 100 or less. Smaller Homes might be less institutionalized.

(3) There seems to be some advantage in choosing a well established Home both because of financial stability and because there seems always to be things that are "wrong" in a newly finished Home. The auspicies—the backers with the financial setup—should always be investigated.

(4) People who have lived in cities should be sure they will be contented before choosing a Home in a rural or semi-rural setting—and vice-versa.

(5) Length of waiting list may suggest how well the Home is thought of—and that the application and deposit may be a good insurance policy since one may postpone, or even cancel when one's name reaches the top.

(6) Men may want to know how many men are among the residents, (women always predominate, of course) and if couples and men have any priority in admission.

STATISTICAL NOTE

• Half the respondents had moved to their present home after they had retired and half were living in the same home they occupied before retirement. The older respondents had a much higher proportion of people who moved following retirement than did the younger respondents but, of course, many motives for moving are related to advancing age. Almost three-quarters of the respondents who had moved had changed residence around the date of their retirement, while the remainder had moved sometime during the retirement period. Twenty-four percent of the movers had changed residence more than once following retirement, and 9 percent had moved more than twice.

• The respondents were well distributed across communities of different sizes: 36 percent were living in a small city, 10 percent were living in a small town, 8 percent were living in a rural area, and 15 percent were living in each of a large city, a city, and a town. Seven percent of the men and 10 percent of the women lived in a planned retirement community, with the proportion being much higher for those in the older age ranges, e.g., 12 percent of the men and 24 percent of the women age 78 and older lived in a retirement community.

• The respondents' housing type was primarily a function of their marital status: 79 percent of all marrieds and 47 percent of all non-marrieds were living in single-family homes; 12 percent of all marrieds and 35 percent of all non-marrieds were living in apartments; and, 9 percent of all marrieds and 18 percent of all non-marrieds were living in multiple-family residences, retirement homes, or other types of housing. Age also influenced housing type: moving up through the age ranges found a steadily declining proportion of respondents who were living in single-family homes and a growing proportion who were living in apartments or retirement homes. Almost all the respondents who lived in single-family homes were owners and almost all the respondents who lived in apartments were renters. Eighteen percent of the respondent homeowners had a mortgage, with the percentage declining among the older respondents.

Chapter 5: Financial: Status, Problems, and Advice

Financial Status.

The questionnaire sought more information concerning the financial conditions of the annuitants than concerning any other subject. The answers were remarkably full.

Two questions of a qualitative nature were asked, namely, "In general, how well does your income permit you to live?" and "How does your present standard of living compare with your standard of living before retirement?" In response to the first question, 55 percent stated that their incomes permitted them to live "well" or "very well," and another 36 percent responded "adequately." Of course the answers were highly correlated with the amounts of income. The lowest total monthly income range at which 80 percent replied "adequately" or better was $400-$499 per month; up to the $800-$899 level the most frequent answer was "adequately." From that level up to $2000 per month the most frequent reply was "well"; and beyond that, "very well." Less than a quarter of the respondents said that their standard of living was lower now than before retirement. Nearly two-thirds reported that it had not changed, and some 10 percent said it had improved. Again, these replies are related to income.

One might be tempted to attribute the rather happy answers to the same refusal to pity one's self that, as described in the next chapter, seemed evident in reporting on health. Although this

may be the reason for a few optimistic answers, I believe it is not a significant factor in general since only 15 percent of the respondents said that their savings had decreased since retirement, and the majority of both men and women reported that their savings had increased. Even in the lower income brackets the savings of a significant proportion of the respondents had increased and this was the case for over half in every bracket above $600 a month. It is interesting that the proportion of those who have increased their savings goes up with age: 46 percent, ages 60-70; 59 percent, ages 71-77; and 65 percent, ages 78 and above.

None of this takes away from the fact that there are a number in truly desperate financial condition, for instance, a man, age 89, wrote:

> [My wife] and I were married in 1919. It was a very happy marriage. She was a brilliant wife. She was a saver instead of a spender. We had saved from my salary and concert playing about $52,000.
>
> In 1952 (two years before I retired), she suffered a severe stroke. I had her in the hospital for seven months with three 8-hour nurses, then brought her home and a 24-hour nurse. She died in 1957. It cost me almost $30,000.
>
> In 1955 the strain to see her suffer so much, I had a stroke—a blood vessel in my right eye burst and I became blind. Have only a slight sight in my left eye (bad case of glaucoma).
>
> I have lived 15 years alone and now have only $4200 left. With my teachers' annuities which you raised from $127.57 to $137.50 two years ago.
>
> Those annuities have been a godsend and with those annuities and with what little savings I have left, I might be able to live about three more [years]. [Estimated income $140 per month.]

Only about 2 percent did not report concerning their total income (in a few cases there is internal evidence that the spouse's income was not included as requested); nearly 4 percent had income under $250 per month; and another 18 percent under $500. Slightly over one-third had incomes between $500 and $1000 per month; slightly under a third, between $1000 and $2000; and 10 percent above $2000. Of the total monthly income of about one and one-half million dollars received by the respondents, nearly one-third was derived from annuities or pensions— about equally divided between those received from TIAA-CREF and those from other sources—and something over a quarter

from Social Security and almost that much from investments. Within the neighborhood of 10 percent of income came from current employment (since only about one-fifth were currently employed, this represents an important portion of their incomes), and 5 percent from other sources. The importance of these various sources of income differs with income level, age, and sex.

For persons with incomes under $500 per month, more than two-thirds got at least 50 percent of their income from Social Security. Investment income obviously went mostly to those in the higher income ranges; and the current employment income to younger retired persons. Of course the TIAA-CREF annuities were substantial chiefly for those who had been for a considerable time under a retirement system making use of TIAA-CREF. Although there are many very small TIAA-CREF annuities due to short-term participation, there is ample evidence of how important these annuities can be when based on adequate contributions made throughout a career.

It is clear that the basic support of the elderly annuitants comes from Social Security and annuities, with investment and, to a lesser degree, current employment often making the difference between merely meeting the basic needs and comfort—or even luxury.

There was a great variety of circumstances that have led to either prosperity or financial difficulties. Marriage accounted for some of each; thus one woman retired early "to marry a successful professional man, well able to support" her; and a man reported that he had inherited a good deal from his first wife and that his second wife was still working—with prospects of a substantial annuity. However, there were men whose wives, sometimes second wives, were considerably younger than themselves, with young children still to be educated. The retirement annuities for such younger wives are costly. Inheritances frequently helped and, in at least one case, gifts from children. Even misfortunes may have profitable side-effects, such as the accident whose settlement provided enough to yield "considerable" permanent interest income, or the multiple coverage of medical insurance which helped with a new roof; yet on the average these are losing ventures. The decrease in expenses after retirement, but while still in good health, was mentioned by a number of both men and women. However, some financial restrictions

resulted in compromises between generosity and new clothes. A widower attributed his solvency to not driving an automobile since 1935.

VOICES OF EXPERIENCE

The sources of the following quotes range from the very well-off to those who are in financial difficulty and include some who can adequately meet current requirements but worry about the future.

This is the first time in our lives when we have had no financial worries.—*Male, married, age 69.*

Surprisingly, we find that our present income is about as large as my salary was when employed. Much credit must go to TIAA-CREF. Also, Social Security and Civil Service Retirement help, and a few fortunate investments. With our essential obligations reduced, e.g., insurance, we find our income adequate to do most things that we want to. [Estimated monthly income $2000, TIAA-CREF annuity $871 per month.]—*Male, married, age 76.*

The aspect of retirement which I like the most was that through the grace of God and a fine lawyer I received an unexpected inheritance in 1968 which I have invested, and this has brought me relief from a lifetime of pressure due to lack of income.

The aspect which I like the least is the thought of what I could have done on the amounts which I have received from Social Security and annuities without the inheritance.—*Female, single, age 78.*

During ill health for the last year and a half I have been well covered financially by health insurance along with investments that provide income. This, in spite of the fact that, retiring in 1955 from a position as department head, I retired at a smaller salary than inexperienced instructors are getting now and the first few years were a little difficult, in spite of the fact that I had invested money in two houses and was debt-free at time of retirement. Since then, living costs have steadily mounted, but fortunately the state pension, which was very small to begin with, is now three times the original amount, due to a revision which keeps step with rising salaries.—*Female, single, age 82.*

We were not sure our income would be sufficient for our retirement, but we were happy to discover that what we saved in daily train fares,

less clothes, etc., has enabled us to live quite as comfortably as before.—*Male, married, age 67.*

We can hardly believe how much more economically we can live now that we are both retired. No daily expenses of getting to work, lunches, office contributions, wear and tear on clothes, use of car for business, etc., etc., all add up to a very considerable sum over the year.—*Female, married, age 69.*

Financially, due to saving and careful planning we seem to be better situated than during working years. Whichever of us may survive the other should have no financial problems—a great satisfaction. Social Security as a supplement to our regular income has been a big help.—*Male, married, age 75.*

. . . unless Social Security had come along in the 1950's we would have been very hard pressed to make ends meet since retirement. . . .
Because [of] the combined income from TIAA, CREF and Social Security, plus interest from the relatively small savings we have accumulated, we have had adequate income to live without financial worries, but we have had to be careful in our expenditures and avoid frills. We are deeply grateful for our many blessings.—*Male, married, age 80.*

. . . Accepting the fact of an increased cost of living during an average life expectancy, we assumed our economic needs would be met by an annual income of about 30 percent above our cost of living at retirement. To meet such a need we added to our TIAA investment, up to the allowable maximum. Thus, we could have lived on the TIAA annuity without any need for outside resources. Other savings and fortunate investments removed any worry concerning excessive increases in the cost of living. [TIAA annuity $1306 per month.]—*Male, widower, age 78.*

I will be able to live on my Social Security and TIAA. Our savings have been all used with my wife's long and expensive cancer illness. One never knows what is ahead. [Estimated monthly income $311.]—*Male, widower, age 68.*

The main problem was to accumulate enough savings to pay for eventual residence in a retirement home for my wife or myself, or both, and for a long illness and hospitalization. Additions to the savings account came slowly in the first years. Because I have lived long, interest grew appreciably each year and so the problem has been pretty well solved

without any unusual planning on my part. [Still lives in pre-retirement home.]—*Male, married, age 86.*

I like the least the diminution in my income, which for the time is quite sufficient but, if I should live as long as my mother or father, will be insufficient on account of the continued inflation and the general increase in taxes.—*Male, married, age 70.*

. . . handling our estate, which is over a million dollars, takes up much of our time.—*Male, married, age 76.*

Medical, hospital, dental, drug costs; rising cost of living. Used up my reserves, then borrowed.—*Male, married, age 71.*

Problems.

The above section on the general financial status of annuitants gives only a slight insight into certain special concerns which the annuitants have for the future and certain problems they are facing in the present. These are sometimes admittedly caused by the persons themselves as in the case of a man who, after retirement, built too expensive a home with accompanying swimming pool; or those who admitted they could have saved but did not. But such instances are not typical. The following sub-sections deal with general inflation, with taxes, with medical expenses, as well as a potpourri of other financial problems.

Inflation. A great source of financial distress among retired persons is inflation and its consequences. To an even greater extent it is the cause of worry about the future, not only as the cost of daily living rises, but also as future medical expenses come closer and loom larger. The rise in taxes is another element related to inflation, and in part caused by it. Inflation is ever present in the consciousness of many people, and by some is expected to be a continuing phenomenon.

VOICES OF EXPERIENCE

Chief problem is inflation. This is the one terrifying danger hanging over us.—*Male, married, age 71.*

Increasing cost of living in this pleasant place is becoming a serious burden to many of my friends, if not yet to me.—*Female, single, age 87.*

. . . My income is becoming to be too small to keep up with the rising costs. I could not have anticipated the rapid rise and with a father and mother to take care of for several years, I could not have done anything about it if I had.—*Male, married, age 78.*

By abnegating economy (no car! nickel watching) and rigorous saving I managed, over a life-time, to accumulate investments designed to make retirement independent (re-investment of all dividends was part of the plan).

Saving and re-investing was to stop with retirement, but inflation has taken away security. If we ever have to live in nursing homes, it will eat up all our resources. So I am still saving and re-investing, hoping that inflation will not get out-of-hand.—*Male, married, age 76.*

. . . It was a disappointment to realize that a life-time of savings through CREF and TIAA was giving us a meager return for living in a modest way in today's economy. This makes us recognize the importance of social security in our present budget. However, should the present rate of inflation continue and the rise of all kind of taxes we would be forced to cut and trim on even essential items.—*Male, married, age 69.*

Inflation has not helped, but an increase in social security a blessing! (Unfortunately the TIAA annuity, while as faithful as Gibraltar, has not kept pace with rising costs.)—*Female, single, age 78.*

. . . You rent an apartment for $155 a month. At the time you feel you can take care of your bill. Then every year the rent is raised. So you feel you have got to get something cheaper, but you are afraid to live where the rent is lower. You inquire about the Apartments for Senior Citizens. You cannot get an apartment in these Government subsidized [units] if you have an income of $5000 a year. You are even asked to pay Federal income tax the same percent as if you were working.

I do not feel we should have to pay Federal or State Income Tax when you have less than $10,000 income a year. My income a month is less than $500 a month. We pay tax on everything we buy. I love my country; I want to take care of myself, and help others to live.—*Female, widow, age 74.*

No problems showed up. Increase of TIAA and Social Security payments have so far taken care of inflation.—*Male, married, age 75.*

Pensions very inadequate—should be tied to changes in dollar value and changes in salaries in teaching institutions, instead of to very low early salaries in all branches of teaching, especially those in public schools

which as now arranged are entirely inadequate to meet present living conditions.—*Male, widower, age 83.*

The least pleasant part is watching and fearing the constant "inflation." There was hope that wage and price control would hold the line— but—power politics of labour unions are breaking it down. Only a solid union of retired people could combat it and that's a bit too much for me now.—*Male, married, age 70.*

Taxes. Many persons are distressed by the increase in taxes. A note of anger often crept into the statements on this subject. Besides the cost of taxes, the decisions made by others as to what one should pay, like the mandatory aspects of a fixed retirement age, are resented by those brought up on Henley's "Invictus." The fact was pointed out that when people retire taxes are no longer cared for by payroll deductions, and hence are harder to meet. Although a number complained of taxes, some realized that there are tax and similar savings due to age and retirement. Often, in reporting the taxes upon their residences, they said that in their state there is a marked reduction in real estate taxes for the elderly. This is borne out by the fact that the median value of the residences of those who owned their own houses was $31,900 and the median annual tax on these houses was only $586. A number of respondents expressed surprise (also disapproval) that the major portion of their retirement annuities was taxed.

VOICES OF EXPERIENCE

. . . I do not have any taxes to pay now except Washington State sales taxes which are quite high.—*Male, married, age 69.*

Our main problems have been and are those that confront everyone— inflation and rapidly rising taxes, taxes on both income and real estate (including a summer place in Vermont, acquired in 1947, on which the tax has risen from about $80 to $1400).—*Male, married, age 76.*

The main problem I did not expect was the small monthly amount TIAA alloted me for my retirement and the 80 percent of this, which I must include in my income tax with only 20 percent deductible.—*Female, single, age 80.*

State and Federal income taxes on the annuity payments that you send me should not be charged by our governments when at the same time they so lavishly pour out welfare payments to individuals who will not help themselves.—*Male, married, age 75.*

Necessity to plan everything around U.S. income tax deadlines.—*Male, married, age 69.*

Trying to discover what income tax I owe. I can't deal with it. My accountant and the Inland Revenue are supposed to—but they don't. I have never before appreciated the excellence of the mechanism of the U.S. Federal Internal Revenue Service by comparison with some other systems. [Resident in England.]—*Male, married, age 61.*

[Problem] How to escape taxation—current and final.—*Male, married, age 76.*

Medical Expenses. The financial problems created by the cost of medical services are caused not only by inflation but also by the great impact of expensive illness at any time. Many persons face medical expenses that without insurance could not be met within their normal annual budgets, especially since severe illnesses are episodic rather than usual. "It is the unexpected [or at least the untimeable] that is hard to deal with." In recent years medical and hospital insurance, giving protection against both ordinary and catastrophic medical expenses, may be secured by the individual or by institutions for a group. TIAA pioneered in this field. Moreover, after age 65, Medicare now cares for a large share of the costs of expensive illnesses, and this may be supplemented by insurance which meets most of the costs not covered by Medicare. Almost all of the respondents over age 65 were enrolled under the Medicare A program and about nine out of ten of these had the supplementary Medicare B which covers a large portion of the doctors' bills in addition to the hospital bills covered by Medicare A. Since Medicare B is voluntary, some who wished to have it have failed to secure the coverage, either because of personal carelessness in missing enrollment periods or of difficulty due to the red tape involved. Eighty-six percent of those covered by Medicare had other health insurance, two-thirds under a group plan, and almost one-half under individual policies—obviously some were covered both ways.

Nearly 90 percent believed that their health insurance coverage was "good" or "very good," and 9 percent said it was unsatisfactory. The fact that the cost of dental care and of eye glasses is not covered by Medicare, and usually not by other health insurance, led in some cases to serious financial problems. Evidently, provisions for remaining under some form of group health insurance after age 65, or if one retires before that age, differ from institution to institution. These in many places appear from reports to be improving but not always available. One man complained that the cost of individual health insurance goes up faster than that of group policies.

The difficulty of handling the paper work connected with Medicare and health insurance was complained of by many. Lack of help from hospitals, perhaps caused by the hospitals themselves not understanding differing insurance plans, left those not used to reading the "fine print," even if displayed in bold type, with severe difficulties—which I would judge have sometimes resulted in persons securing less than they were entitled to or would have received if they had understood the necessary processes. "It is all quite an enigma, with reams of paper work."

With current insurance programs, the financial problems of continued disability, involving nursing homes, etc., may be greater than those of either a terminal illness or one from which a person recovers, as was the case of a man with a wife in a nursing home costing $1000 per month.

VOICES OF EXPERIENCE

Again the following "Voices of Experience" relate the experiences of certain annuitants and contain suggestions for action on the part of the individual or of society.

Probably the most unexpected item that is facing us is the sharp and continuous rise of health and medical care. If health fails or if accidents occur, hospital and doctor's fees can wipe out moderate savings and income in a few months.—*Male, married, age 69.*

My greatest need is in knowing how to manage possible medical expenses of a catastrophic nature. I am not able to evaluate insurance policies. I have Medicare A and B but with present hospital costs I could be in serious financial circumstances—yet I do not want to move into a

retirement center which would provide full care as needed. One feels forced to that decision—and delay may mean disabilities that would close the possibility. I wish I had help on knowing how to insure for catastrophic illness—costs and companies.—*Female, single, age 68.*

Sickness and disability—you think you have enough saved and something comes along and you can spend $10,000 in six months; for instance, I have a brother who is paraplegic and has been for almost 20 years. I have no luxuries and practically do without necessities to help my brother.

When there are six children you have little chance to save for retirement. Now eighteen grandchildren and four great grandchildren.—*Female, married, age 68.*

. . . Indeed until two years ago when I was 73 I was not aware of any problems. Then and since I have been faced with a series of medical problems, first pneumonia, then a myocardial infarction, then a fractured hip and, most recently, a cerebrovascular accident and consequent hemiplegia. I don't know how one can plan to meet the problems that such a series of medical problems engenders. While Medicare has been very helpful my various illnesses over the past few years have required the expenditure of approximately $20,000 over and above the contributions from Medicare. [Considers her health insurance program as "good."]—*Female, married, age 75.*

The experience of using savings of 20 years, to provide care during a prolonged illness in my family, is the source of my fear of becoming dependent if I should be ill. Recent contact with Medicare and state insurance (similar to Blue Cross) was not encouraging. Charges so far exceeded allowances that my payment was 75 percent of the bill, instead of the 25-30 percent expected. More health insurance is a solution.—*Female, single, age 67.*

. . . Since retirement it has been necessary for me to obtain medical assistance from Public Aid to supplement what is not covered under Medicare.—*Female, widow, age 68.*

The Medicare program was a godsend. During a three-month stay in hospital (my wife's) they covered most everything. I don't know what I would have done without them. The Company retirement policy took care of the items not covered by Medicare.—*Male, married, age 70.*

Be sure and carry Health Insurance in addition to Medicare. I had hip joint implant surgery in 1970 at a cost of $5600. The hospital payment

by Medicare was fine. I paid only $60. But the doctor was not paid in full. It cost me $1800. My group insurance at the college was cancelled when I was 65. However last year they picked it up again. I pay $18 per month.—*Male, married, age 70.*

. . . Now a serious problem of many older persons is the lack of any help pertaining to oral and optical needs. Teeth repairs and replacement as well as changed eye glasses are two very expensive needed items of older persons.—*Male, married, age 71.*

I also feel that health care program where preventive measures are available is important. I now get this through University health service but such services are not widely available.—*Female, single, age 66.*

I believe the consensus among retirees would be to continue to liberalize Hospital and Medical coverage.—*Male, married, age 67.*

The possibilities of prolonged disability or medical care are somewhat alarming. Hospital and medical costs are fantastic. The lack of a nationwide health insurance plan for everybody, and some adequate control over medical costs seems to us outrageous. Even with Medicare and several sorts of health insurance (all with highly complicated provisions), we are not at all sure that we would be adequately protected under certain circumstances. One can only hope to avoid prolonged disability, whether terminal or not. My wife and I have signed a statement to the effect that if there is no reasonable expectation of recovery from physical, mental or spiritual disability, the patient should be allowed to die and not be kept alive by artificial means or heroic measures.—*Male, married, age 79.*

Advice.

Savings and Investments. There are two times when people frequently give advice: (1) when they have been successful and proudly wish to serve as an example; (2) when they have failed and, perhaps humbly, wish to serve as a warning. Both of these causes have resulted in many respondents discussing the value of savings or the methods for building an estate. Although a few warned against impoverishing one's life during the working years by excessive penny-pinching, the general tenor of the advice was to be sure to save enough so that there are resources beyond Social Security and the annuities which are derived from belonging to a retirement plan.

For a large number of those who find it practical to save, invest-ment is a problem; although for some, it is a stimulating activity which they do well. In the first group, many have wisely decided either to buy additional annuities or to rely on the services of a trust company. Some have found taking the advice of brokers and investment counselors a disastrous course or have had both good and bad experiences. Investments in real estate, income-producing or speculative, were used by a small proportion of the annuitants. Some who have worked at this have succeeded. However, these are not investments you can make and then neglect. One reported enthusiastically about the stability of real estate demand in a univer-sity town and the resulting profits from investing in homes. One person advocated using mutual funds which do not invest in tobacco, alcohol, or war materials.

The questionnaire did not separate investments in "stocks, mutual funds, bonds, and other securities" from each other, but the consensus of the articulate minority was in favor of stocks—although some advised this for the young (under 65) but more conservative investments, with less potential growth but greater yield, for the retired.

TIAA and CREF was the basis for the additional savings of a number of persons. However, I am somewhat surprised at how few mentioned the purchase of tax-deferred annuities, perhaps because these were not available or were infrequently used at the time of retirement of the older annuitants or, in some cases, because now they are paying full taxes on these annuities and do not recall how largely these represent past tax savings.

Of course, it must be recognized that one of the "growingest" investments, especially considering the small amounts that the older beneficiaries have contributed to it, has been Social Security.

We have mentioned at the beginning of the chapter the large proportion of annuitants who have increased their savings since retirement. This deserves further comment. This statement is subject to a qualification: some of the increase is due to growth in the money value of investments, modified, however, by the loss in the purchasing power of the dollar. One man pointed out that the actuarial value of an annuity decreases with age.

It is interesting to note that the total reported assets in cash, securities, and real estate (other than domicile) of the respon-

dents to the relevant questions were in the neighborhood of one-hundred-thirty-million dollars of which two-thirds belonged to under one-third of the group. The income from this property was the major source of income for the few wealthy, an important source for the middle group, and almost negligible for those with incomes under $500 a month—except for a few who may be without Social Security and with very small annuities. It should be noted that if the value of Social Security payments and of the annuities, including those from TIAA-CREF, were capitalized, their total would probably exceed the amount in other investments, and the distribution would be much more uniform than the distribution of the ownership of stocks, bonds, etc. However, almost all of this value will disappear upon the deaths of the members and their spouses.

We were especially warned against the "many plans to entice old people to give up savings."

VOICES OF EXPERIENCE

In the following, the first quotes are chiefly concerned with the value of savings, followed by those dealing with methods of investment.

. . . Begin 40 years before retirement to save, save, save. . . .—*Male, single, age 73.*

I have no trouble in spending, but I don't understand saving!!!
In 1932, I met a German girl in USA, whose father made her save 10¢ out of each dollar earned. I had no such training or urge—sad at this point. Think what might have been!!! . . .
Will budget seriously January 1. [Retired 1970; received small bequest, already spent.]—*Female, single, age 67.*

A pitifully small early savings and investment program can really do a great job.—*Male, married, age 70.*

Do save all you can.
Don't live on too high a scale so that retirement makes you come down and you're unhappy.—*Female, widow, age 73.*

Don't blow your savings for the fanciest house you can get. Some of our neighbors are pinched from trying to keep too much house for their total means.—*Male, married, age 68.*

In pre-retirement don't worry about financial security. You will probably have more than you think you have.—*Female, single, age 66.*

One of my problems in investing for retirement was that my advisors were too conservative. I took the advice of a very well meaning and highly successful investment counsellor about 20 years ago and tied up much of my savings in blue-chip stocks which ought now to be producing a good deal more income than they are. On the advice of a distinguished economist friend of mine I stayed out of CREF all through the 1950's and missed out on the appreciations of that period. (I'm in now, fortunately!) My economist friend simply didn't want to see me the victim of a depression.—*Male, married, age 70.*

Put your money (if you can save any) into Good Growth Common Stocks starting as young as possible—after providing yourself with adequate Life and Health Insurance, and a cash nest egg for emergency.—*Male, married, age 72.*

I saved part of every pay check I ever received. Upon receipt of an endowment from an insurance policy in 1950, I invested in growth stocks. As these rose in value, I passed some of them on to my heirs, thus avoiding a very large inheritance tax.

My most important suggestions are:

1. Invest in leading growth companies.
2. One never gets rich on dividends, but one can get rich from growth.

[Monthly income over $2000 of which about 60 percent comes from investments.]—*Male, married, age 76.*

Invest your savings in safe conservative areas. The older you get, the less you can afford to take risks.—*Male, married, age 74.*

I'm still "plowing back" all dividends but if inflation ever overtakes us, we can still draw on this income to supplement. . . .

In investing, always split investments for growth (to hedge inflation) conservatively in case of depression. TIAA-CREF 50-50 is a fine example. Don't overload with insurance. That money works better in other investments. Term insurance is ok when you're young, to protect the family. As the beach signs in Hawaii say: "This is your beach! Have fun!!" (That's what retirement is all about.)—*Male, married, age 63.*

We recommend the use of a living trust arrangement with a reliable bank or other suitable agency. In this way one can avoid the details of managing his property and be sure his will is carried out properly. Many people fail to prepare their wills. Do it now, is our advice.—*Male, married, age 79.*

We have two revocable trusts, with equal value in the beginning. Survivor can use income or even draw upon assets in case of dire need.— *Male, married, age 77.*

. . . The Government E Bonds that I bought 25-30 years ago and now own, surely have been a poor investment for me. The same amount of money invested in land or growth stocks would have done better. Of course that is hind-sight. Fortunately, I did not buy too much life insurance (some is necessary for all young folks). But as a means of savings I feel it is a poor investment. My real estate investments over the 45 years have been the most productive.—*Male, married, age 74.*

1. Be sure to start a retirement savings program early in life. In the early years invest in securities that will appreciate with inflation.
2. About five years before retirement change your securities, at favorable opportunities, from long range investments to dollar yield securities.—*Male, married, age 71.*

We have found our investment in real estate (city lots) a good one; their value increases with rising prices. The sale of a lot adds to our income as much or more than would investment in stocks or bonds.— *Male, married, age 75.*

Do think about saving but don't hesitate to spend when needed. In particular, look critically at continued expenditure for life insurance if no one needs the protection any more. We have put most of ours on a paid-up basis and have borrowed heavily on it, on the theory that it's cheaper credit than we can buy any other way, and this goes particularly for our fine five percent loan against TIAA life.—*Male, married, age 80.*

. . . If I had it to do over again I would purchase term insurance and put balance in good reliable securities.—*Male, married, age 71.*

Be careful of people who wish to invest your money—especially these Mutual Funds advocates.—*Male, widower, age 71.*

. . . Broker proved to be incompetent—knew nothing about safe investment for retired people, so after investing $15,000, I lost not only $12,000 of the capital, but all the income from it. A different broker salvaged $3,000 of the capital and now after several years I am just beginning to receive a small income from it. This experience and having to manage on a limited, fixed income almost drove me out of my mind. All people who earn should have training in investment.—*Female, single, age 76.*

I was fortunate in that the investments my husband made before his death have been in the hands of an excellent "Trust Company" and have grown considerably in value.—*Female, widow, age 81.*

. . . While working I paid little attention to money but my wife stowed it away. Lucky investments grew while I wasn't looking. $1500 in G.M. became $10,000. . . . I have just bought, closed my eyes and held. Much of it grew. I've been lucky. That is my unexpected experience!—*Male, married, age 70.*

. . . I have been much impressed with the remarkable success and enjoyment of several women who were widowed early, had very modest means, and set out to learn how to invest in equities. Indeed, the best way to succeed in the market is to be an intelligent widow with limited means, a canny skepticism about all brokers and a firm plan for building an estate.—*Male, married, age 75.*

Anyone who gives too much thought to retirement is starving his golden years—30 to 60. A man should make sure that his wife will not be indigent after he dies and that neither should become a burden to the children—and that's all.—*Male, married, age 71.*

I regret the change in attitude among so many people old and young that it is not necessary to save, for the government will take care of you when you are old.—*Male, married, age 83.*

Miscellany.

There was a large amount of testimony concerning the financial status of respondents which could not be classified under the main headings or which crossed several of them. Some of this is given below. A few of these quotes indicate that a standard of living once attained is hard to relinquish even if the new level is one that others might envy. It will be noted that the problem of keeping annuities increasing with the cost of living was mentioned.

VOICES OF EXPERIENCE

A professional person should be able to retire financially able to carry on at approximately the same level as he has enjoyed in later years prior to retirement. In planning it should be noted to what extent one's real way of life is made possible by concessions not available

after retirement without extra costs that should be taken into account in planning for retirement. For example, a retired University president needs more than his regular salary to permit him to continue living at the same level he had attained as president. . . .

Not having a salary in retirement equal to my salary the last few years of employment has a psychological impact hard to describe. I do not feel able to join the country club I would like to join and I have not yet seen fit to spend the $1000 initiation fee and $300 membership fee per year to join the University Club in town.—*Male, married, age 66.*

For family reasons we could not begin savings and investments until rather late in life, but we have fared well in that area, my wife being an astute financier. . . . We have not spent nearly as much as many of my colleagues on travel, theatres, etc. (and my answer to Question 27 is probably unique) [car date 1947]. This reminds me that talk about "unearned income"—that is, dividends—I resent; our dividends have been earned.—*Male, married, age 76.*

Main problem is the payment of alimony. . . .—*Male, married, age 67.*

I believe I should have arranged to have part of my annuities left for my spouse. We talked it over before I made my decision, but I found afterwards that she was approaching a nervous breakdown and remembered nothing of what we were talking of.—*Male, married, age 69.*

In 1959 I faced the fact that I was not going to have adequate money to live on someday. . . . I was almost sixty. I told the president I would eventually have to return to a state school in Ohio or Michigan and get all my years from various states together so as to qualify for a pension. Social Security was low also then. I had no other source of income except what I would receive from this college. . . .

I got information on TIAA and CREF and finally decided on having $100 a month taken out toward TIAA and CREF.

To do this I did not even have a telephone, I did not take a cab when I could walk. I did not have a car. I spent as little as I could in order to do this. At 65 I, as planned, left this college position which I loved so much with all its wonderful young girls to work with and returned to Michigan where I secured a position in a high school. . . .

By delaying retirement until I could afford to retire, I happened to get in more years at higher salary, a benefit for size of state pension and Social Security.—*Female, widow, age 73.*

In order to solve the problem of inadequate income, I decided to see if I could get placed in a college elsewhere. I applied to at least twenty

schools, and finally was fortunate enough to be accepted by the University of [X, a major institution]. Here I am now engaged in my fourth year of happy and contented teaching amidst harmonious relationships with both fellow faculty members and students. It has been a most challenging and satisfying situation in helping to develop a new department, with new courses, even though it has been one of the busiest periods of my career.

During this time I have been able to provide adequately for the family, put my elder daughter through college, and finally to clear the mortgage on our home!—*Male, married, age 68.*

We faced eventual retirement on an income equal to about half the average of our last twelve years of active service. We also faced five to seven years of retirement in which at least one son would be a university undergraduate (two at once in '72/73). Our solution ten years before retirement was forcible saving and living on an amount roughly equal to what we expected our retirement income would be. With some pains this has more or less worked.—*Male, married, age 71.*

. . . One reads and sees the salaries of the active teachers going up constantly in the last few years.

But is there anything done for the retired teachers? Their retirement is today what it was 15 years ago.—*Male, married, age 76.*

Fight for higher wages, preferably through unions to assure adequate wages in order for an adequate fixed income upon retirement.—*Female, widow, age 72.*

. . . There are retirement plans in industry and some education systems in which the retirement payments are scaled to the last or highest salary. They are real retirement plans. TIAA-CREF university plans leave much to be desired. Without a considerable amount of foresight, faculty members can be left stranded; there should be more serious planning and warning; the universities together with TIAA and CREF should spell it out—tell them really what they are going to get.—*Male, married, age 69.*

[Problem] Getting out of the habit of saving. Learn to spend income.—*Female, single, age 61.*

Do your planning early, save as soon as you can by buying excellent stocks and by putting money in good savings and loan associations. Save in both about equal amounts. Buy some real estate when a good opportunity arises. Don't speculate on the stock market. If you smoke, give it up; drink only very moderately.—*Male, married, age 69.*

Never bought anything unless we had the money to pay for it. Therefore I have never had any credit rating.—*Male, married, age 71.*

Start early to plan for retirement. A pension fund or annuity is only as good as you want to make it; be sure it is a vested fund.
Try to have your home paid for; have as much savings as possible and some investments.
Stay away from the G.D. credit cards; all they do is put a noose around your neck.—*Male, married, age 70.*

STATISTICAL NOTE

• The financial status of the respondents was generally strong, especially in comparison to the overall population of retired persons. For example, according to the Bureau of the Census, 5 percent of all men age 65 and older had a total annual income of $15,000 or more in 1972, compared to 40 percent of all men in the respondent group; on the low side, 38 percent of all men age 65 and older had a total annual income below $3000 in 1972, compared to just 3 percent of all male respondents. The median of the respondents' reported total incomes was $862 per month, excluding the 2 percent who did not give income information. The respondents' holdings in cash accounts, securities, and real estate (excluding a main residence) had a median value of more than $30,000, excluding the 10 percent who did not report complete asset information. General comparisons of income and assets showed the retired faculty and administrators to be consistently better circumstanced than the retired clerical-service group. The older respondents were disadvantaged in comparison to younger respondents as regards income, but had about the same general level of assets as the younger people.

• In the aggregate, the respondents' level of debt was low. Sixty-nine percent of the respondents reported no debt (excluding, possibly, small current bills), and only 11 percent had obligations of $500 or more. Seven percent of the respondents did not indicate their level of debt.

• Other data supports the respondents' report of relatively high income and asset positions and relatively little debt: more than half the respondents said their income allowed them to live very well or well; less than one-quarter of the respondents said their present standard of living was lower than their pre-retirement standard; more

than half the respondents said their savings had increased during retirement; and, just 14 percent of the respondents said they had to reduce savings or sell an asset within the past year to meet current needs.

• The extent of health insurance coverage, of course, influences financial status. Ninety-eight percent of the respondents had health insurance coverage, 1 percent did not, and 1 percent did not indicate whether they did or did not. Seventy-eight percent of the respondents were enrolled in the federal Medicare program and also had other health insurance coverage, i.e., a group policy of a former or current employer and/or an individual policy purchased privately; 13 percent were covered by Medicare alone; and 7 percent were not enrolled in Medicare but were covered by other health insurance. Eighty-eight percent of the respondents rated their health insurance coverage as very good or good, while just 9 percent rated it as poor; 3 percent did not rate their health insurance coverage.

• The median of the amounts that respondent homeowners paid monthly for property tax and mortgage payment was $60, and only 18 percent of the respondent homeowners had a mortgage on their home. The median of the amounts that respondent renters paid monthly for rent was $150.

Chapter 6: Aging and Health

Persons who have had an academic career have had either better than average health in their old age or they believe that most other people have poorer health, for on a scale of "very good," "good," "average," "poor," or "very poor" (in comparison with others of the same age group), 73 percent classified themselves as having very good or good health, 20 percent as average, and only 7 percent as in poor or in very poor health. I would have expected the replies to be a little more reflective of the maladies and malaise of age than they were. There was evidently great reluctance to indulge in self-pity; for instance, the woman, age 69, who wrote "I broke an ankle (just a slip on wet autumn leaves) my last year of teaching. Result: shock, to be told my bones are bound to be more brittle because of age. I have been playing tennis for over fifty years and had had no thought of stopping. Now I am constantly worried lest I break something and become a care to others, as when my leg was in a cast. It has shaken my whole airy feeling of physical competence and adequacy. I do not feel I can burden anyone else with this feeling," reported herself as in very good health. So did the man, age 70, who said: "Standard of living has declined, not because of income, but because of physical limitations; e.g., can no longer dine out because of gastro-intestinal troubles, no longer enjoy long auto trips because of rheumatoid arthritis. In general, wants fewer, which helps offset reduced income."

There is a tendency, but not very marked, for the older people to grade their health at a slightly lower comparative level than those in

the younger age group of retired persons, and for respondents to consider their spouses to be in poorer health than themselves.

Few of the factors which we have been able to isolate through the questionnaire appear to predispose a person toward considering himself healthy or in ill health. Previous types of academic work such as teaching, administration, or clerical work have slight, if any, effect. Men and women said they were healthy or unhealthy in about the same proportion. Of course, the condition of one's health has a good deal to do with one's present occupation. Thus, those in good or very good health are more apt to be presently employed, either for pay or on a voluntary basis, than those in poor health. (The cause and effect may at times be reversed.) Those in very good health have a tendency to live in single-family dwellings. Those in poor health have frequently given up driving a car. Those who retired because of poor health are apt to remain in poor health—though there are exceptions. And one can continue to draw other expected conclusions.

The attitude toward unavoidable aging, when accompanied by health that is as good or better than those of the same age, was often written about in an interesting fashion. For instance, a man, age 84, wrote: "I like retirement. My tastes are ones which can be satisfied by a sedentary existence in a pleasant village community, and the same can be said for my wife. The least 'satisfactory' aspect is the process of physical aging which one takes for granted and to which it is possible to make the gradually necessary adjustments." And the oldest respondent, age 99, (who had his son reply for him) was blind, had had a prostatectomy at 87, suffered from arthritis, and had a weakening heart, and reported himself in good condition for his age. Perhaps he is correct.

As a person ages, even if in comparatively good health, the care of an invalid husband or wife becomes more difficult. It matters not which is the annuitant.

Advice as to the care of one's health, and descriptions of the costs this involves are scattered through other chapters.

VOICES OF EXPERIENCE

From Those Reporting Very Good Health (35 percent of males—36 percent of females).

I feel that a program of activities is essential. The saddest thing I have ever seen is a great number of old men sitting on street benches in St. Petersburg,

Florida, waiting to die. I have also seen retired people who can't seem to find anything to do except to sit around playing stupid card games all day every day. I think retirement is no excuse to fail to learn new things every day. At present, for example, I am studying the historical period of the American Revolution, not only through books but by going to the sites of great battles, etc. The keynote of happiness in retirement is activity when and where you desire.—*Male, married, age 64.*

Don't run to the Senior Citizen or Golden Age groups. When old people get together they grow old faster. They all deteriorate at the same rate without noticing it. You keep on your toes when with the young.—*Male, married, age 70.*

If my wife's health was good we would have no problems. As it is she is as she has been for more than 50 years a competent, unselfish, dependable helpmeet. Today she is as courageous as any person I have known. What more could a man want.—*Male, married, age 77.*

I am afraid I shall live too long and I do not anticipate inactivity with pleasure.—*Female, single, age 86.*

From Those Reporting Good Health (38 percent of males—36 percent of females).

Least liked aspects:
Declining energy, shortness of breath, some loss of hearing. God!—to think I almost forgot!!—declining sex energy!!!—*Male, married, age 66.*

Difficulty of finding doctors at all interested in problems of older people —until the point of death is reached and then they try desperately to prolong life. It would be more satisfactory if they would try to make one feel better earlier.—*Female, single, age 67.*

What I like least about retirement is beyond the scope of TIAA or anyone else to remedy—the irrevocable passing of time (in the spirit of Dante's "nessun maggior dolore che recordarsi del tempo felice nella miseria"). —*Male, married, age 67.*

Least of all I like the medical-dental problems of aging, especially the annual medical check-up. This attitude may derive from subconscious insecurity—awareness that the machine must break down sooner or later. I suspect it is also due to the loss of human dignity resulting from medical mass processing.—*Male, married, age 70.*

I dislike the unmistakable fact that I am (despite valiant resistance) aging and requiring more time to accomplish some unattractive routines disposed of readily before. I miss students' problems, new courses, and a vote in

university affairs. But such malaise grows fainter every year.—*Male, married, age 71.*

Increasing forgetfulness—I'm 78. . . .—*Male, married, age 78.*

Though I'm not on a diet, there are more things I can't eat without remorse.—*Male, married, age 78.*

I like least the process of aging, living with "ailing and aging flesh." As some one has said, "Old age is not for sissies."—*Female, single, age 82.*

The first 10 years of retirement I called the Velvet of my Life:
Because of freedom of time. No more schedules to meet! Can plan vacation trips any time of year.
Because finances planned, so no worry about earning.
Because I lived where I already had friends and now I had more time to enjoy them, and belonged to a number of organizations.
After these years of considerable vigor pass, then comes what no one likes—physical decline. This calls for courage, to meet it and adjust without complaint.
One problem: They say "Don't overdo"—but you do not know where your changing limits are, until you have overdone.
I see this in my own experience, and those around me.—*Female, single, age 80.*

. . . That left me an exchange from my home to an apartment—third floor and no elevator. I like the idea, but one does grow old and stairs become a burden to 90 year old legs.
[Explains delay in answering by being in hospital for a few days. About a third of replies came later.]—*Male, single, age 91.*

From Those Reporting Average Health (19 percent of males—20 percent of females).

. . . considering the alternative, growing old isn't so bad.—*Female, married, age 72.*

So far, I don't know how to sympathize with people (young or old) who find time heavy on their hands. But since I became an octogenarian last May, 1972, and since my eyesight is gradually diminishing and my hearing is becoming more and more defective, I may find out ultimately that time can be "heavy" on one's hands.—*Male, married, age 80.*

From Those Reporting Poor or Very Poor Health (7 percent of males—7 percent of females).

About five years ago I discovered I had Parkinson's Disease. It became

worse and I had to retire last summer (1971) at age 64. My illness completely changed our retirement plans and we have had to make some fairly radical adjustments. On the whole, I think we have adjusted fairly well.—*Male, married, age 65.*

Illness has been a major problem. I retired July 1st, 1969, became ill October, 1969, with severe bronchitis. This required three separate hospital sessions (intensive care) because of bronchospasms. Then osteoparosis developed in spine and ribs and there was another hospital session. Now I am constantly under the care of two doctors—chest and orthopedist. Medicare does not recognize the lung specialist's right to charge $15 a call; they grant $10. But they do pay the orthopedist $15 a call. Health is a major problem —physically and financially.
Now in a brace, I have learned to walk and get around quite well but am not allowed to lift or carry. This means I cannot live alone.—*Female, single, age 70.*

[Like] Least of all? I suppose when people ask me how I am feeling and show no concern whatsoever. I always answer that I am fine, because I know how boring it would be to tell the truth. Lack of concern from everyone, including my relatives, is the aspect of retirement that I enjoy least of all.—*Female, single, age 72.*

I like the least just getting old and having an increasing number of physical ailments. Right now I have tired blood, a tired prostate, a tired bladder, a tired heart and tired legs.—*Male, widower, age 74.*

. . . have not driven a car since age 85.—*Female, single, age 89.*

STATISTICAL NOTE

• The respondents considered themselves to be in comparatively good health, even those at advanced ages. In comparison with people their own age, almost three-quarters of the respondents evaluated their health as very good or good, just 7 percent thought their health was poor, and the remainder classified their health as average, with 1 percent not reporting on their health.
• Married respondents evaluated their spouses' health in the same positive way; 67 percent said their spouses' health was very good or good, 8 percent said it was poor, 23 percent said it was average, and 2 percent did not report on their spouses' health. Married women gave their husbands a slightly higher percentage of poor evaluations than married men gave their wives.

Chapter 7: Activities during Retirement

Few things are as important to a healthy, retired person as activity—work for pay, organized volunteer work, work for organizations (social, political, religious), research (organized and individual), cultural activities (including travel), care of home and garden, hobbies, and a host of other enterprises hard to catalogue. What one man likes most is the "leisure to be busy."

The replies to certain questions along these lines lend themselves to statistical analysis. Forty-eight percent of the respondents have worked for salary at some time since their first retirement. Over a fifth of these persons have worked full time during such a period; over one-third of those who have worked since retirement were still doing so. About one-third of those who worked after retirement did so chiefly for financial reasons and about one-half because they desired to work for its own sake. Many in each of these two categories indicated that the other feature was important. Just about one-half of the respondents have done voluntary, unpaid work; two-thirds of these continue to do so. A few (7 percent) worked full time on a voluntary basis. Of the statistically segregated types of service, nearly one-third were classified as "Educational/cultural," followed closely by "Community," "Church related," "Hospital/health related," or "Work for the aged."

A witness to the ability to keep active related: "My wife was telling the lady next to her how busy we were. The lady said rather wryly, 'if you think you are busy now, just wait until you retire.' And that's the

way it is." A recommended compromise was "Take it easy—not more than 60 hours [of work] per week."

Paid Employment.

The most frequent paid employment of those who worked for pay after retirement was "Teaching"—39 percent, followed by "Consulting"—22 percent, and "Research"—14 percent, and a large variety of other employments. Some of these were: revising college texts, being an ombudsman, starting a debt-collecting agency, working in a travel agency, using a cellar workshop to earn enough money to preclude the receipt of Social Security payments, saw filing, transcribing into Braille, being a receptionist in a doctor's office, and serving in the state legislature. One man, past 80, still made over $350 per month from consulting; another has been trail chairman for a 120-mile trail; and one woman helped her husband start a retirement home but now lives in a different one. Additional activities can be gathered from the quotes which follow. Although some saw the need of tapering off, this was not apparent to others.

It is interesting to note that some persons retired early to accept appointments with later retirement dates, such as 70 instead of 65. Clearly many believe that it is one's lifetime professional work that one can do most effectively after retirement and that one should continue to attend one's professional meetings.

One barrier to post-retirement employment is the limit on the amount of earned income a person may receive without affecting Social Security payments. This is resented.

Sometimes a tapering-off process is facilitated either by part-time, post-retirement reemployment, or by a reduced load prior to retirement.

VOICES OF EXPERIENCE

If possible find a transitional job which is less demanding and yet will eliminate unemployed feeling—even if it has to be with a non-profit or charitable organization.—*Male, married, age 71.*

My university has aided me in that up to now, and probably for a couple of more years, I have been able to offer a favorite course on an elective basis and have been able to keep my office in my department. Since retiring I have also

written one book. I attend most faculty meetings when I am in town and in other ways try to stay a part of the university life. Some of my winters I have spent in Arizona, but I do not stay away long enough to lose contact with my university.—*Male, married, age 71.*

I expected in my last years of teaching before retirement to retire to a small town, do a modest amount of research, and live what remained in peace and security, and above all in serenity. Nothing of that has happened in my case except the modest amount of research. In the seven years of my retirement I have taught every year save one (when I was recuperating) in some eight institutions. I am, of course, not complaining; I have been really glad to have the opportunity to continue some kind of activity which requires a regular schedule. I merely point out that what I expected to find I have not found, while what I never even contemplated as possible became possible.—*Male, widower, age 76.*

Having known that retirement from professorship was mandatory (on account of "statutory senility") I accepted an invitation to serve in a government agency, and began services there on leave of absence from the university a year before official retirement.—*Male, married, age 83.*

[Chief problem] Inflation.
Solution: Writing. During first two years of retirement, wrote an institutional history for a flat fee. Next two years, wrote an historical work for Harper and Row; modest advance, followed by royalties. Past two years, wrote historical work for Scribner Sons, for flat fee. By writing three hours daily, six days per week, I have during the past six years averaged between $1000 and $2000 per annum, easily enough to meet medical bills, greatly increased real estate taxes, and other rising costs.—*Male, married, age 74.*

I chose the job that would allow me to work until 70 and start a challenging new School of Engineering at a state college. This also helped my pension situation a great deal as I had been in the state pension system for 10 years previously when I was much younger.—*Male, married, age 79.*

In the fall of 1962, about 18 months prior to retirement, I was offered an opportunity to work in my professional field overseas for a minimum period of two years with the U.S. government. I applied for and was granted a Leave of Absence from the university until June 30, 1964, the date for my scheduled official retirement. . . . Both prior to and following my retirement I continued to make regular payments to TIAA and CREF; I continued these payments until age 70 and was retired from Government employment with an additional annuity. . . .
After a total of nearly ten years overseas and eight years of full time

post-retirement employment, I have retired for the third time, as of last July. However, if my health permits, I expect to continue part-time consulting work, occasionally overseas and here at home in the community and the state. Also I plan to continue volunteer activities, in some of which I was engaged before going overseas.

Thus I faced the twin problems of : (1) wanting to continue to work after retirement; and (2) the desire and need to earn additional funds to build up resources that would enable my wife and me to live more comfortably in retirement. Even more importantly and significantly the nature of my work, in spite of many frustrations, continued to be stimulating, challenging and rewarding both to me and my wife.—*Male, married, age 74.*

The freedom from required schedules and duties has been delightful. I have taken on a new career—medical education has shifted to education of two-year-old children—and it is so delightful and stimulating that I wish I had found the latest career at an earlier age. A book on the subject is nearly ready to go to a publisher, and I consider it the best contribution I have ever made. Other projects related to the area are waiting and I look forward to tackling them with great pleasure. The days are not long enough, and my energy limits me to about 15 hours of active work with children plus 25 hours of writing and study.—*Male, married, age 71.*

I did not face any problems, but was already engaged in developing and marketing a new voting device, which was placed on the market in 1964 and sold to IBM the following year. For five years I served as a consultant to IBM and am still receiving royalties. During several years after retirement I worked harder than ever before and was greatly rewarded, both financially and in satisfaction. My post-retirement activities were closely related to my research and publications, for I was a specialist in election administration and published two books and many reports and articles dealing with elections, particularly in my early academic years.—*Male, married, age 76.*

I have enjoyed doing some private duty and relief nursing. While I was working I so often felt I was so far removed from the patient that it has been a real satisfaction to go in and give bedside patient care. It is fun to do things on the spur of the moment and so I never go to bed without a uniform and white shoes clean and ready to get into in case they call me during the night—and they often do.—*Female, single, age 74.*

Since my retirement from teaching I've made and repaired violins. All "profit" goes to some charity. (Plenty of income from investments. Still working.)—*Male, married, age 87.*

[Like] Least—Necessity to work part time, since if I depended on $250/month Social Security, I would have to curtail spending drastically.

Also feel resentful that at age 69 I cannot draw on my Social Security, since I must make more than $200/month for a decent living, and meanwhile I must continue to make FICA deductions—even though I can only collect payments in July and August.—*Male, married, age 69.*

Voluntary Work and Organizations.

I suppose it is almost tautological to say that the work people do on a voluntary basis is the work they wish to do. It is clear that one of the great dreads just before retirement is that one may not have enough to do after retirement. This fear is seldom justified. It is true that as the debilities of age increase, some find that their spirit is more willing than their flesh; but in the period that immediately follows retirement, there is usually ample opportunity to continue to be active, and many find that they become involved—some say too involved—in various organizations or types of voluntary service.

A leading kind of voluntary work is helping the sick and aged through hospital service such as giving health examinations, acting as hostess at the hospital, or monitoring the coffee cart. There were those who drove for "Meals on Wheels," read to the blind, taped sermons for shut-ins, or catalogued the church library. Another group were on boards of non-profit organizations—sometimes as officers as, for instance, vice president of a roadside protection group or "Chairman of the Board of Pacific Tropical Botanical Garden" or president of the "Society to Save Venice." One described himself as a "Board old man" since he served on several. One woman directed a chorus, another acted as a museum science guide. A number of people did voluntary work for governmental or quasi-governmental agencies such as town finance committees, or a state's Commission on the Status of Women. Related to these were political survey polls. One man of 82 wondered if he should give up his work in a boys camp. There are many elderly persons who care for those who are still older or more infirm, such as the woman who reported that she bowled, knitted, crocheted, played bridge, and cared for a father—age 98. Other sorts of experiences in voluntary work are indicated below.

Post-retirement religious activities are discussed elsewhere.

VOICES OF EXPERIENCE

At present I am president of the Goodwill Industries in our city and serve on the Board of Directors of the Bixby Hospital, the Associated Charities, and the Rotary Club; I am chairman of the Annual YMCA Membership Drive and of the International Rotary Foundation committee of the local club; I serve on the Greater Adrian Area Inter-Club Council; I am chairman of the Inter-Church Activities Committee for the local Council of Churches and chairman of the Friendly Callers Committee of the local Methodist Church; I belong to the YMCA and the Methodist Men's Club, and am interested in Birding and Covered Bridges. I give two afternoons per month to the County Historical Museum. I enjoy LIFE!—*Male, married, age 65.*

We are confronted constantly with the question, "What are you going to do with yourself? Don't you miss going to work?" My husband is a leading layman in our local church, and thus has many responsibilities there. I am having an opportunity now to work in organizations that are daytime oriented—something I have never been able to do all of my working days. When we have gotten our feet on the ground sufficiently, I shall probably do hospital volunteer work in the same hospital in which I was employed. Service for others, I believe, is one of the key words in happiness in retirement.—*Female, married, age 65.*

Teaching English to foreign born students in primary grades.—*Female, single, age 69.*

The first year the days were long and I was quite unhappy in spite of keeping quite busy. The second year I took a Laubach workshop course in teaching English to illiterates. I taught a Mexican young man in the U.S. Medical Center for Prisoners for seven months. He was in for illegal re-entry into the U.S. He learned to speak English fairly well. But more important, since he had to return to Mexico, was that he learned to write legibly, to write Spanish more correctly and he finally read well enough to read for pleasure. He had stopped school after the fifth grade and had never read anything for thirteen years. Teaching him three or four mornings a week gave me much satisfaction and joy. I am teaching at the prison again this year.—*Female, single, age 72.*

During the last half of my teaching career, I developed special interest and competence in international education, and as a climax I taught for four years in Taiwan and Korea as a U.S. government contractor and a Fulbright lecturer. When I returned to the U.S. at the end of 1970, I felt that my qualifications were at their peak, and I was eager to use them in full-time

volunteer work. Therefore I applied to nine organizations in the field of international education, with most of which I had been associated professionally, and most of which were seeking contributions to support their work. To my great surprise, none of them could think of a way to use my services. Since then I have talked with a number of highly qualified retired educators who have encountered the same problem. I feel that organizations and institutions serving the public should plan how they might use retired volunteers, for they are overlooking a valuable source of manpower. In fact, I looked into the possibility to doing this job myself—finding openings for retired educators and retired educators interested in working with the organizations. However by that time, after a search of six months, I had found very satisfying opportunities for volunteer work in the School of Education, the Center for Chinese Studies, and the English Language Institute of my alma mater, the University of Z [a major institution]. I am working there at present.—*Female, single, age 72.*

I moved into a strange community but I was living with a sister and had lots of time on my hands so I joined the League of Women Voters and it was not long before I was chairman of the Foreign Relations Committee. Through that I became very much interested in United Nations Organization. I joined several groups who were working for the Red Cross. Next thing I got into was working with the Girl Scouts and for 16 years I was Juliette Low Chairman of the Girl Scouts in Wilmette. At the same time I was trapping and banding birds for the Fish and Wildlife Service of the United States Department of the Interior.—*Female, single, age 95.*

My main problem was what to do with my time. I feel that volunteering my services to the United Nations Association and the League of Women Voters has been a good solution.—*Female, single, age 73.*

[Like most] Time to invite neighborhood children in to make puppets and give puppet shows. We have given puppet shows on Saturday mornings in the children's department of the Public Library, both here and in Cedar Rapids, in the Music room of the Iowa Memorial Union, before 200 people in a church in Lone Tree—near Iowa City.—*Female, single, age 81.*

. . . in our case we spend two days a week for seven months working with boys and girls voluntarily teaching the Bible.—*Male, married, age 74.*

. . . I have always found that there is plenty of work to be done if you don't have to be paid for it. In our retirement residence there is always much to do. I am still connected with a non-profit agency in New York, and have done frequent volunteering in Greece for the charitable work of the U.S. National Council of Churches. So the days are still too short, even to answer promptly this questionnaire.—*Male, married, age 76.*

I became involved in work for the American Friends Service Committee.—*Female, married, age 74.*

. . . I am the treasurer for a large day care center. I don't get a salary —because that is my contribution to public welfare. I recently had to have an eye operation that makes me write very poorly and keeps me from using the typewriter and driving my car. These are the natural handicaps of age but I have been blessed in so many ways that I don't ever complain.—*Female, married, age 84.*

For five years I was President of the Dutchess County Association for Senior Citizens which I was instrumental in developing.—*Female, single, age 86.*

I make myself available as a consulting engineer at no charge and I am called upon quite frequently for advice. This is good for my ego and keeps me in the swing of things.—*Male, married, age 73.*

Perhaps there was another problem. We became much involved in The Port Charlotte Cultural Center where I was director of "retiree education" part of the program for five years and my wife also helped in many ways. This limited our freedom to some extent. Some people would say that we became too involved as retirees. We have no regrets for the time and energy we expended. The Center is wonderful and we are happy to have been a part of it during the formative stages. To others this might have been a problem but it was no problem for us.—*Male, widower, age 77.*

Find some organization in your community that you think is worthy of support and go in and volunteer to help at anything you can do. The demand for free labor on the part of worthy causes is boundless and you will meet some very nice people with whom you have a common interest. If you are not careful they will make you a director or trustee even if you can't give any money and then you will be back in the same old routine of attending meetings.—*Male, married, age 72.*

. . . Especially disturbing is the amount of time I give to volunteer work in charitable and social service organizations. . . . I find it difficult to say "no" to good causes.—*Male, married, age 71.*

Like the least:
Too much volunteer work is not intellectually stimulating.—*Female, single, age 72.*

Work for world peace!
Work for "Common Cause" (Political)—"Gardner."
Work in some religious faith!—*Male, married, age 82.*

Research.

For many a scholar upon retirement the greatest desire, after health of self and family and an income providing reasonable comfort, is for the opportunity to continue his investigations. There were many expressions of gratitude for those who made this possible by providing laboratory, library, office facilities, and other aids for such work. I suppose every major institution and some smaller places can boast of some emeritus faculty members who have made notable contributions to knowledge after formal retirement. There is ample justification for a fixed age limit for retirement, but the man who has the capacity and willingness to continue as a productive investigator without pay should be given the means of carrying on his work. Frequently, perhaps usually, this is done.

The quotations, which follow, do not even indicate the scope of post-retirement research and come from both those who have and those who have not received some pay for such work. They are given to show attitudes towards research after retirement.

It might be well to add that there are some who, though desiring to continue to teach (and often doing so on a voluntary or paid basis), are happy no longer to pretend to increase knowledge or to publish; and there are also those who, not desiring to teach or to. investigate extensively, have material they wish to prepare for publication. Some reported that they had accomplished this. Perhaps one of the blessings of retirement for a still active person is to concentrate on those phases from the complex of professional duties which are most to his taste.

VOICES OF EXPERIENCE

. . . Indeed, research has continued uninterruptedly and, except for absence of routine classes, etc., life is no different than formerly.—*Male, married, age 68.*

As my retirement is applicable only as far as finances go, my experience is probably atypical. A brief description of my activities during the past few years is in order, therefore, to make my answers to these questions as relevant as possible. I retired as a college president in 1968 at the prescribed

age for that institution of 65. On the basis of a previous arrangement with another institution where I had been employed earlier as a regular faculty member, I returned to that institution in 1968 as a senior research associate at a considerably reduced salary for a three-year period, working on a research project in anticipation of completing a book. When the research salary ceased in 1971, I continued as a research associate, without salary, working regularly on completing the manuscript and I intend to continue to do so for at least another nine months. This arrangement permitted me to postpone the date for the beginning of my annuity payments, thus increasing their amount, and also gave us a three-year period in which to adjust to a lower income. It also eliminated, to a large extent, any unexpected problems, and means that I am still continuing my former role as a research scholar. . . .

For anyone who has carried on research and writing during their pre-retirement years, I would strongly recommend their exploring the possibility of becoming a research associate, either with a greatly reduced or no salary, to enable them to complete a previously planned project. . . . By the end of the project, I anticipate moving to the country and spending most of my time working outside on the place.—*Male, married, age 69.*

. . . I determined at least ten years ago to remain in the same town, and if possible to retain some kind of active membership in my university. The latter was achieved by a research grant on behalf of my wife and myself from the Rockefeller Foundation, administered by one of the research centers of the University. Thus, following retirement from teaching professorship in 1969, my wife and I were appointed research associates in the center that administers our grant. Our responsibilities to the center amount to approximately one-quarter of a full schedule. In actual fact we devote at least one-half time to our project which has already yielded several publications.—*Male, married, age 71.*

I used to wonder whether I would work as hard as I was doing if I had sufficient income to live without working. The answer is "yes," if you are able to do the things you most want to do and how and when you want to do them. [Cancer research nearly full time.]—*Female, single, age 75.*

I would prefer planned work for retirees.
No folderols like crocheting, scrap books or doll clothes. Research: for instance!—*Female, single, age —.*

I have a research problem in mathematics that I have worked on for the past forty years. It is difficult and it is altogether unlikely that I will find a complete solution. But I have made a most interesting discovery this last year which really delights me.—*Male, married, age 85.*

Care of Home and Garden.

The care of home and garden may be one's chief post-retirement activity. At times the garden really is a farm acquired about the time of retirement. Some enjoy such work, while others find it a means of saving or even making money; still others, because of the illnesses of their spouses, take on greater responsibilities around the house than is their wont (or want). One suggested that a major disadvantage of retirement homes is the lack of a place to do "real dirt gardening." The following quotes chiefly emphasize the garden.

VOICES OF EXPERIENCE

I have a very large garden, mostly flowers, which keeps me busy and out-of-doors a great deal during many months of the year. I find myself constantly busy and never at a loss for something to do. That is probably the most important aspect of a happy retirement.

[This is same person who served as an ombudsman.]—*Male, single, age 68.*

I decided that I would not make any effort to continue in my medical specialty after I retired and would do something entirely different. The result of this decision has been that I have spent my time improving our property. I have cleared out underbrush, removed trees, transplanted trees and done landscaping. Removing, pruning and transplanting large trees have been done by professional people. I have planted and transplanted 125 dogwood trees, also some oak trees, planted redbud trees and flowering fruit trees, camellias, azaleas, etc. Oak trees that I transplanted are now 30-40 feet tall, dogwoods and redbuds up to 20 feet tall, magnolias 50 feet tall. I thoroughly enjoy working with trees. The lawn work has been disappointing due to pearl bug infestation for which there is no known insecticide.

I have ample time for reading and continue reading the journals of my specialty.—*Male, single, age 83.*

In the spring of 1972 I constructed a small greenhouse in our back yard. My wife and I are using this structure to give us something to do any time we have time on our hands. In a way we are more fully employed now than we were before we retired.—*Male, married, age 71.*

I decided to take over our lawn care and garden work. This keeps me well occupied from March to November—other chores in winter.

Costs: Invested well over $2000 in lawn equipment—10 hp. riding tractor with rotary mower and snow blower, smaller mowers, edgers and sweeper, all gas-powered.

Our lawn and snow removal had been costing $700 per annum.

Into the fourth year the investment has more than paid for itself—both on our property and in my health.—*Male, married, age 70.*

. . . My wife and I decided on a rural community (which has since become almost suburban) about ten miles from a university city and about four hundred miles from the place where I had taught. I was able to buy an old, well-built farm-house with enough land for a garden and a few apple trees. This has provided food which could now be estimated at $500 annually. . . . As I expected, property values and taxes have both advanced considerably of late. We have liked the opportunity for reading and have been able to use the city and university libraries to advantage. The medical and hospital services are quite satisfactory.—*Male, married, age 77.*

I think the transition from a life-time career of employment was so easy for me because I began to think practically in such terms by my 50th year and planned for the change. I even purchased a country home and acreage to indulge my passion for gardening and nature-observation near enough to New York City, where I was teaching in a college, in order to spend very long weekends there preparing for the time I would live in the country permanently.—*Female, single, age 70.*

We enjoy our gardening and our little cabin in the woods of Southern New York State. I can not think of a thing I don't like about retirement.—*Male, married, age 64.*

Travel and Reading.

At first-thought, travel and reading might seem somewhat antithetical, but they are closely related because of the many cultural cravings which both satisfy. They are also akin in the difficulty of working them into a busy professional life.

The chief advice of a bibliophile is to stay close to the library, and of the wanderer, is to travel early—to "gallop while yet there is time." However, travel was extended well beyond retirement by some, as in the case of a woman of 76 years who, in spite of four serious falls, still found long sojourns in foreign countries both a cheaper and pleasanter mode of life than staying home. There are also those who do not plan a permanent move, who, nevertheless, believe it is best for them (and for their institutions) to have a prolonged period after retiring

away from the milieu of their previous work. Various suggestions concerning the manner of travel were given, some focusing on the pleasures of trailers or motor homes. The advantages in both comfort and price of off-season travel were pointed out.

VOICES OF EXPERIENCE

Don't wait too long for travel and fun. The courage wanes with increasing years.—*Female, single, age 78.*

Do not put off TRAVEL too long. It is best to do it before retirement. One cannot take the RUSH of guided tours, which operate on a timetable. One is unable to deal with unexpected illness without being miserable in trying to deal with such complications and the tour won't wait. [He seems to assume that all travel is by tours.]—*Male, married, age 77.*

The difficulties of retirement were, in my case, mitigated by spending the first year after I retired in Europe with the two friends I was living with. I think it is probably a good plan to do something entirely different in a different place in order to bridge the gap between job life and retirement life. One acquires new interests, new perspectives, renewed vigor.—*Female, single, age 82.*

If means permit (in a cold climate) try to work out a schedule of winter travel or going south. It will make you more interesting (provided you do not bore the hell out of your friends with your damn slides).—*Male, married, age 73.*

I felt at age 75, when I retired, that my savings were large enough to allow me to dip into them to (a) take a tour by plane around the world; (b) take a plane trip around Africa including safaris; (c) travel in all of Europe including Russia; (d) I plan next year at the age of 80 to take a plane tour to Australia, New Zealand, Tahiti and Fiji; (e) I read extensively, and spiritually I live in the whole world.—*Female, single, age 79.*

One is driven to seek the company of the great. And I am particularly interested in those who have a vital vision of the future: Julian Huxley, Albert Schweitzer, Pierre Teilhard de Chardin, Hermann Broch.—*Male, married, age 76.*

We both looked forward to my retirement, and we have not been disappointed. I thoroughly enjoyed teaching at my alma mater, but I had grown

sick of reading and grading the many papers an English teacher must require, and sick of committee meetings. I wanted my nights especially to be free to be home and to read again for pure pleasure rather than the somewhat restrictive reading and research for my courses. I wanted to go on trips to find antiques for her shop and to accompany her to the several antique fairs in which she participates. Twice when the association of Professors Emeriti asked whether I wanted to be listed for a possible position in some college I promptly and emphatically replied NO.

I have bought more books and read more in these five years—in that long list of books which I wanted to read but never could find the time while teaching—and in magazines and periodicals which keep me more or less abreast of today's activities and thought than in any other period of my life.—*Male, married, age 75.*

I have found much interest in some books on archeology such as those on the discovery of the world of the Hittites, the books by Ardrey, and numerous magazine articles. There is plenty to do till I find myself "treading the verge of Jordan."—*Male, widower, age 88.*

I retired to a rural community which I enjoy because of opportunity to garden, hike and enjoy the out-of-doors. Do miss the lack of library facilities for professional study and research.—*Male, married, age 75.*

My wife would like to move to the country, while I wish to be close to a great library, in fact to the old library where everyone is eager to help and please me.—*Male, married, age 67.*

Hobbies.

A large number of retired persons testified to the value of a hobby, as a supplement to professional work or as a means of remaining active after retiring. The hobbies range from the trivial to those which have grown from pastimes to serious occupations, as was the case with one man who, starting long before, by retirement had developed professional competence in water colors. It would be interesting to make an inquiry into the full scope of post-retirement hobbies. The list of those mentioned by respondents (even with no direct questions on the subject) is long. Besides the miscellaneous group there are several distinct categories, each with its devotees. (1) collecting: stamps, coins, pewter, portraits, etc.; (2) crafts: weaving, woodworking (for one in connection with wife's rosemaling), helping son rebuild sports cars, brass polishing, lapidary work, and photography—mentioned by many; (3) games: cards, lawn bowling, golf, shuffleboard; (4)

studies: for instance, geneology (both one's own and that of others), or Washington (George, not D.C.); of course, hunting and fishing or, perhaps best of all, sailing. One man recommends "garden, golf, decoupage, etc." which is a pretty good start for an et cetera.

There are those for whom hobbies hold no charm or have begun to pall—golf is better once a week than every day, and even the zest for fishing attenuates. "Hobbies leave me cold."

VOICES OF EXPERIENCE

Before retirement, become involved in two hobbies (or activities): one, centered in a collection; the other, centered in some type involving physical creativity, e.g.: (1) stamps, minerals, coins, shells, etc.; (2) wood or metal crafts, painting, needlecrafts, etc.

(The important point is that the two types of activities, collection and creativity, be begun before retirement begins.)—*Male, married, age 73.*

Can only advise the obvious—a valid preoccupation with some engrossing hobby—I don't much care what. But it must be continuous, time-consuming, and fascinating.

. . . Being a person with little urge for competitive recognition, and no overriding drive for accomplishment, I accept the condition of "retirement" with considerable equanimity.—*Male, married, age 72.*

[Problem] Ennui:

Coped by diversion of my prior interest and competence in certain aspects of my prior professional engineering activities, to the fundamental and technical analysis of stock market equities. This has proved to be an ever-interesting and, fortunately, rewarding "hobby," to which I can devote as much time as I wish, yet coast along at times with very little effort. Furthermore, it is not dependent upon others to make up a game, as in golf.—*Male, married, age 80.*

When I was 54 years old I had some time on my hands and I took up sketching. After some time I discovered that if I had some help I might make progress. So I took a French correspondence course in drawing and painting. (This because I had no access to help at hand.) I followed this course for 3-4 years. This was completed in 1964. Since then I have:

(1) had an Exhibition in the school in which I was teaching (before retirement—my subject was French); (2) had an Exhibition in my home last year; (3) am in the throes of another; (4) make greeting cards for sale.—*Female, married, age 66.*

Also take adult education courses to learn or to improve your bridge, chess, etc.—*Female, married, age 68.*

... My hobby is playing shuffleboard. We have many retired persons in our community who are enthusiastic about the game.—*Male, married, age 83.*

I had two hobbies that I pursued for years before I retired: these were collecting pewter and portraits of ancient doctors. I also collected some old glass, both American and European. I still add to my pewter and glass collections but now that I do not travel abroad, I have stopped collecting portraits of ancient doctors, and except for 15 of the portraits I gave the collection to the last medical school where I worked.—*Male, single, age 83.*

Don't count on your stamp collection to keep you busy if you have neglected it when you were working. In general, this kind of thing will have less appeal as a time filler than it had when minutes were snatched from sleep. There is more hope in new crafts and skills related to some new central purpose.—*Male, married, age 80.*

One activity that my husband and I have enjoyed after retirement is compiling our genealogies. Fortunately, both of us had well documented ancestral lines, going back to the Mayflower, so we have been able to find records of several hundred ancestors, with fascinating stories of their experiences. Ancestor-hunting does not require physical exertion, nor much money—only writing letters. And, these letters lead to interesting new acquaintances, so I warmly recommend this as an occupation for the older generation.

Also, writing letters to grandchildren is well worth-while. Their letters are so naive and so full of surprises, that each one is a source of great pleasure. If one does not reply to your letter, it is a good idea to write again, saying you enclose a check, and then forget to enclose it. This is almost certainly going to be answered soon.—*Female, married, age 79.*

Collect materials for a history of your family, including yourself. Many objects and facts of interest to your children and grandchildren can be removed from oblivion.—*Male, married, age 68.*

... I have six hobbies and enjoy them all.—*Female, married, age 66.*

I can now do the many things I've wanted to do but couldn't find time to while working. My job came first and I worked at it 70 hours per week if necessary. I like retirement so much that I even hate to go back to the office when they call on me for help. I can fish, hunt, go canoeing, boating, hiking, bird watching, do a lot of photography work, catch up on my stamp and coin collection, find time to do some carving and lathe work, read the things I've saved up for 25 years, etc., etc. We can visit our children in Texas and New Mexico when we choose, go camping anytime we like, sleep late if we desire (but we never do—not even on Sundays: there are too many things to do)!

What aspects of retirement do I like the least? Days, weeks and months are too short.

. . . Anyone who can't develop a knack of liking to do a great many things must have a poor imagination.—*Male, married, age 61.*

Miscellany.

There are some post-retirement activities or situations that do not fall under the other headings of this chapter, or would naturally come under so many that they are best gathered together in one section. Is "making coats-of-arms" a craft, a study, or a service? "Computerizing the operational data of the Royal National Life-Boat Institution" is unique, fascinating, and useful. Certainly the advice to "keep up a lively interest in theater, concerts, reading, politics, and social affairs" sets a manifold objective. But there are those who like most "no list of things to do" and "no necessity for making speeches."

VOICES OF EXPERIENCE

Don'ts . . . Don't think you need a year of rest, doing nothing. You probably don't need it as much as keeping active.—*Female, single, age 74.*

If you have been wrapped up in your work and will not be able to continue it part time LOOK OUT! You are apt to be LOST. Our next door neighbor is in this "boat." He is becoming meaner and more grouchy by the day.—*Male, married, age 67.*

Retirement provided me with many aspects that I like. Part of my vocation became an avocation. Until administration made it impossible, I was a very good pianist. Teaching, research and administration pushed piano practice aside. So, one of the big pluses of retirement was the daily time to put in at least two hours a day on piano practice. Now I am back in shape. Another plus was much more time for research—in which in times prior there was a deadline. I now have time to catch up on my reading in general history. Also to cook which I like. The pluses in retirement far outweigh the minuses. . . .

To date, retirement has been very pleasant.—*Male, married, age 68.*

During the last four or five years preceding my retirement I served not only as professor but (then completely without pay) as editorial director of a series of books published by our university press, a project important not only for the press, but for the national and international "community" our university serves. This job must, then, be done by somebody. It had come to me largely as an informal ex officio supplement to my regular professorial duties but I

[could] find no way to shed it. . . . The problem is really this—how to effect a complete retirement, not only from the central job but from the informal appendage that thus far occupies too large a part in my working day.—*Male, single, age 66.*

Do something absolutely new and different. For example, I took up Dog Obedience Training at the age of 71. In the past year and a half since I began training my Shetland Sheep dog, Shelley, she has graduated from Novice Training and earned her CD (Companion Dog) degree. In her last trial meet she took first place honors in competition with 42 other dogs. My wife and I joined the local Dog Obedience Club and have enjoyed immensely the fellowship of its members, most of whom are much younger than ourselves. I still hope to take up water color painting.—*Male, married, age 73.*

. . . Our policy is to play golf on all good days and work when and if we feel like it on rainy days.—*Male, married, age 63.*

The second problem was how to keep busy. I have solved this in several ways. (a) I had long planned to write three books, and I immediately set to work. Two have now been published, and the third is ready for the publishers. (b) I had long wanted time to read far more than my teaching and administrative work permitted. Since retirement I have read scores of books and have kept up with journals in various fields. (c) Before retirement I had made two European trips and travels in Canada. We have since been traveling more in our own country and contemplate further travels as time permits. (d) I have also kept busy with church work and correspondence and with various social activities. So time has thus far not been a problem.—*Male, married, age 77.*

I expected to have difficulty using my leisure time, but even now, seventeen years after my official retirement, I never have time to do all the things I want to do. Every morning I have to make a list of the most pressing needs in the order of their importance, and then try to get as far down the list as possible. Because I am a victim of what I call "the cult of accomplishment," I find myself spending too much time answering the call of those "pressing needs" without allowing enough time for relaxation and quiet reading.—*Female, single, age 82.*

After a bad six months I decided I was trying too hard—that a dusty house was better than a dopey wife. . . . —*Female, married, age 69.*

Wife's duties remain about the same. Wife not used to you being around the house. I used a space in the home as an office—desk, files, tape recorder, Hi-Fi, records, etc., and tried to stay from "underfoot."

Built house (second house) in mountains, added rooms on main residence, also on two rentals.

Now at 70 intend to build one house per year in mountains to keep busy. Am taking course for Private Pilot's license.

Keep busy maintaining two homes and five rental homes 1500 sq. ft. and larger. . . .

Sometimes feel like I am somewhat "useless" compared to former life.—*Male, married, age 70.*

I expected to do considerable writing, but bad eyes and nerves have almost stopped this. I take walks to keep down nerves. I tend to get depressed which can be terrible.—*Male, married, age 75.*

[Problem] I did not expect to give nursing service but our internist advised my caring for my sister in the last four months of her terminal illness, with good visiting nurse help. He was probably right but I was long on good will perhaps but short on skill. Reading and questions helped. I had not foreseen this and wish I had had some training. It is a more common experience with many aging in the population.—*Female, single, age 74.*

Think of all the things you like to do—then do them. I sat down one day and put down all the things I love to do.

Walk—at least 1-½ miles a day.

Read—several books every week.

Sew—at least one garment a week.

Play bridge—at least twice a week—often more.

Baby sit for my granddaughters.

Cook—never miss a meal—nor nibble—cook lots of good food.

Go to see a good show now and then.

Watch game shows on TV—not Soap Operas.

Have company and go out a lot. Never sit at home and feel sorry for yourself. Keep real busy.—*Female, single, age 74.*

I usually work in the morning and retire in the afternoon—I'm semi-retired.—*Male, married, age 64.*

STATISTICAL NOTE

- About half the respondents had worked for salary or wages after they had retired. Twenty percent of these respondents had full-time employment and 37 percent were working at the time they completed the questionnaire. Respondents who were retired faculty and administrators had a higher percentage of workers in retirement than did those with a different career background. Retirement employ-

ment fields corresponded closely to pre-retirement career emphases with the exception that consultation was introduced as a popular work area. Teaching (39 percent), consultation (22 percent), and research (14 percent) were the three retirement work careers reported most often by the respondents, especially the men; women indicated strong involvement in librarianship and clerical-service employment as well.

• As the primary reason for working after retirement, 29 percent of the respondents wanted the extra money, 17 percent wanted simply to work again, 14 percent received an offer too attractive to refuse, 11 percent were asked to return to a designated assignment, 10 percent missed work, and 19 percent gave other, less specific reasons.

• About half of the respondents had performed voluntary, non-remunerative service after they had retired, although only 7 percent of these people had performed voluntary service on a full-time basis. Sixty-nine percent of all those who performed voluntary service after retirement were involved in such service at the time they completed the questionnaire. Proportionally more women than men had voluntary service experience during retirement, 55 percent compared to 46 percent of the men. Also, the retired faculty and administrators more often reported voluntary service experience than did those with other work career backgrounds, and the older respondents had a higher percentage who performed voluntary service following retirement than did those who were younger. Respondents' voluntary service activity covered a variety of interests, and some were involved in two or more areas. Thirty-one percent of those who reported post-retirement voluntary service performed an educational or cultural service, 30 percent were in community service, 23 percent aided a church or religious organization, 14 percent were involved in hospital work or health service, 8 percent helped the aged, and 23 percent served a professional or political organization, helped private individuals, or engaged in voluntary service too general to classify.

• Twenty-seven percent of the respondents worked for pay *and* performed voluntary service following retirement, 21 percent worked for pay but did not perform voluntary service following retirement, 21 percent performed voluntary service but did not work for pay following retirement, and 28 percent neither worked for pay nor performed voluntary service following retirement. Three percent of the respondents could not be tabulated on both the variables.

Chapter 8: Relations with Other People

The general rule that much of the contentment in life depends upon one's relations with other people is as true for the retired as for the more active. The importance of pleasant pre-retirement relationships was emphasized both by the woman, age 84, who wrote, "Fortunately, I have not learned to hate anybody," and by the man who asserts, with reason, that "good relations during one's active life contribute more to a satisfactory retirement than any other factor that can be identified. . . ." The absence of companionship is discussed in connection with loneliness in the chapter on "The Unhappy Side of Retirement." In this chapter neither the pleasant nor the unpleasant aspects are emphasized, but rather the nature and importance of relations with certain groups of people, particularly with one's former employing institution and its administrators, with one's former colleagues, and with one's spouse, children, and other relatives.

It is my impression, after reading the questionnaires, that many persons are too self-conscious of their relations to other people and too afraid that the elderly are not welcome, an attitude that may become self-realizing. The joy of those who acting naturally find their personal contacts becoming ever richer is the other face of the same coin.

Former Employing Institution and Its Administrators.

I fear it is a human trait to complain about what is not done well, rather than to praise good performance. Hence there were numerous

expressions of dissatisfaction with administrators and some words of commendation. Perhaps the fact that most people said nothing about their institutional officers is evidence, both of a fair degree of approval and of a belief, which I share, that, after all, administration is not too important. A few evidently have been unhappy with their situations for a long period and, as mentioned in Chapter 3, some even explained the decision to retire early as due to the "arrogance" or the "corruption" of their administrative superiors.

The experience of the last year or two before retirement leaves a permanent taste. This is particularly unsavory if the individual was retired without sufficient warning, either by an action in his particular case or by changing the retirement age of the institution, effective within a short period. I think the resentment of the man whose shoes were filled by many new feet was mixed with pride. The attitude of the institution at the time of retirement is also important. The person who received an honorary degree felt very different from one who retired "with[out] as much as a goodbye."

Perhaps partly because an explicit question was asked concerning pre-retirement counseling, a number of respondents commented on this subject. To the question as to whether the last employer before retirement had provided counseling or assistance in retirement planning, only 22 percent replied "Yes." I guess it had been available but sometimes not known about or not used in many other cases. Of those who used the service, 94 percent said that they had found it helpful. The quotes which follow are over-weighted towards those who were unhappy with the counseling, finding certain counselors uninformed, others "harassed," and in some institutions, even large ones, non-existent. There are those who emphasized the importance of counseling, one even saying that ". . . every employer should give so many minutes per week to employee training for retirement."

Among the subjects on which it was suggested that information should be given are: the dollar amounts of such items as annuities and post-retirement insurance coverage (health and life), financial planning, part-time employment and voluntary work opportunities, income tax information concerning annuities and other retirement benefits, useful organizations for the elderly, investment programs, Social Security benefits and work rules. Others urged special courses on retirement with spouses included. Although some of these proposals indicate too great faith in the competence of others to give universal advice, they do represent strongly sensed needs.

In contrast with the dissatisfaction with counseling were the large number who greatly appreciated the post-retirement privileges which they received, ranging from library and office privileges to free parking. Facilitating the work that an emeritus professor wishes to do and is capable of doing, usually without pay, is not only a morale-builder but often a productive investment in scholarship. Those not retired also look more calmly at the future if they expect to have the means to continue their work as long as they wish.

It is clear that a little effort on the part of the administrator combined with a great deal of human understanding can significantly enhance the life of the retired employee of a college or university.

It is somewhat disturbing how seldom in spite of having enjoyed teaching, missing students, and retaining an interest in their disciplines, the retired spoke with affection of the institution they had served. There are too few love affairs between colleges and scholars.

VOICES OF EXPERIENCE

My transition from an active career to a passive retirement could have been serene instead of stormy if my employers had only been more understanding and less domineering. I was, of course, well past the canonical age of 65, but my first warning came on March 10, 1971, when a minor functionary called me to his office and told me I was finished at the end of that semester. That "radicalized" me in about five seconds. I told him I'd fight, and I did. I won another year, and retired in June 1972. I have no complaint about that date, but I am still bitter about the manner of my dismissal. This is outside the scope of TIAA, but I wish someone those administrators would listen to with some respect, would tell them that the people they hire and retire have human emotions. It would in many cases, including mine, alter the emotional color of the remaining years of the retiree's life.—*Male, married, age 73.*

I had expected to be a full-time college faculty member until I reached the age of seventy years. The sudden decision, initiated by the college president, to retire all faculty members who had reached sixty-five, caused me to become resentful. Therefore, I was discontented with the idea of retirement. I was not ready for retirement and resisted forced retirement. I am still teaching college classes part-time and I am involved in voluntary adult education. I am "busier" than ever, but I still reject the thought of retirement. This is my main problem.—*Male, married, age 68.*

Retirement age was lowered from 70 to 65 with only six months notice and the adjustment in daily living was too abrupt.—*Female, single, age 65.*

The university should notify employee at least five years before retirement and not one year as they did to me and others.—*Male, married, age 69.*

As my retirement was at my own choice I had no feeling of resentment which I think is an important factor.—*Female, single, age 74.*

Beware of the so-called "counseling" offered by some (maybe most) University Personnel Divisions. You can probably get better help from insurance agents, or an accountant, or lawyer. These people will work for you, admittedly for a fee, but will at least be informed and helpful on the subject.—*Male, married, age 67.*

University helped in explaining how to apply for the annuities like Social Security and TIAA and the Iowa one.—*Female, single, age 86.*

In addition to pre-retirement counseling I feel there are many things an institution can, and should, do after employees retire. Just good public relations would suggest: mailing certain material to keep former employees up-to-date; inclusion in at least one function annually, etc. It would seem to me just prudent for an institution to retain the good will of former employees and not "brush off" this group as no longer useful.—*Female, single, age 66.*

I wish the employer had given us more information on pros and cons of going into TIAA-CREF when it was made available to us, and how it would benefit us in our retirement. Even though I was approaching retirement (within five years) perhaps I could have benefitted more by making a personal deposit with TIAA or CREF even though my employer did not contribute.—*Female, single, age 68.*

Insist upon being given clarity and definiteness in pension plans of the institution well in advance of years of retirement.—*Female, single, age 74.*

I am now sorry I worked for a church related college in the middle South that paid very low salaries especially to single persons. This college also showed preference to certain single persons by paying higher salaries to some and lower salaries to others even with the same teaching load. I taught because I enjoyed teaching young people and made thousands of friends. After retirement one cannot live on former friendships but it takes money to pay necessary expenses.
Be very much aware of the college you teach in. Even church related colleges are not always honest with their employees.—*Male, single, age 74.*

Have experienced no real personal problems. However, my employer had our TIAA medical insurance and group life insurance cancelled out—for

retired employees—and replaced it with a group policy of no benefit to retired faculty employees with other medical and hospital insurance.—*Male, married, age 73.*

Have become a second-class citizen: moved to a much poorer office; have no secretary; no telephone; no longer consulted. All this has had effect on my morale.—*Male, married, age 73.*

The College with which I was connected for 41 years (1924-1965) allows its Emeriti to keep their office in the Library if they so wish. My special field of research is in the contemporary period. This enables me to keep up with the times.

Moreover, the College provides more interesting lectures, plays, films and exhibitions than one person could possibly keep up with.—*Female, single, age 73.*

You might ask also what a university could do to ease its faculty's retirement. Here perhaps one tenth of former full-time faculty take advantage of the opportunity to stay on for slight remuneration and occupy former quarters, and work as they like. I think more would do so if it were considered "normal." Some seem to think they "ought" to get out, and that the younger people do not want to have them around. That is not my position nor my experience. It's true I don't try to give advice or interfere in the current work of the department, but I never did that much anyway.

It seems to me a great pity that people in intellectual work should suddenly be expected to give it up, when they may be wiser than they ever were before.

My own office is in my department. But the University has one house given over entirely to retirees, who are provided with secretarial service and who work as they like, whether they are paid or not. One man spends most of his time promoting the United Nations, and at least two of the others, who have worked abroad, carry on their contacts with other countries and with students from other countries on our campus.

To my knowledge, no one who stayed on has made himself disagreeable to others.—*Female, single, age 79.*

I have no real problems. My department includes me in its activities. As am emeritus I have the old privileges plus a new one; free campus parking. An office and furnishings has been provided on the campus. One unfortunate feature is that no private laboratory is now available. (I am a chemist.)—*Male, married, age 66.*

Always do your best at your job so that your employer will "keep you on the job" several years past retirement time.—*Male, married, age 81.*

Former Colleagues.

There are many who believe that the ties with one's job should be broken as completely as possible upon retiring, but there are also many who think that would be a great mistake. Some of the latter had words of wisdom as to how one should behave in keeping in touch with one's former colleagues, especially when on campus. Although a few resented not being consulted, the general advice was to stay away unless you can accept change and to avoid making suggestions to one's successors. One man of 84 recommended an attitude of "kindly nonchalance" promoted by being "tolerably indifferent." Some institutions have given special, perhaps specially created, positions to certain members of their faculty after retirement with varying degrees of satisfaction on the part of the recipients—in one case even in the same person, who, finding that continuing on the campus planning committee brought him into disagreement with his successor, had a sense of fulfillment in his subsequent position as university archivist.

VOICES OF EXPERIENCE

Don't: Cut your ties with the community (friends, neighbors, associates) where you have been living and working. [Don't]: Live in the past, nor talk in terms of "when I. . . ."—*Male, married, age 76.*

Make a retirement plan that is right for you. I think there is something sad and inherently painful about trying to hang on in a profession in which you have been a leader when you are no longer able to carry leadership responsibilities. I knew always that having been Dean, for example, I would not continue on the faculty, teaching a "course or two." The Elder Statesman role has never appealed to me . . . particularly in this Youth Dominated age. The way to end is to end . . . at the height of your powers and accomplishment. But that is my philosophy. Others may wish to "hang on." I believe however that they constitute a problem and embarrassment to the new administration and continuing faculty and are demeaning themselves.— *Female, single, age 69.*

Recognize before retirement that after your retirement persons who sought advice, guidance, or opinion will no longer listen attentively to "the voice of experience."—*Male, married, age 66.*

Don't go back to the office after you retire to see how your successor is handling the job you retired from. He will do many things differently to the way you did them but why let this concern you. When I retired I left the office and have never been back. I know this was best for me and I am sure that my successor probably felt the same way.—*Male, married, age 72.*

Do not feel you are the only one who can do your job. Every position needs a new and fresh viewpoint.—*Male, married, age 74.*

. . . Naturally I miss the daily contact with young people in the classroom and the feeling that I may be giving them information and ideas that will be helpful to them. I miss also the friendships which these contacts brought, for now when I cross the campus, students may speak, but few know me and I know few of them. They are busy with their own affairs and would find little interest in trying to bridge this "generation gap." But after all this is quite natural, and one would be as foolish as Lear to expect the same attention after he has surrendered active responsibilities as when he carried the full load.—*Male, married, age 77.*

. . . Don't, like a fool, hang around where you used to work. . . .
Don't be meddlesome—don't take the attitude that advanced age means advanced wisdom.
Don't be garrulous. Practice the "listening ear and the silent tongue."— *Male, married, age 76.*

[Problems] I might say a lack of amenities for retired faculty such as library facilities, a place to park on campus, and a general lack of respect from younger members of the faculty.
I am not bothered too much about these, however.—*Male, married, age 72.*

. . . Why should the gains of seniority in position be snapped when the employee reaches the age of 65? If the employer is foolish and callous enough to break the last thread, then the older employee should look for a new job or make one for himself.—*Female, married, age 72.*

In a sense I retired gradually, giving up the department chairmanship one year, getting off most committees the next year, and teaching only half time the final year. During my second year of retirement and a part of the third year, I acted as ombudsman. In a small college when a new Dean of Students was appointed, this position became unnecessary, and I put an end to the office by giving it up. As an alumnus I also became a member of the Alumni Council. A number of Faculty members also live in my immediate

neighborhood. Hence I am still generally informed and interested in the college activities, but I am careful not to interfere: I am retired.—*Male, single, age 68.*

I have an office in my college department, close to a fine departmental library and laboratories. All this is wonderful.—*Male, married, age 82.*

Spouses.

No other relation is as important, as intimate, or usually as rewarding as that of marriage. There are those who in their eighties are nearing their sixtieth wedding anniversaries and are happy and contented. Satisfaction is also expressed by the woman who had the "sting" taken out of retirement by a "favorable opportunity to get married at age 73." Marriage, however, is not devoid of problems—problems which are different when the children are growing than when the grandchildren are developing. It would be false to stereotype even the point of view of the husband or the wife, but they are not the same. This section suffers, not only from being written by a man, but also from the fact that among the respondents there were 792 married men, 86 percent of the total men, but only 123 married women, 21 percent of the total women. As is natural, at least in a society as reserved as ours, the most touching tributes to a husband or to a wife were from those bereaved by death. This is also mentioned in the section on loneliness in another chapter. Here we discuss the couples where both are living.

In addition to, and among those, who expressed their pleasure in their life together are those who recognized that retirement brings problems—especially the problems that a man's retirement brings to his wife. If he stays home and does what he wishes, this may be resented. If he tries to help, he may be more underfoot than if he does not. Many husbands seem to believe that it is wise to have some activity which regularly will take them away from home for a part of each week day—a retained office helps. It is natural for the expert housekeeper to tend to direct the less skillful. What one man liked the least about retirement was working under orders on what he called "Honey do jobs." I was somewhat surprised that no annuitant quoted the current saying, that she married him "for better, for worse; for richer, for poorer; in sickness and in health; but not for lunch."

A few found that their views, especially about retirement and

where to live, were quite different from those of their spouses. This is borne out, not only by the experience of respondents but by a thesis written under one of them which reports finding "a number of couples in which the inner visions of one concerning retirement were opposed to the other's, and neither one was aware of this."

There are those who appreciate the financial conditions of their helpmates. Some have different viewpoints as to saving, the wife frequently being more thrifty than the husband.

All of us have observed married pairs who are more anxious about the health of each other than about their own. One woman's most emphatic advice is to " . . . find some way to get your husband to put himself under a doctor's care."

I suppose most married people wish they were more skillful in being considerate of their partners and also wish the same for them.

VOICES OF EXPERIENCE

Try to arrange for retirement in advance by choosing a wife who will be companionable.—*Male, married, age 81.*

. . . We have almost NO social life outside ourselves. However, I suddenly found my WIFE to be a darned good companion—really hadn't NEEDED all the others.—*Male, married, age 67.*

More opportunities for enjoying home life and companionship with my wife—while at the same time each of us has certain interests and activities of his (or her) own.—*Male, married, age 79.*

. . . After 22 years of commuting, arising at 6:30 A.M. and returning at 7 P.M. or later, I find it very pleasant to get up when I want to get up, to spend time over the morning paper before dressing, and to be free for afternoon or evening engagements. In particular, having time to share in my wife's activities and interests has been very satisfying.—*Male, married, age 68.*

My wife has been retired only four plus months and hasn't been able to adapt to a new life style and is very jealous of mine which I enjoy so much. When I'm busy and she has time on her hands, she is unwilling to take on tasks I was glad to do when she was teaching and keeping house. I put most of our resources into guaranteeed income, but she worries, frets and stews about reduction in income and possible confinement in a nursing home for many years and the cost.

Unfortunately, since we have absolutely no interests in common, retire-

ment brings far more strain between us than was present when we were both employed.—*Male, married, age 68.*

My problems in retirement seem little different from what they might have been in any case—the problems of aging, of reduced capacity to remember, to absorb and to function. There is, however, an unanticipated problem of my wife's inability to accept these realities. Having a greater commitment than mine, both professionally and socially, she feels frustrated for both of us.—*Male, married, age 71.*

My retirement is a bigger trial to my wife than to me, in spite of my prior awareness and my conscious efforts to minimize the annoyance.

My wife finds it more difficult than I do to get out of the habit of saving; she can't seem to realize how well off we are and how few years we have in which to enjoy our assets.

. . . The average woman survives her husband by six years (actuaries, please correct me if I have the figure wrong).

. . . teach your wife to be a widow. Get her to participate in banking, will-making, purchase and sale of securities, and other transactions. On your death she should have in her possession a document listing bank, brokerage, and Savings and Loan accounts; the name of the attorney; the location of the will and of stock certificates, bonds, and other valuables; the annuity and insurance policies with advice about the options most appropriate for settlement; the persons and agencies to be notified of your death; and any other pertinent information likely to be needed to settle the estate.—*Male, married, age 68.*

My wife and I can't be in but one place at a time—me—I'd rather be here. [Florida.]—*Male, married, age 68.*

The adjustment requires a new sharing and understanding each others' needs. One selfish partner who will not share can create quite a problem.—*Male, married, age 68.*

. . . My wife must still care for the house as I do the grounds and we work together happily, both with less worry than in our early years when we both worked extremely hard and with much sacrifice to save for just these years. I looked forward to retirement and pity those who cannot give up their jobs or find interests to occupy themselves beyond working years. My wife actually is growing reconciled to my retirement, which she envied at first, now that she senses its satisfactions through me.—*Male, married, age 69.*

. . . Then, there is the problem of wife and husband adjusting to being together all day, every day, and becoming a one-car family.—*Male, married, age 78.*

The husband especially needs to continue in part-time work or have some hobbies, recreational pursuits, and/or volunteer service projects or positions to fill his time and make him feel needed—or useful—and also keep him out of the house at least part of the time and from driving his wife mad by being underfoot, or taking over her usual responsibilities, unless necessity requires such.—*Male, married, age 73.*

From my husband retiring and beginning new work or no work, I would suggest married couples try to plan their lives to have some part of each day apart. No matter how congenial they are, this change of schedule curtails privacy and is a new area of adjustment which I see many people have difficulty with, and I see enough change in schedule to understand.— *Female, married, age 62.*

. . . To my great surprise I was married again just over a year after my retirement. Obviously, if I had had any idea that this was going to happen, I would not have chosen a one-life annuity.—*Male, married, age 66.*

If your wife is still alive, try to make up to her some of the sacrifices she had been called upon to make in your behalf.—*Male, married, age 74.*

Our type of life would not appeal to many other families. At ages of 85 and 87, after 17 years of retirement we have settled into a quiet routine. We keep regular hours, up before 8:00 and to bed at 11:00. We tend to housekeeping and garden chores in the morning, and after lunch are free to do shopping and run other errands, visit friends, or put in our time reading and/or playing a little cribbage. Soon it is time for dinner, and after, the newspaper, TV, and lately a game or two of Scrabble.

We get all of our own meals—the wife is a good planner—in preference to eating out. We have balanced meals and we save money in addition.—*Male, married, age 87.*

Discuss everything with your wife—she does not retire. She is the custodian of your serenity.—*Male, married, age 72.*

Children and Parents.

One of the most poignant satisfactions of life is to have one's children grow up. No reward is greater than to see children reach maturity with the kinds of bodies, minds, and characters one would wish; but such maturity involves independence, both in ability and in spirit, and one finds that one has cherished their dependence. You wish they would cling to you but you are proud they they do not. I was the

youngest of a large family and my mother was a firm-minded woman, but I remember the tears in her eyes when she said to me, "I guess my last baby is too big to sit on my lap." It is natural to fear the growing separation from one's children, yet be almost passionately resolved not to interfere with their lives especially after they are married. Phrases similar to "They have their own lives to live" were used frequently, and, as quoted below, this exact phrase by at least two people. I fear that sometimes the resolution is so extreme as to trouble the children for whom the parent is making a renunciation.

I would be interested in knowing to what extent this is a new approach, since we often hear of the roles of several generations in a single household when America was an agrarian nation. We also often learn or even read of cases where men and women have fond memories of grandparents or aunts who lived in their homes when they were young. It is true, of course, that when the children have increased independence, the parents also have. I sometimes wonder if approval of this mutual independence of the generations may not be one reason why workers are willing to pay the present heavy Social Security taxes. The quotations which follow give an inkling of the spectrum of emotions in regard to the relation of elderly people to their children and grandchildren.

It is interesting to note that I recall no case of any of the respondents complaining of their own parents, some of whom lived in close association with them even into retirement years. It is equally interesting to note that although there were frequent complaints and some diatribes against the young, these young always appeared to be other people's children and grandchildren.

Several persons had special advice to give on money relations with children, this advice differing markedly from person to person.

VOICES OF EXPERIENCE

Don't interfere with your children's lives, and don't give them advice unless asked. As adults they will make their own decisions. Don't visit them unless specifically invited.—*Male, married, age 74.*

Do not expect too much of your children. They have their own lives to live. Do not sit at home, afraid to go out for fear of missing a telephone call or a visit from one of them.—*Female, single, age 73.*

. . . Don't expect your children to cater to you—they have their own lives to live. Help when and where you can, but don't take sides, nor interfere with the household.—*Female, widow, age 72.*

. . . If one has children, don't be a bore to them; this probably means don't live in the same town unless this has been the case before retirement.—*Male, married, age 71.*

Many retirees are looking forward to intimate contact with children and grandchildren. If for no other reason than the increasing mobility of the young generation, you should not count too much on it.—*Male, married, age 74.*

Don't let your family run your life until it becomes necessary and you can't take care of yourself.—*Male, married, age 73.*

Most important—to have a family of children who like you!—*Male, widower, age 92.*

My retirement has given me time to be with my family more than I could when working. It so happens that I feel very close to my wife, children and grandchildren and now I can see them more often than previously.—*Male, married, age 72.*

Three grandchildren (so far!) and they are a joy. My only observation is that I don't believe that grandparents should live with their children—near for frequent visits, but far enough away to make one's visits looked forward to.—*Male, widower, age 63.*

I was exceptionally fortunate to have a son in Chemistry patent work who provided me office space and opportunity to do library research in that field (without compensation).—*Male, married, age 81.*

We hope to discard the parent-child relationship; that we can trade opinions on a par with each other, our offering of advice only when it is asked for; to help each other when needed, if possible; to enjoy each other as people. We appreciate our chance to learn about the world and its people from them, and hope our experience may in some way serve them.—*Female, married, age 69.*

Don't give or loan money to your children.—*Female, widow, age 76.*

I regret, however, that I cannot do more financially for my children and grandchildren.—*Female, married, age 65.*

Don't move in with one of your children unless there is no alternative. You need your privacy and so do they.

Make a will—but keep your money and your property.—*Male, married, age 71.*

Advise any prospective retiree if his nondependent single children are not covered by hospital insurance to get it for them if they (child) can't afford it. It will be much cheaper for the retiree in the long run.—*Male, married, age 72.*

Don't become dependent upon your children, they don't want an added burden and you don't want to become a glorified baby-sitter.—*Male, married, age 68.*

When I retired at 65, I went back to my mother and father, and had the time to take up handweaving which I really enjoyed. I also worked at a research problem in Middle English, which I had neglected while I taught.

Within a year, my father died, and my mother's health gave out. For the next six years I looked out for her and ran the house.—*Female, single, age 85.*

In this rural community there were a lot of grandfathers and grandmothers when I was a child, and elderly farm workers, and masons, and handy men. They did a surprising amount of work at their own pace. Now there's nothing to do but sit and rock into oblivion. They used to mow and hoe practically up to death's doorstep.

I mow and hoe only when I please and I am spoiled rotten by retirement. I am also entirely grateful to my forebears for contributing to me an ability to enjoy. This I would gladly pass on to others if I only could.—*Female, single, age 68.*

Have been fortunate to share living arrangements with my mother—whose income is much bigger than mine!—*Female, single, age 62.*

My grandmother lived to be almost 105 years old. As her generation passed away, she continued her interest in people of the next generation and in my generation. Being blessed with a good memory and a keen mind, she never sat back and moaned about her "rheumatism." Instead, she kept active: cooking, sewing, reading, knitting for all ages, and, through her interest in people, gave them a great deal of pleasure.—*Female, married, age 68.*

Relatives and Friends.

Living with relatives, other than parents or children, was seldom recommended although there are cases where it has worked well,

especially if the persons had lived together before retirement. The advice on this subject often was emphatic.

There were a considerable number of single women who by living with a friend had solved financial problems and precluded loneliness. Such arrangements sometimes started well before retirement and seemed to involve less inherent strain than living with relatives.

VOICES OF EXPERIENCE

[Problems]
A. Getting along with other members of the family.
B. I have had to adjust to several personalities.
C. I like most living in the country; least with relatives.
D. Don't, if possible, go to live with your relatives.—*Male, married, age 86.*

[Problems]
Incompatibility in single home with independent sister used to working separately and planning alterations to allow continued independency in use of home by both—constantly living in four rooms—altered with twin kitchen and extra plumbing plus closing carport for utility and storage space. (Loan for alterations just paid in full.)—*Female, single, age 67.*

. . . I decided to leave Arizona, an adopted land, to return to New England. During the period of finding a new place to live I've allowed myself to live with members of my former family. This has been a difficult situation. I don't recommend it. However, when I move into my new house I should again have the freedom I crave and/or need. I have many interests which do not coincide with my family at present—creative and intellectual—which should give me a measure of contentment and a sense of accomplishment.—*Female, widow, age 67.*

My only real problem is that I am very much tied down with the care, both physical and financial, of a much older sister. She is very crippled from two severe accidents but is perfectly clear mentally (although 90 years old) so that I would never consider placing her in a nursing home.—*Female, single, age 73.*

Do—Retire with a companionable brother who is a widower.—*Female, single, age 75.*

Mostly Advice.

Below is a small selection from a great deal of advice on how to get along with others, ranging from "Stay young" to "Be your age," and from rules of a type given by Dale Carnegie on how to make friends to those in the spirit of Whistler's "Gentle Art of Making Enemies."

One of the points emphasized by both advice and example is the desirability of remaining independent of others as long as possible.

VOICES OF EXPERIENCE

Don't expect younger people to include you in all their activites. Today's middle-aged as well as its youth and also its aged, are very "peer" conscious, and many have not learned to adapt to those of other age groups. They feel uncomfortable except when among their peers.—*Female, single, age 71.*

If you involve your actions with those of the present group of young people, you will get not only a lot of satisfaction, but also a different set of notions as to "what it's all about." "Try it. You'll like it."—*Male, married, age 78.*

Be patient with those who are ahead of you in years.—*Female, married, age 64.*

Try to be interesting to yourself so that you may become more interesting (and less boring!) to other people.—*Female, single, age 72.*

Enjoy persons with whom you are in contact in a new existence. Remember: Faculty people are not the only informed and intelligent persons.—*Male, married, age 61.*

Be cordial to others, but not overly so.—*Male, married, age 89.*

. . . but I probably rub other people the wrong way, too.—*Female, single, age 72.*

Don't worry about needed friendships—retirement offers the luxury of determining friendships by choice, instead of by expediency!—*Male, married, age 73.*

What I enjoy least is the barrage of advice to older, retired persons. Much of it is an insult to their intelligence.

Probably the readers of this will not remember "Misther Dooley"—a

character created by Peter Finley Dunne. When people asked him why the end of his nose was so red (expecting him to confess to a love of liquor) he would reply in his Irish brogue, "Sor, it is glowing with pride because it is kept out of other people's business." Perhaps I remember this so clearly over the years because the end of my nose tends to be red. So I have no advice for persons about to retire or already retired—it is already too late for it to be helpful.

Anyhow, this all sounds pretty smug, and I'm not really. Thank you for making me count my blessings.—*Male, married, age 76.*

Perhaps the most important lesson we may learn in old age is that it is more important to be able to love others than to be loved.—*Male, single, age 68.*

Chapter 9: Religion and Churches

A large number of respondents wrote of their religious faith. Some of these (and also others) described their church activities. It is clear that for many persons the chief source of comfort and strength lies in their belief in a personal God. These often expressed their desire that others share in this blessing, and their conviction that this can be done: for example, "I firmly believe the hand of God is always at my elbow for guidance just as he is always present for everyone to lean on." "It is time to devote some thought to eternity." "Get plenty of sleep, at least eight hours, and above all have faith in God for this is where your strength comes from." This is reminiscent of the command of Cromwell's to "Put your trust in God; mind you keep your powder dry." There were others less articulate as to their faith who found their churches were not only places of solace but also congenial environments for their voluntary services and social activities. This mixture of advice as to everyday activities and reliance on religion represents the practical value that many place on faith and is illustrated in several of the quotations that follow.

Emphasis was placed by some on reading the Bible and other religious books, as well as on regular attendance at church. The religion of certain others was more generalized, for example, "find your Supreme Being (in church or with nature)."

VOICES OF EXPERIENCE

I have been a widow for ten years. I have never sat around and grieved about my past. Thankful I am alive, healthy and able to take care of myself. Thank God for another day in this beautiful world God has made for us. We have a choice of making it beautiful or ugly, which will it be? As for me through God's love for me I am going to try to make it more beautiful every day God let's me live. May God be with you all.—*Female, widow, age 74.*

But we older ones must look ahead and know sometime we will be going beyond. How much does one's religion really mean? Mine is essential for every day and I have keen sense of wonder about the future. It will be the greatest experience in my life. [This reply is given in full in Appendix 1.]—*Female, single, age 82.*

Don't overspend your income. Get rid of all charge accounts. Keep active physically and mentally. Arise every a.m. at your usual time and give thanks to the Lord for your health and his love which manifests itself each day in your life.—*Female, married, age 66.*

Do love your neighbor as yourself. Do love Jesus Christ, the Son of God and the Holy Spirit. Do believe in the Triumph of Good over Evil. Learn to live with your Conscience. Do not lie in any situation—always tell the Truth. Be innocent—be like little children—for of such is the Kingdom of Heaven. Be cheerful and joyful. Contribute to all good causes. Act as though—that this day may be your last. At last may you hear—"Enter the joy of the Lord." May you hear—"Well done, my good and faithful servant."—*Male, married, age 74.*

My advice to those about to retire, if not too late, is to develop other interests and don't believe that life will cease after one's travels on this earth. Thank you for the opportunity of allowing me to express these few simple ideas.—*Male, single, age 76.*

. . . Be truthful, keep your word at any cost and depend on God to lead us into the paths of righteousness.—*Female, married, age 84.*

Give away! Give away to the Lord. He will* return much much more than you have given!
Enjoy living!
*I did receive two unexpected inheritances.—*Female, married, age 79.*

Friends are the most important. Well, no religion is the most important —knowing what you believe and belonging to a group of like believers. My church is very important in my life. The rector and his wife (Episcopalian) are really friends. Friends are second in importance and interests third. . . .

. . . The ability to enjoy what you have is important. I have a rule I don't drink alone so I won't become an alcoholic. . . .

My father was a clergyman and we never had any money 'though we did have social position. I've never made much money in any of my jobs. I've never saved any money. I trust God to look after me and He does. I have on occasion been out of money and nearly out of food. But I'm not in any way one of the slum dwellers. I've never had a mink coat but don't want one.—*Female, single, age 65.*

I am president of a temple. I have 750 voluntary workers. . . .

All people in their sixties should have a sustaining faith in God who answers prayers and gives one wisdom and motive and no fears about the future. They need programs to keep them wanting to live the rest of their life. I would suggest that a faith to live by is most important—otherwise you'll get problems. . . .

Study and work and pray for a faith in God and his eternal plan. Know that death is a part of that plan and determine to fit into that plan. The knowledge that there is a literal resurrection and a life hereafter through Jesus Christ should spur you to learn all you can as long as you can. No man can be saved in ignorance of the good things of this life and the things of God.—*Male, married, age 70.*

I moved to the country just prior to my retirement, commuting for the last 2½ months. I immediately began attending my church where I made friends and joined the choir, for which I was eligible since I had sung in a large New York church for 27 years. Since then I have taken on a job in the church office to which I give two days a month and I have recently been asked to edit the Church Newsletter. I also joined a needlepoint (another of my interests) group in church which is working on a sizable job for the chancel. And, even though I was never a joiner, I am a member of the Women's Club and its Literature Group. And with my other friends, I have a social life that is very satisfying.—*Female, single, age 64.*

Three churches have been erected. A community church is the melting pot for protestants. The building of the churches has provided occupations, good thinking and light work for many people. There has been a good feeling that this is our church. [She lives in a retirement community.]—*Female, married, age 73.*

The churches of all faiths afford rest, tranquility, and promise.—*Female, widow, age 77.*

Chapter 10: The Unhappy Side of Retirement

In spite of the fact that the general tenor of the replies was remarkably happy, retirement isn't all fulfillment or all "beer and skittles." Between religion and a well-developed philosophy of life, many retired persons lead lives of serenity, but I believe that only a minority prefer retirement to their former lives. Of course, the greatest curse is not retirement itself, but decreased energy and the illnesses which come with increasing years. These arrive earlier for some than for others; and there are a fortunate few who retain their vigor and their clarity of mind into very advanced years and then die with little or no warning except from the calendar.

Perhaps loneliness, loss of status, and lack of routine, coupled with boredom, are mentioned more often than other unpleasant circumstances; but there are other complaints, ranging from those that are rather general to those which might be labeled "pet peeves."

Other chapters also deal with certain misfortunes, such as unsatisfactory places to live, financial restrictions, and ill health; hence these are only lightly touched on here.

To try to isolate the types of unhappiness, though useful, is rather artificial. The ill, the idle, the bored, and the lonely are overlapping categories.

Loneliness.

A large proportion of those who wrote of their loneliness had lost a husband or wife, some other close relative, or a friend who had been a

constant companion. Mealtime may be especially poignant as more than one widow attested. Like least: "Eating alone since husband's death. Companionship of husband and intellectual stimulation greatly missed." The ability to recover from such a bereavement differs greatly from person to person and is less in the aged than in the young.

A second cause of loneliness is moving away from the community where there are many friends to a place where there are few. Such a move does not always, perhaps not usually, result in loneliness as many respondents bore witness. The consequences of a move depend on the type of community to which one goes and upon one's temperament. Moreover, the effect may be different upon the husband than upon the wife. Even without a move, the daily association with students and colleagues can be sorely missed.

Loneliness was mentioned more often by women than by men; perhaps this is because among the respondents there were more single women than single men. Moreover, because the wives, on the average, are younger than their husbands and more long-lived, there are more widows in the general population than widowers.

VOICES OF EXPERIENCE

The main problem was the sudden death of my wife ten months prior to retirement. We had planned our retirement years and everyone should at least ten years prior to retirement. Ours were broken—I have made none since and live day to day following my hobbies which are numerous, and everyone should come to retirement with preferably life-time hobbies. Hobbies cannot be developed overnight. Loneliness is the worst enemy especially when your life partner is suddenly taken away. It should be remembered that there is no formula to cover all people—it (retirement) is a very private and personal affair.—*Male, widower, age 75.*

My life now is very lonely. I live alone with my son near by. I keep the house, yard and flowers and enjoy, the best that I can, my friends. I, also, work with community projects.—*Male, widower, age 70.*

I think widows and widowers should seriously consider remarrying. My wife died shortly before retirement and I have remarried very happily. Of course this is much easier said than done.—*Male, married, age 76.*

The loneliness: My sister and I lived together. She died shortly after we retired. We bought the house together.—*Female, single, age 82.*

What I like the least is the sharp reduction of social contacts—the "built-in" kind—those associated with one's job. My hobby interests have been solitary—reading, needle-work, gardening. I've never liked bridge or other games, club work, big parties—or the like.—*Female, single, age 73.*

. . . I moved away from the area I'd been in for 15 years and I miss old friends and college activities—consequently—loneliness.—*Female, single, age 70.*

Had always made friends easily in the States; had not expected it to be different. Acquaintances were made easily but new friends were not. Credited this as partly due to ages and partly to normal Canadian reticence.

Had not expected to spend as much time alone—especially evenings. Had to develop interests and jobs to keep me actively busy and interested at home.—*Female, single, age 77.*

Loneliness: I moved back to Columbus, Ohio, after living in New York for 30 years in order to be near my sister. I have found it hard to make new friends and I also miss the cultural activities provided by New York.—*Female, single, age 73.*

I do not like my present role as a spectator rather than participant and do not at present see how I can change that role even if I recover my health.

I did not expect so many of my closest friends to die before I did. My younger friends have also been reduced in number. It is difficult to establish more than a superficial relation with new contemporaries. Real companionship seems difficult to achieve.—*Male, married, age 75.*

My close friends are either dead or live at a great distance and I have no interest in making new ones. . . . I have never welcomed forced association with others and I have no interest in such groups as the "golden age clubs." It seems best simply to adjust to the inevitable.—*Female, single, age 68.*

Having had no "home base" for many years, I expected major adjustments in a new environment, chosen for the reason of living close to my only relatives—a brother and his family. During this first year of retirement the differences between their interests and activities and mine have come into clear focus. To avoid irritations I've almost isolated myself. To my dismay, I've been unsuccessful, so far, in developing enthusiasms for inner-family and inner-community activities. The fault is mine. I had not guessed the width of gulfs between aged spinsters and members of a closely knit family of three generations. The great change in mode of living has brought knowledge of myself—of my habits, characteristics and theories which fit uncomfortably

among people who are considered to be living "normal" lives.—*Female, single, age 67.*

. . . I had not realized how seriously I would miss daily contacts with students and others. An unexpected silence descended on my world.—*Female, single, age 73.*

A lonely life with no hope of betterment.—*Male, married, age 79.*

I was very lonely at first but kept so busy during the days that it was only in the evenings that I was depressed. Got a young cat, and believe it or not, he has helped a lot! So glad to welcome me home.—*Female, single, age 80.*

. . . I spent a great deal of time planning activities that would be suitable for an old woman. But there has never been a lonely moment—perhaps because my friends were (and are) kind, but also, I think, because I had provided myself with good books, periodicals, phonograph records, puzzles, games like the Saturday Review double crostics. Among books dictionaries (English and foreign languages) are invaluable.—*Female, single, age 85.*

Change of Status.
Loneliness is hard to bear but usually not blamed on others, whereas frequently, but not always, a change of status—real or imaginary—is resented as caused by the inconsiderate, the patronizing, or the unwise attitudes of past colleagues, new acquaintances, or that catch-all of all evil, the "young." Sometimes a sense of uselessness is not the result of the opinion of others but of the feeling of guilt, or at least of uneasiness, in oneself. This was complained of particularly by the recently retired, and some described how this complex had either faded away or been mastered through the development of a more mature philosophy or through finding activities interesting in themselves and valuable to others. One of the "pet peeves" related to status is the euphemistic, often patronizing, language used concerning retired people. The phrases "senior citizen," "golden years," and their ilk appear to be particularly obnoxious. To me, they are trivially disgusting. But it is well to remember that the words "senior citizens" have become big business. Another source of anguish is the surprise retired persons encounter that they are still around or even alive. It is annoying to remain on the appeal but not on the invitation lists.

VOICES OF EXPERIENCE

"A workless worker in a world of work."—*Female, single, age 69.*

My greatest problem was a temporary one—that of adapting to the transition itself; i.e., shifting from a heavy-pressured, overly structured life to one of free form choices, and from a situation in which my usefulness was taken for granted both by others and myself, to one in which my usefulness demanded definition and appraisal.

. . . What proved most distressing was the ever present feeling of guilt which characterized those early weeks and months; the sense that I was wasting time and energy, that others were doing the work of the world all around me, and I alone was shirking. The effort to combat these feelings led to several initial volunteering ventures which were less than satisfying, but taught important lessons on what not to do. Time and experiences such as these did bring perspective, and made it possible eventually to move freely and with real enjoyment, but the early stages of my retirement experience, personal and individual though they may have been, were peculiarly painful, and of surprisingly long duration. . . .

I would urge that the prospective retiree plan ahead, so far as possible, in terms of what occupations he is retiring to. Ideally, make a choice beforehand, and even set a starting date. But even with these decisions made, allow for some transitional turbulence. Emotions are tricky parts of us, and they don't always give notice of their needs and plans!—*Female, single, age 74.*

. . . After a lengthy career in education, government and foundation work, I found it hard to accept the situation of not being needed. . . .

A concomitant of the first problem was another: that when I had something which seemed to me to be a valuable contribution, I had no effective outlet which would put my ideas into practice.

. . . It is very easy to fritter away hours and days without accomplishing anything which is satisfactory to oneself. By this I do not mean that one should always devote oneself to the highest pursuits. Playing music with friends who are also amateurs can be very satisfying, but it requires self-discipline to practice, to rehearse, and to arrange times for meeting. If left completely to impulse, nothing happens.

On the other hand a rigid schedule is merely a reversion to pre-retirement days and can produce the same symptoms of regimentation as occured at that time.—*Male, married, age 68.*

The discovery that nothing any longer depended on me for its success or even its continuation. This was not a sudden, but a dawning discovery. The

family no longer depended on me for making a living; it was—thanks to TIAA and CREF—already made. No students depended on me for instruction. No university depended on me for guidance. It did not matter whether I was a success or not, what did matter was that carrying such responsibility over so many years made it a part of my personal "life-support system." Of course, it is a trite discovery, but like most of the great facts of life, it had little genuine reality until it happened to me. It is not an experience that can be learned vicariously.

Retirement suddenly withdraws one from a role of responsibility to one of non-responsibility, from activities useful to others, on which society places great value, to the "hobby," leisure time activities which serve only oneself—golf, gardening, fishing, furniture-refinishing—on which society places a very low value. And, by comparison, such activities have no taste; they do not satisfy.

Recognition of this fact and adjustment to it is almost universal in retirement communities, and is among the most difficult problems. Its solution may require a fundamental modification of one's previous philosophy of life. Among these changes could be a more modest estimate of the role which an individual can or should play in the lives of others, a greater appreciation of the diversity of life from which can flow other kinds of satisfactions, a willingness to accept a kind of excommunication from the things from which one formerly derived satisfaction. . . .

Be prepared to relinquish one's position, status, influence and even one's views, gracefully. The world does not stand still and younger people have the same right to establish their relationship to it which you asserted for yourself.—*Male, married, age 69.*

Least: You'll laugh at this, I'm certain, but only after returning for a short luncheon visit did I realize my greatest need—I once took it for granted—and that is the constant love and support of a faculty and staff who gave me deep appreciation and respect.—*Female, single, age 68.*

. . . it seemed to me that what I did or did not do was of significance to other people—and therefore that it really mattered where I chose a wise course in a particular situation and whether I did or did not do my job well. Once I had retired, it suddenly seemed not to make any difference to anyone (except, of course, my immediate family) what I did or thought, or indeed whether I did anything at all. This came as something of a shock that gave me a feeling of futility associated with retirement.

. . . Gradually, I found that it was pleasant to work under conditions of less strain and with more leisure time to pursue other interests, than I had known in the past. These leisure interests involved some lecturing and work in my own professional field along with a "branching out" into other activities, e.g., assistance to refugees, travel, and travelogues at schools, churches and

retirement homes, research in local history and landscape work around my house.

These leisure pursuits were satisfying to me, partly because I enjoyed them in themselves and partly because it seemed to me that many of these leisure activities were meaningful to others besides myself.—*Male, married, age 67.*

The aspects I like the least can be put in one sentence: I miss so much being a part of the mainstream. Sometimes I wonder if the one who wrote "Grow old along with me, the best is yet to be" had arrived at that point.—*Female, married, age 65.*

Forget your previous status, and be open to new possibilities where your status, degrees, etc., don't matter.—*Male, married, age 69.*

. . . Strenuous activity of a mental or argumentative nature is good but not too easy when retired. Most people will let the old bird have his views without argument. This amounts in another way to being put on the shelf.—*Male, married, age 73.*

. . . did not fully realize the impact of losing status (as teacher, director and actress). Here, I was merely my daughter's mother.—*Female, single, age 64.*

. . . (We have been accustomed, unconsciously perhaps, to the Orientals' attitude of respect toward age. They value the "elder statesmen," they consider the eldest the head of the family.) It seems to us that many retired people live—physically and psychologically—in a world of their own. Younger people have either encouraged or accepted this attitude, so that it is being built more and more firmly into our social thinking. Older people are politely, and with relief perhaps, relegated to this "other-worldliness"— often self-centered, almost always non-productive, and without the real respect of the younger, productive group. My husband and I are trying not to be swept into this backwater, even though it is alluring in many ways.— *Female, married, age 69.*

There is a disturbing feeling, in my case, that my occupational group, the local immediate one, continues without much sense of loss in my retirement. They are busy professionals, of course, and have no time for pure sentiment.—*Male, single, age 71.*

As you get older people tend to call on you less and less for advice and help. Finally some of them seem to be asking, "What! Are you still here?"—*Male, married, age 79.*

Retirees in this community are too often considered extra baggage; e.g., two questions I am constantly asked are (1) "How do you fill up your time?" and (2) "When are you going to Florida (or Europe)?" This is an aspect of retirement which is disagreeable.—*Male, married, age 70.*

Also, in our youth-oriented culture, I find it very irritating to be talked down to by a variety of people from receptionists to physicians.—*Female, single, age 73.*

Problem:
Childish or absurd entertainment considered suitable for the senile.—*Female, —, age 81.*

Community benevolence and disposition to segregate by age—canting talk about "senior citizens."
Unsolicited and unwanted altruistic interference.—*Female, married, age 72.*

The least:
1. Being called a senior citizen.
2. No chance for attending a convention with expenses paid.—*Male, married, age 68.*

The aspects I like least:
1. The daily reminder by post, Insurance Companies, and news media of the forlorn and pitiful state of retirement.—*Female, widow, age 77.*

Freedom and Boredom.

> *Regained his freedom with a sigh.*
> *–Byron, "The Prisoner of Chillon."*

It takes a great deal of self-discipline not to be bored by freedom. The work of most faculty members is interesting, strenuous, and time-consuming. They know it is useful. If it is a relief not to work so hard and to have a reasonable amount of free time, it is difficult to find an occupation as interesting as teaching and research or as rewarding through a sense of accomplishment. The result can be an uncomfortable lack of direction and boredom. It is sometimes difficult to distinguish between those who feel the loss of status when they lose the job and those who miss the work for its own sake. During most of my life when bored, it has been chiefly either by inactivity or by certain kinds of people. I am surprised to find how few reported the second of these causes. It, perhaps, is not surprising that boredom, especially im-

mediately after retiring, was more frequently reported by the obviously energetic than by those whose physical condition precluded much activity. Perhaps I should have placed, along with the quotation from Byron, a statement of a man, age 72, who wrote concerning retirement, "If you are lazy, its good. If not, Blooey."

VOICES OF EXPERIENCE

Like most—freedom.
Like least—the loss of being a part of a team in a useful project.—*Male, married, age 74.*

Being in perfect health, I resent retirement and the "loafing"—my previous work can only be done in college or a university and at 65 years no one wants you.—*Male, married, age 67.*

I like most the freedom I have to pursue my interests.
I like least the lack of stimulus to make the most of my time.—*Male, married, age 70.*

. . . I missed the pressure of deadlines to meet, did not take easily to leisure and had a guilty feeling when I "wasted" time. There was still plenty to do but no time limit.
I expected this but it has taken longer than I thought to adjust to it.—*Female, single, age 70.*

The unscheduled life, denied me for so many years, is such a sheer joy to me (even after two years) that I really revel in it! For there is time at last to watch the flowers grow, to observe the goings-on in the world about me—and to read about them too—to go to museums, to attend concerts and lectures at the college in our town—to take courses at adult night school which have nothing to do with music—even to go to church now and then. . . .
. . . For my own satisfaction, apparently, I cannot lead a totally unscheduled life—enjoy it though I may. Retirement removed the necessity, and I shall have to restore it—a psychological one.
I may be mistaken, but I should suspect a good many retirees have, or come to have, the same mixed feelings about their lives as I have described—that is, if they have no regular working hours, and are in effect, "living the life of leisure." I should suggest, therefore, that they devise a self-imposed framework for their lives—a much restricted and less rigid one than their full-time job required, of course—but still a recognizable framework.—*Female, single, age 67.*

Probably the thing that I miss most is (or are) my captive audiences. Very ego-nourishing to have 50-60 people listening to me for 50 minutes at a stretch, six or nine times a week. No replacement for this.

On the other hand, it is wonderful to be able to thumb my nose at the alarm clock. And it is sheer joy to know that I will no longer have to:

(a) Make up examinations, with original questions.

(b) Grade them (or instruct my graders, and verify the grading).

(c) Sit in judgment on the poor devils who (for example) will be barred from medical school if I give them the low grades they deserve—but will make very poor doctors if I am too generous with them.—*Male, married, age 71.*

. . . I and others seem to think retirement meant unlimited time. Thus the first year, and well into the second, was filled with meetings. Volunteer work and attendance at a few classes depleted all my energy and time. Perhaps fear of boredom entered into this rushing about initially instead of a realistic selection of interest which gradually followed.—*Female, single, age 71.*

The least? Boredom, few contacts such as you have when working. Walking for exercise. Pointless striving, to hell with golf, and bridge. When you retire you begin to get the idea of how very transitory and brief the whole sojourn through life really is; therefore some personalized philosophy is in order. Seek beauty, comfort, be kind (feed the birds) etc. Look for God in all things.—*Male, married, age* —.

Boredom. Took a couple of volunteer jobs, but find them both dull and uninspiring. . . . There is a pervading sense of uselessness.—*Female, widow, age 68.*

I expected to be bored. I don't know whether I would have been or not, because I desperately avoided the problem by working ever since. I am 75 and still working. But I am getting bored with working. So next year I think I will stop teaching and see if retirement bores me.—*Male, married, age 75.*

I suppose the aspects of retirement I like the best are the freedom to go and come as I please—travel when I care to and, as they say, "take life easy." None of this really interests me a great deal. So the aspect I like the least is simply too much idle time on my hands.—*Male, widower, age 75.*

Too much time on my hands as I am getting elderly.

Bored some of the time. Lonely.—*Male, widower, age 83.*

. . . it was good to be free to sleep in if I wanted to (which I don't do now that I could).—*Male, married, age 71.*

I do like the unlimited leisure—a lessening of pressure—but sometimes the leisure is too much.—*Female, single, age 74.*

Miscellany.

It would be as hopeless to try to list all the complaints of the aged, including being classified as aged, as those of any other section of mankind. A few quotes are given below, chosen because they are well-stated, humorous, or typical (as in the case of men's dislike of household chores) of a number of responses.

VOICES OF EXPERIENCE

I expected to find time on my hands. This has not been so.
I thought my wife would dislike having me "under foot." This has not happened.
I wondered if my neighbors would act differently. This seems not to be.
Minuses:
Fear (mild) of future infirmities.
Need to keep weight under control (and that's no joke!).—*Male, married, age 63.*

If I had to pick on something I like least it would be the absence of the best and most efficient secretary anyone ever had. For one thing, she could deal with questionnaires like this without ever showing them to me.—*Male, married, age 72.*

The least—maintenance jobs about the house, for which I have too little "know how" and skill.—*Male, married, age 69.*

These I like the least: Mowing lawn, pulling weeds, killing bugs and washing windows.—*Male, married, age 69.*

The aspect I like the least? Well, I guess I would have to say: there's no future in it!—*Male, married, age 72.*

(Least)
The attempt by "well wishers" to turn over all committee work and offices in various organizations because "Now that you have nothing to do."—*Female, single, age 80.*

Aspects I like least:
1. So much advice from friends who believe they have just the right place for me to live and to join.
2. High rent and drug bills.
3. High cost of living, in general.
4. Loads of junk mail.—*Female, widow, age 73.*

The main problem I face is constant harrassment from salesmen—someone always wanting to sell you something like a new roof—siding—cars, etc. Magazine and book salesmen—they call only on retirees.

You have to use firm but polite answers to these pests.—*Male, single, age 65.*

Increased trivia of bookkeeping caused by the de-personalizing, dehumanizing practices of our machine-controlled economy. The individual retiree cannot solve this problem, which is a major one.—*Female, married, age 72.*

. . . I find confusion in high places to be one of the most upsetting aspects of modern day living. There is little respect for authority, dress is horrible. Young people think they know everything and many of them are disillusioned and drug users. Persons in authority capitulate to their ridiculous demands and instead of being guided by the wisdom learned from the past, we hurry on to use temporary palliatives to appease the furor of large groups. I seek in my old age dignity, decency, respect, love and understanding and I detest violence, hate, and all false pretences. So, I am pleased to enter a new world where I can seek these values.—*Male, married, age 68.*

You have asked enough questions!
What do you think we want to do with our time? Write essays?—*Male, widower, age 75.*

Chapter 11: Special Situations and Problems

We have described some situations and problems under such headings as Where to Live, Health, and Finances, but the variety of human experience is not readily classified. Besides the topics already discussed, there are a few that arise with considerable frequency—for example, transportation, the new-found opportunity to sleep late, the necessity of caring for sick friends or relatives, and, of course, questionnaires.

Transportation presents serious problems to those who have become too old to drive at night, in the winter, or at all, or who have never driven. One woman declared, "When I am born again, I plan to learn to drive first thing." Others found taxis expensive and buses inconvenient or nonexistent and were naturally reluctant to impose on friends or relatives. The absence of sidewalks in certain residential areas cause special concern both for the elderly and for children. On the other hand, retirement has eased the burden of commuting for a good many persons—one, at least, having found this the best aspect of retirement. There was one man who gloated over the fact that his car was a 1947 model. I presume depreciation has by now changed to appreciation. Transportation difficulties include those of getting meals brought in.

I like the attitude of the resolute woman who said: "I get up at 8:05 a.m.! For twenty-nine years I had to be at work at 8:00 a.m. So I deliberately rest until 8:05!"; and I have a fellow feeling for the man who enjoyed not only sleeping late when he wanted to, but also

shaving less frequently. One man found that his wife wished that he had an eight-o'clock; while another who was happy not to have to make a schedule still said "we have our traces tight." This is matched by the man who longed for "the harness."

There were a great many, besides those who cared for an invalid husband or wife, who cared for some other relative—sometimes a parent or a sister. These persons rarely complained but they did recognize the sacrifice in freedom, and sometimes of money, that was involved. One had her mother, age 101, as a beneficiary of a life insurance policy. A widow lowered her medical expenses by being a guinea pig. Another annuitant wished there were prescribed vacations. Furthermore, we were warned not to "fall into the habit of starting the day late."

One problem that was reported more frequently than I anticipated was the difficulty of adjusting to retirement in a country different than one had been in during one's active career. This sometimes was the result of returning to the homeland of a man or of his wife after teaching in this country. Even the man who was in love with Mexico in general and Guadalajara in particular warned not to plan to live there "unless you have lots of patience. When the tailor says you can have the suit he made for you, he normally doesn't say which week. May take 30 minutes to cash a check. Customs are different—learn to enjoy them."

More than one person mentioned the difficulties of understanding foreign tax regulations. However, some of those living in the United States found that tax regulations and keeping wills up-to-date may pose difficulties.

It was suggested that a special survey of annuitants with foreign residences would be of interest.

A traumatic experience that at least two respondents have faced is eviction: one, twice within twenty months; the other, at the time of retirement from a home where they had lived for 30 years to make way for a freeway. Akin to this was the loss of much personal property and great damage to the home caused by a flood—her advice: "Do save for a rainy day."

The freedom to express personal opinions without institutional responsibility was appreciated by at least one person and presumably by a good many others.

Perhaps this is the best place to make one comment: The most quoted lines of poetry among the replies are:

Grow old along with me; the best is yet to be,
The last of life for which the first was made.

This was quoted with approval by a woman who had recently attended the fiftieth reunion of her class at Wellesley and reported cheerfully concerning her classmates. One man, age 78, however, said, it "is bunk, or at least wishful thinking"; while another demanded with indignation to know how old Browning was when he wrote "Rabbi Ben Ezra." (He was about 52 when it was published.) It was an annuitant, age 97, who said he had no problems but did have "more leisure time to write."

One man was prepared for leisure time since, as a younger man, he had taught classes in its use; and another, by growing up "in a Border State where there is a tradition of leisure."

Some of the foregoing are illustrated, and other subjects are added in the quotations which follow.

VOICES OF EXPERIENCE

How to insure adequate transportation. This problem has not been solved to my satisfaction. I depend on buses, and taxis, and, of course, on relatives and friends. My relatives and friends have been kind, but I don't want to impose.—*Female, single, age 71.*

Like least: . . .spending so much time on voluntary jobs. I once read something that applies to me: "The big trouble with your leisure time is keeping other people from using it." (Like this questionnaire, which took a lot of time! But don't misunderstand me. I don't resent it a bit.)—*Female, single, age 76.*

. . . My older friends who are unable to drive have trouble finding someone to take them to doctors, etc., also the ones who live alone have meals that are not well balanced; often settle for cereal, soup, or a sandwich with tea.

Not driving to work when snow is deep is best aspect.—*Female, married, age 66.*

No 7:00 or 8:00 A.M. classes to meet. "Oh! how I hate to get up in the morning." Doing things now, that I wanted to do for 30 years, matching wits with three year olds for instance. These I like.—*Male, married, age 78.*

. . . I especially enjoy the freedom from schedule—being able to sit up and read till three and sleep till noon, to shop at leisure, to take off for several days on a trip, to do nothing at all.—*Female, single, age 69.*

[Problem] Adjusting to irregular hours.—*Female, single, age 65.*

[Like least] The amount of time and energy expended to aid spouse's mother and aunt to change from independent living to two separate retirement homes in different geographical areas, as well as expense to us.—*Male, married, age 70.*

Sickness and disability—you think you have enough saved and something comes along and you can spend $10,000 in six months: for instance, I have a brother who is a paraplegic and has been for almost 20 years. I have no luxuries and practically do without necessities to help my brother.

When there are six children you have little chance to save for retirement. Now eighteen grandchildren and four great grandchildren.—*Female, married, age 68.*

Main Problem: An invalid, widowed sister whose husband died very suddenly of a heart attack, or coronary, just before I retired. I have had the main responsibility for managing her business affairs, with Power of Attorney, for the duration of her widowhood. She has asthma, emphysema, etc., and has been in an excellent but expensive nursing home (about $665 per month) since September 15, 1968—except for a policy-required annual absence of at least 60 days; I have cared for her each summer from 63 to 73 days until this past summer when the explosive noises, the drilling, and the continuous dust from the urban renewal projects completely surrounding my place of residence made this vicinity impossible for my sister's lung condition. Her insurance was cut off last September; but after I wrote countless letters, etc., the insurance was finally paid up through January 31, 1972. Since then, she has had no insurance, but I am still waging a battle to collect. I had complete care of her from the summer of 1966 until September 15, 1968, when she went to a nursing home. Of course I am still responsible for all her expenses, her clothing, etc.

By March 1971, I was in the intensive coronary care unit of an excellent hospital: angina. But with medication, I am doing quite well now. My family know nothing about my angina.—*Female, single, age 77.*

. . . Not having any children of our own (our son was lost in World War II) we have aided our numerous nephews and nieces on both sides to send their sons and daughters to college, and have made gifts to our Alma Mater [and to other major universities]. We plan to increase our gifts in the future.—*Male, married, age 76.*

. . . This [invalidism of husband] meant I had to maintain a home and educate my girls alone. This added burden no doubt, was the cause of a stroke [at age 67]. We were left with no income except what I could earn, or which I

had saved during my employment. The dependability of TIAA and CREF, as well as regular payments from Social Security, have assured my survival. Frankly I have not enjoyed retirement. I was very happy in my work, I miss the association with professional teachers. It has been hard to find a real purpose in life after the previous heavy demands. My physical and mental restrictions, of course, account for much of this feeling.

All of these unusual circumstances, make my experiences a poor addition to a survey—but I am glad to make the effort to grant your request, since I am most appreciative of your help to me.—*Female, widow, age 79.*

I feel that I am not in a position to give advice to future retirees, for my husband and I faced problems which persons who have spent their working lives in the U.S.A. probably would not. Our careers were spent in the Near East Colleges so that retiring in the U.S.A. first of all presented the problem of deciding where to locate. The first year was spent visiting the East coast as well as the West, and finally settling in the Middle West where my husband's boyhood home was located. I believe it is helpful to have one's roots somewhere among former friends.

We decided upon a rural community in order that my husband might pursue his agricultural hobby of raising trees and landscaping.

Securing labor for landscaping almost impossible.

Provincialism of community not expected—uphill task to widen their horizons. . . .

Aspect—disliked most:

The attitude of people that retirement means being placed on the shelf, in spite of the fact that we spent our lives working with young people overseas and had much to offer.—*Female, widow, age 77.*

. . . No matter how reasonable are the present provisions, we spend much time worrying about taxation, inflation, sickness and crime. If I have too much leisure time, my worries increase. If I apportion my work badly, my worries also increase. If I cannot find anything to worry about, I begin to wonder what is wrong. These things occurred long before retirement; they merely became more acute with age.—*Male, widower, age 76.*

. . . Frankly, my classroom teaching—in which I have taught more than 8000 students in the one university where I worked—has been my most satisfactory reward. When I look back in retrospection, I am proud that some little part of my life has gone into the careers of those whom I have instructed. Today, many of my former students stand high in positions of respect and honor, and commencements are times when I am told that I have contributed to their successes.—*Male, married, age 75.*

Be sure to have been born enough years ago to have lived through—and remember—the "Depression." It was of great help in planning for retirement.—*Male, married, age 72.*

I like the freedom of retirement. I am slow as hell and always have been. Now I have no one to push me except my wife but she is coming around to my speed and may surpass me in this respect.—*Male, married, age 70.*

Do have a very definite and formulated program to increase your options in life after retirement. We have noted so many retired colleagues who limited their options on retiring—curtailed them—with subsequent rapid deterioration and a spiraling diminution of options and interest in life. Sad.

For instance, we live in Southern California. On retirement we first got a beach trailer. This sold at a profit, by which we bought a beach apartment. Similarly on selling this at a profit we bought an Hawaiian apartment—and now have two apartments on Maui. They give good income and provide us with the "need" of checking them for a couple of months twice a year in the off-rental seasons. In the meantime we have built a high desert "Den." All of which, together with travel (61 countries past 15 years), keep us very active.

We design and build much of our own furniture, and practically all household maintenance and repair we do ourselves. It helps us make a house into a home.

Maybe pre-retirees should have a course in "domestic mechanics!"—*Male, married, age 77.*

Our children had warned us against accumulation, and that we needed to sort and discard as we went along. We never seemed to "find the time" for it! We allowed a few weeks for it—and nothing could have been more foolish or bewildering. We could not afford to move it all. Time ran out. We shipped a great deal of personal memorabilia—letters, pictures, records, etc., irreplaceable—giving up furniture, precious books and phonograph records to reduce weight. As we have been traveling, we still have the problem of sorting, reducing and organizing what remains of our last twenty years of family life and planning for its ultimate disposal.—*Female, married, age 69.*

One completely unanticipated problem of retirement was the sudden appearance of a starving, handicapped kitten, eating birdseed in our back yard. Now, four years later, she is a member of the family, and "cat-sitting" as well as house-sitting (or rental) is a problem whenever we leave home.—*Male, married, age 79.*

We really have a ball until we get pooped out.—*Male, married, age 73.*

Chapter 12: TIAA and the Questionnaire

In spite of the fact that there was no request in the questionnaire that annuitants comment upon TIAA and CREF, many did so. There was a great deal of praise, but also some complaints. Suggestions were numerous.

The praise was more concerning the quality of the service than the amounts of annuities, although some, especially those who had made considerable contributions, found the financial aspects most rewarding. The promptness of payments often received favorable comment, along with "Knowing that all I had to do was to live" for the payments to continue. The advice and information given by TIAA was considered excellent, especially when compared to what some recipients received within their own institutions. Evidently, a very favorable impression has been made by the uniform courtesy of TIAA-CREF.

As the analysis given elsewhere shows, for the respondents as a whole, the annuity from TIAA-CREF was not usually the chief source of income but, when combined with Social Security and other annuities (presumably in most cases derived from retirement systems other than TIAA), formed the basic support of most of the respondents and, for most persons who had spent the greater part of their careers in institutions with retirement provisions using TIAA-CREF annuities, these annuities along with Social Security were the chief source of post-retirement income. Clearly, therefore, the provisions for retirement annuities based on employment and Social Security

should be planned so as to provide reasonably adequate incomes. This will not be the case if any large portion of such income is forfeited through lack of vesting provisions in any of the systems under which a person works, or if too long a waiting period is imposed before contributions to the retirement plan begin. This is particularly true if a person has moved several times to places with required initial uncovered periods. Several persons complained of suffering from such delays in coverage, and in some cases blamed it on TIAA rather than—as they should have—upon decisions made in their own institutions.

The opportunity to invest in CREF was greatly appreciated. I think it would still be—even with the lower level in the stock market—though possibly with slightly less ardor. Some expressed the wish that CREF had come into being sooner, or that the individual had learned about it earlier. One person recognized that "CREF is being widely imitated and many faculty members don't really understand and appreciate what a wonderful development that was by TIAA." Perhaps few realize that variable annuities are now offered by many life insurance companies and form a multibillion-dollar business. Although many companies are making more frequent variations, up and down, in the annuity payments, the basic ideas worked out by CREF are unaltered.

The suggestions volunteered for changes of policies and practices on the part of TIAA-CREF ranged from wishful thinking, such as "raise the value of TIAA and CREF twenty or thirty percent," to making sure that everyone knows that if they leave an institution with a TIAA plan they may still contribute to the annuity on a personal basis.

There is still the problem of getting advice and information about pensions and financial matters. Even if in some cases it stems from lack of curiosity on the part of individuals during their more active years, it is real. The paucity of the information obtainable (or at least obtained within the colleges and universities) led to various suggestions, e.g., earlier and more adequate information on taxes. There were also requests for giving information which, in fact, is already being furnished. More than one person suggested that TIAA establish regional offices, largely for advising on retirement and insurance matters. Having experienced on a large campus how many more people will seek advice if it is available in the same or a nearby building than if a few hundred yards away, I doubt that regional

offices would materially improve a service already recognized as excellent.

Quite a few realized that it was the employing institution which should have informed them about the retirement plan with TIAA and that it was the college which determined the amount contributed and therefore almost directly the amount of the annuity. Many, although blaming no one, pointed out that inflation had eroded the true value of the annuities based on contributions made years ago; and at least one liked the formula plan of the state he served better than the TIAA plan.

There were suggestions for additional services which the retirees believed should be established or encouraged by TIAA, such as housing specially planned for retired college teachers or meal services for the elderly.

Very few expressed anger at TIAA; however, one man, who after shifting his CREF funds to TIAA was not allowed to shift some of them back, wrote, "I suspect that bureaucrats have one trait in common with dictators—the propensity to use straight-jackets," and another revealed a false belief concerning TIAA by writing "I do not think companies like yours should give out lists of retired persons."

There are those who do not like questionnaires. In many cases they made an exception of this one. This was not always done, especially if the recipient felt that the questions concerning finances were "an invasion of privacy." Kindly feeling towards TIAA was the reason for some answers, e.g., "You are a good outfit so I'll comply." TIAA-CREF was frequently complimented on making this study for "the study is a wise one and may be helpful." It was made clear that a report on the study was desired by those who answered. A number spoke of the amount of help the questionnaire had been to them in making them analyze their own situations; and it was suggested that a prospective filling-out of the questionnaire would be useful to those nearing retirement and perhaps also a "challenge." The questionnaire is given as Appendix 2.

VOICES OF EXPERIENCE

... I can remember very well my deep resentment when I was forced to enter TIAA at the age of thirty and how silly I thought it was. Now it is the very fine frosting on my cake. It is my TIAA income which makes my life

very pleasant in retirement. I urge all my young friends to undertake an annuity plan very early. I consider it essential for a happy retirement.—*Female, single, age 69.*

I think your people have done a great job in both TIAA and CREF.

Having been a broker, I have always looked askance at investing in bonds. To me that was why most widows ended up broke. Inflation took over. Your CREF came along just in time for me. I would have put all my program into CREF if I could have with a "good as cash" cushion to tide over a year or two.—*Male, married, age 70.*

As indicated earlier, I should have just kept up at least a minimum monthly payment to TIAA—the best retirement program for teachers.—*Female, widow, age 68.*

The pension from you people has been the difference between selling our home and staying in a home we worked so long and hard for.—*Male, married, age 70.*

Owning TIAA-CREF annuities affords me a certain peace of mind.—*Female, single, age 68.*

Establish a series of non-profit retirement centers in Florida, Texas, Arizona, California—consider Mexico, on one of the Caribbean Islands, also England, Italy or Spain, also Vermont, New Hampshire, with the right to change from one to the other.

Each center should be made up of cottages, living room, bedroom, bath and kitchenette, complete maid service, dining room, store to buy supplies, medical center and recreation center, office, open once a week to cash checks, bus service to churches. Check existing successful center sponsored by churches, unions, etc.

Offer advice—service of investments.

Offer advice—service in how to prepare wills and set up trusts, etc., when one becomes unable to handle finances.

In other words expand beyond the usual activities of an insurance [company].

TIAA should follow Federal legislation of interest to retirees and inform them through newsletter, also developments in medicine of interest.

How about auto insurance where insurance company has cancelled because over 65.—*Male, married, age 81.*

If the retirement system had been explained to me from the outset I would have put in three times the amount I had withheld each pay period. This way the retirement income would have been a bit more worth-while. There are so many aspects of the TIAA-CREF plans that are not understood by the

Faculty or by the Staff at this particular University. No one in the departments responsible for the system seems to know exactly the answers to the many questions we have asked them. I do think it a very good way to provide for retirement—especially if the monthly input is sufficient.—*Female, married, age 67.*

Contribute as much as possible, as soon as long as possible to TIAA and CREF—over and above funds or matched contributions by your employers. . . . TIAA and CREF should emphasize and clarify this option in more detail. Be sure you understand tax options on annuity incomes. TIAA and CREF should revise and clarify their literature on this subject, using an absolute minimum of legal jargon.—*Male, widower, age 75.*

(This questionnaire asks many questions about income, but none about expenses!)—*Male, married, age 67.*

Sorry to be so prolix, but you asked for it.—*Female, married, age 75.*

You manage superbly. Thank you!—*Male, married, age 75.*

STATISTICAL NOTE

• A common characteristic of the respondents was their participation in the TIAA-CREF retirement system and receipt of income from TIAA-CREF annuities.

• All the respondents were currently receiving income from TIAA whereas 55 percent of the respondents reported current income from CREF. Those not reporting CREF annuity income may never have had the opportunity to participate through their institution in the CREF program.

• Respondents reported receiving income from TIAA and CREF annuities in monthly amounts ranging from under $10 to more than $1500. Variations in the amounts depended mainly on the following factors: length of the pay-in period, salary level during the pay-in period, the contribution rate(s) under which premium payments were made, the annuity income option selected, sex, and the participant's age when annuity income was begun.

• Retirement fund payments to TIAA-CREF were contributed on behalf of some respondents for a long period, for others for just a short time. In general, men reported longer retirement fund payment periods than did women. The median time for men was 15 years, and for women it was 11 years.

• Forty-three percent of the respondents selected a single-life income option for their TIAA annuity, i.e., an annuity terminating at the death of the annuitant or continuing after death to the expiration of a guaranteed period. Fifty-four percent of the respondents chose a survivor option for their TIAA annuity, i.e., the annuitant and his or her spouse (or other second annuitant) both receive a lifetime income. Three percent of the respondents did not indicate the income option they had selected. Seventy-one percent of the men and 28 percent of the women chose a survivor option, reflecting the higher proportion of men who were married. However, 20 percent of the married men and 41 percent of the married women selected a single-life annuity, which would give a higher regular payment from the same original accumulation than would a survivor annuity. Also, 4 percent of the single men and 16 percent of the single women selected a survivor option.

• Twenty-six percent of the respondents began receiving income from their TIAA-CREF annuities at age 65, 17 percent started their annuities when younger than 65, and 50 percent said they were older than 65 when they began their annuities. Seven percent of the respondents did not report their age at the time they began to receive TIAA-CREF annuity income. Women and the retired clerical-service group reported generally younger ages at which they began TIAA-CREF annuities than did men and the retired faculty-administrator group.

Chapter 13: And They Gave Advice

Just as the situations that retirees are in defy classification, so too, although much advice falls into patterns, there are many points both well-taken and well-put that are more the expressions of individuality than of general counsel. Sometimes even a rather short dictum reveals a good deal about the writer, for instance, "Get a dog or cat or someone dependent on you"; or "Keep your hair dyed—whether people admit it or not, people don't like grey hair"; or, again, "It is never too late to learn another foreign language."

Advice cannot always be separated from a description of what one does since example is the elder sister of precept. Many who were willing to write about their experiences were reluctant to give advice, one having "never felt like a Solomon" and others believing that people differed too much to make advice worthwhile, except one said to have a "central purpose." It was frequently stated that any useful advice, especially about saving money and developing hobbies, should be addressed to those who still have many years of active service before retirement. We were also warned it was useless to advise a professor. A psychologist pled retirement as a good excuse for no longer giving advice. There were those who were more willing to help guide society than to advise individuals. They wanted laws to ban employment discrimination on the basis of age, or special provisions to facilitate the finding of work by the elderly. Some declared that all medical expenses should be tax deductible for the retired.

Much advice is devoted to pre-retirement planning, not only con-

cerning finances but also about activities, where to live, etc. Some of this appears in other chapters. The length of time ahead when planning should be done was stipulated: "At least three years before retirement plans should be made and a monthly budget prepared"; "Begin to plan approximately ten years before retirement." Some extended the period to forty years, while one said, "Be sure to plan ahead at time of very first paycheck."

Many persons of course wrote about organizations to which they belonged. The national association serving exclusively the elderly most frequently mentioned is the American Association of Retired Persons. The comments were favorable.

A number, particularly women, stressed appearance. The windup of some very extensive advice was: "Brush up 1) hobbies, 2) old interests, 3) your figure, and 4) sense of personal worth." The only one underlined was 3). Another, "Continue to dress well—look sharp!—Have fun, but don't be a silly ole fool!!"

The concern for having wills and other business documents in order is inextricably connected with the attitude towards death. In addition to the impact of religion on the idea of death, several changes occur with age that bear on the subject. I mention two. Although a large proportion of people say they are content with retirement, many even declaring it the best period of their lives, no respondent said that his retirement years would improve as they go along. This makes death seem less grim in comparison with life; and it is clear that a few, but very few, had reached the point where it would be welcome. The other marked change that comes with years is that, whereas people in middle life recognize that death would be not only a bereavement to those they love but also an added burden, one sees in later years that the second aspect has diminished and that, when one dies, sorrow might be accompanied by easing of responsibility on the part of others. Thus there was a great deal of emphasis on having one's affairs in order and then being unworried, even carefree. "Get your financial and personal affairs in apple-pie order so that if and when you become ill, or pass away, you won't leave a mess for someone to attend to. Once this is done, ENJOY LIFE ANY WAY YOU WANT TO!!" Another in the same vein: "Don't: Be afraid of death; have your affairs in good order for your passing and then go ahead with life." Although one declared that getting older beats dying, another recommended dying between 70 and 75 and referred to that early actuarial table, Psalm 90, verse 10. Another light-heartedly

recommended euthanasia as a means of easing medical expenses, but added "it will be harder to legalize than even abortion."

There were other topics that attracted a good deal of attention: the general attitude towards retirement; having or developing an open mind and, akin to this, keeping a sense of humor; budgets—along with the virtues of spending or skimping; and a good many remarks about not taking or not giving advice.

One woman, after advising to stop "keeping up with the Joneses," wrote re retirement: "Don't fear it—don't fend it off—enjoy it. There is much to enjoy, and you'll find much that still needs to be done. Find it, choose it, and do it with zest and a willing heart." A different woman gave the assurance that even the few who dislike retirement soon get over it. We are reassured by another "Retirement is totally a 'condition' of the mind. You've earned your reward—enjoy it."

Although there probably are some very earnest people with open minds, intellectual flexibility usually is associated with a sense of humor. It is true, of course, that some rigid people have a sharp wit. We got such advice as: "Stay loose and have fun. Don't spend all your time with other old people—the young are very worth watching!" "We are all funny if we'd only allow ourselves the luxury of laughing at the mirror image." A number picked up the fact that the questionnaire was printed on recycled paper, with such remarks as, "I feel recycled, too!" or "For recycled lives!" A good deal is summed up in the brief remark, "Don't get grumpy!"

Almost every quote given below was selected as meeting at least one of the following criteria; 1) it is a prototype; 2) or, contrariwise, it is strongly individual; 3) it is pithy or witty; and 4) it could easily be overlooked such as taking plenty of vitamins or organizing an address list.

VOICES OF EXPERIENCE

Some do's:

a. Analyze financial resources for retirement and understand thoroughly the benefits and options available. This should be done at least five years prior to anticipated date of retirement.

b. Have a specific or general idea as to how retirement years will be spent.

c. If possible, or feasible, work out a program with employer for semi-retirement a few years prior to anticipated or mandatory retirement date.

Some don'ts:

a. Retire prior to mandatory retirement date unless a specific program has been worked out for use of time.

b. Depend entirely on employment benefits as sole source of finances. Some savings should be accumulated to supplement retirement benefits.—*Male, married, age 67.*

Respond to the invitation, which you probably will receive, to attend occasional sessions of pre-retirement planning. I know that my professional organization (for retired teachers), of whose state board I am a member, holds an annual all-morning session on pre-retirement planning once a year, and the teachers who are nearing retirement flock into it.—*Female, single, age 80.*

A single person probably should find a friend with whom to live. Then the two could care for one another. People about to retire are often in vigorous health and they naturally plan for a healthy retirement. They should look way ahead to possible (probable) illness, eye trouble, inability to drive, or care for themselves—dismal as the prospect is! They should live a busy, active, happy life, as I am, while they are well, but they should plan for the probable inevitable sickness and incapacity which I have not done!—*Female, single, age 67.*

People approaching retirement should certainly plan for it, but they should not worry about it as much as many do. To them I would offer the advice of the well-known advertisement: "Try it—you'll like it."—*Male, married, age 70.*

And take care of one's appearance and one's clothes. How well it makes one feel to be complimented on the way one appears—even if the skin is wrinkled!—*Female, single, age 69.*

Make your will. If you have done so earlier, as you should have, see if it meets the present situation. If not, make a new will or a codicil to your present one. But it must be done by a lawyer.—*Male, married, age 76.*

Give your bank power of attorney to receive your Social Security, dividend, income checks. They will add them automatically without charge to your account. It will save a lot of time and worry.—*Male, married, age 71.*

Do clean out your drawers and closets—sort through your treasures and possessions—give away or dispose of those you really don't want. Decide to whom you will leave special items.

Do make a new up-to-date will—leave one copy with your lawyer and one in your own desk. See that all personal papers are in order (bank statements, securities, Social Security and Medicare records, income tax statements, etc. and etc.).—*Female, widow, age 70.*

If you know your faculties to be slipping don't wait too long to establish trusts and reliable management for your finances before you are too far gone to do it.—*Male, married, age 70.*

Be sure annuity income is planned to provide maximum income for spouse if you die first.—*Male, widower, age 75.*

. . . I wanted to live a little before I died a lot.—*Female, single, age 63.*

Retire with a comparatively new car.—*Female, widow, age 72.*

There must be something about yourself that you respect other than your income.—*Male, married, age 73.*

Don't follow anyone else's advice.
If you don't know your strengths and weaknesses by retirement, you are probably in for a bad time.
If you do, it's not so bad.—*Male, widower, age 74.*

. . . If a man reaches 65 or 70 and feels life is empty without work, his education has been faulty.—*Male, married, age 78.*

. . . I think that the person who stops learning stops living.—*Male, married, age 71.*

We need a different Ph.D. preparation program, one that puts the stress on imagination, innovation, discovery, critical analysis of the status quo. The aim should be to equip one for a life of continuing development so when reaching retirement age the person is more creative than at say, 30.—*Male, married, age 81.*

I am learning—organ, ceramics, sewing, Bible, etc.—*Female, widow, age 70.*

To have an open mind about the way things are done; to cooperate in making it a pleasant, attractive, active community [of elderly persons] and above all, to accept changes and avoid bickering.—*Female, married, age 73.*

Don't think of yourself as, nor confine yourself to, "Senior Citizens," "Golden Agers," "Geriatrics," or "Ancient Mariners." I realize that many

have no choice. But I suggest that contact with the age-range of the general community, as found in church, service-club, or similar organization, is helpful; and blessed indeed, if still possible, is contact with the young.— *Male, married, age 70.*

As you approach retirement, prepare to face it and to accept it with faith in God, with dignity, with gratitude, with courage, and also with a sense of humor!—*Female, married, age 79.*

. . . Make a budget so you know what you can afford and won't have to worry about living expenses. An extra fund set aside for "specials"—the fun kind—is a great help. I have a savings account that I don't count in my budget and use only for special things I want to do. It is a great morale booster.—*Female, single, age 70.*

I think a retired person should live up to his income. Some people have saved all their life and will continue to do it after retirement. We are frugal, not wasteful, and enjoy life with our neighbors and loved ones. We try to share what we have with others. We raise enough in our garden for three to four families—what we do not use, we give away to our neighbors. We live simply but "high on the hog."—*Male, single, age 76.*

Live simply, not lavishly, even if your income is large. You can devote the excess amount to good works of various kinds. But spend on the few things you find really important.—*Male, married, age 67.*

If you expect to write, don't wait till you are retired. Make your plans and collect materials while still on the job. Writing must not wait. It will never be easier.—*Male, married, age 72.*

If you must endure a Retirement Party or Dinner, make it an enjoyable one—help with the planning. Make sure the people you like are invited (some of mine were omitted by the Committee!).—*Male, married, age 71.*

I should have put more of my tennis years in golf.—*Female, single, age 74.*

Burn all credit cards if you have any and say "No" to all committees, etc., unless you like credit cards and committees. If so, its your own "look out."—*Male, married, age 61.*

Don't give your possessions to your children or to others until you are certain you will no longer need (or want) them for yourself.
. . . Read and carefully study the social security laws and their interpretations. Help is available, if you need it, at your local HEW office.—*Female, single, age 71.*

Use only your name—not titles.—*Male, married, age 68.*

Travel all you can possibly afford to do before you retire! My memories of trips abroad are a great resource since I feel I would not be discreet in going now!
Take good care of your eyes so that you can read—as much as I do!
I hope you've already achieved a sense of beauty—if you weren't blessed with it from childhood—it's everywhere!—*Female, single, age 83.*

Do live for the present to a reasonable extent. To save everything for retirement years may be too late!—*Male, married, age 68.*

The advice that I would like to give to anyone, middle age or older, who is looking to the day of his retirement is—Don't pass up all of the opportunities of the present to save for that grand and glorious day ahead. It may not be there when you turn in your keys for the last time. Save for a rainy day yes, but not everything, life is too uncertain.—*Male, widower, age 70.*

Do what you have wanted to do; if it's lawful. If it's just loafing, do so and don't feel guilty. Never mind about leaving the children anything. This can foul up your using money as you like. We save between trips; then blow it in a short time. Why build an estate as long as you can enjoy this looking at what God hath wrought. . . .
Learn to listen a little (dammit) pretend you are interested if you're not; he has a story too. Keep it light and funny even if your gut is hurting.—*Male, married, age —.*

Above all, keep in mind that life without a purpose is a pretty sure way to promote both physical and mental deterioration.—*Male, married, age 80.*

Don't get so stuck with Bridge day in and out that your world gets limited to that.—*Female, single, age 80.*

In these days when so many people need help, I find myself growing a bit impatient with older people who feel useless.—*Female, married, age 66.*

Don't make a fetish of being useful or needed.—*Male, married, age 67.*

I've learned to enjoy not having to do anything.
I've learned to hate being lazy—although I enjoy it.—*Female, single, age 67.*

While reserving the right to express opinions, remember that in these times older people should not aspire to public activities, e.g., elective offices,

advisory groups, etc. The day of the "elder statesman" is gone and attempts to counteract this trend will only cause hard feelings. [See Appendix 1 for opposite point of view.]—*Male, married, age 68.*

Don't depend only on reading, traveling and activities without responsibilities.—*Male, married, age 71.*

Do remember Parkinson's Law that "work may be expanded to fill any period of time allotted for its completion."—*Male, married, age 69.*

Leave stock market alone—use mutual funds rather—now such that charge no fee. Do not patronize any Mutual Fund that invests in tobacco, alcohol, or war material. There are such funds now that avoid these items. . . .
Do not let material success have first priority in your life. Human values are more important and giving them priority over everything else will make for real happiness and satisfaction.—*Male, married, age 81.*

Reduce the cocktail hour to a quarter-hour.
Find ways to be helpful to young people, but don't push.—*Male, widower, age 71.*

I found that continuing my daily association by going to the University Club for luncheon, playing billiards and keeping out of the house several hours a day provided the solution. [Much like me. MHI]—*Male, married, age 74.*

Take exercise every day. If you don't play golf or swim, at least walk as far as you can, as fast as you can, before breakfast (and before dinner if possible). . . .
Happiness is like a butterfly.
The more you chase it, the more it will elude you.
But if you turn your attention to other things,
It comes and softly sits on your shoulder.
—Beverly Sills . . .

If you are going to use any quotations, since so many of your members are, or have been, teachers, don't forget to remind them of Sir William Osler's . . .
"No bubble is so iridescent or floats longer than that blown by a successful teacher."—*Female, widow, age 69.*

. . . Try helping someone that you know that is trying to get to that point that you have just passed by. And you will find that you will enjoy your retirement more passionate.—*Female, widow, age 66.*

Napoleon, it is said, used to enquire of officers whose names had been submitted for promotion to field rank, "Is he lucky?" The answer to a similar question is just as good a basis for the prognosis of the outcome of one's retirement as it was for a successful military career under Napoleon. My best advice is "be lucky": in your investments, in your health, activities, and friends.—*Male, married, age 67.*

. . . don't discard too much of your library. Many books are difficult or impossible to replace, and they won't have your marginal notes.—*Male, married, age 70.*

Talking Books for the Blind and the Handicapped. Few people seem to understand that this wonderful service is for the Handicapped too. It costs absolutely nothing.—*Male, married, age 90.*

Keep your health and ride the wave!
And be a little frugal.—*Male, married, age 80.*

Almost each day, I ride a bicycle four miles (30 min) or walk two miles (30 min).—*Male, married, age 76.*

[Question 40c. "No money invested in real estate"] (except a cemetery lot!)—*Female, single, age 66.*

Don't deprive yourself of the things you need as you don't want to be the richest man in the cemetery.—*Male, married, age 69.*

Someone has said, "There are two kinds of fools: those who give advice and those who don't take it." Admitting my guilt, I offer the following.

Retirement is prepared for unwittingly long before the event (inherited outlook and character; up-bringing and circumstances; education and nature of career; managerial ability; inherited, acquired and accidental health; fortune; personality of spouse and fundamental character of marriage). These are such highly individualized factors, singly and in combination, that arbitrary advice on preparation for retirement has no place. The individual must have worked out his own destiny long before detailed decisions are to be made, and not on the basis of an arbitrary formula.

Hence, you can't reasonably or wisely volunteer advice to a prospective retiree. The fundamentals are already determined and what is left is application of the given to the opportunities available. Range of choice depends on breadth of outlook and variety of opportunities.

An example is that of the retiree (professor of music) who in exasperation exclaimed, "Do I have to do something?" He remarried, his new spouse was wealthy, and he had a happy and financially successful life in raising cattle.

To those anticipating retirement: Don't take advice (seriously), including this!—*Male, widower, age 77.*

The two quotations that follow contain interesting advice on many subjects and might be called "omnibus" or, to change the metaphor, "shotgun" advice. So might the final one.

1. Don't worry about it.
2. May as well relax and enjoy it.
3. Do not eat heavily.
4. Do not drink (liquor).
5. Get plenty of exercise in some manner. Don't overdo.
6. Realize the world can get along without you.
7. Keep weight to proper level.
8. Cuss the government and taxes.
9. All any old person has to do to get along is to keep his mouth shut and and have a good time.
10. Enjoy grandchildren if you have any.—*Male, married, age 68.*

1. Look forward to the time of retirement early in life and plan for it.
   a. Save part of your income.
   b. Invest some savings in (1) insurance or (2) real estate; insurance for protection, real estate for future financial security.
   c. Join the Social Security and Medicare program.
   d. Carry hospital and medical insurance for emergency protection.
2. Live right. Maintain Health.
   a. Eat a variety of wholesome foods.
   b. Drink clear, cold water.
   c. Hold weight near normal by controlling amount of food eaten.
   d. Drink no liquor of any kind.
   e. Do not smoke tobacco.
   f. Get regular exercise.
   g. Avoid extremes and excesses.
   h. Get enough sleep.
   i. Get frequent health check-ups.
3. Overcome worry.
   a. Make decisions and then carry through on them.
   b. Don't spend your life "stewing around in your own juice."
4. Don't retire.
   a. If you are a farmer, dairyman, livestock man, small business operator, contractor builder, real estate broker or any other independent operator, keep going. Don't quit.

    b. If you are an employee and have to give up your job, don't retire. Switch to a hobby and develop it, or to some independent line of work—keep busy.

5. Travel.

6. Write—give the world the advantage of your knowledge and mature wisdom. If you think you are "over the hill" you soon will be.—*Male, married, age 77.*

In a nutshell . . .: To Each His Own.—*Female, single, age 69.*

Chapter 14: Summary

It is almost a shame to try to summarize material whose most striking characteristic is diversity; yet, like the Supreme Court, the majority of the annuitants agreed on certain matters even if for a variety of reasons. In this chapter we emphasize the common, or at least the frequent, rather than the individual. We freely plagiarize former chapters; repeating key sentences or phrases without scruple and also without quotation marks. However we have not followed the same sequence as we have in the rest of this study in order by a different arrangement to reveal certain additional interrelations.

Most of the annuitants were in good health when they retired and had remained so for a considerable length of time thereafter or were still well at the time they replied to the questionnaire. Although asked only concerning comparative health, most respondents showed satisfaction with their health; and the great amount of activity described by them clearly indicated much vigor on the part of the majority. Of course in most elderly groups there are those who are suffering from serious maladies and TIAA annuitants were no exceptions. A person in good health when retiring should of course try to be prepared by insurance and medical arrangements to care for illness, but should also plan to lead a life of satisfying activity.

Although a few in the group had incomes below the theoretical "poverty level," this was unusual. Many were well off, but only a small number could be classified as wealthy. Three-quarters of the respondents said that their incomes allowed them to live at about the

same or above their pre-retirement levels. The proportion that said they were inadequate was less than 10 percent. Over half had increased their savings since retirement; and only 15 percent reported decreased savings. Although for a majority the amount coming from annuities, including Social Security, was over half their income, a very large number would have found their standard of living substantially reduced if they lived on these alone. Investment income is significant in that it represented at least 10 percent of the total income for 58 percent of respondents and over 25 percent for 32 percent of these. There is strong consensus that persons should save beyond required participation in Social Security and in retirement systems, although there are warnings against impoverishing the younger years to build up financial resources for a period which may not arrive or—when, if it does—may involve lessened incentives for spending. However, the usual advice is to save. The elderly who have done so are glad that they did, and many others expressed regret that they did not. A common complaint was that the habit of saving, which had been a virtue in earlier years and formed the basis for individual security, can become too compulsive in either one's self or one's spouse, so that the style of living is cramped even when reasonable financial security has been attained. The then present adequacy of income for the majority was accompanied by fear of inflation, especially of increasing medical expenses and dread of the possible cost of long-time illness or debility.

TIAA-CREF cautiously asked no questions about themselves. However, there were many comments volunteered. The uniform courtesy and the promptness shown by TIAA-CREF personnel in contact with policyholders were praised time and again. The size of the annuities was often a disappointment. Few seemed to realize how much money must be put aside during 30 years of earning to take care of 15 years of retirement; and it is disappointing to find how many had had little idea of the size of the annuities which they would receive, even after the constant series of statements (evidently unread) which had been sent to them. In many cases it would have been more effective if these had been mailed to their wives. There is certainly quite a compliment contained in the suggestions that TIAA could raise the amounts of the annuities, create retirement centers around the world, give pre-retirement counseling, reform the laws which concern retirement, and operate superior "Meals on Wheels." But as one person said, "You are a good outfit. . . ."

Forty-eight percent of the respondents had worked for salary at some time since their first retirement, frequently full time. About half of the respondents had done voluntary unpaid work, some full time. Of course those who had worked for pay and done voluntary unpaid work were overlapping groups. The Social Security rule which decreases the benefits of those who, before the age of 72 and after having started their Social Security annuity, worked for pay, was (and is) resented by many. Although teaching, consulting, and research (often unpaid) were in that order the most frequent, paid post-retirement occupations of respondents, a long list of other ways of earning money was reported. With the ages among the reporting group ranging from 60 to 99, it is natural that the voluntary work of many was to help those who are older than themselves. A good deal of the activity of a sizeable group was devoted to religion and the church. There is no way of knowing for how many this was true; for although a considerable number mentioned both the comfort and the stimulation of religion, it would be unfair to assume that silence meant the absence of such an experience. The "board old man" is typical of those who served on committees and boards of associations, leagues (woman voters, etc.), or conservation groups (to protect roadsides or to save Venice). The list of voluntary work indicates imagination, good will, and usefulness. Travel was a favorite occupation of the younger elderly and sometimes of those not so young as, for instance, the woman of 79 planning a tour of the Southwest Pacific after having recently completed safaris in Africa. There were those for whom gardening had its charms. The nondescript classification of hobbies contains activities that are the passion of some and the defense against boredom for others.

About a quarter of the respondents retired before the age of 65 and about 5 percent after the age of 71; a quarter retired at 65; and over a third between 65 and 70. Slightly over half of those who retired did so because of reaching a mandatory retirement age, most often at 65 and frequently at 70. There was a considerable and vocal group who believed that mandatory retirement ages are undesirable, some thinking that age discrimination is of the same unethical nature as discrimination on account of either race or sex. There was even greater resentment felt by those who had been retired under a flexible plan before they believed that they should have been. There seemed to be no consensus as to the best time to retire; but the number who believed that one should retire early and do something that yields

more satisfaction than their previous work and the number who believed that one should continue as long as permitted and that the permission should be to a late age, were both large. In spite, however, of the fact that there was a fairly sizeable group dissatisfied with when they retired, this was far short of the majority and represented only a few of those who were in financial conditions to make it easy to retire. Some would conclude that people are fortunate to have retired while there are still zestful years in which to enjoy their new status. Others believe, as I do, that early mandatory retirement has forced many who could still be productive to stop work or to work under less satisfactory conditions than if they had not retired. I would judge that my opinion is that of a numerous minority.

You could get up a fine debate between those who believe in remaining in the same house (or near it) as lived in at retirement and those who would recommend moving away; but it might be as hard to choose a place for such a pow-wow as to select the location of a "summit conference." A majority of the respondents lived where they did before retirement and another 10 percent in the same general location. However, by the time persons had reached 77 the picture had changed a great deal as to whether they still lived in the same home but much less so as to locale—the majority of those over 77 still living within 10 miles of their former residence. Up to age 70 three-quarters lived in single-family dwellings and less than 20 percent in apartments; whereas after 77 only 59 percent lived in single-family dwellings and 11 percent in retirement or nursing homes. We have no statistics on the cause of moving or staying put, but a great many volunteered statements or advice. From these we would conclude that the chief reasons for moving were: 1) to not interfere with successors, especially if the move was that of an administrator made immediately upon retirement; 2) to go to a warmer climate; 3) to find a type of residence which would take less effort to keep up than a single-family dwelling.

It is almost accurate to say that most retired persons believe they would not mind retirement if they did not have to grow older and suffer the decreasing energy and the illnesses which come with advancing years. After lessening vitality, perhaps, loneliness, loss of status, and lack of routine coupled with boredom were mentioned more often than other unpleasant circumstances; but there were other complaints, ranging from those that are rather general to those which might be labeled "pet peeves." A large proportion of those who

wrote of their loneliness had lost a husband or a wife, some other close relative, or a friend who had been a constant companion. Change of status is sometimes accompanied by a sense of guilt due to imagined uselessness. There is a general dislike of euphemistic phrases such as "Senior Citizen" or "Golden Years." Boredom was sometimes emphasized, but more often merely mentioned as a drawback that accompanied the delight in a new freedom.

For many the attitude towards retirement is largely conditioned by relations with others. Most of those who spoke of their marriage did so with great appreciation of their wives or husbands. The affection for one's children was overwhelming, but led in a few cases to almost pathological self-abnegation, in order to guard against interfering in the children's lives. The former relation with administrative officers and colleagues, in part self-determined, had colored the lives of many after retiring, usually (but not always) happily. There are many who reject "the young" (not their children or grandchildren), but there are also many who seek them along with, or sometimes even in preference to, the elderly.

Among the topics frequently discussed, but not rating a chapter, were transportation, especially local transportation, for those who no longer drive; the necessity of caring for sick friends or relatives; the new-found but often unused opportunities to sleep late; and questionnaires. The last topic was especially dwelt on by those who explained why they did not fill out the one from TIAA or by those who explained why it was an exception and they did so.

Advice impossible to epitomize in a brief summary was given in profusion, much of it for the benefit of those far younger than persons "about to retire" as suggested in the questionnaire.

The attitude of respondents was usually, in the absence of ill health or recent bereavement, one of contentment and serenity. In the cases of many this was bolstered by religious faith—a faith they yearned to share with others.

After reading all the questionnaires I have developed a real affection for my fellow annuitants. They are likeable, witty, and courageous. It has been a privilege to become acquainted.

Appendices

Appendix 1 consists of four answers to the open-ended questions. They are given in the order of their receipt. Three of these are complete and the fourth, "1500," omits only a final section containing some scattered quotations. "733" and "1435" have become names to some of us. All four of these stirred me, but in different ways.

Appendix 2 consists of a copy of the questionnaire.

"733"

[What are the main problems you faced in retirement, including those you expected and those you did not expect, and how did you deal with them?]

No special problems. Been completely happy—especially happy my sister and I bought this little house in Maine and been able to improve it little by little.

From childhood we were led to appreciate that the eternal and intrinsic values were of greatest worth—therefore education held a priority. Thriftiness was essential in our childhood home and has always seemed the better way. Things—or to be like our neighbor—were not important bases for living. When I began teaching on a yearly salary of $580, my father said, "Begin regular saving with your first check." Therefore I invested $3 a month in Building and Loan. This enabled my sister and me to have a down payment on our first home. My father had a stroke eight years after I began teaching and my sister and I had complete support of mother and father.

This childhood gift of our parents of joy in eternal and lasting values continued through life has laid the foundation of happy retirement.

Thriftiness and spending less than one earned has been the asset to my low retirement income (from salaries under $5000).

Our purchase of our little summer home here in Maine was most fortunate as shore property has increased so greatly in the last ten years.

Living on the whole is much less in this tiny rural village. Building costs were much less than in cities. I raised all our vegetables, freezing many till six years ago—now buy them from a nearby farmer and freeze enough for winter at a very low cost.

So—where have my problems been?

[What are some of the aspects of retirement you like the most—and the least?]

Living on the edge of a little rural community on the shore—with the beauty and wonder all about us—away from so much man-made things—to think God's thoughts with him—to reach out, ponder, think deeply.

Living with these good fisherfolk—listening to their wisdom, stories of birds and nature they see on their lobstering—talking over news. Their friendliness and helpfulness—yesterday two young lobstermen came at different times: one to put in the glass panels of the storm doors; he took in the heavy bird bath; new bulbs in two ceiling lights; the other to see what he might do and say he'd put down the board walk to the garage next week. Their wives say they might as well be our granddaughters.

One older couple include us each year for Thanksgiving (you are family) together with married daughter and her family.

I love them, just as they are and enjoy them—surprising them with hot bread, rolls, cake, etc.

More time to read.

[What are some do's and don'ts you might suggest for persons about to retire or already retired?]

Look forward with joy to change the joys of the past: opera, concerts, theater, social clubs do not need to be continued; other things will prove a joy.

Be broader than one's job; have things to do and enjoy by one's self. I learned in my youth to sew, crochet, tat, knit, embroider, cook. Did little in busy adulthood. Now evenings by the fire, knitting sweaters for some of the thoughtful folk here, for hospital fairs, Christmas gifts, is pure joy and fun.

If one changes his community and way of living, enjoy people as they are. Be simple and friendly; keep still about what one has done, one's education, achievement. Become a part of the new situation. Make a humble contribution to community by working with—not big giving.

Don't be afraid to do something new. I designed the additions to our home here; drew blueprints to scale; worked with the local carpenter about details.

In a small community use local people if possible even tho it may take lots of patience. Expect joy and some difficulty.

One other thing: As we grow old expect that there may be changes and

illness that will bring disappointment—sometimes temporary—but when they come, let one's "wings of the spirit" lift one to the blue sky overhead and the song. After a life of almost perfect health, first I had a very badly broken hip—a year out. I learned a lot; expected to walk—and it's fine. I had shingles—didn't know any one could have such pain or be so sick (3½ months in bed) and three times after the first, tho not so severe. More learning —deeper meaning of God and his nearness—surgery three times. All is well.

But we older ones must look ahead and know sometime we will be going beyond. How much does one's religion really mean? Mine is essential for every day and I have keen sense of wonder about the future. It will be the greatest experience in my life.—*Female, single, age 82.*

"*1214*"

Main problems—accidents: (1) After walking skillfully through icy streets during an unusually cold winter, on a bright spring day a month before retiring, I fell (stepped off a kerb unexpectedly) and shattered my left elbow. The operation to set it (or remake it) lasted two hours and a half. My whole body seemed to be affected. Several months of physical therapy, begun in the U. S. and continued in England, helped to straighten the arm. In my crippled condition I went on with plans: freighter passage across the Atlantic, three months at Crosby Hall, London, and an indefinite stay in Europe. October, South of France. November 1962-September 1963, Italy. November 1963, South of France. December 1963-February 1964, Portugal. March-July, 1963, Spain. (2) Second accident (I shall not go into details, merely say that the circumstances were similar to [1]—except that the right arm bone near the shoulder was broken).

July to October 15, 1964, London. I had thought of returning to the U.S. to look for work, teaching or translating, but had the opportunity to make an overland (coach) trip, London-Bombay, and join a friend for travel in India during December. After the rugged but fascinating bus trip to Bombay, I flew the rest of the way to San Francisco with generous stops in Bangkok, Cambodia, Hong Kong, Korea (a month in the home of friends), Japan and Hawaii. Then came a 99-day, $99 Greyhound journey through Canada and the U.S., which included visits with my family and friends. Next, 18 months in Mexico (with two trips to the border to renew tourist permit; a second $99, 99-day Greyhound trip, and a second (post-retirement) trip to Europe, beginning in April 1967 with tulips in Holland, then first trip to Berlin West and East, two months in Munich, two months in Vienna, then Italy, Switzerland, the Midi of France, then Paris (in these places many visits with friends). Called home because of a death in the family; remained six months. Mexico once more for six months, 1968. Christmas, 1968 with family. Back to Mexico to begin flights to the countries of South America I had not yet visited

(including a delightful month in Brazil). To the Canary Islands, five or six months, 1969 (with stop-over in Dakar), Madeira, Ireland, London (three months, 1969); Paris, nine months, 1969-70, Italy, one year. (3) A third accident in Siena spoiled a most interesting program (two months); Spain, France, back to New York on the S. S. Raffaello (cyclone, fire alarm, etc. Thanksgiving last year); U.S. home town and other places, December-April, 1972. Mexico, April 21—till the present.

Sheer self-indulgence, but this has turned out to be the only pleasant life that I could afford. It is still possible (but becoming rarer) to find outside the U.S. boarding houses, pensiones, etc., and small hotels, which [are] delightful and also inexpensive. (Examples: 1. In Florence, my hostess was a very pleasant marquesa. 2. Above Lake Lugano—the old mansion of the Consul General of Holland. 3. A dream of a place in Taormina.) Prices are high in the U.S. The only hotel in my home town costs three times+ what I pay in a private home (very genteel and amusing) here in Mexico. I admit that this is the only such place I happen to know about in this city.

It seems late in life to set up housekeeping (buy furniture, linen, silver or even stainless steel, etc.). The obvious solution would seem to be a retirement home. When I finally "settle down," I want to be in Tennessee (or not farther away than North Carolina) in order to be near my family. We are on good terms, but I cannot stay in their homes. There are few retirement homes at all suitable. The only one in my home town is on the gloomy side. I should like to find one which is not church-sponsored and which is within walking distance of a first-rate library.

And now for accident (#4)—the one from which I am suffering now, and which I offer as an excuse for the delay in answering your request for information, and for the illegibility, lack of cohesion, etc., etc., etc., with which the answer finally reaches you.

On October 29 I took a train to Guadalajara to fit in a concert on Monday, the 30th, between engagements here on Sunday and Wednesday. For years I had been wanting to hear Pablo Casals play. Of course it was now too late from a strictly musical point of view, but at least I could see him. I sat so near him that I could see every facial expression while his two friends were playing the violin and piano. When after intermission it was his turn to take part in a trio, I watched with great interest his 33-year old wife help him tenderly and unobtrusively to the platform with the big cello. My friend and I did not stay for cocktails, even though there might have been an opportunity to exchange a few words with this great man and his lovely wife (after seeing her, I approved of the marriage—96 vs. 33 years).

I was glad there had been no cocktails. The fall down stone steps leading from my bedroom directly into a hall, would have been misinterpreted. The next evening I was carried by two porters in a chair to the train in Guadalajara, and after twelve hours, from the train to a taxi in Mexico City. I preferred being ill here rather than in Guadalajara. For one week I had to remain in bed,

and for the whole month I've had to keep close to my room. No bones were broken, but no spot in my body seems to have escaped injury!

Please forgive this. I know it is not what you want, and that it will not fit into a calculating machine, but you have always attended to my requests promptly and courteously, and I felt you deserved a reply, even such as this one.

Of course I have no advice to pass on to others—except perhaps that it is never too late to learn another foreign language.

And now, how to get this mailed?—*Female, single, age 76.*

"1435"

I believe that the problems of retirement are basically Health, Happiness, and Security. They have to [be] prepared for long before retirement. This has been our experience in setting them up.

Health. Includes longevity and we prepared for that as much as possible by choosing partners in marriage whose families carried it. We had both trained in biology so we knew the important facts. We visited in each other's families, understood our cultural differences, and governed ourselves accordingly. We didn't expect health problems and we have not had them.

Happiness. In both work and marriage. We wanted and have had what is known as a companionate marriage: Equality and independence and co-operation. I was an only child in an eastern family of above average means; she was eighth of nine in a midwestern farm family of slightly below average means. Fortunately we lived at considerable distance from either family and for three years were thrown very closely together in a foreign country.

I had covered the eastern U.S. with Chautauquas and conducted a party in Europe; she had had farm life until college years when she worked for board and room.

I started college at Rensselaer Polytechnic Institute, moved to Syracuse to be near home before entering service. Volunteered for orderly service as a pre-med, had a summer at Harvard with a navy friend, transferred to Washington University. There I found biology and psychology more to my liking. As a junior I did field work at the Child Guidance Clinic for the City of St. Louis and was Clinical Psychologist there for three years. We decided that as graduate students we could afford to marry, both having jobs. A month after marriage I was in New York State in jail having been loaned to the New York State Crime Commission by the National Commission on Mental Hygiene. This was my first working with adult criminals. It opened my eyes to conditions in corrections (1922). I moved to University of Minnesota to work with Dr. Karl Lashley in his work with rehabilitation from brain injuries. We didn't like being in Minneapolis and St. Louis and decided that if we were ever to travel it would be now before we started our family.

We taught three years in the outer provinces in the Philippine Islands. We

were the only American couple and one year the only Americans in our assignments. It threw us very close together and gave us the good start in being companionate or else.

Returning to the U.S. via Asia and Europe we found positions I wanted scarce. I was interviewed at Middlebury to substitute for a biology professor on leave and hired. Next year I was asked to stay on in another department. I instituted courses in sociology and two years later was able to persuade President Moody to establish a department of sociology, one of the early ones in New England. I taught 21 hours a week to give the range of courses I wanted for two years until I was given an assistant. Since I had had experience in a wide variety of application of the subject I instituted field trips in all courses much to the horror of my academic friends. All over the state and in four-day vacation trips fall and spring my students saw in practice what they were learning about in classes. New York, Boston, Washington. Both my students and I made many contacts over the state which have led many of them to present positions in state government and on boards and commissions.

On my Sabbatical in '40-41 our family of five trailered thru the 48 states, Canada and Mexico. I studied migrating families where and how they lived. The children went to school in 30 states. On return I was given the position of co-ordinator with the Navy V-12 unit and my teaching was cut to a number of seminars in Marriage and Family Relations for the coeds whose men had gone into service and the men who were expecting to go.

I served on a number of boards and commissions and my students got the benefits of participation in many of them during the next years. My next Sabbatical I spent in 30 state and federal prisons examining the methods of vocational training, education and rehabilitation being used.

Upon return to college the Governor, a former student, appointed me to the Vermont Board of Institutions and the State Parole Board. This allowed real information to my criminology classes and I was able to have seminars in several state institutions.

I was still on these boards when I retired in 1963. Meantime I had served on several municipal boards. I appeared before several sessions of the legislature to advance corrections programs and construction. One senator told me "you could exert more influence if you were one of us." Apparently that caught on and in 1968 I was asked to represent my district in the House. I have just been re-elected to my third two-year term.

I have used the experience of my teaching in the legislature and find that they respond just as mature students do. For example, over a number of years I had work with corrections on a Corrections Code, to bring all the laws together in revision and needed advance. It came together as a technical 76-page bill. Using seminar technique I presented it to each Democrat and Republican caucus, explained it, answered all questions and answered why it was needed. Committees of both the House and the Senate visited our

correctional facilities and when the bill came to the floor of the House there were no votes against it. That action carried over to the Senate which passed it also. I hadn't retired; I was just teaching in another institution.

If there was a let-down when I retired in '63 I didn't feel it. The next morning after it I started in on a year's work as Governor of Rotary for Vermont, New Hampshire and Quebec.

There is not happiness in work and family unless both partners feel it, and have a part in it.

Our family started in 1917 and we have raised three children who are now happily married and have their own families. They all finished college and our son has gone on to his Ph.D.

My wife was, as she said, a housewife until the children were of sufficient age, then she returned to teaching. During this period she was active in both local and state affairs. She retired from teaching science at our Union District High School two years after I retired and for a year tried retirement with only her other activities to keep her occupied. The college then offered her the position of supervisor of student teachers and that is her present activity. So both of us have continued on in retirement doing work which we liked, merely shifting to other bases after the formal proceedings. This September our children surprised us with an anniversary party at our 50th and we had a gala celebration. (50ths are not at all unusual in Vermont.)

Security. This also is something you prepare for over the years. We have our home long ago paid for, our children are college educated, we have the security of both TIAA and Social Security but during all the years of earning we had a strict system of saving, a budget that we could control but did not control us. We did not go wild on insurance but had enough for necessary protection.

Although we both have paying positions now it is only a small amount for either of us but it allows us to make larger contributions to what we are interested in, allows us to continue to both have our own cars and in good New England style keeps us from spending our capital.

Perhaps our greatest security is the fact that we are able to and are asked to continue to work in what has been our professions.

We really haven't found anything we don't like about retirement but rather enjoy the opportunity to continue in what we have liked over the years.

We have about the same amount of free time we had while teaching and have been able to do a bit of traveling. We enjoy visiting our children and grandchildren who live at considerable distances from us.

I'm on the road over 20,000 miles a year but I don't enjoy winter night driving as I used to.

We don't spend all our time on our work because we have the reserve of our experience to live on. We have lots of diversions both together and as individuals. Right now I'm building a color TV set and my wife has a class in pine-cone creations.

If we have any Do's or Don'ts for retirement they would be:

Find a way to use the knowledge and skills you have built over the years. Have a hobby and make the most of it.

Attend the cultural offerings not only in your field but those you missed during teaching. There is a lot you don't know about and it is important.

Enjoy what you are doing or else get out of it.

Get to know the young marrieds around you. They have a lot of refreshing ideas and mostly welcome exchange of ideas with maturity.

Both of you make wills and get the best possible legal advice for what you want to accomplish.

DON'T sit down and think that it is only a matter of time now.

If you have lived with northern winters don't expect to be happy with perpetual sunshine and no stimulation.

Stay out of politics unless your field of experience really has something vital to offer in the legislative process.

Mr. William T. Slater, TIAA

I wouldn't be able to get it finished today but for the fact that I have been temporarily grounded by a slip on the ice so I am nursing three cracked ribs. We are leaving to drive to Toronto this afternoon and it's snowing.—*Male, married, age 74.*

"*1500*"

Thoughts About Retirement: Planning for It and Experiencing It.

Underlying the problems facing the "retired" elderly is the conception of old age prevailing in modern society. More emphasis on a full life in retirement for the elderly could be given by our society and its institutions in preparation for retirement, in counseling citizens about retirement, in pensions, in social security policies, in taxation policies, and in social organization if there were a societal interest in making full use of our older human beings. Such a change in attitude is likely to come in due course as it is realized that the survival of our culture depends upon the civilized use of all of its parts. Life and living continues after the career and after life-time work. This period need not be a "pasturing," as our culture seems now to think of retirement, and certainly it should not be a "shelving" of the aged to get them out of the way to serve an ever increasing production pace whereby profits and products become more important than the society of human beings. Conservation of human resources, of skills, of experiences, are essential to the survival of any culture. And especially at this time in history when other systems lay claim to better use of human beings.

If our society fails at this time in history to make its aging population an integral part of throbbing societal participation, prospective retirees are bound to make out their own schedule of purposeful, meaningful work as

basic to their own good health and social well-being. This requires some personal planning and innovating a place in life so different from prevailing concepts which many, if not most, retirees themselves unthinkingly absorb—concepts that carry with them, it seems, a notion of sanctions: that prevailing ideas about retirement are natural, dictated by common sense, and that reasonable persons find them acceptable. Current counseling and preparation for retirement seem to be more concerned with the use of leisure time instead of with continuation of purposeful living. If the relationship of living continuity to physical and psychological well-being were more widely disseminated and if there were societal backing of options including this kind of continuity, more elderly citizens would, I think, choose it (living continuity). I am optimistic that this will come about—that more information about the proper place of the elderly in society and the relationship of this to their well-being as well as to the well-being of society as a whole will be available and that the options will then materialize. We could clear the obstacles to this a little quicker and we could speed up process toward a more civilized view of the aged and of their "retirement."

The vogue now is for oldsters to join with other oldsters in mutual associations and aid—the "peer" group organization idea carried out to the end. Spurred by the enterprisers who have discovered a new and profitable market in providing homes for the aged, condominiums for the aged, whole towns just for them, the prevailing concepts of retirement get attached to new but questionable symbols of "social recognition of the needs of the elderly." Counseling prior to retirement seems to have overlooked the new problems arising from these trends. I observe that the salesmanship is so effective and that the planning in accordance with the fads takes on an obsessive determination that warnings now in the magazine and in books and newspaper media are not seriously considered.

Some retirees find volunteer work in libraries, hospitals, social welfare offices, charitable institutions, citizen action groups, political party work satisfying. One keeps busy this way and much of the drudgery carries rationalized or even real purpose. I think of this activity in general as a parasystem in a capitalistic society which offers work for no pay. Are they not getting social security and pensions, medicaid and other "free" or "near free" services? But it is a further segregation of the aged from active society even from its economic benefits. And a surprising percentage of them need additional income for basic necessities. Since the aged are not needed for production, they become subjects of the Welfare State. There they may eat and live but not as well as those active.

Our culture has, evidently, separated work from personality—a consequence, no doubt, of our mechanistic, mass production age. To mass mentality, there seems to be no recourse. Work for many is submergence; leisure (non work) is presumably freedom from this. For a few, retirement is a sort of "drop-out" from a system which underrates human beings. The promised

leisure seems to provide a chance for regaining self-respect, independence, assertion of self. Those who are victims of the system as factory hands or as organization persons certainly need relief from the system—the earlier the better—65 years or younger—say 55 or sooner. But the organization person and the mechanized culture worker are ill prepared for independence, self assertion, or even self respect. Traits of courage, self assertion, self respect are from consistent choices in the struggle against submergence. And significantly, a culture which justifies and condones submergence of personality is hard put to prepare prospective retirees for a self-respecting life.

Work for me always carried purpose, different purposes as life matured. My independence and my free choice were my precious assets which I protected as I reinvested them in new endeavors. I do not know when I became conscious of this, but by the time I did I found I had already established it in countless decisions. My work and the activity I choose gives my existence zest to this day. Doing what I like to do for the purposes I choose is my strength and the struggle has added to my competence. An ebbing energy is somewhat annoying now, but I have found or am finding that extra exertion, even pain in overdoing, up to now at least (age 75), is not too harmful to my health. Indeed, I have come to think that the extra exertion, as long as it is not reckless, is part of the price for good health in old age.

The main problem I faced when my university work came to a close at 69 arose from my sudden disengagement from my academic associations, from students as they come and go, and from campus life. The on-the-shelf climate is quite a shock, and it takes a bit of doing—more than I expected—to adjust. I should have been prepared for this. I had observed that those of my associates who retired before I did suddenly "disappeared." I kept wondering what they were bitter about. I did notice that some of them carved out another way of life—busy, purposeful, productive. It turns out now that they were too busy to return for nostalgic visits. The thought that they disappeared and left sulking, I now see, merely fit into the prevailing thinking about retirees.

To create a full life on different terms from those we were familiar with and habituated to tests resiliencies. Different goals, new points of view, different kinds of friends and associates, and environments not accustomed to thinking out loud, or even thinking, make for a sort of existential experience; the day takes care of itself and the quality of life and of associations, new purposes and the means employed continue the self-esteem and self-respect that the career just closed carried with it. An unexpected dividend comes: the activities keep the memory responsive, the talents exercised, new facets of wisdom developed, and all keep the metabolism close to normal. The associations are with people of all ages, of all classes, of all education levels. Fellowship with them gives an intimate sense of comfort. They are kindly, humble, independent, and wise. What I am now is more important than what I was, and this makes for a logical continuity to the past and provides a

timeless view of the future. I find myself working out plans as though life has no end, and, indeed, it foreseeably hasn't, though I, of course, shall pass on. What is surprising to me is that I did not predetermine this philosophy; it grew out of experience, a confidence and security that comes from purposes to which I commit myself.

To draw anything from my experiences into do's and don'ts, as the questionnaire invites, is to ignore I think, the great variety of needs, outlets, dispositions, well-being, and choices. Still, I say this: if society does not know how to use me for human purposes at my older years, I harbor ideas, as I always have, on how to use my life for social purposes as my talents, energies, and health guide. The culture into which I was born and the institutions and professions in which I worked never had complete say over how I was to be used. Why should they now? I resist the trend of segregation, of shelving, pasturing, or Welfare State dependent citizen, and as long as my health comes up to it, I shall find some continuing purposeful work (at least to me) to do.—*Male, married, age 75.*

Appendix 2

November 1, 1972

Survey of Retired TIAA-CREF Annuitants

Teachers Insurance and Annuity Association
College Retirement Equities Fund

Educational Research Department
730 Third Avenue   New York, N.Y. 10017

Special Instructions

1. So that all information will remain confidential, anonymity of the respondent is essential. *Please do not sign your name.*

2. Please fill out and return the questionnaire only if you are *now retired* or, if now employed, *have previously retired* from your main working career.

3. If you have *never retired*, please do not fill out the questionnaire. Please just write "Never Retired" on this page and return the questionnaire so that we can count the annuitants in this category.

Not much is constant in this rapidly changing world, including the way people live in retirement. This survey is being conducted to obtain current, first-hand information about retired persons receiving income from their TIAA-CREF annuities, information that can be useful to us at TIAA-CREF, to you personally, and to other participants in the TIAA-CREF retirement system.

You are a member of a group selected at random to represent all TIAA-CREF annuitants. By completing and returning this questionnaire you will

- help us (1) become more informed about our retired annuitants and their retirement planning and experience, and (2) define areas where we might provide more information to our annuitants on retirement and on planning for retirement.

- contribute important data on the actual experiences (both favorable and unfavorable) of retired annuitants, data which we can communicate as instructive guides or examples to participants retired and not yet retired, and to retirement counselors.

This questionnaire seeks two kinds of information: first, biographical data on employment, finances, insurance, health, housing, and residential mobility; second, your observations on the problems and pleasures of retirement.

Please answer all the questions. You may have to look up information to answer some of them. We hope that your work will be rewarded by the knowledge that you are participating in a study to benefit present and future generations of retirees.

We will be most grateful to you for taking the time to fill out and return the questionnaire. A postage-paid return envelope is enclosed.

WILLIAM T. SLATER
Vice President

PART I—GENERAL INFORMATION

CARD 1
1-5

1. Month and year of your birth:

	Month	*Year*
	6-7	8-9

2. Sex:

10-1 ☐ Male
  -2 ☐ Female

3. Present marital status:

11-1 ☐ Married
  -2 ☐ Widowed or Widowered
  -3 ☐ Single, Separated or Divorced

If presently married, what is the month and year of birth of your spouse?

	Month	*Year*
	12-13	14-15

4. Main emphasis of your working career:
(*Check as many as apply*)

16-1 ☐ Teaching
  -2 ☐ Research
  -3 ☐ Academic administration
  -4 ☐ Librarianship
  -5 ☐ Clerical or secretarial work
  -6 ☐ Maintenance or service work
  -7 ☐ Other: (*Specify*)

5. What type of organization was your **last** full-time employer before you retired? (*Check one*)

17-1 ☐ University
  -2 ☐ 4-year college
  -3 ☐ 2-year college
  -4 ☐ Primary, intermediate, or secondary school or academy
  -5 ☐ Educational organization other than a teaching institution
  -6 ☐ Foundation
  -7 ☐ Research organization not affiliated with any of the above
  -8 ☐ Other: (*Describe briefly, e.g., law firm, bank, government agency*)

6. Was your last full-time employer before you retired under public or private control?

18-1 ☐ Public
  -2 ☐ Private

7. Month and year of retirement (initial retirement if more than one):

	Month	*Year*
	19-20	21-22

8. Did you retire because you reached a mandatory retirement age?

23-1 ☐ Yes
  -2 ☐ No

If no, please indicate briefly the primary reason(s) for your retirement, listing them in approximate order of importance, if more than one:

9. Over your career, for how many years did an employer or employers contribute to TIAA-CREF on your behalf?

	Years
	27-28

10. What was the month and year that you started to receive your TIAA-CREF annuity income?

	Month	*Year*
	29-30	31-32

11. Which type of TIAA-CREF annuity income option did you select? (*Check one box in each column*)

	From TIAA	From CREF
Survivor Annuity You and your spouse (or other second annuitant) receive a lifetime income	33-1 ☐	34-1 ☐
One-Life Annuity You only receive a lifetime income	-2 ☐	-2 ☐
No CREF Income		-3 ☐

-2-

12. Have you worked for salary or wages at all since your retirement?

35-1 ☐ Yes
-2 ☐ No

If yes, please answer the following questions in regard to this work:

a. Are you **presently** working for salary or wages?

36-1 ☐ Yes
-2 ☐ No

b. What was (is) the main emphasis of your **post-retirement** working career? (*Check as many as apply*)

37-1 ☐ Teaching
-2 ☐ Research
-3 ☐ Academic administration
-4 ☐ Librarianship
-5 ☐ Clerical or secretarial work
-6 ☐ Maintenance or service work
-7 ☐ Consulting work
-8 ☐ Other: (*Specify*)

c. How many hours in a week did (do) you normally work in your **post-retirement** working career?

_____ Hours
38-39

d. How many weeks in a year did (do) you normally work in your **post-retirement** working career?

_____ Weeks
40-41

e. What do you consider your main reason(s) for working after you retired? (*If more than one reason, please list them in the approximate order of importance.*)

☐ 42
☐ 43
☐ 44

13. **If you are now married,** does your spouse currently work for salary or wages?

45-1 ☐ Yes
-2 ☐ No

14. Have you done unpaid, voluntary work at all since your retirement?

46-1 ☐ Yes
-2 ☐ No

If yes, please answer the following questions in regard to this work:

a. Are you **presently** doing unpaid, voluntary work?

47-1 ☐ Yes
-2 ☐ No

b. How many hours in a week did (do) you normally do unpaid, voluntary work?

_____ Hours
48-49

c. How many weeks in a year did (do) you normally do unpaid, voluntary work?

_____ Weeks
50-51

d. Describe briefly the type of unpaid, voluntary work:

☐ 52

15. What type of structure is your **main** residence? (*Check one*)

53-1 ☐ Single-family dwelling
-2 ☐ Small, multiple-family dwelling (2-4 units)
-3 ☐ Apartment
-4 ☐ Mobile home or trailer
-5 ☐ Hotel or boarding house
-6 ☐ Nursing home or hospital
-7 ☐ Other: (*Specify*)

16. Do you own or rent your main residence? (*Check one*)

54-1 ☐ Own (including joint ownership) (*Go to Question 17*)
-2 ☐ Rent (*Go to Question 18*)
-3 ☐ It is owned or rented by a relative or friend (*Go to Question 19*)
-4 ☐ Other: (*Specify*)

Please answer Q.17, Q.18, or Q.19 depending on your answer to Q.16.

-3-

17. **If you own your main residence:**

    a. About how much do you think your main residence would sell for today, i.e., what is the current market value of this property?

        $_____
        Current Market Value
        55-60

    b. How much are your annual taxes on this property?

        $_____
        Per Year
        61-64

    c. Is there a mortgage on your home?
        65-1 ☐ Yes
        -2 ☐ No

If yes:

    (1) How much do you owe on the remaining mortgage principal(s)?

        $_____
        Amount Owed
        66-71

    (2) What is the current monthly mortgage payment exclusive of property taxes and insurance?·

        $_____
        Per Month
        72-75

    (3) How many years from now will your scheduled mortgage payments be completed?

        Years
        76-77

78-80 BL
CARD 2
1-5

18. **If you rent your main residence:**

How much do you pay monthly for rent?

    $_____
    Per Month
    6-9

19. **If you live in a dwelling owned or rented by a relative or friend:**

How much, if any, do you pay monthly towards mortgage or rent?

    $_____
    Per Month
    10-13

20. Do you share your main residence with anyone? (*Check one*)
    14-1 ☐ No, live alone
    -2 ☐ With spouse only
    -3 ☐ With spouse and others (another)
    -4 ☐ With others (another); no spouse

If others (another) besides a spouse share your main residence:

    a. How many others are there? ____
        15

    b. How much, if any, do they pay toward monthly costs?

        $_____
        Per Month
        16-19

21. How satisfied are you with your main residence?
    20-1 ☐ Very satisfied
    -2 ☐ Satisfied
    -3 ☐ Neutral
    -4 ☐ Dissatisfied
    -5 ☐ Very dissatisfied

If dissatisfied, please indicate the principal reason(s), listing them in approximate order of importance, if more than one:

21
22
23

22. How long have you lived in your main residence?

    Years
    24-25

23. Is your main residence the same one now as before retirement? (*Initial retirement if more than one*)
    26-1 ☐ Yes
    -2 ☐ No

If no:

    a. How far do you now live from your pre-retirement main residence?

        Miles
        27-30

    b. Did you move at (or about) the time you retired?
        31-1 ☐ Yes
        ·2 ☐ No

    c. How many times have you moved since you retired?

        ____
        32

-4-

24. In what size community is your main residence located? (*Check one*)

33-1 ☐ Large city......(over 500,000 people)
  -2 ☐ City..........(100,000—500,000 people)
  -3 ☐ Small city.....(10,000—99,999 people)
  -4 ☐ Town..........(4,000—9,999 people)
  -5 ☐ Small town.....(Under 4,000 people)
  -6 ☐ Rural community

25. Do you live in a "planned" retirement community?

34-1 ☐ Yes
  -2 ☐ No

26. Do you have a driver's license?

35-1 ☐ Yes
  -2 ☐ No

If you are now married, does your spouse have a driver's license?

36-1 ☐ Yes
  -2 ☐ No

27. Do you have a car (or cars)?

37-1 ☐ Yes
  -2 ☐ No

If yes, what is its year? _____
                                      38-39

If no, what is your **main** means of transportation? (*Check one*)

40-1 ☐ Other peoples' cars
  -2 ☐ Taxi
  -3 ☐ Bus
  -4 ☐ Subway
  -5 ☐ Other: (*Specify*) _____

28. How do you regard your health (and that of your spouse, if married) in relation to other people your age?

Yourself	Spouse
41-1 ☐ Very good	42-1 ☐ Very good
-2 ☐ Good	-2 ☐ Good
-3 ☐ Average	-3 ☐ Average
-4 ☐ Poor	-4 ☐ Poor
-5 ☐ Very poor	-5 ☐ Very poor

29. Are you enrolled in the Federal Medicare Program?

43-1 ☐ Yes
  -2 ☐ No

If yes, which part?

44-1 ☐ Part A only (hospital insurance)
  -2 ☐ Part A and Part B (supplementary medical insurance)

30. Do you have other health insurance coverage?

45-1 ☐ Yes
  -2 ☐ No

If yes, how was the insurance obtained? (*Check as many as apply*)

46-1 ☐ Under the group health insurance program of a former (or current) employer
  -2 ☐ Under a health insurance policy purchased on your own

31. How would you describe your total insurance coverage for medical expenses?

47-1 ☐ Very good
  -2 ☐ Good
  -3 ☐ Poor
  -4 ☐ Very poor

32. Do you have life insurance?

48-1 ☐ Yes
  -2 ☐ No

If yes:

a. What is the total amount of your coverage?

$_____
Amount of Coverage
49-54

b. Who is the primary beneficiary (or beneficiaries) of your life insurance? (*Check as many as apply*)

55-1 ☐ Spouse
  -2 ☐ Children
  -3 ☐ Other relatives
  -4 ☐ Estate
  -5 ☐ Other

56-80 BL
CARD 3
1-5

-5-

33. Did you have savings accumulated when you retired?

    6-1 ☐ Yes

    -2 ☐ No

34. Has the amount of your total savings changed during retirement?

    7-1 ☐ Yes, increased

    -2 ☐ Yes, decreased

    -3 ☐ No, remained about the same

35. **Income.** Please indicate about how much income you currently receive **monthly** from each of the following sources. If income is received less frequently than monthly, please estimate a monthly figure.

    If married, include any income your spouse receives.

    If no income is received from a source, enter a zero on the corresponding amount line and check the box to the right of the line.

    For TIAA and CREF annuities, include those bought individually as well as those provided through an institutional plan.

Sources of Income	Amount Per Month		Check Here if NO Income is Received
1. Social Security	$_____	8-11	36-1 ☐
2. TIAA annuity(ies)	$_____	12-15	-2 ☐
3. CREF annuity(ies)	$_____	16-19	-3 ☐
4. Other pensions or annuities	$_____	20-23	-4 ☐
5. Income from current work	$_____	24-27	-5 ☐
6. Interest or dividends	$_____	28-31	-6 ☐
7. Other, e.g., royalties, gifts, income from rent	$_____	32-35	-7 ☐

36. Considering all sources, please estimate your average total monthly income:

    $_____

    Average Total Monthly Income

    37-41

If you are now married:

a. About how much of your average total monthly income would continue to your spouse in the event of your death?

    $_____

    Monthly Income of Your Surviving Spouse

    42-46

b. About how much of your average total monthly income would continue to you in the event of your spouse's death?

    $_____

    Your Monthly Income as Surviving Spouse

    47-51

37. Are any other persons besides yourself (and your spouse, if married) **mainly** supported by your income?

   52-1 ☐ Yes
   -2 ☐ No

   If yes, how many? _____
   53

38. In general, how well does your income permit you to live?

   54-1 ☐ Very well
   -2 ☐ Well
   -3 ☐ Adequately
   -4 ☐ Not too well
   -5 ☐ Poorly

39. How does your present standard of living compare with your standard of living before retirement?

   55-1 ☐ Much higher
   -2 ☐ Higher
   -3 ☐ The same
   -4 ☐ Lower
   -5 ☐ Much lower

40. **Assets.** Please estimate the value of your assets in each of the following areas.

   If married, include any assets of your spouse.

   a. What is your total cash balance in savings or checking accounts at banks, savings and loan associations, or credit unions?

      56-1 ☐ No money in savings or checking accounts
      -2 ☐ Less than $1,000
      -3 ☐ $1,000—$2,999
      -4 ☐ $3,000—$4,999
      -5 ☐ $5,000—$6,999
      -6 ☐ $7,000—$9,999
      -7 ☐ $10,000—$19,999
      -8 ☐ $20,000—$29,999
      -9 ☐ $30,000—$49,999
      -0 ☐ $50,000—$99,999
      -x ☐ $100,000—$250,000
      -y ☐ More than $250,000

   b. What is the market value of any investments you have in stocks, mutual funds, bonds, and other securities?

      57-1 ☐ No money invested in securities
      -2 ☐ Less than $1,000
      -3 ☐ $1,000—$2,999
      -4 ☐ $3,000—$4,999
      -5 ☐ $5,000—$6,999
      -6 ☐ $7,000—$9,999
      -7 ☐ $10,000—$19,999
      -8 ☐ $20,000—$29,999
      -9 ☐ $30,000—$49,999
      -0 ☐ $50,000—$99,999
      -x ☐ $100,000—$250,000
      -y ☐ More than $250,000

   c. How much is your equity in real estate?

      Exclude any equity in your main residence already covered by Q.17. (*Equity equals market value less mortgage loan(s) outstanding.*)

      58-1 ☐ No money invested in real estate
      -2 ☐ Less than $1,000
      -3 ☐ $1,000—$2,999
      -4 ☐ $3,000—$4,999
      -5 ☐ $5,000—$6,999
      -6 ☐ $7,000—$9,999
      -7 ☐ $10,000—$19,999
      -8 ☐ $20,000—$29,999
      -9 ☐ $30,000—$49,999
      -0 ☐ $50,000—$99,999
      -x ☐ $100,000—$250,000
      -y ☐ More than $250,000

   | 59 |
   | 60 |
   | 61 |

41. Within the past year have you used savings or sold securities, land, or other property to meet current necessities (but not to purchase something special)?

   62-1 ☐ Yes
   -2 ☐ No

   If yes, about how much money did you use from these sources?
   $_____
   63-66

42. **Debts.** Please estimate the sum of your debts in the following areas: total amount outstanding on bank, personal, and other loans you have received; total amount you owe on installment purchases; and total amount you have unpaid on charge, credit, and investment accounts.

    If married, include any debts of your spouse.

    Exclude any mortgage debts on your main residence already covered by Q.17.

    67-1 ☐ $000 (no debt)
    -2 ☐ Less than $100
    -3 ☐ $100—$499
    -4 ☐ $500—$999
    -5 ☐ $1,000—$1,999
    -6 ☐ $2,000—$2,999
    -7 ☐ $3,000—$4,999
    -8 ☐ $5,000—$6,999
    -9 ☐ $7,000—$9,999
    -0 ☐ $10,000—$14,999
    -x ☐ $15,000—$20,000
    -y ☐ More than $20,000

    68

43. In general, how satisfied are you with the preparation you made for retirement (financial, housing, leisure, other activities, etc.)?

    69-1 ☐ Very satisfied
    -2 ☐ Satisfied
    -3 ☐ Neutral
    -4 ☐ Dissatisfied
    -5 ☐ Very dissatisfied

44. Did your last employer before retirement provide counseling or assistance in retirement planning?

    70-1 ☐ Yes
    -2 ☐ No

    If yes, did you use the service?

    71-1 ☐ Yes
    -2 ☐ No

    If you used the service, did you find it helpful?

    72-1 ☐ Yes
    -2 ☐ No

    73-79 BL

    80

PART II—YOUR RETIREMENT EXPERIENCE

We believe that people about to retire might better anticipate the problems and satisfactions of retirement if they could learn from persons already retired. We would appreciate your advice to present and future retirees based on your experiences, advice we plan to summarize and distribute in printed form.

We are especially interested in your comments on:
1. The main problems you faced in retirement, including those you expected and those you did not expect, and how you dealt with them,
2. Some of the aspects of retirement you like the most—and the least—and finally,
3. Some do's and don'ts you might suggest for persons about to retire or already retired.

We have provided some space for your comments on the following pages. If we didn't provide enough space, please attach additional sheets. [To conserve space, all three questions were placed on this page, but on the actual questionnaire they were spread over four pages.]

1. What are the main problems you faced in retirement, including those you expected and those you did not expect, and how did you deal with them?

2. What are some of the aspects of retirement you like the most—and the least?

3. What are some do's and don'ts you might suggest for persons about to retire or already retired?

After you complete the questionnaire, please return it in the enclosed postage-paid envelope. Thank you for your help.

This is 100% recycled paper